I0682391

The April-May June Series – Book 2

Mad About Magic

Patricia Srigley

Join the author's mailing list to win monthly
give-aways and receive author/artist updates at
SrigleyArts.com

WigglesWorth Press & SrigleyArts.com

Additional Titles

The April-May June Series:
1 – A World Apart
2 – Mad About Magic
3 – Message in a Bubble
4 – April Fooled

Deeply
The Storyteller Series
Universe Idol
Fire-scape
All Planetary Shipping
One Crooked House
The Top-Secret Life of Timbuktu Kalamazoo
Blue Wings
Moody Gasping Middle School Adventures

Library and Archives Canada Cataloguing in Publication:
Please contact the publisher for this information
ISBN 9780973856545

Published by: Wiggles Worth Press, Montreal, Quebec, Canada

Contents

1. Outside Interference 1

2. Hairy-Melon and Peachy Leechy.............................. 16

3. Mice with Teeth... 31

4. Plants Alive... 45

5. Decoy 64

6. Imps and Leprechauns.. 79

7. Fire and Water 89

8. Basketberry 103

9. The Ant Test... 115

10. Brag... 131

11. Midnight Picnic.. 145

12. River Surfing... 162

14. Upside-down.. 191

15. Fairy Lights and Flower Petals 204

16. Heap of Gold 222

17. The Best Laid Plans... 237

18. Final Destination.. 252

19 – Hibernation 265

1. Outside Interference

"Quick, run! We have to hide!" Raina whispered in a panic, eyes darting around wildly.

"I know! I heard them too. Hide where?" Airron demanded, equally distraught.

"Anywhere! Move." Peter shoved Airron aside and took the lead, randomly heading left.

Raina tugged April by the wrist to hurry her along. "Come on!"

"Why are we whispering? And why are we hurrying? And why are we hiding?" April asked and promptly stumbled over a stick.

"Some elves are looking for you—again." Raina ducked under a large fern. April had no choice but to accompany her friend. Raina's grip was very firm.

"Why are elves looking for me?"

"How would I know? But I don't want to find out. Let's try and manage one day without being bugged. Summer is almost over, school starts tomorrow." Raina scowled fiercely, wrinkling her slightly turned up nose and collecting her freckles closer together. Her expression probably had more to do with school starting than the fact that elves were looking for April—yet again.

"Summer is never over," April contradicted, since it was always perfectly warm in this magically-guarded world of elves. And as far as the months were concerned, it was spring that was almost over. New Haven had mixed up the seasons in the eons it had been isolated from the outside world. It was an easy enough thing to do, given that all four of New Haven's seasons had exactly the same weather—summer.

Until recently, April had been the only elf who had ever seen that outer-world, which had officially come to be known, rather unimaginatively, as the Outer-World. She had grown up in the perilous place. And when her already endangered home was destroyed by explosions and fires, April had been left lost and alone. It had taken her five long years of searching to find other elves—to find the magically-guarded realm of New Haven.

Hauling April along, Raina jogged after Airron and Peter. The boys ducked behind a raised tree root, and Raina did too, taking April with her. The root was covered over by an umbrella of leaves. Airron yanked a leafy branch closer, hiding their small group completely. He all but disappeared when his raven-black hair and dark robe blended into the shadows.

"Perfect," Raina decreed. "Now quiet, I want to hear if we were followed." Their four sets of pointed ears perked up and listened hard.

"I think I hear someone coming." Peter leaned silently out to take a peek, his golden-brown curls camouflaged by the leaves.

Airron was not as quiet. "We wouldn't have to hide if April would learn to say 'no'—it's a very useful word. Comes in handy! *April, will you do magic tricks for us? 'No!' April, can you tell us about that giant furry purple-spotted, three-legged, one-eyed hopping critter that we saw in the Outer-world? 'No!'* It's not that hard to say 'no'!" Airron mimicked, ranting to himself.

Raina elbowed him in the ribs. "Shush, Airron. You're going to give away our hiding spot."

"Ouch! You have very pointy elbows," he griped.

"I'll elbow you again if you don't shush!"

"I've never seen a purple-spotted creature like that, Airron. I don't think they exist," April whispered.

"Quiet!" Raina hissed, louder than anyone.

Soft footsteps drew closer and closer. No-one said another word. April held her breath but … she felt the overwhelming urge to sneeze. "*Ah-ah-ah-choo!*" The footsteps stopped. Everything was silent for a moment, until— "*Ah-choo. Ah-choo. Ah-choo. Ah-choo. Ah-choo!*"

"Hello? April-May June? Is that you sneezing? Are you in there?" an impatient voice called out.

"*Ah-choo. Ah-choo.* Yes. *Ah-choo.* I'm here. *Ah-choo.*" April rubbed her nose and stood up, rather embarrassed.

"She should have said 'no'." Airron rose and brushed bits of foliage off his behind.

Raina accepted Airron's proffered hand and stood, too. "I don't think that would have helped. I think there must be some sneezeweed in here."

The branches were shoved aside and three elves stared down at them. April didn't recognize them. "What are you all doing in there?" The

2

shortest elf and owner of the impatient voice made it sound like an accusation. He seemed to be the leader of the trio.

"Um … playing hide-and-seek," April said lamely, climbing over the root and out into the open.

The elf eyed her with skepticism and took one step back, flanked by his companions. These elves were older than April's fifteen, and older than Raina's brother Salm even, who was seventeen. They looked about eighteen and had probably finished school, which would explain why April didn't recognize them.

"Were you looking for me?" she asked.

"Yes." The elf squinted at her eyes as if to make sure it was really her. The crystal-blue colour confirmed her identity, since every last elf in New Haven had dark brown, almost black eyes. Every elf except her. It was only one of many differences between April and the New Haven elves, but it was the most obvious one, at first glance anyway. Although her long streaky hair came a close second, since it included the unfortunate colour of green. New Haven elves never had green hair.

"Greetings, April-May June." The elf gave a bob of his head.

"Just April," she said. "Please."

"Greetings, April. My name is Figgy, Figgy Forester. I present Robin Sky and Cedric Greenthumb." Figgy motioned to his friends in turn. "We have recently returned from an extended camping trip in the Outer-World. We encountered something that we have never seen or heard about. We hope you might be able to help us identify the creature."

"Was it a giant furry purple-spotted, three-legged, one-eyed hopping critter?" Airron asked with a very straight face.

Figgy lowered his carrot-orange eyebrows as if trying to recall such a thing, as if he could have possibly forgotten. "No, we didn't see anything like that. And I can assure you that we saw many strange sights on our adventure!"

His companions nodded their heads eagerly. Robin had a scrawny build, dark brown hair and he wore robes. He was clearly a winged elf— a fairy. Cedric was of an average height with shaggy brown hair and a happy face. He was most likely an earth elf, a pixie, as was Figgy. Their names gave it away.

"Airron is only joking about that purple-spotted hopping thing," April said. "No such creature exists. At least, I don't think it does. What did you see?"

3

"Well, it is hard to describe. It was alive, certainly. Twice our height in length, but much rounder. And it walked on four stubby legs, very slowly. I don't know if you will believe me, but it carried on its back a sort of flattened helmet which was as hard as rock. It could actually disappear inside it, as if the creature was no longer there at all. We were truly amazed when it entered the water. It didn't sink under the weight of this helmet, but swam more quickly than a gilled elf, a merrow. I can draw you a picture if that would help." Figgy plunked down on a stone. He yanked a square of birchbark and a charcoal stick from his pack, and started sketching with fast strokes. "I think it might be a magical creature," he added.

At over six inches, Airron was the tallest in the group, even taller than the three older elves. Using his height to advantage, he stared pointedly down his very straight nose at the interlopers, crossed his arms and tapped his toes. April got the message.

"Figgy, there's no need to draw a picture," she said hastily. "I know what you're talking about. They are quite common, really, and not magical at all. They're called turtles, and come in different sizes and varieties. The helmet is really a hollow shell, but it's very thick. It protects the turtle from creatures that would eat it. You didn't get too close to the turtle, did you?"

Figgy shared a guilty glance with Robin and Cedric. "Um, well, we did poke at the helmet—shell, with a stick. But the creature moved so slowly, it didn't seem dangerous. And I only rode on the turtle for a short distance, to see what it was like. It was too slow, no fun at all ..." He trailed off uncertainly when he noticed April glaring at him in outrage. She would have been surprised to know how ferocious she looked.

April was amazed that all the elves who ventured bravely, and in her opinion foolishly, into the newly accessible Outer-World had managed to return safely. After thousands of years of being trapped by the same forcefield that protected New Haven, elves were eager to see, for the first time, what lay outside their own world. The magical barrier still protected the elven realm from everything large and dangerous that would enter it, but elves could now come and go as they pleased. And since it was April's doing that the barrier had been altered, when she had saved it from failing completely, she knew that she would blame herself if any elves came to harm. Figgy and his friends were lucky to have returned after riding on a turtle.

"Are you completely nuts?" April cried. "Have you no more brains than a squirrel? Or a Giant? 'Not dangerous'? Did you go near the turtle's mouth? Did you try swimming with the creature? Just to see what that was like? For … for fun?" April strode angrily toward Figgy to emphasize her point.

Figgy backed away, shoving his sketching materials into his pack haphazardly. "No, no! None of us are gilled elves. No merrows here. So we didn't try to swim with it, honest!"

"If you had tried swimming with it, you wouldn't be standing here now. Not with two legs anyway. 'Not dangerous'! Ha! You saw how the turtle could move in the water, and their jaws snap closed with enough force to crush a stick twice the size of your leg. Their jaws aren't slow, believe me. They aren't called snapping turtles for nothing. They're fast enough to catch minnow fish, elves are no match. And you don't even have any magic to protect you or—"

"Okay. Okay, well…um …thanks." Figgy backed further away, his pack held protectively in front of him like a shield.

Robin inserted himself between April and Figgy, as if his friend needed rescuing. "Yes, we'll be sure to stay away from those dangerous turtles next time we go camping. That's all we needed to know. Nice to meet you, April-May June." Robin grabbed Figgy's arm and the trio lunged into the leaves as if a vicious snapping turtle was lumbering towards them.

"Just April! And nice to meet you too," April called out to the empty air.

"I don't think they'll ride a turtle again." Peter stared after them, grinning.

"You did a super job getting rid of them." Airron patted April on the head. He liked to rib her about her short stature. "Scared the heck out of them. I don't know if they were more afraid of you or the turtle. That was way better than 'no'. They'll never ask you another question again."

"But I was only telling the truth. And it is my fault that elves are travelling through the barrier. If something bad happens, I'll feel responsible. Sometimes I think it would be better to take the thunderwand and reset the forcefield to the way it used to be, when no elves could leave New Haven and you were all safe."

"I think you're getting a Franken complex," Airron said. "When he founded our world, he managed to outlaw magic for eons, didn't he? Think of all the elves that were banished because of his own fear of magic. Elves shouldn't be trapped again because you're scared of what will happen to them outside. You're not the boss of all the elves."

"I know, but still -"

"And it's not your fault if elves decide to visit the Outer-World," Raina cut in. "Head-Sage Falcon has warned them of the dangers. And even King Skylar issued a statement about the risks. The mayor recommended elves limit their travel to the transitional outer layer of the forcefield, where there is less risk of coming face-to-nose with a forest cat." Raina shuddered, she had been dangerously close to a cat herself, not so long ago. "If any elf goes outside or leaves the safety of the barrier's second layer, it isn't your fault. By the way April, why didn't you ever tell us about snappy turtles, when we were stuck on the wrong side of the forcefield? I'm sure you never mentioned a word about snappy turtles when we were walking around out there."

"We weren't exactly walking around." They had been desperately trying to get home. "And I probably didn't think of it," April added.

"I'm starting to wonder exactly how many other things you forgot to mention besides snappy turtles, arrow shooting porkypines, baby boars, forest cats, giant raven birds, can't forget those …" Raina listed. None of those animals existed inside New Haven, so they were new to everyone except April. No animal larger than a mouse lived inside the elven realm. Even the trees were shrunken versions of what grew outside the forcefield.

Airron looked up and checked the position of the sun. "I better fly home, can't be late for dinner. My mother invited company, the Risings." He pulled a face. "I think she has hopes for me and Starla, you know— *the fairy*." That said it all. Airron's mother wanted him to associate with other fairies, not his friends of choice.

"But that's not fair, Airron." Raina frowned. "Your mother can't pick your friends!"

"I know, but that doesn't stop her from trying. Anyway, I have to go, have to keep her happy or she won't let me out of the house at all," he complained. April had met Airron's mother, it didn't look like she had ever been happy, or wanted to be.

Airron removed his robe to free his wings, said he would see them at school tomorrow, and soared away. With his arms spread wide, his wings were huge. Winged elves didn't exist outside the forcefield, and April was still amazed whenever she saw a fairy fly. Their wings were as varied and decorative as butterfly or moth wings, but structured more like bat wings, attached from elbow to shoulder, and down the spine. April watched with admiration until Airron's beautiful amber and black-banded wings disappeared into the leafy canopy.

"Come on, we better get home too," Raina said. She veered left to cut through a clover field, complaining nonstop about Airron's mother.

April couldn't help but smile at her best friend's grumbling. April had never even had a friend until she arrived in this world and now she had three, Raina, Peter and Airron. Four if she counted Salm. And still more if she counted friends from school. And she had a family, Raina and Salm's family. It was wonderful to not be alone anymore. April often walked around grinning foolishly because she was so happy to have a home and friends and a family after five years of loneliness. April's true parents had been gone ever since she was a small elf. They had disappeared into the treacherous Outer-World never to come home again, a tragic and too-common occurrence outside the barrier.

They ducked into a band of thicker undergrowth and Raina's voice disturbed several insects—and something larger. A dark shadow caught April's eye, moving through the trees ahead of them. April squinted, trying to bring it into focus, and then it was gone. It had probably been a trick of the dappled light, but April concentrated her magical senses on that part of the woodland anyway. The area proved deserted except for a few perfectly innocent bugs.

They hadn't traveled many more steps when an acorn plummeted through the air and almost landed on April's head. She dodged it in the nick of time. The acorn dug into the ground. It seemed to have fallen with unusual force.

"Be careful, April," Raina said absently.

"I'm only walking, I don't have to be careful."

Less than a dozen steps later, a grasshopper pelted out of the brush and rammed April to the ground—hard. The insect took off without any sort of apology. It was a very rude grasshopper. Raina offered a hand to pull April to her feet. "I was being careful," April insisted. "The grasshopper wasn't."

This time April managed a grand total of twenty steps before the ground gave way beneath her right foot and half of her fell into a mole's muddy tunnel. The rodent must have burrowed too close to the surface. This time Peter hauled her up from behind.

"Not having much luck, are you," he said.

"I'm having lots of luck—bad luck," April said. What was going on?

She advanced cautiously now. Around the next curve in the path, April tripped and fell on her face. Somehow her foot had gotten tightly tangled in a vine, the thing wrapping around her ankle like a snake. She kicked it off and stumbled up, unaided. She was known to be clumsy on occasion, but she wasn't usually this bad.

For a few moments, April held her small spot of ground, leery of moving even one step. When a hummingbird buzzed by, April could not believe what landed on her previously clean hair. Raina collapsed in laughter. Who could blame her?

Peter was more polite, as always. He handed her a leaf to clean her hair, as much as it could be cleaned.

Even standing still had not helped. April stepped hesitantly forward, alert for another mishap. There wasn't one—not *really*. But April started to have the most peculiar sensation. She couldn't remember ever feeling this exact same thing before. It wasn't the crawling sensation that she got along her spine when she sensed danger … but it was similar. And she couldn't say with any certainty that she wasn't sensing danger. Her feet stopped unbidden. She opened her mind to the surrounding forest, straining all her magical senses.

"April, what's up?" Raina touched her arm. "I've spoken to you three times and you haven't answered once. Did you rattle your brain that last time you fell down?"

"I didn't fall, I tripped. And I'm not listening because I'm sensing—magically checking the area." April should have felt reassured that she couldn't detect anything, but somehow she didn't. She felt itchy.

Peter glanced nervously over his shoulder now. "And do you sense anything?"

"I don't know. It might be my imagination, but I have a funny feeling. I can't sense anything that shouldn't be here, but …" April turned in a circle to look around with her eyes. She was surrounded by the green of the forest and sunlight flickering through the leaves. Shadows were lengthening as the afternoon edged toward dusk, but they seemed to be perfectly normal shadows, nothing more.

"April, I'm sure everything is fine. We are inside the barrier and it is functioning perfectly. Nothing dangerous could be here. So you had a few accidents, it doesn't mean anything," Raina said.

"I know that." April bit her lip, then sighed. "Look, stay here for a minute, okay? I want to look around and try and figure out what this weird feeling is." She knew New Haven was safe, but she wanted to discover what was unsettling her.

"We'll come with you, don't want you to fall down a mole hole and disappear," Peter teased.

"No. I can concentrate better if I'm alone. And this feeling is tough to figure out. I'll be fine, so wait here, okay?"

"Well, don't be long." Raina sounded impatient. "There's nothing wrong, you know. There can't be. And I want to get home for dinner."

April headed directly into the thickest undergrowth and it closed around her. She lost sight of her friends after only five steps. Ignoring the persistent feeling of unease, April spiraled out from where they had been walking, circling around the spot where Raina and Peter waited. She scanned the ground for unusual tracks. After a thorough search, she discovered some fresh scuff marks, exposing the damper ground underneath. The scuffs looked bigger than elf prints, but not by much. April decided that the marks had probably been made by an elf with exceptionally large feet, nothing more. Her search proved a waste of time. On the bright side, she came across a trickle of ground water and washed out her hair.

It took April awhile to get back to her friends. She had wandered farther away than she had realized. When April pushed through the vegetation and rejoined them, Raina eyed April's dripping head. "It took you long enough. What did you do? Hike all the way to the lake to wash your hair?"

"No. I just searched the ground around here, around us. I didn't find anything except some scuffs, and some ground water," April said. They resumed their hike home and April tried hard to relax, but she couldn't. At least she stopped having accidents.

"What does your feeling feel like, exactly?" Peter asked, not quite ready to forget the incident.

April struggled to find the right words to describe it. "Sort of like when I sense danger, but not the same. I feel kind of itchy, like bugs are crawling under my skin."

Raina shuddered. "Yuck."

"Maybe it's invisible," Peter suggested. "Do any invisible creatures live in the outside world?"

"No. None that I know about, anyway. And being invisible wouldn't stop me from sensing it. You didn't feel anything?" April could use some help figuring this thing out.

He shook his head. "No, but I'm not likely too, am I?"

"Well, we don't know what sort of magical ability you'll develop. Or when it will happen, maybe you could sense something." They knew that Peter would be one of the rare New Haven elves gifted with a touch of magic, since April had been able to see his magical aura at the changing ceremony three months earlier, when Raina had gotten gills and Airron had gotten wings.

"Well I can't sense anything. You're making me nervous," he said with a quirk of his lips.

"I think I'm making myself nervous, too. It will be nice to get home."

They picked up their pace. The sun was setting when they spotted the tall white towers of the Pooles' house, perched on the side of a small lake. Some of the towers jutted right out of the lake's edge.

"Are you going to stay for dinner?" Raina asked Peter automatically.

"No, I better get home. I really do have some stuff to get ready for school, tomorrow." He grimaced. "Thanks anyway."

"What is there to get ready?" April asked. "We didn't have homework over the summer, did we, Peter?" She didn't remember being assigned anything.

"We had some reading, but not real homework. I like to be organized, that's all. It makes school easier. See you tomorrow." Peter waved and disappeared down the path.

As was customary, they rinsed their feet in the basin by the door before entering the house.

"Reading? Did you do it?" April asked, as she scrubbed up to her knees. Half of her was muddy from the mole tunnel.

"Yes. Didn't you?" Raina hopped out of the basin when the water turned dirty brown.

"No, I forgot." Oh, well, it was too late now. April hadn't grown up going to school and tended to be less concerned about the whole thing than her friends. They dried their feet with the little cloths stacked nearby and entered the cozy comfort of the house.

Familiar noises and delicious scents were coming from the kitchen. It smelled like turnip and crabapple casserole, one of April's favorite dishes.

In the kitchen, Mrs. Poole was busy stirring something over the coals. "You're back. I'm surprised you made it in time for dinner. Is Salm with you?" She smiled as warmly as the banked fire in front of her.

10

Soothed by the scene, April began to relax fully inside, unaware until that moment of the tight little knot of disquiet inside her chest.

Raina automatically started laying places at the table. "No, Salm went to Big Lake, with Sprite." She waggled her eyebrows and sampled a snippet of parsley.

"Sprite is it? Well, I do hope he hurries home. You all have school tomorrow, you know," Mrs. Poole reminded them.

"As if we could forget." Raina handed April the stack of shells to distribute.

They put everything they could think of on the table, stealing bites all the while. Salm had not turned up by the time Mrs. Poole called the rest of the family to the table.

"We might as well start." Mr. Poole eyed the food hungrily. He began serving DewDrop, Raina's little sister, and the rest of them served themselves.

April was enjoying her second serving when a wild-eyed Salm pelted into the kitchen as if a forest cat was on his heels. He was a mess. His clothes were torn and his skin was raw and bruised. All of him was covered in mud. He looked like he had been dragged through a prickly hedge backwards in the rain, at least ten times.

He made a beeline for April and glared down at her so fiercely that she almost slid off her cushion to seek shelter beneath the table. He pointed an accusing finger and demanded, "Why did you do it? Was it a bad joke?"

"Me?" April asked.

Salm's eyes grew so wide that they showed more white than dark, and his freckles stood out on his pale skin like muddy spatters. "Well it couldn't have been any other elf, could it?"

He looked like he wanted to shake her and April drew back as far as she could. She had never seen Salm lose his temper. He was normally so easygoing, but at this moment, he was frightening.

"Salm, that's enough! You're scaring April. Sit down, calm down, and explain yourself." Mr. Poole guided Salm over to a cushion. In spite of being so mad, Salm looked ready to collapse.

"Well, it's nothing compared to how much she scared me, and the others."

April had no clue what he meant. She hadn't scared elves since before the summer holidays, and she had never scared Salm. "I don't know what you're talking about, Salm," she said timidly, hoping he wouldn't jump

11

down her throat again. "I don't know how I could have scared you. I don't understand."

"But it couldn't have been any other elf. Only you could have done it," he said.

Mr. Poole sat down on his cushion. "Salm, what could only April have done?"

"No other elf could have made the lake spin and turn it into a gigantic whirlpool. If I didn't have gills, I wouldn't even be alive. Sprite, either. We couldn't swim out of the whirlpool. We were pulled under and trapped. We kept being tossed into rocks and other debris, and the water wouldn't stop spinning. The whole of Big Lake was spinning. What else could have caused that, besides powerful magic?" Salm's voice shook.

Mr. Poole frowned deeply. "Were any other elves hurt?"

"No, Sprite and I were the only elves in the lake when it turned into a whirlpool and our gills saved us. But we got really banged around." Salm stared fixedly at his empty shell. He wouldn't even look at April now.

"What about the elves on the shore?"

"They watched, they couldn't do anything to help. But they weren't hurt. The land didn't spin, only the water." Salm sighed and seemed to deflate.

"Um, Salm? Did the water in the lake drain out, like one of your basins, until there was no water left?" April asked, "Or did the water stay in the lake and spin?"

"Well, you should know," he muttered bitterly.

She felt like Salm had kicked her.

"Don't talk to April that way," Raina cried. "She was with me all day. She couldn't have made the lake spin, and she wouldn't do that anyway. You're wrong."

"Salm, did the lake drain or merely spin?" Mr. Poole pressed, "It could be important."

"The lake spun around, the water didn't drain out."

Mr. Poole looked disappointed. "If the water had drained out, there might have been a natural cause, but I can't think of one rational explanation for the water in the lake to spin like a whirlpool. That is certainly unprecedented."

It sounded like powerful magic, even to April. Mr. Poole glanced at her briefly. Were his eyes accusing now?

"What happened to Sprite? Is she all right?" Mrs. Poole placed a comforting arm around Salm's shoulders. She squeezed too hard and he winced.

"I took her home. She was really upset and bruised. Some date!" Salm said bleakly. "I don't understand what happened. You were with April, the whole time?" he asked his sister, still not looking at April.

Raina nodded firmly. "Yes."

"Well, except when we separated in the forest," April said. She should have kept her mouth shut. Raina thought so, too, and shot her a quelling glance.

"But that was only for a few minutes, if that," Raina lied. "Certainly not long enough for you to have gone to the lake and back."

"Well, I have no explanation, not one that makes sense, anyway. How many elves witnessed the event?" Mr. Poole sounded official now.

"Me and Sprite, Paddy and Twiggy. Cherry and Marigold had left a few minutes before it happened. All the others had gone home."

Mr. Poole nodded, his face set in grim lines. "I am going to report this event to Falcon at once. We will send some scientists over to examine the lake at first light. Salm, I'll have a look at those bruises and scrapes before I go."

"Don't bother, they're only bruises. I'll go shower off the mud in the waterfall, even though water is the last place I want to be right now." Salm wilted into his cushion like a plucked flower under a hot sun.

Mr. Poole disappeared briefly and returned with two vials of cream. "For scrapes. For bruises. Apply them where you need them," he instructed, setting them on the table.

Mrs. Poole served Salm his dinner onto his platter, as if he was DewDrop's age, before he could do so himself. She said, "Eat your dinner, Salm, you must be famished after your ordeal. You can shower later. I'm just very glad that you are safe and that no elves were seriously injured. We will get to the bottom of this." Poor Salm looked so banged up and sore, he might not make it to the waterfall.

Mrs. Poole started to clear up even though the rest of them had not finished eating.

Salm's face was set in mutinous lines. It was obvious that he believed he had already gotten to the bottom of it.

Her appetite gone, April carried her shell to the basin to rinse. She didn't want to keep sitting at the table with Salm, since he thought her capable of harming him and other elves. How *could* he think that? They were friends—more than that, he was like a brother. April couldn't decide if she was more angry or hurt by his attitude. Hurt, she realized when the emotion tightened her throat and threatened to choke her.

"The rest of you go and get ready for school, then get to bed early. I'll clean up tonight." Mrs. Poole urged them out of the room and away from Salm.

DewDrop didn't go. She moved her cushion closer to her brother and sat right beside him, sweetly comforting. He put an arm around her and tucked her close.

April felt funny inside, watching the gesture. It almost felt like her heart was being squeezed. "Come on, April." Raina tugged her up the spiral staircase.

They had a lot to talk about. But April didn't feel like talking, she felt more like crying. And she hardly ever cried, almost never. Neither said a word until they were installed in Raina's room with the door securely shut.

"My thanks for believing me," April said, as soon as they were seated cross-legged on Raina's bed.

"Of course I believe you. Why would you make the lake spin? That's the stupidest thing I've ever heard. Salm must have hit his head on a rock and knocked all the sense out." Raina looked April straight in the eye. "Try not to let it bother you. By tomorrow, Salm will realize how foolish he's being. Okay? Try not to be so sad about it."

"I'm not sad," April said.

Raina didn't call her on the white lie. "I didn't want you to say anything about when we separated in the forest," she said. "Since you didn't make the lake spin, there's no point in anyone thinking it was you. And if Salm could believe you did it, so could other elves. They should try to find out what really happened, and not waste time thinking it was you."

"I can't imagine anything in your world that could make a whole lake spin. You know, if I didn't know it wasn't me, I would probably think it was me," April said with dismay.

Raina rolled her eyes at April. She used to do it all the time, but now that April was more familiar with living in New Haven and amongst other elves, Raina did it a lot less. "April, I just thought of something else. Do you think the water spinning might have had something to do with that strange feeling you had in the forest?" she asked.

14

"Oh." April hadn't connected the two. "Maybe. But that doesn't really help, does it? We didn't know what it was then, and we still don't."

"True, but it is a good starting point. I know I dismissed it at the time, but after what happened to Salm, maybe your clumsiness even meant something."

"I don't know, I can be clumsy," April said. But there had been that strange dark shadow and the scuff marks, which probably had been too big to be made by elven feet.

"But you're not usually that clumsy, April. I think you were sensing something significant," Raina said. "Something that was really there."

"Well, I wish I knew what it was then." But sadly, April didn't know. The day had certainly ended on a sour note. The holidays were officially over, and to top it all off, Salm hated her.

2. Hairy-Melon and Peachy Leechy

April had forgotten how hard it was to crawl out of a cozy bed much too early in the morning. More asleep than awake, she stumbled over to her tower window and groaned. The sun was well over the horizon. She had slept in. Why hadn't Raina woken her up? April could only think of one reason.

Grabbing a dress off the floor, she tugged the wrinkled cloth over her head, twisted her long tangled hair into a big knot and ran out the door. So much for getting organized in the morning. She spiraled all the way downstairs, then all the way up to Raina's tower room, only to find her friend cocooned under blankets, oblivious to the fact that it was the first day of school.

"Raina, wake up. Get up. Stop sleeping." She shook Raina several times. "School starts today. We're late and I don't think we're organized."

"Huh? Oh no!" Raina sprang from her bed and dashed for her closet. "Why didn't my parents wake us?"

"It's very quiet. I'm pretty sure everyone is still asleep."

"They must have been up really late because of the spinning lake. Go wake them up! Wake everyone up. I'll meet you downstairs. Oh no, where did I leave my books?" Raina started rummaging frantically through piles of assorted junk in the bottom of her closet.

April had forgotten all about books. She would have to go back to her own room and search since she didn't remember where she had stashed her books three months earlier. April suddenly understood why Peter wanted to be organized to start school—it would make everything run more smoothly.

April woke DewDrop first, since the little elf was easy to rouse.

"Yippee, I get to go to school today. I'm in a bigger grade this year," DewDrop informed April importantly, as if April didn't already know.

"Are you really?" April gave her a hug to start the day and sent her off to disturb her parents. DewDrop was very good at waking elves. She would make a loud screechy noise right in their ear. If that didn't work, she would jump up and down on top of them. April had first-hand experience of being woken up by DewDrop and felt a pang of sympathy for Mr. and Mrs. Poole.

She climbed the stairs to Salm's room. She hesitated in his doorway, flooded with the memory of how angry he had been with her last night. "Salm, time to get up for school. We're late," she said, without crossing the threshold. Salm continued to lie like a lump. "Salm, we're late for school. Wake up," April said louder, not moving a muscle. Neither did Salm. Why hadn't she enlisted DewDrop's help with Salm? No, given his injuries, that would have been cruel. As much as Salm's attitude had hurt her, April didn't want to cause him further pain.

Gathering her resolve, she crossed the room and gazed down at Salm. Up close, his bruises looked painful and plentiful. He really had been badly banged around. He was going to be sore when he stopped sleeping. Her heart got that funny squeezed feeling again, looking down at him.

April touched his shoulder. "Salm, time for school."

Salm yelped as if he had been stabbed with a sharp thorn, and leapt to his feet. He backed away from April, groaning and clutching his ribs.

"Everyone slept in, we're late," April repeated. "I wasn't going to hurt you, you know. I was only waking you up." She wished the ache trapped within her own cage of ribs would ease, but it went too deep. It felt like she had lost a treasured friend, and maybe she had. April turned and fled.

Salm watched her go without saying one word. He didn't call her back to apologize for his accusations. He didn't say he now knew better. He didn't say anything at all.

Back in her own room, April collected some books scattered in the bottom of her closet and stuffed them into her sack. Back downstairs, she assembled lunches while she waited for Raina to appear. She took a long time, given that they were late, and when she finally walked into the kitchen, she was all dressed up.

"I thought we didn't dress up for school. We didn't dress up last year," April said.

"Well, yes, but it is the first day back. It's okay to dress up on the first day." Raina smoothed her perfectly tidy shoulder-length brown hair and adjusted a neat fold in her pristine pink dress.

April stared down at her crumpled grubby clothes with regret, disheartened about how the day was developing, and it had barely begun. Raina also surveyed April and looked doubtful. "I should have told you. I was half-asleep before. Do you want to change? Maybe you should change."

April shook her head. "There's no time."

"Well, we might still make it before the gong, then. Come on!" Raina grabbed a berry for breakfast, put her lunch into her pack, and they hurried outside.

The official gong did sound before they could make it into the school meadow. Headmistress Hawthorn was waiting by the front door, arms crossed, frowning at their tardiness. The head-elf had seen them several times over the summer, so she did not ask about their holidays.

"Salm is still coming, we all slept in, even my parents." Raina said breathlessly. She was passing the blame.

Headmistress Hawthorn raised her eyebrows and tapped her fingers on her forearms. Her grey hair was pulled back severely for this first day of school, making her look extra bossy. "It does help to start the school year in an organized fashion," she advised. "Report to your old classroom, where you will be assigned your schedules. There are several new teachers this year, since some have not returned."

"Mr. Parsley? Has he not returned, Heady?" April asked hopefully.

"He has returned," Heady, as she was known to the students, replied without any expression, which was very telling in itself. Mr. Parsley was the meanest and loudest teacher. He yelled all the time, especially at April. "Ms. Summers, on the other hand, has taken the year off to explore the Outer-World. She believes it will be safer than teaching, less stressful. Now, get to class. Off you go."

Off they went, hurrying down the corridor to their old room, where all the girls were as dressed up as Raina, April felt messy and unkempt in comparison. She *was* messy and unkempt in comparison. April was quick to sit down, so that she wouldn't be noticed.

It was a surprise to see Ms. Larkin-LaBois standing at the front of the room—as a teacher. She was quite old to be teaching, let alone starting this year. April hadn't seen the elf since they had last met in secret while trying to save the forcefield.

The teacher did not comment on their late arrival, but continued speaking to the class. "Now, where were we? Ah, yes. As you are already aware, this is the year of school when you are streamlined into three

18

special classes, classes where you will learn about the type of elf you have recently become. If you have developed wings, you are properly called a fairy. If you have developed gills, you are a merrow. And if you are an earth elf, you will be known as a pixie. And of course, there are some of you that fit into none of these categories as perfectly as you should." She meant April. "I will personally instruct approximately half of you, the pixie group. Pixies outnumber both fairies and merrows by about two to one. Mr. Flynn will teach the fairies, and Mr. Leech will instruct the merrows. I understand that Mr. Leech is new to the school this year, as I am myself. This special class will be held immediately after lunch each day. Now, I am going to hand out your schedules, then turn this class over to your regular teacher. And I will see my pixies after lunch."

Ms. Larkin-LaBois handed out the squares of bark as if she had already memorized every single student's name.

April looked around the classroom while waiting. Peter and Airron sat one row over. Cherry Pitt was beside the window, surrounded by her usual group of friends—Marigold Primrose, Lily Waters, and Starla Rising. Cherry, the thorn in April's side, made a point of looking April up and down, before sharing a spiteful giggle with her gang.

Seamore caught April's eye and grinned toothily. April smiled back. She knew all the faces and names this year. It was a good kind of feeling, a belonging kind of feeling—barring Cherry and company.

Ms. Larkin-LaBois placed April's schedule on the table in front of her and tapped it. "We need to discuss your placement, April. Come and see me in the office before you go to lunch. You are an exception," she stated, but not unkindly.

April had never been called 'an exception' before, but didn't take offence. It was a fact that, in many ways, she was different from the elves born in New Haven.

After all the timetables had been distributed, Ms. Larkin-LaBois paused in the doorway with one last instruction. "While you are waiting for your teacher, verify that the information on your schedules is correct. I look forward to our year together." She looked small and rather tired standing there, and the school year was just beginning.

As soon as she disappeared, everyone started talking. April turned to Raina and asked, "Why do you think Ms. Larkin-LaBois is teaching?"

"I don't know. She's kind of old, but she seems okay. Where have you been placed? With the fairies, merrows, or pixies?" Raina asked curiously.

April hadn't checked her bark. She took a look and found she had most of the same teachers as the previous year, but not for the first class. An elf called Mrs. Merry-Helen Joy was replacing Ms. Summers as Environmental Studies teacher. The second class listed was Living in Elf Society with Mr. Parsley, it was written as L.I.E.S. Mr. Bladderwrack was still teaching mathematics, before lunch. Then lunch. The next square on April's birch bark was blank: that was the new special class. It was followed by Mr. Flynn's Literature class, and lastly, Sports with Mrs. Myrrh. They didn't have History with Mrs. Black at all this year. It must have been replaced with the special class. April had really liked learning about the history of New Haven—she would miss the stories.

"April, which special class are you in?" Raina nudged her.

"Oh, I'm not in any special class yet. They didn't know where to put me, I guess. I'll find out when I go to the office."

Raina grinned widely. "What's so funny?" April didn't think she'd said anything funny.

"It's only the first day of school and you have to go to the office already."

"But I'm not in trouble, so it's not the same thing," April stressed.

"I know. I'm teasing. Do you think we have time to talk to Peter and Airron before the new teacher gets here?"

As if to deny her, an ample figure filled the archway. "Well hellooooo! Hellooooo! Wonderful morning. Lovely to see you all so bright-eyed and bushy-tailed. How were the summer holidays, besides much too short?" The elf was as enthusiastic as anyone April had ever met. "I will be your Environmental Studies teacher this year. Lovely to be here, lovely, lovely. Lovely! My name is Mrs. Merry-Helen Joy and I am—merry that is! You may call me Mrs. Merry-Helen, that will do fine! We will assume the Joy."

She made her way to the front table, beaming like the sun. "Now, where shall we start? I've told you my name, now I want to hear all of your names. You there, we'll start with you!" She flapped her hand at Heather, the first student in the first row. Mrs. Merry-Helen held her smile as the first few rows introduced themselves. The smile never faltered; it looked like it was stuck on her face.

When April introduced herself, Mrs. Merry-Helen's smile stretched. It looked like her face stretched, if that was possible. The teacher peered closer. "April-May June, is it? Well, it is thrilling to have you in my class. Thrilling, thrilling, thrilling! We will get on famously, I am sure! April-May June, imagine that!"

"Um … it's just April, Mrs. Hairy-Melon," April said. The teacher's extreme enthusiasm was unnerving. When the whole class burst into laughter, April didn't know why. She had only asked the teacher to call her by the name she preferred.

"My name is Mrs. Merry-Helen, April," the teacher stressed.

"I know. That's what I said."

"No, you called me a Mrs. Hairy-Melon, not a Mrs. Merry-Helen. I'm sure it won't happen again. Now, next student please, what is your name?"

Raina was giggling and trying to be quiet about it. April's face heated up as if she was sitting dangerously close to a campfire. She wished she could disappear into her pillow. She wished she had started the school year on the right foot instead of the wrong one. Mostly, she wished she could talk properly.

The class finished introducing themselves and no-one else messed up.

"Thank you class. A finer crop of students I have yet to see! Now, Ms. Summers left some notes about what she had planned for this year. She hadn't scheduled even one field trip. Well, I will remedy that as quick as a wink! Best place to learn is outside the classroom, isn't it?"

The students nodded, although too many shot leery glances in April's direction. She liked field trips as much as anyone, she'd simply had some bad luck last year on their expeditions. April was sure that it would be different this year, since there was no longer any reason for things to go awry on field trips. She determinedly pushed the mental image of the spinning lake to the back of her mind. She had nothing to do with it and it had nothing to do with her.

The rest of the morning passed quickly, probably because it was only the first day back at school. As soon as the lunch gong sounded, April said to Raina, "I'll meet you in the meadow after I go to the office."

April wove through the crowded corridors, against the flow of students heading outside. Most were quick to step aside, accompanied by a skittish glance and followed by a whisper in a companion's pointed ear. News of the incident at Big Lake must have already travelled through the school. The fact that April was the only elf in New Haven with strong magic pointed a guilty finger directly at her.

It was a relief to reach the office. Mrs. Figwart was installed on her usual cushion, as if she had never left. "Greetings, Mrs. Figwart. How was your spring—I mean summer?" April asked politely, since it was the preferred question for this time of year.

"We work all summer. It is only the very first day of school. Why are you in the office?" Mrs. Figwart didn't bother to rise, not until she heard the details.

"To see Ms. Larkin-LaBois. Is she here?"

April was pointed toward an unfamiliar door. The room on the other side was small and windowless, containing only an empty table and several threadbare cushions. It was the most rudimentary of offices. It looked like Ms. Larkin-LaBois hadn't moved in yet or didn't plan to stay long. She was seated behind the empty table, staring off into space.

"Ms. Larkin-LaBois?" April said, when the teacher didn't move.

The old elf started. "Oh, April, there you are. Is it lunchtime already? Sit for a moment, even though you are one of the few elves around here that I do not have to strain my neck to look up at."

April claimed the cushion across from her. "Same for me."

"It is nice to see you again, April, without the pressure of our last encounter when New Haven was facing a most grave crisis." The teacher studied April intently as if to take April's measure, as if this was the first time they had ever met. Up close, her eyes glowed with life and energy, belying the aged skin that framed them in soft folds.

Ms. Larkin-LaBois got right to the point. "Now, April, it is possible for you to be in any one of the three classes, since you don't come from a specific type of family, as far as we know. Do you have a preference? Or do you need time to think about it?"

"No, I don't need time to think about it, I feel more like a pixie, really, since I didn't even know that fairies or merrows existed until I found New Haven. And I don't have wings or gills, and never will," April said.

A flicker of some dark emotion passed meteorically across the teacher's face, clouding her eyes. She closed them briefly, as if in pain. "Yes. Good. That was all I needed to know. I am pleased that you will be in my class. It will grant us an opportunity to get to know one another better." Ms. Larkin-LaBois studied April closely again. "You attended the changing ceremony three months ago," she stated, out of the blue.

"Yes."

"How did you transform? What changed about you after the ceremony?"

"Um … nothing. Nothing I can figure out, anyway. I felt sort of tingly and I turned fifteen. That's all. But since I'm not from New Haven, the transformation ceremony probably didn't work the same way for me. It probably didn't work at all, even though April the first is my birthday," she said.

"I would not be so certain that the ceremony had no effect on you," the teacher said. It sounded like a hint.

"But I would have noticed if I had changed, and I didn't," April said, not sure why the teacher was even mentioning this now.

"Time will tell, I suppose. I will see you after lunch, since you will be one of my students." Ms. Larkin-LaBois stood and moved stiffly toward the door. April was being dismissed.

She hurried away feeling a bit uneasy. The meeting had seemed odd, somehow, but she put it behind her when she joined her friends outside. They were installed on the same patch of moss as the previous school year. April settled cross-legged on the soft ground and smiled around, ignoring her food for the time being.

Raina leaned close and said quietly, "I told Airron and Peter what happened to Salm at the lake yesterday."

"There is no way you would endanger Salm. How can he even think it?" Peter shot a disgusted glance at Salm, who was perched gingerly on some thick moss beside his friend Paddy, indicating he had some bruising in unseen areas. Sprite was not in the meadow at all. If her condition was equal to Salm's, she was probably at home in bed.

"By the way, could you make a lake spin, April? Do you have that ability?" Airron asked.

It was an interesting question. Could she? April considered what magic could make a lake spin. "I've never tried to do something like that … but I probably could," she realized with dismay. "It wouldn't be all that different from making it snow or rain around me. I think I could do it, as long as the lake was inside the barrier where magic works so much stronger, like it's amplified."

"Don't go around saying that out loud," Peter advised.

"No, I won't." April had already been on the receiving end of all too many dark and accusing glances.

"So, what class did they put you in? Fairies, pixies or merrows?" Raina asked.

23

April was relieved to discuss something else. "I got to pick, so I chose pixies. I'm more like a pixie than anything else, and they don't offer magic-elf classes, do they?" There weren't enough magic elves to fill such a class. This year there would have been three—April, Peter and Tinka, if April's ability to see a magical aura proved accurate. And she wasn't sure about Cherry Pitt. The girl's disturbing black aura, which had also been visible to April at the transformation ceremony, had been anomalous. April didn't know what it meant, unless Cherry took after her late father and had the power of dark magic.

"But why didn't you choose the merrow class? Your family is gilled elves now, and I'm a merrow. We could have taken the class together," Raina cried, clearly not pleased with April's choice.

"Oh. I wasn't thinking about any of that. I was thinking about what I am, and I am a pixie. I don't have wings or gills, and I never will," April said, rather lamely. She should have considered Raina's feelings, but she hadn't even thought of her friend. After five years of looking out for herself alone, April often forgot to take into account other elves' feelings. She still made a lot of mistakes, even though she had lived in New Haven for almost half of one year.

"Oh, I understand." Raina heaved a martyr's sigh and looked very sorry for herself indeed. "Well, I hope Mr. Leech is nice. Imagine if he's another Mr. Parsley? Ms. Larkin-LaBois seems like a good teacher. And Airron gets Mr. Flynn for the fairy group, Flynn is really smart. It would be just my luck if Mr. Leech is a horrible teacher."

April choked on a seed when the name of Raina's new teacher sank in. Peter thumped her back until she could breathe again.

"What's up?" Raina asked.

Much too quickly, April said, "Nothing."

"Spit it out."

"No, you don't want to know." That was the wrong thing to say.

"Oh, yes I do!" Raina insisted. "Do you know something about Mr. Leech?"

"I don't know anything about *him*, not really. It's … his name," April said unwillingly. "Do you know what a leech is?"

"No, it's just a water name. Does it mean something in the Outer-World?"

"Well, yes. A leech is a water creature," April said vaguely and hoped Raina would leave it at that. Of course she wouldn't.

"Describe this water creature." It was an order.

"Do I have too?"

Airron leaned back on his elbow as if about to be entertained. "Your reluctance to describe this water creature is a dead giveaway that there is something wrong with it."

"It is a rather unpleasant thing," April admitted.

"Why are you dragging this out? You know you'll tell me eventually because I'll keep bugging you until you do," Raina said. And she would.

"If you really must know, a leech is a sort of fat worm that lives in the water. It isn't very big by Outer-World standards, but it would be big in New Haven. I've seen leeches as long as three or four inches. A leech feeds by sucking blood from other living things, when they go swimming. Leeches have a strong sucker kind of mouth, actually two sucker mouths, one inside the other. The smaller, inner sucker mouth has the teeth."

"Teeth?" Raina echoed faintly.

"Yes – very sharp teeth. The teeth cut the skin, then the leech sucks blood. But when they bite you it doesn't really hurt, something stops the pain, and it makes you bleed a lot too, for a long time."

"Magic?" Peter guessed.

"No, I think it is something in their saliva or slime. Anyway, it lets the leech suck lots of blood. A sizable leech can kill an elf if they suck enough blood out. Once they latch on, you can't get them off. Well, you can get them off with fire, but you usually end up getting burned yourself. Or if an elf can make magical heat and fire, like I can, you can use that, but even if you get the leech off, it's really hard to stop the bleeding. Magic can't fix that," April described.

"You're making up stories again," Airron said dismissively.

"I am not!"

"Yikes. My teacher is a giant blood-sucking vampire worm, like that blood-sucking vampire bat you told us about—except it's a giant worm! Great, just great." Raina packed up what was left of her lunch. "April, you didn't say anything about giant blood-sucking vampire worms when we were in the Outer-World."

"I didn't think of it," April said. "And we didn't go swimming, did we? I can't remember to tell you about everything. Why do you think I don't want elves exploring out there? It's simply a matter of time before one of them doesn't come back."

The gong sounded to end lunch then. It seemed overloud, making April's words sound even more ominous than they already did. Lunch was over, which was probably a good thing. They had spent too much time dwelling on disturbing topics and not nearly enough time eating. April had completely forgotten about lunch, which wasn't like her at all.

"Well, I'm off to meet my blood-sucking vampire worm teacher. If I disappear, you know where to look for me." Raina slung her pack over her shoulder and strode into the school.

April accompanied Peter to a classroom that she had never seen before. It was still more or less the same as all the other classrooms that she had already seen. They claimed a table together and waited for the lesson to start. Cherry wandered in with Marigold and April realized the main drawback of choosing the pixie class: Cherry was in it.

Their enmity dated back to April's arrival in New Haven, and since Cherry now held April responsible for her father's death, the elf openly hated April. The fact that Drake Pitt had elf-napped April's friends and shutdown New Haven's protective forcefield in a desire to rule the elven realm by force, didn't matter to Cherry any more than the known truth: her father had died accidentally when the thunderwand was struck by lightning and he had refused to release his grip.

Cherry scanned the room for a free space. Her gaze settled on April and she smiled maliciously, almost excitedly. It was a disturbing smile. "April-May June July August," she drawled, tossing her golden curls and bumping April's table on purpose, hard enough to knock the books off it.

"It's just April," April said coldly, and picked up her books.

Cherry moved to the far corner of the room and sat at a table with Marigold. April was really glad that Cherry settled nowhere near her.

"That was strange," Peter whispered in April's ear. "Cherry looked happy about something. You better be careful—the last time she was nice to you, she plied you with fermented baneberries." He didn't need to remind April, she would never forget that night, or trust Cherry again.

Ms. Larkin-LaBois entered the room last, after all the elves were seated. "Good afternoon. We have a lot to cover so let's get started, shall we. This is the largest of the three classes, since pixies tend to outnumber other varieties of elves roughly two to one, as I mentioned this morning."

April looked around; this class contained seventeen students, including herself. The other two classes would be significantly smaller.

"Each of you in this room is primarily a pixie, with the inherent abilities that earth elves are born with. Pixies sometimes have a difficult time discovering where their talents lie. But often, you will develop an

26

ability similar to one of your parents. I would like each of you to describe your parent's abilities. Daisy-May, we will start with you."

April learned a lot about her classmates over the next half an hour. She heard about abilities she didn't even know existed. Who knew it took special talent to fit rocks together precisely to construct stone walls? Or train mice? Or weave cloth? Or grow fruits and vegetables, with what Ms. Larkin-LaBois called 'a green thumb'? April hadn't seen even one elf in New Haven with a green thumb, although she had recently met an elf with that surname.

When it was Cherry's turn, she stood up and announced flatly, "My father, Drake Pitt, owned a mine and could find gold faster than anyone—until he was killed." Her vindictive gaze targeted April.

"And what was your mother's talent?" the teacher asked.

Cherry gave a twitchy shrug. "I don't know, I've never known. She died when I was little."

"You were never told about your mother?"

"No."

"Thank-you Cherry. Marigold ..." Ms. Larkin-LaBois said, moving things along.

April didn't know what to say when it was her turn and sat tongue-tied. "April, what about your parents?" the teacher prompted. "Do you remember anything at all from the world outside?"

"Well, I don't remember my parents. But they both would have been magical elves because all the elves were magical outside New Haven. Although the degree of magic did vary. Some elves had much stronger magic than others. I don't know how strong my parents' magic was." It was all she knew.

"Thank-you, April. Peter ..."

"Both my parents are scientists." Peter didn't volunteer anything about having magic. That was private, except amongst his closest friends. Every last elf already knew April had magic because she had used it to save the forcefield, but the New Haven elves with magic didn't go around boasting about it. Magic had only been allowed in the realm for three short months. It was going to take longer than that for New Haven elves to be at ease with it, especially if lakes started magically misbehaving.

The hour-long class passed quickly since it was new and different. At the end of the lesson, all three groups of elves reunited for literature in Mr. Flynn's room. April was already seated adjacent to Airron when Raina wandered in. She looked to be in a daze, as if she was sleepwalking and having a nice dream. April waved her arm vigorously until Raina finally noticed and came to sit with them, a goofy smile plastered on her face.

"What happened? Did your vampire worm teacher suck so much blood that you're all woozy?" Airron asked, scooting over to make room for Raina at his table. She didn't notice and joined April.

"No! He's not like a vampire worm at all. I didn't see any resemblance to a giant blood-sucking parasite." Raina sighed, with a soft lingering hum as if she was eating something yummy.

"Was Mr. Leech nice?" April asked.

"Mr. Leech—well, he said to call him Wade. Wade was *very* nice." They didn't learn anything else about *Wade* because the next lesson began. Mr. Flynn's class was the same as the previous year, but harder for most of the students. April was probably the only elf who found school easier this year. She had practiced her New Haven symbols for letters and numbers sporadically over the summer and was much improved. School was definitely easier when you could read and write.

In Sports, Mrs. Myrrh spent the entire class talking about the activities they would try in the coming year. They were used to running around for the last hour of the school day, so that sedentary lesson seemed extra-long. By the time the final gong sounded, it felt like the holidays had never been.

Airron said his mother wanted him straight home. He slumped off in the direction of his treehouse, as if his pack was loaded with rocks weighting him down. Peter headed directly home as well, citing homework, even though it was only the first day.

April and Raina walked home together, the forest peaceful around them, especially after being surrounded by a crowd of energetic elves. "Can I tell you about Wade?" Raina asked, as if it was a secret.

"Of course you can tell me about your teacher—you never got to. What's he like?"

Raina sighed and looked dreamy again. "Well, he's young, for a teacher. And tall, with deep, dark brown eyes."

"Raina, everyone in this world has dark brown eyes, except me." It was a fact.

"I know. I like your blue eyes, I've gotten used to them, but his eyes, Wade's eyes, are deeper and darker somehow. And he's very handsome, for a teacher, for any elf. He has muscles like the statue of Ibias Teal, you know the one." Raina's cheeks reddened.

April stopped and studied her blushing friend, finally starting to catch on. "You *like* him?"

"Of course I like him, he's a really great teacher." Raina sounded defensive.

"You're not supposed to *like* him, you like Airron, and Prince Skylar. And now you like Mr. Leech?" April frowned, confused.

"Well, Airron lets his mother run his life, doesn't he? And now that he's sixteen, now that we're sixteen, she's never going to let Airron spend any time with me, because I'm not a fairy like Starla. It's hopeless. And there is no future with Prince Skylar because he can only date a fairy and I'll never be a fairy, so that's hopeless too. At least Wade is mature— he would never let his mother tell him what to do. And he is a merrow like me." Raina scowled and kicked at pebbles with her toes.

April hadn't realized that Raina was so upset about the situation with Airron. Most of the time she laughed it off. She had been keeping her true feelings hidden. They continued along the path, yet suddenly the woodland didn't seem so peaceful. It took April a moment to recognize the same eerie sensation that she had felt the day before, but stronger this time. It made her feel afraid and deeply cold, as if her insides had been turned to ice.

Her feet stopped moving. She forgot to walk. "Raina, something is wrong."

As soon as Raina saw the expression on April's face, she looked frightened and whispered, "What? What's wrong?"

"I don't know, but I think we should run," April whispered back.

"Why?"

"I'm not sure, but it seems like a good idea. Let's get home!" April clasped Raina's hand tight and they took off as fast as they could, sprinting along the path. They ran hard, all the way to Raina's house.

When they reached the front garden, Raina skidded to a stop. "April? What happened back there?"

"I had that weird feeling again, like yesterday—only stronger. It was scary, but I still couldn't tell what was causing it." April magically checked the forest before she felt safe enough to collapse onto the edge of the basin to rinse her feet.

"Let's hope the lake didn't spin again. And at least we were together this time." Raina splashed her feet around energetically, splashing April, too.

"Yes, at least we were together." April scooted back and dried her toes.

They stepped inside the house, and April made sure the door closed firmly behind them. Locking doors were a rarity in New Haven. The safeguard had never been necessary, but April wished for some way to bar the door now. And the windows were worse. The big round holes allowed plants to grow inside and insects to fly through. Except for cloth curtains that could be closed at night, there was no way to shut them. It was hard to feel safe in a house full of holes.

3. Mice with Teeth

Since April and Raina were the first ones home, they started preparing dinner. April was chopping up a long bean sprout when the front door opened and closed. Footsteps padded across the floor and up the stairs—Salm's footsteps. He had gone directly to his room. He always came into the kitchen when he got home from school, except today. It was not hard to guess why. April renewed her attack on the sprout, frustrated and sad at the same time.

Raina paused in the middle of carving up a cherry tomato and said, "He'll get over it, April."

"There's nothing for him to get over," she said resentfully.

"I know." They both kept chopping.

The meal was ready when Mr. and Mrs. Poole arrived home with DewDrop in tow. The parents looked tired in spite of sleeping in. "Long day," Mr. Poole declared, combing his fingers through his thinning brown hair. "There was quite a rash of minor mishaps in New Haven, not serious thank goodness, but lots of cuts needed stitching and sprains needed wrapping. Kept me busy." He helped himself to a bean sprout slice and crunched on it. His words reminded April of her own close calls the previous day. It had to be a coincidence.

"Did you have a good day?" he asked his wife.

"Quiet. Lots of reading and writing, no stitching or wrapping." Mrs. Poole was a Historian, an expert on New Haven's past. "Thank-you girls. It was very thoughtful of you to make dinner, especially after your first day of school. How was it?" She started pouring out drinks.

"School was fine, I guess," Raina said, looking preoccupied.

"It was fine," April agreed, even though it hadn't been. She needed to tell Mr. Poole about the awful feeling she'd had twice now, but she would wait until after dinner.

"Well, that was certainly informative," Mr. Poole commented dryly.

Raina placed the food on the table. "Dinner's ready. Can we eat now?"

31

DewDrop said, "Yes," and sat down.

"Certainly, I missed breakfast entirely." Mr. Poole pulled out his wife's cushion. "Slept right through the most important meal of the day." He ducked out the door, called Salm to the table, and sat down to start serving.

They were all served before Salm made an appearance, sliding onto his cushion and chewing sullenly. When his father asked about his injuries, he just shrugged. He barely spoke a word and left before dessert. It made for a tense and uncomfortable meal.

They were clearing the table when the front door vibrated with urgent banging. "Well, this brings back memories," Mr. Poole commented and hurried to answer it. He returned with company. Head-Sage Falcon and Sage Scarab filed into the kitchen, their faces grave.

"Tea?" Mrs. Poole assumed, automatically putting water on to heat.

Chills traveled down April's spine when Sage Scarab shook his head. Something disastrous had happened if the grumpy old elf was refusing refreshments.

Mr. Poole picked up his medical sack. "Shelly, I must leave to treat an elf who has been injured. Don't wait up. And April, Falcon would like a word with you." He rushed away, as if there was not a second to spare.

"Perhaps it would be best if we spoke in private." The Head-Sage nodded at DewDrop, who backed out of the room with an awestruck expression on her face. Raina stood up as well, uncertain if she should stay or go. "Actually, I think we need you here, Raina." He tucked his robe around him and settled tiredly onto DewDrop's cushion, adjusting his long white beard below the table. "Shelly, you should stay as well. Perhaps private was not the word to use," he murmured.

"What has happened, Welkin?" Mrs. Poole asked anxiously.

"Welly, what happened," April asked at the same time.

"Let us all be seated." He waited until everyone was, then reluctantly delivered his news. "The elf who was injured is Airron."

"Airron?" Raina gasped. "Something happened to Airron?"

"Yes. There was an incident after school, but it was only discovered when his father returned home for dinner. Airron was attacked at the edge of the forest surrounding his house. He was unable to walk home. Luckily, his father found him in time." He reached across the table and clasped Raina's hands. "I have every confidence that your father can heal Airron and that he will make a full recovery," the Head-Sage assured her—assured them all.

April wanted to believe him, but the shadows in his eyes belied his words. "But we're inside the forcefield," she said. "There's nothing dangerous here. What attacked Airron? Surely not another elf?"

"It was not an elf that harmed Airron. He was not able to say very much, but he managed to tell us that he was attacked by mice. We could also tell by the ... bites."

April swallowed hard. "Bites?" Bites sounded raw and painful.

"Mice? But that makes no sense," Mrs. Poole insisted. "Mice do not attack elves, mice have never attacked elves. Never. They are not aggressive by nature."

"But ... but why would they attack Airron? And they bit him?" Raina's voice was thick with suppressed tears.

"Since this type of attack is unprecedented, the best possibility—the only possibility that we have come up with is that these mice were being influenced by something or someone outside themselves, in the same way that Drake Pitt could control other creatures to do harm," The Head-Sage said.

"But what else can control mice?" Raina cried. "Aside from April? April, do you know of anything?"

"No. Pitt could have done it, but he's gone," April said flatly. "And I can't control mice, not like that. I could never make them do anything if they were unwilling. And I can't believe mice would be willing to attack Airron. I didn't do it," she added sickly. She knew how this all looked.

Welly held April's gaze, his own steady. "April, listen to me. We do not suspect you, you are a great friend to Airron. What we have come here to ask you is if you might be able to suggest an alternate possibility. What, other than yourself, could influence mice to this degree? What could cause them to behave so aggressively? We look to you for answers. Nothing more."

"Course you didn't do it. Stupid idea." Sage Scarab glared at April as if she were blaming herself.

April felt a small warm glow, as if a candle had been lit inside her. They believed her innocent, in spite of the strong evidence to the contrary. "I wish to help, but I don't know what could have caused the mice to attack Airron. Or make the lake spin."

"Do you believe that both incidents have the same root cause?" Welly asked, as if this was an important clue.

April nodded. "I'm almost certain."

"April had the same strange sensation both times," Raina said, backing her up.

Welly sat up straighter. "Explain, if you would."

April did her best to describe exactly what she had sensed, twice now—twice before elves were harmed, or perhaps when they were harmed. As soon as she finished, Welly leaned back on his cushion and said, "It seems clear that something is using strong magic in our world, something other than April."

Sage Scarab grunted his agreement.

"Yes, I do believe something magical has entered our realm from outside the barrier, where magic is commonplace," the Head-Sage concluded, "but what? And why? April, any thoughts?"

"I don't know. There are a lot of magical creatures outside, but it would have to be a small one to come through the barrier, something as small as an elf. Since I can't sense what it is, I really don't know."

"Think something followed you here?" Sage Scarab asked bluntly.

"Huh?"

"Never had a problem like this before, timing seems fishy. Maybe you brought some critter with you when you crossed through the barrier," he accused.

April leaped to her feet, feeling betrayed by another friend. "I didn't bring anything with me. I wasn't followed. I was *alone*," she cried.

Sage Scarab arched a scraggily eyebrow. "Might have been followed unawares. You can't sense the thing, can you?"

"No. But I wasn't followed," April would have known if she had been followed, wouldn't she? Surely she would have noticed if she had brought something dangerous into New Haven with her.

"Clayton, I think we will examine other possibilities for the time being. Speak no more of this," Welly said.

"May we go and see Airron now," Raina begged, unable to wait any longer.

"No, Raina," he said firmly. "He is not in any condition to receive visitors yet. Your father will be able to tell you more in the morning. Airron will need a great deal of care and rest. But I am sure you will be able to visit him soon. April, come and see me if you think of anything to explain this attack. And please do not dwell on Clayton's words. They are merely speculation at this point, nothing more."

April nodded tightly. She did know that, didn't she?

Mrs. Poole walked the Sages to the front door and Raina fled to her room in tears. April followed her friend and tried to offer comfort. Nothing she said helped. It was the middle of the night before they went to sleep and Mr. Poole still hadn't come home.

Raina must have been up before the sun. When April rose at first light, Raina was already in the kitchen, completely dressed, with their lunches made and already stowed in their packs. It was a much more organized day than the previous one.

"My Dad's still not home," Raina said tragically, then they both heard the outside door creak open. Mr. Poole entered the room looking years older. "Dad! How is Airron? Did you heal him? Tell me," Raina said desperately.

Mr. Poole sank onto a cushion and rested his head heavily on one hand, staring blankly at nothing. "I did my very best, Raina. My very, very best. He survived the night, so I believe he will recover, but it will take time." He rubbed his eyes as if they hurt. "I had no idea that mice could be so dangerous, so vicious. I think we shall have to eliminate mouse-wrestling from the Harvest Moon Festival, permanently."

"But Dad, where was Airron hurt exactly?"

"He had many bites that required stitching. He lost a lot of blood before his father found him. One leg was worse ..." Mr. Poole trailed off. "That is all you need to know. He can have visitors in a couple of days, if he is up to it. Not before." He gulped down the cup of tea April had set in front of him and pushed to his feet. "I'm going to bed now."

Raina stared at him helplessly, tears welling up in her eyes. Mr. Poole sighed and pulled her into a hug, looking helpless himself. "Maybe you can come with me tomorrow, when I go to check on him. Okay?"

Raina nodded and sobbed.

"Airron should ... I'm sure he will be fine, Raina. The worst is over for him. Now, make sure Salm walks to school with you. Home, too. And don't go into the forest alone, not under any circumstances, not until we find out what is going on around here."

He held Raina against his chest and didn't release her until she said, "We'll stick together. We won't go anywhere alone."

"Good. Good night then. I mean good morning. I'm going to bed." He stumbled out of the kitchen, his face gray with exhaustion.

Raina stood in the middle of the kitchen as though she was lost in her own house, a world of hurt in her eyes. April put an arm around her friend. Trying to provide comfort to someone significantly taller made

April feel inadequate to the task. "Airron will be fine, your dad said so. Airron is really tough, and strong. He won't let stupid mice get the better of him," she said firmly.

"You're right. Airron will be healthy in no time. Of course he will. Now, we better wake up Salm, so we can go to school together."

"You should do it." No way was April going near Salm. He would probably think she was trying to finish him off once and for all. April went outside to wait, so Salm could breakfast in peace.

In the front garden, the world was barely awake. Sunlight glinted off a field of dew, transforming the water droplets into an illusion of brilliant crystals. April settled beside the lake and listened to the waves gently lap the shore. It was hard to accept what had happened yesterday in this very woodland. Tragic events were commonplace outside the barrier, but not inside. Never inside. Had April drawn a dangerous creature to New Haven with her? Was Sage Scarab right? After two near tragedies in as many days, April dreaded what this third day might hold.

When Raina and Salm turned up, Salm was tense and upset. Clearly, Raina had told him the bad news. He didn't speak a word to April, and that was fine with her. The longer Salm treated her like she had rolled in stinkweed, the more resentful she became. Head-Sage Falcon didn't believe she would hurt anyone, and Sage Scarab didn't think she had done anything harmful, on purpose at least. Salm should certainly know better.

"We're early, aren't we?" April said. "Why don't we pick up Peter at his house? He shouldn't walk through the woodland alone, and we can tell him what happened to Airron before school starts, in case he doesn't know."

"Good idea." Raina veered toward Peter's path and quickened the pace, intent on intercepting him before he left.

Peter's home was small and cave-like, recessed into the base of a mature tree. Two exposed roots bordered a path that led right to his door. He opened the door as April was raising her hand to knock. He looked so surprised to see them, it would have been comical on any other day.

"What are you doing here?" Peter said. No-one answered, not sure quite what to say. Peter recognized their silence as a precursor to bad news. "You better tell me on the way to school." He shut the door and they started walking. When nobody spoke voluntarily, he said, "Okay, what happened? You're scaring me."

"Something really bad, Peter. It's Airron." April tried to say it gently. It didn't help.

Peter stopped walking. "Airron? What's happened to Airron?"

"Maybe you should sit down."

"Don't say that," Salm said sharply. "You'll have Peter thinking the worst. Have you no idea how to deliver bad news?" He sounded mad at her.

"Shut up, Salm," Raina burst out and started to cry again.

"Someone better tell me." Peter sat down on a stone then, of his own accord.

Salm took over, since according to him, April was the last elf who should be delivering bad news, and Raina was crying too hard to talk. "Listen Peter, Airron was seriously injured yesterday. He was attacked by mice before he made it home from school. He lost a lot of blood before his dad found him. My dad spent the night stitching up his bites, but he should recover." Salm spoke rapidly. It did seem the best way to deliver the bad news, especially because he finished with the good news.

"Airron? Our Airron? He's hurt?" Peter hadn't quite taken it in. "But mice don't attack elves. They don't. We wrestle mice for fun. I don't understand. Why did they attack him?" Peter appreciated logic and this did not sit well with him.

"No-one knows why the mice attacked. Maybe they were being controlled. But it wasn't me. I didn't make the mice hurt Airron." April shot Salm a resentful glance, aware her statement placed her in a guilty light. Salm already believed her capable of deliberately harming other elves. He might believe this confirmed her crime.

"Of course you didn't. What a ridiculous idea. So, where these mice are now?" Peter asked.

"I don't know, no-one said. The rodents are probably still roaming around." April concentrated hard on the immediate area. "No mice nearby. Oh!" she gasped when she suddenly had an idea. It struck with the force of a firebolt.

"What? That bad feeling again?" Raina asked fearfully.

"No. No, I should have realized something important. Really important." April was deeply disappointed in herself.

"What?"

"If I could track the mice and communicate with them, I could discover why they attacked Airron. I could find out if they really were being controlled—and by who or what!" April said excitedly. "I can find out what's going on!"

"If the mice didn't attack you, too." Raina wiped her eyes and hugged herself.

"But I could sense them. I could climb a tree or something if they got too close. Mice can't climb trees, at least not very high," April declared.

"You're talking about normal mice. These aren't normal mice, are they? I don't want you to get chewed up, too." Raina's voice rose out of control. "Come to school, no tracking mice today."

"But they'll get too far away, I should try right now. I don't *have* to go to school, I'm only *supposed* to go to school." Never having gone to school before she arrived in New Haven, April still thought of school as sort of optional.

"April, you shouldn't go alone," Peter said, supporting Raina's opinion. "Even if the mice aren't dangerous to you, the thing that is causing you to have strange feelings might be very dangerous. Tracking the mice is a good idea, but you should do it with a group of other elves. And there's no hurry, the mice could be anywhere by now. It has been more than sixteen hours."

Peter was right. After sixteen hours the mice could even be long gone from New Haven. April gave in grudgingly. "Okay, I'll go to school— for now. But I'm going to speak to Heady about arranging a group of elves to track the mice with me, as soon as possible."

They reached the school meadow and Salm left them without a word. April ran inside the building on her urgent errand. Luckily, Heady was available. It helped that she had already been informed about the attack on Airron. She listened patiently while April proposed her idea, but she refused to commit to gathering a group of elves to accompany April while she tracked the mice. Heady claimed it was not her decision to make.

"I will present your idea to Falcon this very day, and I promise we will inform you as soon as a decision has been reached. These are very grave circumstances and we must act with the utmost caution. Do not even consider acting on your own, April. It would be risky, not to mention foolish," she said sternly, as if she could read April's mind. "Now, get to class. It is only the second day of the new school year and you have been late twice."

April had been talking longer than she realized. She hurried to class.

The disturbing news of Airron's attack had travelled through the school faster than an Outer-World spring flood. Following on the heels of what had happened at the lake, many students acted frightened of April. Airron was well-liked and everyone was genuinely upset that he was so injured.

Cherry was the exception. She had a strangely smug and self-satisfied expression on her face. She sauntered up to April in pixie class before the teacher arrived, for a few foul words. "April-May June July August, I heard about Airron. Such a tragedy. Too bad your magic didn't help him stay safe. Unless you used it to harm him in the first place? Isn't this stuff your specialty?" she drawled in her nastiest tone.

"Shove off, Cherry," Peter growled angrily.

Cherry wasn't ready to leave yet. "No elves were injured in weird attacks before you came to this world. Makes an elf think, doesn't it?" Her cutting voice was deliberately loud, to be heard by every ear in the room.

"Airron's my friend. I would never hurt him," April denied hotly.

"You've lied before. You lie all the time. Your words aren't worth mud," Cherry taunted. It was lucky the teacher arrived then, because April had been about to leap over the table and stop Cherry's mouth forcibly.

When the final gong sounded to end the school day, students were cautioned to go directly home and not walk through the forest alone. April tried to see Heady again, but she was unavailable.

Raina and April partnered up with Salm and Peter in the meadow. "Come on, we should go straight home. Peter, we'll walk you to your door," Raina said, recovered enough to start organizing her friends.

"You don't have to do that. I'll be fine," Peter said.

"No, it could just as easily have been you yesterday. And Airron's not fine, is he. And Salm is barely fine! We'll all stick together." Raina pointed to the path. They marched tensely through the underbrush and April kept checking the area, stretching her magical senses as far as they could reach. She found nothing to worry about at all.

"Thanks," Peter said when they reached his door. "And be careful going home."

"We will and we'll pick you up in the morning. Don't you dare leave without us," Raina reminded him.

"I won't." Peter stood and watched them out of sight.

The rest of the week followed a similar pattern. It was a great relief when no more elves were harmed. April began to breathe a little easier, and her classmates stopped avoiding her as is she was dressed in poison ivy leaves.

April had caught sight of the famous Mr. Leech between classes and had to admit that he was exceptionally eye-catching, being that much more tall, dark-eyed and handsome than any elf she had ever seen. There was absolutely no resemblance to an actual leech. Unfortunately, he seemed a little too aware of his fine appearance. He walked through the halls with his head tilted up and his chest thrown out, as if on display. His shirt and pants were unusually close-fitting, showcasing his muscular frame. The group of giggling girls that hovered by his side were treated to his brilliant white teeth and dimples at regular intervals, as if the smiles were timed. April overheard the teacher referred to as Peachy Leechy— the nickname was enough to make an elf gag.

No matter how much April pestered her, Heady would not commit to tracking the mice. Airron was not strong enough to receive visitors yet. And Salm didn't speak a word to April unless it was unavoidable. All in all, it was a somber first week of school.

When the final gong sounded on Friday, Raina was animated for the first time in days. Mr. Poole had finally agreed to take them to see Airron. He met them at school, right on time. Salm joined them at the last minute, standing silently beside Peter.

April had never been to Airron's house before, and couldn't believe her eyes when she looked way way up at the formidable structure built into the gnarled branches of an old oak tree. Airron lived in a treehouse! About five times bigger than a regular house, it looked more like a fortress. A wide staircase wound around the thick trunk at least three times before it arrived at a large balcony. The entrance to the house was an oversized archway that was both high and wide enough for a bunny to hop through. It took two doors to close it, split down the middle.

Mr. Poole stopped them outside this pair of doors and issued a sober warning. "Now, before we go in, I must caution you about what to expect. Airron has had a most difficult week. It will not be easy to see him so injured. Try not to be shocked by his appearance, remember he will recover. We won't stay too long. Right now he needs rest to regain his strength." They all nodded. "Okay, let's go then."

Mrs. Fay-Finch answered his knock looking rather tired, but as immaculately groomed as always. She smiled coolly at Mr. Poole. "Thank you for coming. You remember the way?"

Mr. Poole scratched his chin. "Airron's room ... well, now, it's straight, then up, then right, left, up again, left again ... or is it right?"

"I know how to get there," Peter said.

"Yes, yes, I'm sure we'll find the way. We can see ourselves to the room." Mr. Poole bobbed his head and swallowed as if Airron's mother made him nervous.

The heavy doors creaked closed behind them, filling the long corridor with gloomy darkness. The damp chilly air raised bumps on April's sun-warmed skin and she wanted nothing more than to turn right around and run back outside into the sunshine. She didn't want to see Airron other than he had been on Monday, healthy and happy. But she kept following her friends, trying to be strong for Raina.

Mr. Poole did end up needing Peter's directions as soon as they left the first floor. The hallways snaked through the house like mole tunnels, often changing directions where tree limbs blocked the direct path. When they finally reached Airron's door, Mr. Poole halted and turned to face them. "Remember what I said," he warned before he tapped on the wood and said too jovially, "I have brought you visitors, Airron, as promised."

April waited for Raina to enter first. Her friend's horrified gasp was not muffled quickly enough. April prepared herself for the worst.

Poor Airron was propped up in a huge bed and he looked like something from a nightmare. Mr. Poole could not have prepared them for this. Airron's arms were covered in deep bites, sutured together with fine black thread. The bites were swollen and bruised and angry red. He had so many bites that he looked like a patchwork doll, held together with thread. He even had a bite on his shoulder and one on his cheek. April felt ill just imagining what they couldn't see beneath the blanket.

Growing up in the Outer-World, April had regularly witnessed the results of grizzly and often fatal attacks of all kinds, but it always hurt terribly to see a suffering elf, especially when the elf was a close friend. New Haven elves, who lived so peacefully, had to be even more upset by the sight of violence. Peter latched onto April's arm, needing the support. April moved them both forward and tried to smile at Airron, who was managing the feat in spite of a painfully swollen cheek.

"Hey Airron," April said, when no-one else managed a word.

"Hey. I found a way to get out of going to school, extend the summer holidays a little longer," he joked weakly. Raina was trying to present a brave face. She couldn't manage it. Airron was the one to offer comfort. "I know I'm a sight, but it's not as bad as it looks. I'll be up in a day or

41

two," he insisted. "Come in and sit down, there's plenty of room on the bed. Just don't bounce."

Raina perched on the edge as gingerly as if she was sitting on a porcupine. April moved Peter closer, since he hadn't let go of her arm. Salm managed three steps into the room before he turned and fled. He didn't come back.

"Well, I'll have a word with your mother, Airron. Then I'll be back to take a look at your leg. Don't exert yourself, now. Healer's orders! I think I know how to find my way downstairs. If I don't return, you're in charge of locating me, Peter." Mr. Poole moved to the door and paused, uncertain.

"It's left," Peter said.

"Left, right." Mr. Poole nodded as if he had known that and turned left outside the door.

"Left, left," Peter called after him, perhaps misunderstanding.

Airron immediately told Raina, "Your dad has been really great."

"And ... and how are you, Airron?" Her voice shook.

"I'm good. Getting better," he replied, without a lot of conviction.

Peter cleared his throat to speak. "Has it been boring, staying in bed all week?"

"No, it hasn't been boring. I've been asleep, mostly."

"Do you remember being attacked?" April didn't know if she should ask that question, and from the look Raina shot her, she probably shouldn't have, but they needed answers if they were going to figure out what was going on.

Airron turned even paler, if that was possible. "I remember. Wish I didn't."

"But why did the mice attack you? Mice don't attack elves," April said.

Airron didn't argue the point. "No idea why they attacked. Couldn't believe it at first. Then I couldn't get my robe off fast enough, couldn't fly away." He leaned back into his pillow and closed his eyes as if the memory had drained him.

"Airron, did you see or hear anything before the mice appeared? Anything unusual? Anything at all?" April asked, ignoring Raina's shushing motions.

"No, no warning. Then mice with teeth. Three, I think. Three too many." Airron shivered weakly. "I lay there for a long time after, honestly didn't believe I'd make it. Dreamed about you, Raina. Then there were eyes, unusual colour of eyes—blue eyes? No, not blue eyes—green eyes? Yes, bright green eyes. Never saw green eyes before." Airron was falling asleep while he talked and started dozing lightly.

They shared concerned glances over his head. "April, stop making him talk about it." Raina gazed down at him sadly. "Does he look like he's getting better? He doesn't look very good, does he?"

"He's getting better. It will take time, that's all," April whispered. "And I'll stop asking questions."

Airron opened his eyes again, but only halfway. "Sorry, did I fall asleep on you? Keep doing that. Your father says its shock. I think it's that tonic he keeps giving me." Airron made a visible effort to open his eyes wider.

"We aren't going to stay too long, Airron. You need to rest. We just couldn't wait to see you. But we'll come back tomorrow if it's okay, if you're up to it," Raina said.

"I'll be up to it." Airron sounded determined. "What's tomorrow?"

"Saturday."

"Already? How did that happen? Lost some days," Airron muttered to himself. Raina tenderly took his hand in hers. Even his hand had an awful deep bite. He was very lucky to have all his fingers.

"Don't squeeze," Airron said and his eyes closed once more.

They sat silently, allowing Airron to doze until Mr. Poole returned. April finally noticed the rest of Airron's room. It was enormous, matching the scale of the house. A strong bough, growing in through one wall and exiting out another, divided the space in half. A hammock and several swings were suspended from the branch. One large round window showed exactly how high up they were. April shifted her gaze to an elaborate polished desk and several bookshelves crowded with dusty tombs. It looked like Airron had quite a collection of reading material that he never read. Except for the island of a bed, his room didn't look like a bedroom at all.

Mr. Poole returned with an armload of bandages and other Healer's medicines, and a cup of the tonic. "You better wait outside," he said firmly. They didn't argue. They filed out and Salm was there, propped against the wall. His face had lost all of its colour.

"How is Airron doing?" he asked, his voice as strained as his face.

"Not great," Raina whispered.

"Sorry, I couldn't handle going in. Something about the sight of blood …" He swallowed sickly.

Raina didn't tease him as she normally would. She simply hugged him. Airron groaned painfully from inside his room. Salm shoved away from the wall and moved toward the far end of the hall. Everyone went with him.

"What do you think Airron meant, when he said he saw green eyes?" April asked, trying to distract everyone.

"Maybe he was dreaming or hallucinating. Mice don't have green eyes, do they?" Peter said. "I don't think it means anything. He was probably staring at the green leaves overhead or something. A lot of leaves are shaped like eyes."

April wasn't so ready to dismiss the green eyes. "Lots of creatures in the Outer-World have green eyes," she said. They were still close enough to Airron's room to hear cries of pain. Salm put an arm around Raina and started them walking again. He got them thoroughly lost. By the time Peter found the way back to Airron's hallway, all was blessedly quiet again.

Mr. Poole stuck his head out the door. "Come say goodbye. Airron needs to sleep now."

They tiptoed inside and said their farewells while Mr. Poole packed up his equipment. Airron was barely lucid.

"We'll come back tomorrow," Raina promised him anyway, kissing his forehead gently. He mumbled something incoherent, not even opening his eyes.

Peter led them to the front door and outside into the warm sunshine. Raina cried all the way home. No-one could console her.

4. Plants Alive

Airron showed steady improvement over the weekend. On Sunday, he actually sat upright and looked very proud of himself indeed. When Raina, Peter and April took their leave that afternoon, it was with lightened hearts. They ambled through the town circle on the way home, not in any hurry to face the homework they had ignored all week.

Peter stopped in front of a white stone building and said, "Why don't we take a look at the new museum display, the one with the thunderwand. I haven't seen it yet and it is dedicated to us for saving New Haven."

"I haven't seen it either. Let's take a look," agreed Raina. April had never heard of a museum and Raina explained the concept, as they crossed the large, deserted entrance hall. The building echoed with emptiness. It didn't look like very many elves were interested in visiting the museum.

"It's not a very popular place, is it?" April said.

"Not really. Going to the museum is something you're supposed to do, not necessarily something that you really want to do," Raina explained. "The school often brings us here for field trips, but it's not very exciting."

An engraved sign pointed them through a doorway on their left. They toured around the room and stopped to admire the central display. It showcased the three gold and silver rods that formed the thunderwand, a magical device that they knew better than any other elf in New Haven. They reminisced about how they had found the thunderwand inside the Giant-tree's brain cavity and carted the rods halfway across New Haven to repair the injured Echo that was disrupting the whole forcefield. The beautiful gold and silver rods brought back a lot of memories, both good and bad.

"Okay, that's enough museum," Raina declared at that point, and headed for the exit.

From town, they detoured slightly south to walk Peter home. They dropped him off and continued on alone. When April magically checked the forest, as she did all the time now, she sensed an elf nearby, but no danger. She stopped walking.

"What is it?" Raina asked anxiously.

"Nothing's wrong. An elf is approaching, I'm waiting." April hoped it was a particular elf, one who spent a lot of time wandering around in the woods.

It was. Sage Scarab stumbled out onto the path ahead. He greeted them as if he had known they were there all along. "Thought I'd see you the rest of the way home," he grumbled, as if it was an inconvenience. They started walking, and he didn't try to lead them off the trails or take any shortcuts, as he usually did. They did not stray off the path. "You're not mad at me, are you April? About what I said the other night, about you bringing the trouble here?" he said.

"I was. It wasn't very nice. You hurt my feelings," she said frankly. She didn't feel the need to pussyfoot around Sage Scarab. He always spoke plainly and wasn't inclined to be sensitive, so she could speak plainly right back to him.

"Well, had to be said. Got to consider all angles."

"I suppose." But April didn't have to like it. "Have you been patrolling the forest?" she asked. She had several pressing questions, and he was the best elf in New Haven to answer them. Sage Scarab was one of the rare New Haven elves with a touch of magic. Sometimes April suspected that he had more than he let on.

"I have been patrolling, a little bit," he replied modestly.

He was probably patrolling the forest every waking moment. "Have you seen anything or sensed anything unusual?" she asked.

"Can't say for sure. Haven't actually seen anything that shouldn't be. As to sensing something, can't really say. Don't sense things like you, do I? But every so often, I get an itchy feeling ..." He trailed off.

April reached over and picked a burr off his back. "I know what you mean. It's like something is there, but it's not there."

"Yeah. I've had the feeling I'm being watched, once or twice. Not a good feeling." Sage Scarab frowned.

"No. But I still don't understand why we didn't try tracking the mice. It was a perfect opportunity to gain answers. Have you seen any wild mice roaming around?"

Sage Scarab stopped in mid-step and spat out the blade of grass he had been chewing on. "As to that, I'm going to tell you a secret—a big one. Not to be spread around." He lowered his scraggily eyebrows threateningly at both girls. "We tried to track those darn mice that very night. I'm the best tracker in New Haven," he stated factually. April had no doubt that he was. "I found the mice, all right. Three of them. Dead in a pile." April's breath caught in her throat, but there was worse to come. "These mice—they killed each other. Most unnatural thing I ever saw. Don't know what could control mice to that degree. April, could you do that? I'm not thinking you did, I'm curious is all," he said gruffly.

"No, I can only ask a creature to do something. I can't make them. If they don't want to do it, they won't. I don't have a terrible magical power like that." She wouldn't want a dark power like that, either.

"Didn't think so. Anyway, mice won't be any help now. Forget about them."

"Be glad to." But she couldn't dislodge the image of mutilated mice from her head. It wouldn't leave. Raina linked their arms, tightly. They walked like that, both reassured by the contact.

Sage Scarab escorted them right to the door of the house. A delicious aroma wafted out through the kitchen window. "Do you want to come in for dinner? There's always plenty," April said, but hesitantly, since there might not be plenty enough for Sage Scarab's appetite.

He accepted with enthusiasm. "Don't mind if I do."

April ran inside to warn Mr. and Mrs. Poole. Fortunately, there was sufficient food to go around, and it was nice to have Sage Scarab's company at the table. He helped to cover up Salm's continued silence. All disturbing topics were avoided so everyone could enjoy their meal.

Sage Scarab rose to leave after only two servings of dinner and two of dessert. "Thanks for the great meal. Have to get back to the woods," he said regretfully.

"Um … anytime," Mrs. Poole responded, a bit anxiously. There wasn't a scrap left on the table.

April jumped up and walked him out the door. "Be careful, Sage Scarab, really careful." She closed her eyes, pushing her sensing ability to the very limit. The surrounding area proved safe.

"You having a nap?" the Sage asked suspiciously.

April opened her eyes and he winked. She shook her head, suppressing a smile. Sage Scarab snorted and disappeared into the night. Trying not to worry about him, April returned to the house.

The second week of school passed without incident. They visited Airron every afternoon, sometimes accompanied by other classmates. They were all tremendously pleased at his steady progress. Tuesday, he had managed several limping steps around his room, looking as proud of this feat as when he had gotten his wings.

On Friday, Mr. Poole removed all of Airron's stitches while they were in school. It did a lot to improve Airron's overall appearance. The desk in his room was completely overflowing with gifts from well-wishers by then. Every day the pile had grown.

"I didn't know I had so many friends." Airron looked rather choked up as he limped over to his desk and picked out some fruit jellies to share. "These are really good. They're from O'Wing and Skylar—they flew over this afternoon. My mom was so thrilled to have a prince come to call that it was embarrassing." He made his way back to the bed and settled down with a sigh of relief. "At least the mice didn't bite my...posterior. Or I wouldn't be able to sit down at all."

"Thanks for sharing that." Peter helped himself to a grape jelly.

They all helped themselves to the treats while Airron quizzed them about what was happening in the world outside his bedroom. The first question he asked was, "No-one else has been attacked, have they? By mice?"

"No," Peter said, and nothing more. April had trusted Sage Scarab's secret with Peter. But they had waited to tell Airron until he was stronger.

Airron narrowed his eyes on Peter. "Have they found the mice?"

"Yes." Again, Peter didn't offer details—he paced over to the window.

"And?" Airron turned to April, probably because she couldn't lie to save her life.

"They found the mice, Airron. But they were already dead, so I couldn't learn anything from them," she said. Airron did need to know the truth.

"Dead? What killed them?"

"Each other. They killed each other." April sighed. "It proves that something was controlling them, which is why they attacked you. They wouldn't have done it on their own, would they?" April rose restlessly, and settled into one of the swings.

Airron absently traced the healing scar on his cheek. "They killed each other," he murmured as if to himself.

"Please, let's not talk about the mice. It makes me feel sick," Raina said. "The weekend is starting, what should we do tomorrow? Airron, what do you want to do?" She was desperate to lighten the mood.

Airron was happy to oblige. "Whatever you want to do."

"I think we should hang out in your room, there are heaps of treats and lots of games. And your mother doesn't try and throw us out anymore, I think she's getting used to us." Raina smiled smugly.

"I think she is, too." Airron took Raina's hand in his. The two seemed closer than before the accident, in a different way.

"How was school this week?" he asked, relaxing back on his pillow.

"It was a very quiet week. Everything was normal, almost boring. But boring is good," Raina said. After the previous week, boring was wonderful.

"We're supposed to go to the museum on Monday morning for a field trip. You'll miss that," April told Airron.

"Poor Airron," Raina laughed, tongue-in-cheek.

"Are you kidding? I won't miss that trip one bit. I've been to the museum. I would rather stay in bed."

"When will you come back to school?" Peter asked. He had missed Airron's companionship.

"Maybe the week after next. Believe it or not, I want to go back to school. Now that I'm not sleeping all the time, it gets kind of monotonous around here." Airron frowned at his walls.

They left before dinner since Airron still tired easily and Mrs. Fay-Finch had never invited them to stay for a meal. She put up with their visits, no more. The three friends turned toward Raina's house, since it was already the start of another weekend.

"Is Salm talking to you yet?" Peter asked April, ducking under a bright orange spotted toadstool.

"Not if he can help it." April followed him, she didn't have to duck.

"I don't understand how he can think that you made the lake spin. He knows you as well as a brother, as well as any of us," Peter said angrily. "Does he seriously believe that you hurt Airron, too?"

"I don't know."

Raina shrugged helplessly. "He is my brother, but I don't understand him right now. I wish..." Raina stopped talking and they all heard something coming toward them through the underbrush. Too late, April realized that she had forgotten to check the woodland even once since they had left Airron's house. Before they could run, a large fern

49

shuddered and Figgy Forester stumbled onto the path followed by his two friends, Robin and Cedric.

April breathed a sigh of relief, her heart still pounding. "Greetings, Figgy. Were you looking for me?"

He jumped and swung around apprehensively. "Oh, April, I didn't see you there. And there you are! Right there." He backed up and tripped over a curled-up caterpillar. "No, no, we're not looking for you today! No, no, no! Simply helping out, looking for someone else—not you!" He sidestepped towards a nearby edge of thicket.

"Who's missing?" Peter asked, before Figgy could disappear.

"Not missing exactly. But hasn't been seen for a couple of days. Sage Scarab, you know, the nutty old elf that wanders around in the woods covered in earth. I think he's a little bit crazy myself. A few trees short of a forest, if you know what I mean. I don't know why they're so worried about him. Probably meandered off and got himself lost. Probably walking in circles." Figgy smirked.

April gasped in indignation and stomped furiously toward Figgy when her temper took over. "Sage Scarab is not crazy! Not one little bit. He's not missing any trees! He couldn't get lost if he tried. He's one of the smartest elves in New Haven. And what do you mean that he's missing? How long has he been gone?" she demanded, as if it were Figgy's fault. He blanched and looked wildly towards his friends. Did he think April was going to get mad enough to strike him with a firebolt?

"The old coot hasn't been seen since ... uh, Wednesday evening," Cedric said. "Didn't check in on Thursday like he was supposed to. That's all we know, honest. Can we go now?"

"No! Where have you searched for him?"

"Everywhere, here and there, all around, you know." Cedric flapped his hand about as if shooing away a fly.

"No I don't know! How could I? You just told me!" April cried, overwrought.

Figgy latched onto Cedric's arm and gave him a strong tug. "We've got to go now, we're late for ... something, something important."

"Very late!" Robin added, from behind Cedric.

"And very important," Figgy added. The trio scuttled backwards and practically flew into the undergrowth, even though Robin was the only one with wings.

"Oh. Okay, bye," April called, but they were already out of sight.

Raina moved to her side. "Relax, April. They're gone now."

"But Sage Scarab is missing. Something terrible must have happened to him. He would never get lost."

Peter nodded in agreement. "No, he wouldn't get lost. But he's the toughest elf we know. I'm sure he can look after himself."

"Not against the thing that's out there, he can't." April was recalling the mice.

"No elf is safe against that thing," Raina said. "Come on, we can talk at home. Let's get home." They jogged the rest of the way. April didn't forget to check the forest, but now she was trying to sense Sage Scarab as well as danger.

As soon as Mr. Poole stepped through the door that night, Raina cornered him for information while he tried to pour himself a fermented drink. "Dad, what's happened to Sage Scarab? How long has he been missing? Has anyone found a trace of him? Why weren't we told?" All of her questions came out in one breath.

Her father pointed silently at the cushions and finished making his beverage. They all sat down and waited, if not patiently, at least quietly, until he joined them at the table.

"Now, let me see—we don't know what has happened to Scarab, if anything. He has been unaccounted for since yesterday, when he failed to check in. No elf has reported any sign of him, as yet. And you weren't told because there is nothing you can do about it anyway." Mr. Poole answered all Raina's questions in the right order.

"But Dad, we could help find him, especially April—she could sense him, you know that!" Raina raised both her hands in the air, palms up, emphasizing her agitation.

"Raina—all of you, listen to me," her father said sternly. "I don't want any of you roaming the woodland under the present circumstances. The adults are looking after it. It has only been one day since Sage Scarab failed to check in. If we feel he is in danger, we will hold a gathering and decide what should be done. We will enlist April's help if it is necessary, but only with a great deal of supervision. I don't want to have to stitch up any more of you, believe me." He took a big gulp of his drink and thumped it down on the table. "Now, it is Friday. Go out in the garden and play, stop hanging around the kitchen."

"We don't play, Dad. We're fifteen now," Raina declared in an offended tone. They went outside anyway, but they didn't play, they were too upset.

After dinner, Raina ordered April and Peter into the front garden. She even dragged Salm outside. He said he had a date—a double date, and couldn't stay. Raina didn't care. "This is important, Salm! You must have ten minutes to spare. I'm sure your date will wait ten minutes. Who is it anyway?"

"None of your business."

"Is it Sprite?"

"No. Keep your nose out of it. I'll stay for ten minutes, but only if you shut up about my date. Paddy and Twiggy will be here soon to pick me up so if you have something to say, you better say it now." Salm sat down, crossed his arms and waited.

Raina poured out nectar to attract the fireflies. They settled under the countless twinkling stars and Raina was the only one who knew why. She didn't keep them in suspense for long. "I'm calling our own meeting. We need to find out what's going on around here. We need to help Sage Scarab. First of all, Salm?"

He was surprised to be singled out. "Me? What?"

"We all need to work together. You have to stop being mad at April. You must know that she didn't turn the lake into a whirlpool. And she would never hurt Airron. Never! April is part of our family and you're being really mean to her." Raina pinned him with an accusing gaze in the flickering firefly light.

From the look on his face, Salm might have fled if the forest had been a safe shelter. But it wasn't. "Look, I'm not mad at April and I don't think she hurt anyone. I only thought she made the lake spin right after it happened, when I wasn't thinking very clearly," he muttered, abashed. "I've felt like an idiot ever since, and I never once thought she hurt Airron."

"But then why are you so uncomfortable around me?" April demanded. "Why won't you talk to me?"

Salm really did look like he wished he were anywhere else, even in the Outer-World. He heaved a sigh and shifted his eyes to meet April's gaze. "I acted really stupid. I feel bad and I don't know how to apologize for accusing you of trying to hurt me and Sprite. I thought you were … jealous or something, of Sprite. Pretty dumb idea."

"Jealous of Sprite?" April didn't understand.

Salm flushed and didn't elaborate. "Anyway, I've been avoiding you. Seemed easier."

"Easier?" Raina wasn't impressed with his explanation. "Let me see if I understand. You would choose to be miserable and never talk to April again, and make her sad, rather than simply apologize?" she asked incredulously.

"I wouldn't put it like that. And it's not like she could forgive me. April doesn't want to talk to me either."

Enough was enough. "Salm, I forgive you. I do want to talk to you, I've missed you," April said.

Raina rolled her eyes. "Salm, you're an idiot. April, he didn't apologize yet."

"It's okay."

"April, I'm really sorry. I was an insect's abdomen. I don't deserve your forgiveness, but I'll gladly accept it." Salm apologized quite beautifully. April felt warm inside and lighter suddenly, as light as a cloud.

"Well, good." Raina beamed, extremely pleased with herself. "That's much better, isn't it? Now, the real topic we need to discuss is the disappearance of Sage Scarab."

April jumped in. "And whether we should search for him ourselves? Is that why you called this meeting?"

"Yes. No. I don't know, but I feel like we have to do something. I wanted to discuss it. That's all. What do you think?" Raina asked, looking around at all of their faces.

April knew exactly what she thought. "As soon as your parents go to sleep, I should sneak into the forest to search for Sage Scarab. Something terrible has happened if he hasn't checked in, I'm sure of it. He would never get lost."

"April, you can't go alone. We should go together." Raina eyed the encroaching darkness fearfully.

"It's a dangerous idea," Peter said, and fell silent.

"That's why I should go alone," April said firmly. "I have magic, I'll be fine."

Peter shook his head. "No, you definitely shouldn't go alone."

"Not alone," Salm said, backing him up.

"But I would be safe and Sage Scarab needs help. He wouldn't think twice about searching for us if we were lost, would he? I am going to search for him." April had made up her mind.

Raina was in charge of their small gathering and took over. "You're right. Sage Scarab wouldn't think twice about helping us. We are going to help him, but the four of us will go together. April, with your magic, I'm sure we'll be safe. We just have to make sure that we're back in bed by first light. If we're not, I think I would rather face the creature than my parents. So, who's in?" she asked decisively.

"I am, but I should go alone," April said, one more time.

"Forget it. I'm going, too," Raina said.

Peter raised a hand, like in school. "Count me in. And I already told my parents I was sleeping over in Salm's room, since I can't walk home alone. So that works out rather conveniently, doesn't it?"

When Salm stayed silent, Raina asked, "Salm, what about you?"

"I have plans, Raina. If you wait for me to come home, I'll go with you. I'll try not to be too late."

"You should cancel your date, Salm. Finding Sage Scarab is more important," Raina said in a bossy tone.

"Hey, my date is important too. I already said that I'll try to make it home. Just wait for me." It was the best offer Raina was going to get.

"You better not be late, Salm."

"Don't push it."

Raina didn't push it. She knew her brother well enough to know when he could not be swayed. They agreed to slip out of the house and meet where they were sitting, as soon as the adults were asleep. As soon as Salm was home.

That was the end of their planning. Paddy and Twiggy strolled into the front garden to pick up Salm. Greetings were exchanged. When Salm ran inside to brush his teeth, Raina didn't waste a minute. She smiled artlessly at Paddy. "Do you still have to pick up Salm's date? Does she live far away?"

"Blossom lives near town, so it's not far. Don't tell Salm I told you," Paddy said without missing a beat. He knew what Raina was about.

"Blossom, is it? I don't know her from school," Raina mused.

"She finished last year, she's a little older," Paddy said with an exaggerated wink. Twiggy elbowed him in the ribs. Salm rushed out then, breathless. He was either eager to see Blossom, or he didn't want to leave Paddy at the mercy of his sister.

"See you later," Salm said significantly.

"Say hi to Blossom for me," Raina sang out.

Salm shoved Paddy to get a move on. The trio disappeared into the darkness. Raina, April and Peter lay under the stars and talked about what they might face in their search for Sage Scarab, then went to bed early, trying to look tired. DewDrop laughed at them for going to bed before her. They should have stayed up later because it took forever for the household to settle for the night. April must have napped because the next thing she knew, Raina was shaking her awake.

The house was dark and still when they tiptoed downstairs as quietly as two fleas. Peter was already outside. April hadn't heard him at all. He had been very sneaky, or she had been fast asleep. And then they waited for Salm—until they couldn't wait any longer. They gave up on him when the moon started to lower in the sky. Raina didn't rage about Salm, she simply asked if the three of them should risk going without him. Sage Scarab was in trouble; he needed them. The decision to go was unanimous.

They moved cautiously away from the house, away from safety. April knew they had to help Sage Scarab, but that didn't stop her stomach from feeling like she had swallowed a squirming centipede, whole. They hiked a good distance before daring to light one of the torches. Raina said breathlessly, "Well, we made it."

"So far, anyway," Peter said, with less confidence.

"Okay, let's make the most of the time we've got. April, we'll follow you. Start doing whatever you do with your magic." Raina handed over the light and waited, as if she expected April to conjure up Sage Scarab from thin air.

"I'll do what I can." April began to concentrate and walked east, away from New Haven. It was the most logical direction. If Sage Scarab had been hanging around the town, someone would surely have spotted him by now.

They hiked for several hours, weaving between eerie black shapes that pressed too close. Their imaginations were working overtime since they expected danger with every single step. April grew so tired of straining her magical senses that she got a thumping headache, and that was all she got for her efforts. She had yet to discover anything useful.

"Try a different direction," Raina prompted at one point.

April angled left and walked that way for an hour or so. Then she angled right for another hour. No-one knew where they were at that point (not even Peter), but they were increasing their distance from town. And they were fast running out of night. April was almost asleep on her feet when she finally sensed something worth investigating at the very edge of her range. It was too far away to be identifiable, but at least it was *something*.

"This way," she murmured and waded through a shallow bit of boggy ground. Soon, she knew it was an elf that she sensed. There was no way to confirm that it was Sage Scarab, but who else would be alone out here in the dead of night? After several directional adjustments, April raced forward with purpose. When the elf was just ahead, she slowed and turned to her friends. "Okay, this is it. I think Sage Scarab is on the other side of that tree. The other thing might be nearby, too, so stay close."

Raina whimpered and grabbed April's arm, truly frightened now. April felt the exact same way, but she was refusing to acknowledge the clawing fear. If she pretended she wasn't scared, she might not be.

The three friends crept slowly forward, almost joined at the hip, alert for any movement. When they rounded the tree, April could sense the elf strongly, yet she couldn't see him or hear him. She should have been able to do so.

Peter murmured, "Where is he?"

April shrugged against his shoulder. They took more cautious steps forward. Still nothing revealed itself. Was the elf invisible? "Are you sure he's here?" Raina whispered.

"Positive," April answered at the same moment that something snored and grunted. As one, they looked up. An elf-sized bundle was wrapped in vines and suspended from the branch above, at least four feet off the ground.

"Oh dear," Raina breathed. "I guess that's him."

"It looks that way, doesn't it," Peter said.

"Sage Scarab. Sage Scarab!" Raina hissed, trying to be quiet.

The bundle jerked around angrily. "Who's there? I know you're down there, whatever you are! You better stay back if you know what's good for you," said Sage Scarab's querulous voice, making no attempt to be quiet. The bundle swung and twirled, firmly attached to the branch.

"Sage Scarab, it's us—Raina, April and Peter. We've come to rescue you!" Raina called up, since he was making enough noise to make whispering useless.

"About time. Well, look out. Some weird creature keeps coming to check on me. So get me down, fast. We have to get the heck away from here," he ordered.

Peter sighed and looked way way up. "We could really use Airron and his wings right about now. Or Salm and his muscles."

"I can burn through the vine from here, magically," April said.

"No, he's got too much of a drop. He might get hurt. But I can climb up and cut the vine, and try and lower him down," Peter said.

"You have your pocket blade?" Raina assumed.

He felt his pocket. "Yup."

"Well use it!" Sage Scarab said crossly. "I've been hanging here with no food or water for days and days. Like torture, I tell you."

"It hasn't been quite that long, but we'll get you down," Raina promised.

"You two stay here. Guard duty." Peter lit a second torch off the first one and started climbing up the bark, a little awkwardly with only one hand. Raina edged closer to April, so close that they could have been one body.

"And watch out for whatever that critter is. Haven't laid eyes on it yet, but it keeps sneaking around," Sage Scarab reminded them quite unnecessarily. "April, it seems to have magic kind of like yours. I hate to say it, but I think it has stronger magic. It didn't wrap me in these blasted vines, it made the vines grow so fast I could barely see them. Vines wrapped me up all by themselves. Never seen a plant do that before. Vines behaved like serpents! So stay alert, keep an eye on the plants!"

Peter scrambled along the branch from which Sage Scarab was suspended. He held the torch close to examine the tangle of vines. He traced the supporting vine higher. "I think this is it—it seems to be tangled around enough of these branches that his own weight might ease him slowly to the ground, if I cut it through up here."

"Sounds good. Give it a try." Raina shifted nervously from one foot to the other, trying to watch all the shadows at once. Peter sawed at the vine. They really could have used Salm's help in case they needed to catch the Sage. Raina was so upset with her brother that she hadn't mentioned his name even once. He had left them to risk the woodland alone in the middle of the night. Salm's behaviour was disappointing.

The vine snapped without warning. Sage Scarab came sliding down faster than expected. He hit the ground with a thump and moaned dramatically. Peter winced. "I forgot to take into account how heavy he is. Sorry about that," he called down to the lump that was Sage Scarab.

Raina and April worked at ripping apart the tight vines that secured the elf from head to toe. Peter scrambled down to help with his blade. In minutes, the Sage was free. The first words out of his mouth were, "Why did you drop me?"

"We weren't trying to. We were trying not to," Raina stressed. "You could say thanks. We did save you, you know!" All their nerves were wearing thin—it had been a long and stressful night, and it wasn't nearly over.

"Harrumph! Didn't save me yet. Let's get out of here, we can talk on the way back to town. And thanks." The Sage started walking with a pronounced limp, which soon disappeared. They were heading home, after all, and the rescue had gone surprisingly smoothly. Then April started to sense something all too familiar. The creature, whatever it was, must be using magic! That did not bode well for their small defenseless group.

"Uh-oh," April gasped.

"Uh-oh?" Raina echoed. "Why did you say 'uh-oh'?" In answer, the surrounding trees came alive with sound. The peculiar noise hemmed them in on all sides. There was nowhere to run. They stopped walking and instinctively pressed closer together.

"April? What is it?" Peter asked.

"The thing is using magic, but I don't know what that weird sound is." And it was creeping closer, growing louder—a rustling, crackling, crumpled kind of noise. Underlying it was a sort of squishy gushing. The squishy gushing was the most unsettling of the chorus of sounds.

"April!" Raina cried. "Do something magical to make it stop, please. Please stop it." She covered her ears with her hands.

"But I don't even know what it is." April strained her magical senses. Nothing. Then the noise edged overhead.

"April!" Raina's voice was shrill with panic.

"Cripes, could you at least make more light? So we can see what we're up against," Sage Scarab growled.

"Yes. I can do that." April concentrated hard on the perimeter in front of them. A curved line of fire surged along the ground and flared high. It illuminated a scene of absolute normality.

"I don't see anything weird," Sage Scarab grunted. "Let's move." And then there was a new noise—a distinct *plop*. Then another and another and another, like rain, but much bigger and gloppier.

"Okay, I don't know what that was, but I don't want to find out." Peter placed a hand on April's back and propelled her forward, fast. Everyone took off running, but it wasn't fast enough. *Plop.*

"Something landed on me!" Raina shrieked. "Get it off!" She brushed frantically at her shoulder. "Yuck, it's sticky. What the heck is it?"

"Hold still." April tried to have a look, but Raina wouldn't stop squirming. Whatever was falling wetly around them was increasing in volume.

"Keep moving, would you," Sage Scarab snapped, right before a large sticky glob landed on his head and oozed slowly down the side of his face. A familiar smell proved what the substance was—a mixture of tree gum and sap. The ground was fast becoming coated in the stuff.

They tried to run. It proved impossible. The ground had transformed into one big sticky trap. April's foot stuck the next time it hit the ground, then her second foot joined it, sinking up to her ankle bone. She yanked with abandon to unglue either foot and lost her balance instead, falling over backwards. Another part of her anatomy stuck where it landed.

All around her, everyone's feet were stuck. Worse yet, muffled laughter echoed from the dark undergrowth at their backs. That noise definitely came from something alive: animal, not vegetable.

"Creature's making the trees rain this mess," Sage Scarab said. "April, anything you can do to get us out of here before we're buried in the stuff? Or before that critter does something worse." He fought to shake his leg free, yanking on his knobby knee.

Peter held his torch high and forward. The viscous lake did end abruptly, at April's line of fire. Ahead, the green moss looked undisturbed—and close!

With no time to think of anything fancy, April heated the gummy sap around her, as if she was going to make a fire. Hot sap ran a lot thinner than cold sap, and it wasn't nearly as sticky. "Pull me up." April held her arms over her head. Peter and Sage Scarab yanked hard, her bottom came free with ease, then her feet. Long gooey threads trailed off her feet when she lifted them, but she could walk.

"What did you do?" Peter asked.

"Warmed the gum, makes it runnier."

"Well, do us all then! And fast." Sage Scarab ordered.

"I'll try, I'll heat a … a path, straight ahead. Follow my feet exactly and we should be able to get out of here." April concentrated on the surrounding sap until Raina shouted, "Ouch." The sap had gotten a little too hot.

"Sorry. Follow me." April started walking, leading the parade. Progress was slow. They certainly couldn't run. Their pace was more suited to slogging out of thick muck, but they gained ground steadily.

The line of fire had nearly burnt itself out, and the dewy green ground was almost within touching distance when April sensed something truly deadly. A forest cat was loping through the woods toward them, as fast as it could run. Inside the barrier? April forgot to heat the gum ahead of her feet and bogged down immediately. And the cat was closing in with great bounding steps, silent on its furry padded feet.

There was no time to escape. The beast leapt through the air, claws at the ready, fangs bared. April screamed when a huge paw swiped at her, she was still screaming when the cat picked her right up between hot jaws and shook cruelly. Cats liked to play with their prey before they finished it off. April cried out in agony and couldn't stop screaming.

"April, April! What's wrong?" said Peter.

Couldn't he see the enormous cat? Thunder rumbled and drowned him out.

"Stop screaming! Please stop screaming," cried Raina. April was pretty sure it was Raina's hand that slapped her hard across the face. April was still being shaken, but it wasn't a cat doing the deed. The cat wavered and disappeared into thin air, as if it had never been. Raina was doing the shaking now, she had April by the shoulders.

April fell against her best friend, clutching her tight. "Where's the cat?" she gasped hoarsely, trembling from head to toe.

"What cat? April, there is no cat." Raina hugged her hard in return.

"There was a cat," April insisted, but weakly.

"There's no cat," Sage Scarab barked. "Critter's playing with your mind, trying to distract you from getting us free. Pull yourself together. Get back to heating the sap before it dreams up something else."

Sage Scarab was right. And there was no cat. April focused again, as best she could. Luckily, they were near the edge of the trap because she was an emotional mess. Channeling her magic was almost an impossible feat. Raina kept an arm around her and urged April along, supporting her.

In gasping breaths, Raina told Sage Scarab about sneaking away from home to find him, and said they had to be back in their beds before her parents woke up.

He was not impressed. "So, you weren't supposed to come and save me? Huh. Imagine. Think I'll have a word with Welkin about leaving me hanging. And you lot have to be tucked in bed by sunrise? Since you had to sneak away to rescue me? Huh. Well, we can make it. Keep running. I'll say I escaped on my own—looks better for me that way."

April could sense danger nipping at their heels the whole way home, but the creature didn't approach or try any more nasty tricks to trap them. It was almost as if it let them leave, as if it had been taunting them with the sap. And torturing April with the cat.

The sun was peeking teasingly over the edge of the world when they tumbled into the front garden. And Salm was waiting for them, propped up beside the front door. He hadn't slept a wink, his tormented face proved that. "Sage Scarab! You found him. Why did you leave without me?" Salm said, hugging his sister.

"We did wait for you," Raina said coldly, pushing him away. "You never showed."

"You didn't wait long enough! You didn't come back all night, and I heard thunder—figured you were done for." Salm swallowed sickly. "Hey, what's all over you?" He touched Raina's shoulder and his hand stuck to her.

"Sap," she said shortly, and provided a brutal version of their narrow escape.

Salm swore soundly and had to be shushed so he wouldn't wake up their parents. He hugged Raina again, ignoring the sticky mess. This time, she allowed it. "Don't you ever do that again. Next time you wait for me," Salm said hoarsely. He hugged April tight next, and she felt safe for the first time all night.

"Enough of that," Sage Scarab said. "You lot better clean up and get to bed. Sun's almost up."

They showered off the worst of the mess, fully dressed, trying to hide the evidence of their ordeal. They dried off and snuck soundlessly into the house through the back door. April was pulling the blanket over her head when she heard Mr. and Mrs. Poole moving around downstairs. She slept until DewDrop came to wake her up. It couldn't have been more than two short hours.

Raina and Salm were already in the kitchen when April stumbled in, yawning. Raina's eyes were only half-open and Salm was sleeping with his head on the table. He was even snoring. April stifled another yawn and slumped onto her cushion.

Mrs. Poole approached with a platter of hard-boiled hummingbird egg slices and thumped it down loudly, startling Salm awake. She surveyed them all suspiciously with her hands on her hips. "For elves that went to bed so early, you do not look very rested."

"Maybe we got too much sleep. You know how tired that can make you feel," Raina said, yawning widely.

Mr. Poole closed in from the other side. "April, you look as pale as a forest spirit. And if I am not mistaken, you are all somewhat … stickier than when you went to bed." It had been impossible to scrub off all the stubborn gum.

"I wonder how that could have happened." Raina assumed a comically blank expression. "Maybe we were sleepwalking?"

April had to bite her lips together to keep from giggling. She was so tired that she was downright giddy.

"Well, you will be happy to know that Sage Scarab dropped by while we were preparing breakfast and he is fine," Mr. Poole said. April attempted to look sincerely surprised and pleased, as did Raina and Peter and Salm. April thought they carried it off rather well, until she intercepted a suspicious glance shared between the parents. They knew something was fishy.

"Where was he?" Peter asked, as if he had no idea.

Mr. Poole sat down on his cushion, still frowning. "He was attacked by magically controlled vines and tied up for a day or so, before he managed to escape, all by himself, with no help at all. He was very emphatic about that detail. He looked a bit sticky too, come to think of it. Unfortunately, he did not see a thing to help us identify the culprit."

"That's too bad. What's for breakfast?" Raina asked, changing the subject.

Mrs. Poole glowered and pointed at the egg slices already on the table.

"Oh, that looks delicious." Raina helped herself. The fact that they were so hungry they ate two breakfasts each, may also have hinted at an active night. Raina jumped up as soon as she had cleared her shell. "I claim the waterfall first!" she said. It would be a second attempt to clean up.

"Next," April cried.

"I'm going back to bed," Salm said, leaving Peter third in line to shower.

Mr. Poole cleared his throat pointedly. "It is quite evident that something went on around here last night. It seems a bit too coincidental that Sage Scarab turned up at breakfast. He is not a better actor than any of you. If I find out for a fact that you were roaming around in the forest last night and putting yourselves at great risk, you will all be severely grounded. Salm, I could use your help in the garden. You'll have to sleep another time. And get your head off the table."

With slumped shoulders, Salm followed his father outside. Raina, April and Peter showered in turn, then Raina rushed them off to visit Airron. She couldn't wait to tell him all about their exciting adventure.

5. Decoy

As always, Monday arrived long before anyone felt it should have. The fact that the class was going on a field trip didn't make the school day any more appealing, since they were merely visiting the museum.

"At least this is one field trip where you shouldn't stir up trouble," Raina teased April, referring to the previous school year. "I mean, what could possibly happen at the museum, right in the middle of town? No beehives, no rushing creeks, no flying fish, no wild mice or snaky vines or sap. It will be nice and boring."

They barely had time to warm their cushions before Mrs. Merry-Helen sailed into the classroom bubbling over with enthusiasm. "Hellooooo, hellooooo. Did everyone have a mmmarvelous weekend? And isn't this a thrilling way to start the week? With a field trip, my dears! Come now, let us not waste a precious minute. Hop up, nice straight line, pretty please. And march, *hup two three*!" They didn't actually march and their line was as twisted as the hallways in Airron's house, but Mrs. Merry-Helen didn't notice. She led the way, humming and tilting her head first one way and then the other.

"What does a trip to the museum have to do with Environmental Studies anyway?" April asked, wondering what Mrs. Merry-Helen was doing with her head. Could she hear marching music that no-one else could?

Peter said, "Several rooms in the museum are dedicated to nature. You can learn about insects, or wildlife, or plants. There is even a room devoted entirely to underwater life, so the museum has a lot to do with Environmental Studies." He sounded like a promotional leaflet.

"I suspect this is a practice field trip," Raina ventured. "After what happened to Ms. Summers, Mrs. Merry-Helen probably wants to make sure that we'll behave and that everything will run smoothly, before she takes us anywhere more adventurous." Raina was always very good at understanding behavior and motive. "Or else she thinks the museum is really exciting—that could be it, too," Raina tacked on.

April heard a certain amount of grumbling about this field trip from the front and back of the rambling line. With a pang of guilt, she overheard the teacher referred to as 'Hairy-Melon' more than once. April's slip of the tongue had been adopted as the teacher's nickname, it seemed, and it was not a flattering one. It was almost as bad as Peachy Leechy.

The class trickled into the town circle in pairs and small groups, their line nonexistent by the time they reached the museum. Mrs. Merry-Helen halted them and motioned for a proper line before she would permit them to enter the building.

April was standing, perfectly relaxed, in the middle of town when the horrible tingling sensation gripped her, stronger than she had felt it yet. It came out of nowhere, as if a giant wave of icy water were splashing over her. April stumbled and spun in a circle, searching for the source of the threat. Nothing, all appeared normal. Every student was safely in line, except for Cherry. She had detoured over to put her hand in the fountain, but that didn't look dangerous.

Raina steadied her. "April, what's wrong?"

"That weird feeling again?" Peter guessed, reading her expression.

"Yes." April turned in another circle, still searching with her eyes. It felt like danger itself had assumed physical form and was standing beside her, blowing bitterly cold breath down her back. "It's right here. Can't you see anything?" she cried.

The class started forward, toward the museum door. Raina murmured, "I don't see a thing out of place, April."

Every last student entered the building safely, but April was not reassured. "Do you still feel it?" Peter asked.

"Yes, but not as strongly."

Mrs. Merry-Helen clapped her hands for attention. "Yoo-hoo! Gather round! We will start our wonderful tour with the museum rooms that are devoted to our natural world. I would like each of you to pay particular attention to what is most relevant to you, whether you are a fairy, merrow or pixie. I know you will have a lovely time exploring the museum's wonders. I will be circulating to answer any questions you might have, and the museum staff is always available. After we have completed a tour of the relevant rooms, we'll take a quick peek at the newest thunderwand display, just for fun, before we return to school for lunch." The teacher

65

beamed happily and motioned for them to proceed through the first doorway on the right, off the spacious entrance hall.

April followed the elves in front of her, paying no attention to what they were supposed to be looking at. The air smelled stale and the polished stone floor was chilly underfoot. Anticipating trouble, April was first to notice the unusual noise—only unusual because it should never be heard in the center of town.

"Not bees again!" April groaned.

Raina looked at her like she was nuts. "Why are you talking about bees? We're in Seamore's favorite room, fish and lakeweed and watery stuff…" Raina trailed off when it became clear why April had mentioned bees. The angry buzzing grew louder and louder. Were the bees coming to visit the museum?

Students panicked, rushing around the room to seek shelter. Alas, there really was nowhere to hide. The class was in grave danger. A bee's sting was always fatal to an elf.

Mrs. Merry-Helen threw her arms into the air and shouted to be heard. "Get down, lay down. Don't move. If you can find something to cover yourself, do it. Now!"

Most students dropped where they stood. Black darting shadows passed by the open windows in ever increasing numbers, until the room itself darkened. The walls began to vibrate in protest. The museum was surrounded. April remained frozen in place, waiting for the bees, dreading the bees.

"Bees," Raina said tragically. "They've never come into town before. They're being controlled, aren't they?"

"It makes sense." April kept her gaze on the windows. There was no way to close them.

It was still a shock when the first bee zoomed brazenly into the room. The buzzing was so much louder inside, that the one bee sounded like ten. The insect also seemed bigger inside the room—too big for the enclosed space. Peter urged April and Raina toward the wall, until their backs were pressed against it.

More bees entered through the windows, then still more bees. They flew in a circular pattern around the room as their number swelled. When it appeared that the room couldn't possibly hold one more bee, the larger queen landed on the window ledge. April shook her head to clear it. She had been watching the bees in a daze, but suddenly realized what she could do. It was a wonderful opportunity, in spite of the circumstances.

"I'm going to talk to the queen, see if she can tell me something," April cried, before closing her eyes to concentrate. It took a few moments to make contact with the queen bee and it felt like the last time April had communicated with a bee. The insect's thoughts were all fuzzy and buzzy and vague.

April tried to find out why the bees had come to the museum, but it was as if the queen bee couldn't think for herself. There was only one fuzzy thought planted in her royal head: to fly around the museum. Every other thought had been suppressed. In one way, it was great news. April was overjoyed to discover that the bees intended no harm. They had not been told to sting elves. The class was not doomed. Unfortunately, she couldn't find out where the planted thought had come from, because the queen didn't know. Lastly, April asked the bees to go back to their hive, without delay. The queen refused. Her compulsion to fly around the museum was too strong for her to resist.

When April opened her eyes, Raina and Peter were waiting for news with baited breath. She had to shout to be heard over the tremendous volume of buzzing. "We're safe! The good news is that the bees aren't here to do any harm. They aren't going to sting any elves. They're only going to fly around. That's all they can think about. But I couldn't find out who or what planted the idea in the queen's head."

"They're not ... they're not going to sting us?" Raina stammered

"No. They couldn't if they wanted too. Come on!" Fed up, April linked arms with her friends and strode across the room, weaving between the huddled elves that littered the floor. She went right to the door, secure in the knowledge that the bees were harmless. Raina and Peter came along in a half crouch, not feeling nearly as confident with hundreds of agitated bees whizzing by overhead.

April stopped at the door of the room and banged loudly on the door for attention. "The bees won't hurt you, but stay where you are, to be safe," she shouted, as loudly as she could. The other elves didn't move, they stayed curled up on the floor. Cherry was the exception. She was leaning against one wall looking highly entertained by the spectacle. Why wasn't she frightened of the bees?

Outside the front door, a second cloud of bees circled the exterior of the museum. In the surrounding buildings, the windows were filled with horrified faces, peering out at the building under siege. The culprit orchestrating the mayhem was still hiding its sneaky face.

"I don't see anything," Peter said, scanning the town circle with his eyes.

Raina's face was tight with fear. "How can you say that? I see bees."

Across the circle, the Head-Sage was organizing a group of elves in the doorway of his building. April dashed across. As soon as she reached Welly, he gripped her shoulders with icy, trembling hands, his face horror-stricken. April had never seen him so overcome. "Are the bees...? Have they...?" He couldn't say it out loud.

"No! No. The bees aren't here to harm elves. They haven't hurt even one elf in the museum. They're only flying around and that's all they're going to do. They aren't going to sting anyone. It's okay, Welly. It's not as bad as it looks," April stressed.

He took a shuddering breath. "You are sure?"

"She's sure," Raina said. She had bravely crossed the town circle with Peter. The nearest elves calmed visibly, but they kept their eyes on the museum.

"Why are the bees here?" Welly asked. He had pulled himself together in one beat of a hummingbird's wing.

"To fly around the museum. The thought has been planted in their heads. It's the only thought they have, but I couldn't find out who or what put it there." April was disappointed that she couldn't tell him more. She had so hoped that she would learn something important from the bees.

"Do you know when the bees are planning to depart?"

"No. They don't even know."

Welly curled the tip of his beard absently and stared across the square. "Well, I do hope this is a short visit. We will wait it out then, but perhaps we shouldn't stand in plain sight, in case the bees change their collective mind."

"Or something changes it for them," April muttered.

Elves attempted to spread the word that no students had been harmed and all would soon be well. The shadow on the sundial had barely moved before the bees departed the museum. They flew back to their hives with purpose. Before the last stinger had disappeared from sight, elves flooded out of the surrounding buildings and into the museum, eager to see for themselves that no elves had been attacked.

April trailed behind with Peter and Raina, not one of them was in a hurry to join the jostling crowd trying to squeeze into the room with the students. "Let's go somewhere quiet and wait it out," Raina suggested.

The room across the hall was empty. They wandered inside the peaceful space and a small grouping of guest cushions looked particularly inviting. They sat down and made good use of them. "That was quite a field trip. I wonder how Mrs. Merry-Helen is holding up," April mused.

"The field trip curse continues," Raina said. "Do you think she's still smiling? Do you think that will be the first and last field trip of the year? And what about Seamore? Will he ever set foot in his favorite room again?" She was giddy with relief.

Peter rolled his eyes at her and leaned his head back against the wall, gazing across the room. "Have they sent the thunderwand out to be polished?" he asked idly.

"The rods looked pretty spiffy the other day. And wouldn't they simply polish them here," Raina said.

April felt like she had been dumped off a raven in mid-flight. "Oh no!" She leapt up and stumbled over to where the three beautiful metal rods should have been proudly displayed. It was nothing but a glaringly empty space, except for the finely carved base, built to support the rods that weren't there anymore.

"No, it's not possible!" Peter groaned beside her shoulder. Apparently he couldn't see the rods either.

Raina was slower to catch on. "What's wrong with cleaning the wand? Oh. Oh, I see. The bees -"

"Were a decoy," Peter finished.

"They did a great job," Raina commended.

Before they could move, Welly peeked into the room. "Ah, there you are. You will be pleased to know that all is well. Your class is about to be escorted back to school." He strolled up smiling and started frowning. "Has the museum relocated the thunderwand?" he asked.

April bit her lip and shook her head. "I don't think so."

He squeezed his eyes closed as if he had a painful cramp. He opened them and asked, "Do you know where the rods are, by any chance?"

"No. They're gone. Just gone."

He could see that for himself. "Very clever, very cunning." Welly sighed from deep in his chest. "What better to distract us than a swarm of bees?"

Sage Scarab marched in. "Hey, we're ready to walk the students back to school. You three coming? Or you going to stand here all day gawking at...nothing? Oh crap!"

Mayor Bushy-Finch was right on his heels. "There you are Falcon, lots of elves are looking for you. Aah! The wand has been stolen!" The mayor was quicker on the uptake than all of them. "Clayton, round up the rest of the Sages and the High Court. We'll hold an emergency gathering as soon as we can … can gather everyone together."

The mayor had a lot of faith in meetings. He and Sage Scarab jogged out of the room together. The mayor, at least, was filled with purpose. Welly watched them go, then turned urgently to April. He gripped her shoulders. "April, if you can think of anything … anything at all that might help, inform me immediately," he said and rushed away, too.

They were probably all thinking the same thing. The vile creature that had entered this world had coldly hatched a plan to obtain the thunderwand. Given the intruder's powerful displays of magic, it might be capable of shutting down the forcefield. The end result would be disastrous for the whole of New Haven and every last elf that lived within the protected world.

Peter and Raina moved toward the door. April didn't follow. She was not going back to school. The rods hadn't been gone all that long. It was the best opportunity to try and track them magically. It didn't matter if April went into the forest alone. No elf was safe while the creature had the thunderwand. And it had stolen their thunderwand—it was a personal affront!

Raina turned around. "Come on, April."

"Raina, I'm not going back to school. I'm going to try and track the wand. The wand belongs to us! Cover for me, okay? Say I went home sick or something."

Two pairs of eyes looked at her is if she was a whole lot of trees short of a forest. "Do you really think we would let you go alone?" Peter asked.

"Well, it was worth a try. It could be dangerous—"

Peter didn't let her finish. "We'll use the backdoor. The rods didn't go out the front, so they had to go out the backdoor."

April hadn't even known the museum had a backdoor. Together, they made good use of that discreet exit. They snuck out of the building without encountering another elf. April had never been behind the museum and was surprised when they stepped directly into thick and tangled undergrowth.

She concentrated immediately on the forest around them. Nothing was there now, except a whole lot of vegetation and the usual collection of insects. April shook her head in frustration. "I can't sense the creature, I never can unless it is using magic."

Peter got a peculiar expression on his face and pointed between two overlapping ferns. "Did it go that way?"

"No idea," April admitted sadly. "I was going to search the ground for tracks or something, and hope for some luck."

"I think we have some luck. Come on." Peter ducked between the two ferns and took off running. Raina and April chased after him, puzzled but hopeful. He wove unerringly through the green maze, as if there was a marked trail only he could see.

"Peter, where are you going?" April called, trying to keep up.

He shouted, "It went this way, we need to hurry."

"But how do you know?"

"I don't know how I know, but I do. I think it has to do with the metal. We can figure it out later." He sprinted even faster. The two girls ran like mad trying to keep Peter in sight, and had no breath left for talking.

"We're close," Peter finally called back to them.

It was great news, because April honestly didn't think she could keep going, not at the pace Peter had set. He slid to a halt with no forewarning. April and Raina barreled into him, catapulting them all forward and into a pile.

There was a flurry of movement directly ahead. Too close. April fought to be free of her friends in case they were about to be attacked. She rolled into a crouch, hoping for a glimpse of the creature, but it was already gone. What she did not expect to see was one of the thunderwands floating in front of her face—inside a large bubble!

Raina leaned closer. "It's inside a bubble!"

"A magical bubble—it has to be to float the weight of the wand." Peter stepped forward for a better look. The bubble didn't like that. It shot away, aiming for a gap between branches.

"Stop that bubble," Raina screamed.

April was the closest, so she took a flying leap and managed to land on top of it, kind of draped over the thing. It kept on going, unaffected by her added weight.

"Puncture it with something sharp," Peter yelled, when April and the bubble drifted ahead.

The sphere was soft and squishy. It would have been fun to ride, if the situation had been different. This bubble could not get away—they had to save the last rod! The survival of New Haven depended on it.

"April, burst it before it's too late!" Raina shouted.

Already the bubble was wafting higher. April didn't have anything sharp in her pocket. She only had her fingernails and the unfortunate habit of biting them down to nothing. Already as high as her tower room, April stabbed the bubble forcefully with her finger. Her finger wasn't sharp enough. Frantic, she tried to burst the bubble magically. Her magic had no effect.

"April, come back." Raina's voice sounded awfully far below.

"Weasel whiskers," April groaned, refusing to look down. But she did look sideways. The bubble was floating between trees, close enough to brush branches. April scanned for a thorn or sharp branch, anything. A pointy broken limb loomed ahead, almost within reach. April leaned way over, trying not to slide off the precarious bubble. She had intended to yank off a sharp sliver of wood, but when she grabbed the branch and pulled, the bubble came along. It was pressed hard against the point, and that was the end of the shimmering globe. It popped with a *whoosh*. April ended up dangling in mid-air from the branch she had grabbed. The metal rod made it all the way to the ground. Too petrified to move, April watched it fall. It was a long way down.

Peter appeared beside the wand and stood over it. Was he expecting another bubble to materialize out of the air? He looked up. "April? Are you all right?"

"Yes." As long as she held on, she was safe. If it wasn't nearly drowning, it was heights. Always one or the other, as if she was cursed.

Peter shouted, "Are you coming down?"

"I'll be down in a minute."

"April, hurry. We still have to find the other two rods!"

She knew that. Arms shaking, April hauled herself over the branch. She climbed down, down, down. It took a long time. "Peter, can you still track the other two rods?" April gasped, as soon as her feet touched earth.

"I think so. Raina, stay with this one, you'll be safe. We'll keep chasing the other rods." Peter took off like a cricket. April groaned and followed, doubting her legs.

The thunderwand thief could move much faster than an elf, and the trail became increasingly hard to track. Peter lost it several times and then he couldn't find it again. He slowed to a stop, shaking his head. "I can't sense it anymore. It's probably too far away."

April was determined to look on the bright side. "Well, it's not so bad, Peter. It can't turn the barrier off with only two of the rods."

"Right. Then we better get back to Raina, in case it's doubled-back for the third one." Peter brought up a good point.

The possibility of Raina in danger gifted April's exhausted legs with energy. She matched Peter's pace all the way back to Raina. She was safe and guarding the rod. She was actually sitting on it.

As soon as she spotted them, Raina jumped to her feet. "Did you get the other two? Oh, I guess not or you would be carrying them." She looked devastated.

"At least we have one, that's as good as having three. Well, not as good, but they don't work without the full set," April reminded her.

"Oh, I didn't even think about that. Well, we did it, then! We stopped the barrier from being shut down! We saved New Haven—again," Raina declared triumphantly.

"We did." They all shared a satisfied smile.

April would have stood there all day, grinning and recovering her legs, if Peter hadn't glanced into the shadows and said, "We better get this wand safely back to town." He hoisted the metal rod over his shoulder and they retraced their steps. The more leisurely pace gave them a chance to talk and April was extremely curious about one aspect of their chase.

"Peter, how could you track the creature, anyway?"

He looked thoughtful. "I wasn't tracking the creature. I was tracking the rods. It had something to do with the metal, the gold. It must be part of my magic developing. I could almost smell the gold, isn't that weird?" He was clearly trying not to look too pleased with himself.

"That's great, Peter! You're going to be super rich if you can find gold like that," Raina declared.

"Hey, didn't Cherry say her father could find gold faster than anyone. Maybe he could do this, too?" April remembered Cherry mentioning her father's ability in pixie class. But Drake Pitt's magic had been of the darkest sort. Peter's touch of magic could be only good. This was *Peter* after all.

It was almost noon when they arrived back in the town circle, only to find it deserted. It seemed extra quiet after the mayhem of the morning. "Everyone must still be at the gathering," Raina said, pointing to Seelie Court.

They hurried toward the most impressive building in the square. The dark wood façade was trimmed with gold, and flowering vines clung to the wall, bursting with big crimson blossoms.

The guards posted outside the front door took one look at what Peter carried and stepped hastily aside. April led the way to the same vast room where she had met with the Sages and the High Court in the past. The door was firmly closed, but an urgent hum of voices came from inside. A pair of large guards in the King's familiar red and gold were stationed outside that door. Trained to be stoic, both their strong jaws dropped at the sight of the rod. One of them rapped sharply on the door before he threw it opened with a flourish.

Raina nudged Peter first into the room. There were at least fifty elves scattered about. They had been in an uproar until Peter stepped into view. Judging by their expressions, they couldn't believe what he was carrying, slung so casually over his shoulder.

Head-Sage Falcon rose straight up off his cushion and met Peter halfway. He beamed and touched Peter's shoulder, then the metal, as if to make sure it was truly solid. Peter's parents looked to be bursting with pride, off to one side. Even Heady was present, right in the middle of the school day. She was gazing fondly at her three young students, as if unsurprised by their latest accomplishment.

"How did you manage this miracle," Welly asked the three of them.

Peter shrugged bashfully, he could be rather shy. Raina glanced wildly around at all the elves, and her eyes widened with alarm when she spotted both her parents. Mr. and Mrs. Poole were about to hear all about how they had placed themselves directly in harm's path.

"April, would you like to explain?" Welly said, when her two companions didn't utter a word.

"Sure. Peter was able to track the wands, so we followed them, and the creature that had taken them, through the forest. It was floating the rods in magic bubbles. We managed to stop this one from floating away, by popping the bubble. But the creature did escape with the other two." It was the short version.

"You saw the thief?" Head-Sage Falcon asked.

April shook her head regretfully. "No. We didn't even catch a glimpse."

"Ah, well, the creature is no longer able to shut down the barrier. That is the most important thing. Your quick thinking and brave actions have saved New Haven, again." He lifted the wand out of Peter's arms and passed it off to Sage Scarab. Then his voice lowered to a confidential tone. "Peter, how did you track it?"

"I think it was … my magic developing. I could sense the metal rods, not the creature. It was the metal, the gold I think," Peter responded, just as quietly.

"Intriguing. We are indeed fortunate that you were able to do so. And April, were you able to use your magic against this creature?"

"No. I'm beginning to believe that my magic is useless compared to this thing's magic," she said with regret. Thank goodness for Peter's new ability. If not for him, all the devices would be gone and New Haven would be facing another crisis, before it had fully recovered from the last one. Even with her magic, April hadn't been able to help New Haven at all.

With no forewarning, Head-Sage Falcon took April by the arm and walked her straight out of the room, alone, just like that. "What is it?" April asked, when he stopped at the deserted end of the hallway.

"I prefer to speak to you without an audience. The members of the High Court have enough exciting news to keep them buzzing until my return, if you will pardon the pun. Now, April, this is most important."

"It is? What is?"

Head-Sage Falcon's expression was inscrutable beneath his beard. April had no idea what he was thinking, and she wished she did. His intensity scared her a bit. "You, April, have more to offer than you realize. You must not think otherwise. It is important for you to have faith in your own abilities, in yourself. I have no doubt that you are more than worthy to confront our unknown adversary, and it may not all rely on the strength of your magic," he said. "Remember, it is how you think of using your magic that is as important as the power of the magic itself. Do you understand?"

April wasn't sure that she did. Head-Sage Falcon hadn't been vague exactly, but he hadn't been overly clear either.

"Whatever is causing such harm in our world is a thoughtless being, a destructive force." Although he had never met this creature, Welly spoke with a loathing that was personal. He was judging the creature by its actions. "You and your friends are very brave and noble elves." He tapped his heart gently. "I like to believe that good has the upper hand over evil, especially in our special world. Have faith in this goodness, April. Have faith in yourself. I do."

April tried to feel heartened by Welly's confidence in her. Alas, there was an underlying air of desperation, or perhaps even anguish, to his message that caused a knot of foreboding to tighten around her heart. She nodded and didn't know what to say, except, "I'll try. I'll do everything I can to stop this thing."

"I know you will. I do know that. I have no doubt that you will always place New Haven's welfare before your own." He reached out and touched her cheek with a strangely chilled hand. "Heed my words. We will all survive this creature, every last one of us. Humour an old elf and speak no more of being useless. Come." He started back the way they had come.

When Head-Sage Falcon re-entered the room, it fell as silent as a guilty classroom is guaranteed to do when the teacher enters. He addressed the assembled elves briskly. "We must find some way to safeguard the remaining device, since all our lives depend on it. And our three young heroes should return to school now." He winked at April. "I would offer an escort, but with the amount of time that you spend roaming the forest ..." He exchanged a significant glance with Sage Scarab, who must have spilled the beans about his own rescue. "You do seem to manage well enough on your own."

They were sent on their way with heartfelt applause and even a few cheers. Peter couldn't stop grinning all the way back to school. Raina, on the other hand, fretted and fussed about what her parents would have to say when they got home. The school meadow was empty when they arrived in the middle of lunch. Students were being kept safely inside the building, while teachers monitored doors and windows as if they were guards, not teachers at all.

Mr. Leech was in charge of guarding the main entrance and he was taking his duty very seriously. He had crossed his bulging arms over his bumpy chest, and his hair had a tough, windblown look about it, as if he had deliberately ruffled it up with his fingers. He was attentive, but he was not thinking clearly. "No elves in or out until the gong sounds," he said when they tried to walk through the front door.

"But, Wade, I'm one of your students, remember? Me?" Raina pointed at herself, and tried to step around him. He blocked her with his massive shoulders.

"Stop right there! I am charged with keeping the students safe. No elves in or out." He didn't seem to recognize Raina, even though he had been her teacher for weeks now.

Raina looked at him like he was nuts. "But I am one of your students. Don't I need to be kept safe?"

"I have my instructions."

"But … surely your instructions aren't to keep students outside, where it is dangerous," Raina reasoned. "Can't we come in and be safe?"

He pondered the question for several moments, ruffling his hair a little more while he had the chance. He hadn't decided if they needed to be kept safe when Ms. Larkin-LaBois happened by. She observed Mr. Leech barring them from entering the school as if she couldn't quite believe her eyes. When it became obvious that Raina's question had stumped him, Ms. Larkin-LaBois stepped closer. "Excuse me, Mr. Leech. I don't mean to interfere, but I do think these three students would be better off inside. And I can personally vouch for the fact that they do attend school here and are not intending any harm. They are most trustworthy, I assure you. I will take full responsibility for allowing them entrance into the building." Ms. Larkin-LaBois smiled at him as if he was about five years old. If she could have reached the top of his head, she might have patted it.

"Oh, well, fine. Good, good." Mr. Leech was transparently relieved to have the matter decided for him. He stopped using his body to block the doorway.

"I would like a word with the three of you. Come with me," Ms. Larkin-LaBois ordered.

Were they in trouble for giving Mrs. Merry-Helen the slip? They followed the old elf into the same small bare office that April had visited previously. It hadn't changed in three weeks. The door was firmly closed, ensuring privacy.

"Thanks for getting us in," Raina said, straight off. "I can't believe Mr. Leech didn't recognize me. I'm one of his students." She was clearly offended.

"When one's eyes are turned inward, they do not see out," Ms. Larkin-LaBois said with a quirk of her lips. "Now, I have been somewhat apprised of the morning's events. But I have some questions about what transpired, if you wouldn't mind answering them."

"No, we don't mind." April knew that Ms. Larkin-LaBois was in Welly's confidence, from when they had saved the forcefield, the first time around. She must be involved this time, too.

The old elf proceeded to ask a seemingly endless stream of questions, until she knew every tiny detail of their morning as well as they did. If she came to any conclusions, Ms. Larkin-LaBois kept them to herself, but her expression reminded April of Welly's melancholy.

Ms. Larking-LaBois concluded by saying, "This information has been most helpful. Now, I am sure I have delayed you from your lunch for long enough. You can use my empty classroom if you would like to eat in peace. I do hope that Mr. Leech wouldn't allow you outside to eat in the meadow." She pursed her lips. "But perhaps I am wrong."

They hurried away, quite starved. Ms. Larkin-LaBois' classroom was not entirely empty. Several groups of students were playing games on the tables and generally running amok. April had expected her classmates to be more traumatized by the morning's events, but that was not the case. They were having too much fun to be traumatized. And they didn't seem to blame April for the field trip disaster at all. She had been in plain sight the whole time and was thereby judged innocent.

When they tried to leave school at the end of the day, there was a backlog at the front door. Students weren't being released until they had partnered up and been thoroughly cautioned about going directly home. Luckily, Mr. Flynn had replaced Mr. Leech at the door, or they might have been trapped in the building all night.

6. Imps and Leprechauns

At home, dinner was waiting. So were Mr. and Mrs. Poole—waiting and angry. DewDrop must have been sent to her room to play, so they could speak plainly, or shout plainly. Salm wasn't home yet, or he had made a run for it.

"Pursuing that creature into the forest alone today!" Mr. Poole raged, as soon as Raina and April sat down. "What were you thinking? Obviously you weren't!"

The food was thumped into the middle of the table—a variety of chopped vegetables that looked haphazardly mixed together, and some sort of dirt-coloured liquid with brown floating lumps. Fungus soup, nobody's favorite.

"But Dad, we weren't safe anyway, any of us. The creature had the thunderwand!" Raina cried. "You should be proud of us!" She swished her soup around with a wrinkled nose. "Did you cook this to punish us for saving New Haven?" she asked her mother.

"You are lucky to get fed at all, so don't you dare complain. Your father wanted to send you both to bed without any dinner." Mrs. Poole sat down with a 'harrumph' worthy of Sage Scarab.

Mr. Poole picked up a shell to pass around the table. He set it down instead and sighed, seeming to deflate. "We are very proud of you for your quick thinking and brave actions, but we are more concerned about the great risk you took. Things could have turned out very differently," he stressed. "Our world seems to be changing around us, and frankly, it frightens me. This is not talk for the dinner hour, but it needs to be said. In all my years as a Healer, I have never been called upon to treat an elf with such grave injuries as Airron's. He is lucky to be alive, and I never want to see such tragedy in our world again. But until this creature is caught, every last elf in New Haven is at risk. You," he eyed Raina and April in turn, "more than most, because of your propensity for danger. What I am trying to say is that I do not want any of you to be hurt in any

79

way and I wish I could ensure that. But I can't. Each of you is responsible for your own actions, so please do not seek out trouble," he said, almost pleading.

"But, Dad, we did the right thing. We would have to do the same thing, if it happened again." Raina sounded pleading, as well, begging him to understand.

Her father studied her as if she was changing before his eyes. "I forget how much you have grown up," he said simply, and rather sadly. He picked up the shell again and handed it to Raina. "Let's eat." The conversation was clearly over for the time being—there was no easy solution given the present threat.

After such an unforgettable Monday, the rest of the week was filled with perfectly normal days. All classes ran on schedule with the requisite amount of work. At lunch, elves were so closely guarded, Raina said it was like being back in kindergarten. Every day, the teachers joined them in the meadow, sitting together in a circle. Mr. Leech had a habit of ruffling his gleaming black hair repeatedly, much to the delight of many admiring girls. The teachers were not so impressed with his hair or actions. Mr. Flynn kept edging away as if Mr. Leech had a contagious scalp condition. And Mr. Parsley almost came to blows with Mr. Leech one day, although the students couldn't overhear why, as hard as they strained their ears.

Each day when they visited Airron after school, he was reading with great concentration, as if he had discovered the books in his room for the very first time. Salm accompanied them on Friday. Now that Airron wasn't leaking blood, Salm could handle visiting him. And Airron had a wonderful announcement. As soon as they entered his room, he cleared his throat dramatically, rose and sauntered across the room saying, "I am going to attend school with you on Monday. I can walk and my appearance shouldn't cause any elves to run screaming from the classroom."

"Oh, Airron, that's not funny! Don't say such a thing. You look great." Raina was exaggerating, but compared to last week, he did look fantastic. The scars were merely thin red lines, and the bruises and swelling were all but gone. "I would take you over Wade, any day!"

"Well, I should hope so. Who's Wade?"

"Mr. Leech, my new teacher, remember?"

Airron shook his head. "I have a few blank spots. Have I met him?"

"No, you've only heard about him, before … the mice. He teaches the merrows. You have Mr. Flynn, who teaches the fairies. Mr. Leech isn't really the best teacher," Raina admitted.

"I guess I'll meet him for myself on Monday. I wouldn't mind getting out and about on the weekend. I need to practice being back on my feet. Nothing too strenuous," Airron added apologetically.

"Airron, your wings weren't torn up, were they?" Raina asked, then clapped a hand over her mouth as if she could stop the words. It was too late.

"What?" His face fell, stricken. "My wings? Of course I can still fly. I'm sure I can still fly. I haven't looked … no-one has said anything about my wings. Wings don't heal, they're not like skin!" He struggled to untie his robe with desperate fingers. He gave up, ripped the ties apart and dropped the robe to the floor. He stood there in pajama bottoms, trying to see behind his back. He really couldn't. "Have a look," he ordered his friends, spreading his arms to open his wings as fully as possible while his feet were still planted on the ground. Salm and Peter each moved to examine a wing, especially the edges.

April touched the wings' powdery, soft texture. She had never felt wings before. They did seem incredibly fragile, almost as if they weren't there. They felt almost magical.

Salm let go of Airron's wing and nodded. "Nothing wrong with your wings. You'll be able to fly fine as good as before."

"Yes," Peter said, backing Salm up.

Airron collapsed onto the edge of his bed and dropped his head into his hands, overcome with relief. "I was so worried about walking, I didn't once think about flying. I could jump out the window and test my wings right now, to make sure."

"No, Airron. It's too soon. You don't want to reopen your wounds. Let's just go for a walk, a short walk," Raina said.

She was right. It was much too soon for Airron to try flying. At least he listened to reason. They took him for a walk around his house instead. He needed a nap after that and they left.

It was an unusually quiet Friday night. Most elves were being kept close to home, due to the obvious dangers. The Pooles were adamant about all their offspring staying home after dark. The strict supervision had all to do with their latest exploits. Peter was allowed to visit, but he would have to sleep over again.

Dinner was a subdued meal. Mr. Poole ate quickly then rose. "Well, I'm off. See you in the morning." He kissed his wife absently on the cheek.

"Be careful, dear," she murmured back, enfolding him in an unexpected embrace.

"Where are you going for the whole night?" Salm asked curiously.

"Guard duty. There are at least three elves from the High Court watching over the thunderwand at all times, in addition to the guards. Falcon isn't taking any chances," Mr. Poole explained. "Tonight is my night. Be good for your mother." The 'or else' went unsaid, but was crystal clear nonetheless.

After they tidied the kitchen, there was nothing to do. "Well, this is boring," Raina declared, almost petulantly.

April smiled. "I thought you liked boring these days."

"Well, yes. But not too much of it," Raina said. "Let's play a game. There's nothing else to do and we can't even leave the front garden."

"I don't think we're even allowed in the front garden," Salm said, looking out the window.

"Safer in here, I should think," Peter said.

"We'll play upstairs, in April's room," Raina said in her bossy voice. April's room did have the most space since it contained the fewest things. The four of them traipsed upstairs and played sticks and stones without a lot of enthusiasm. Peter kept winning and Salm kept yawning.

"Well, this is boring too!" Raina complained, after several lethargic matches.

Salm smirked. "You just miss Airron."

"I do not! Well, yes, I do but …" She didn't know what to say.

"We could bet on the game, that would make it more exciting," Salm proposed.

"Except April is the only one with gold, if she still has any."

"She does, a whole bunch. Right in the top drawer of that box dresser." Peter pointed out the exact location. He was showing off.

April frowned at him. "That's my hiding spot. Now you've told!"

"It's not much of a hiding spot. It's the first place I would look if I was going to steal your gold," Raina said with a laugh.

"Me, too," Salm said. "Hey, let's see if Peter can find hidden gold!"

"That would be fun. Can we use your gold, April?" Raina asked.

"Peter, do you want to find hidden gold?" she asked him.

"Sure, it would be good practice."

82

April went over to her drawer and lifted out the sack of coins that she had won at the Harvest Moon festival. Peter was sent outside the room. They took turns hiding ten of the coins and then April placed the sack in plain view on top of the dresser. Raina called Peter back in and told him, "We've hidden ten coins."

Peter seemed eager to test his new ability. He pointed to the sack, then ignored it while he toured around the room once, silently. On his second circle, his brow was lowered and he kept closing his eyes. He was really concentrating. He eyed April's closet, then ducked inside. He came out carrying one coin. "I can guess who hid that one. Tricky spot, April—in the pocket of your overalls."

It was incredible that he could track such a tiny amount of gold so accurately. Or he had made a lucky guess. They were April's favorite overalls, after all. But that possibility was disproved when Peter sauntered over to the bed and lifted up a cotton ball pillow, revealing a second gold coin. "Not a very original spot. That's where the Tooth Fairy would put it."

"What's a tooth fairy?" April asked.

"Actually, it's a myth. When you lose a tooth, you're supposed to put it under your pillow and a magical Tooth Fairy will turn it into gold," Peter replied.

"You do seem to have a myth for every occasion," April said.

Peter handed April both gold coins and grinned appreciatively. "You are sneaky," he said, and slipped a hand into her hair above her ear. His fingers emerged holding a third gold coin. "You didn't think I would find that one, did you?" April shook her head and smiled back. It was a fun game.

Effortlessly, Peter found the coin on the window ledge, the one under the bed, the one behind the dresser, the one under the pile of game pieces, the one in Salm's pocket, and even the one in Raina's cup of berry fizz. April's magical ability to sense other creatures and communicate with them did not work at all below water. Apparently Peter's magic did, or maybe the amount of liquid was simply too small to mask the gold.

He was momentarily stumped in locating the tenth coin, but he used his brain to find that one, not his magic at all. After beginning to look truly puzzled, he strode across the room to the dresser and lifted up the sack of remaining coins. Sitting underneath was the last and tenth coin. And April realized something important. Welly was right. Thinking cleverly could be every bit as important as how an elf used their magic.

"That's amazing, Peter. You can find gold anywhere!" Raina cried. "Did you know that you could find gold so well?"

"I was beginning to think so. The sensation has been getting stronger. I always know when April is nearby, because of her gold chain, the magical one that changes every year on her birthday."

"Can you sense the magic or just the gold?" April asked.

"Just the gold," Peter said.

They didn't repeat the game again. It was obvious that Peter could find gold coins wherever they hid them. Even though it was Friday night, they went to bed early. There was nothing else to do.

The next day when they went to pick up Airron. Salm came along. Mrs. Fay-Finch answered the door and greeted them as she always did, coldly polite and with a frown. "You know the way," she said with a vague flick of her hand.

Airron was installed on his bed, completely surrounded by books. "Hey, Airron. Ready to go?" Peter asked, even though they hadn't decided where they were going.

"No, not yet." Airron was flushed with excitement. "I have to tell you something first. Something important. Really important. You better sit down. You better close the door." They did. "Okay, you have to believe what I am about to tell you because I know I'm right."

"Of course we'll believe you, Airron. Why wouldn't we?" Raina said.

"Because it is a little farfetched. Okay, it's a lot farfetched, but I know I'm right," he repeated.

"You already said that. Tell us."

He still wasn't quite ready. "I have to prepare you first. It's like when April said that Giants really exist. It was hard to believe her because we thought of them as characters from myth, not real at all."

"This has something to do with Giants?" Raina asked fearfully.

"No, it has nothing to do with Giants, I'm making a point."

"Well, it's a confusing point," she said.

"Okay, I'll get to the real point. I have figured out the identity of the creature that has entered our world, the one that is causing all the trouble," Airron declared. The news caught them all off guard.

"From the books?" Peter guessed. "Is that why you've been reading so much?"

Airron glanced at the field of books surrounding him. "You noticed? There are some great books on my shelves. Some of them are really old, one of a kind. Hand scripted and inked. A few of them are about myths, mythological creatures and the like." He paused to make sure he had their full attention. They were all pointed ears. "I was able to discover the identity of the creature because of the green eyes that I told you about. It is supposed to be a creature from myth, not real at all—like Giants." He was back to his previous point.

April couldn't wait to hear. "So, what is it?"

"It's an imp, sometimes called a goblin. Have you ever met one in the Outer-World? Like you've met Giants?" he asked April.

"You don't meet Giants, Airron. If there's a Giant around, you're doing everything you can to not meet it! And yes, imps do exist. They aren't quite as loathsome as Giants, but only because they're smaller, almost as small as us. They are smarter than Giants, but not nearly as smart as elves. I haven't seen an imp in six or so years. Not since I was little, before I was lost in the forest."

"You know that imps exist?" Airron asked incredulously.

"Yes. They are supposed to be a sort of distant cousin to elves. Lots of things exist outside the barrier that don't exist in New Haven—like Giants," she emphasized.

"So you believe me?"

April hesitated. "Why do you think an imp is in New Haven causing trouble?"

He dragged one of the largest books closer, already opened. It held both text and an illustration. Four heads leaned in close, all trying to see at once. The detailed picture showed a town path, lined with buildings. What was unusual about the scene was the mayhem occurring from one end of town to the other. Elves were falling down stairs, elves were being attacked by plants and insects, elves were even throwing pies at each other. One elf was hanging upside-down in midair trying to hold her skirts down—or up. These elves were not having a good day.

Peter pointed to the attacking plants and insects. "Some of these events look rather familiar."

Indeed they did. "But what does this have to do with an imp?" April asked.

"Look there." Airron touched his finger to the end of the street, where the edge of the forest encroached on the town. Gleaming green eyes were camouflaged amongst the leaves, but once Airron pointed them out, they were impossible to miss.

"Green eyes!" Raina exclaimed.

"Green eyes. This is the tale of how an imp destroyed a whole village, just because some elves trampled through his garden. Quite by accident, I'm sure," Airron added.

"April, you knew about imps," Raina said. "Why didn't you think an imp might be causing all our problems?"

"Because I'm not so sure it is an imp. They are very rare creatures, and I haven't seen one in years. And I've never seen one with green eyes. The last one I remember had blood-red eyes, and it had just – just done something awful. And imps really aren't very bright. No imp could have planned what happened at the museum, using the bees as a decoy to steal the thunderwand. They do have scary powerful magic, but they're not clever enough to think of something like that. Not even close," April said firmly.

Airron looked crestfallen. "But I'm sure I'm right, I saw green eyes and this book shows imps with green eyes. Look, there's even a picture of a whole imp." He flipped pages to an illustration of an imp peering down into a hole. It did look like the imp April remembered, except for the eyes. It was generally evil-looking, with odd tufts of patchy hair in random places. It had a wiry, tough body and crouched like an animal, curling its lips to reveal a crowd of pointy teeth. It didn't look bright, even in the drawing.

Raina wrinkled her nose at the picture. "I wouldn't want to meet one of those in a dark forest. Is that what your imp looked like, April?"

"It wasn't my imp. And it did look the same, except for the eyes."

"Well, maybe imps come with different colours of eyes. We're both elves and we have very different eye colours," Raina pointed out. "Our eyes are so dark and yours are like lights."

April couldn't argue with facts. "Yes, that would explain the eyes, but not the being clever. That's a lot harder to explain."

Raina took a second look at the picture. "Well, maybe this imp is smarter than your average imp," she said dubiously.

"Imps are never smart," April said. Facts were facts.

"Still—I don't think we can dismiss Airron's theory," Peter said, supporting his friend.

"Provided an imp could travel through the barrier into New Haven," Salm said.

April considered that. "I don't see why not, they're small enough. And if they really are somehow related to elves, how would the barrier know the difference? Maybe it wouldn't," she said, answering her own question. "Okay, so maybe it is a super smart imp." She didn't have a better idea.

Airron perked up. "Good! Well, let's get out of here, we can talk about it on the way." Now that he had delivered his news, Airron was anxious to escape from his room.

"Talk on the way where?" Peter asked. Since Airron could only walk a limited distance, they probably couldn't go further than his lawn.

"Well, I do want to try jumping out my window to test my wings, before we do anything else." Airron stacked some books so he could slide off his bed. "I can't wait any longer."

"But Airron, are you sure you're strong enough? Does it have to be today?" Raina sounded like her mother

"I'm plenty strong enough to fly down to the ground." He removed his robe to reveal long pants, hiding the scars on his legs. Clearly, he had been planning this before they arrived.

Raina stroked one amber wing gently. "Be careful, Airron."

"I will." He climbed onto the edge of his large window as if he had done it plenty of times. Airron stepped forward as if he was taking an ordinary walk, right off the window ledge into space. He opened his arms wide and glided smoothly away. Gaining confidence, he turned several showy circles over his trim green lawn, and even a somersaulting dive. There was no doubt that he could fly just fine.

His whole face lit with joy, Airron soared back toward his small audience. It was the best moment and they all cheered enthusiastically. "I'm going a little further, wait for me!" He looped easily away over the treetops. Raina watched to keep him in sight for as long as possible, then fretted until he returned safely. Airron was panting from exertion when he coasted in and landed gracefully on his floor.

April was impressed. "You fly really well, Airron."

"I've been practicing," he said. "Well—before the attack. At least we can really go somewhere now that we know I can fly." He sank wearily onto his bed, as if the short flight had drained him.

"We don't have to go anywhere, Airron," Raina was quick to say. "Let's hang out here. I like your room."

They hung out in Airron's room, talking and leafing through Airron's books for more clues about imps or other creatures that might be responsible for New Haven's problems. Raina made an interesting discovery in the same book as the imp. "Hey, look at this," she exclaimed in amazement, shoving the book under Peter's nose. He stared at it for several minutes, then started laughing so hard he fell over backwards.

"What is it?" April peered over his shoulder. "Hey, Peter, you're a Leprechaun! Imagine that."

"What's a Leprechaun?" Salm asked, leaning in. "That's a Leprechaun? It does look kind of like Peter, doesn't it?"

"Does it?" April couldn't see the resemblance at all. The depicted elf was short and fat with a bulbous nose and wild head of hair.

"That was a joke, April," Salm informed her.

"But what is a Leprechaun, and why is Peter one?" Airron was reclining comfortably, not inclined to move.

Raina was scanning the text. "It is supposed to be a mythological elf. A Leprechaun is an old name for an elf that can find gold. They are a specific type of magical elf, but they are always pixies. I guess Drake Pitt was a Leprechaun as well," Raina mused. "But the picture of a Leprechaun really doesn't look anything like Peter." She held the book up so Airron could have a look.

Peter stole the book from Raina. "So I guess I'll have pounds of gold and keep it hidden in pots under my bed, or do I have to find a rainbow? The book says something about hiding my gold at the end of a rainbow—is that something in the Outer-World?" he asked April.

"Yes, and it's very beautiful." She did her best to describe an indescribable rainbow while the rest of the books were collected and piled on the desk. Airron was nodding off. They left before Mrs. Fay-Finch could chase them away.

It was hard to believe that almost a month had passed since Airron had been able to attend school. But he would be back on Monday, and everything would be perfectly normal again.

7. Fire and Water

Airron was welcomed back to school as if he was a great hero. There was a tremendous fuss of cheering and applause when he glided down and landed in the meadow. His father hovered overhead, and only flew off when Airron was safely on the ground.

A flustered Airron quickly pulled his robe out of his pack and dressed over his pants, right there in the middle of the meadow, laughing when elves hooted at him. When the commotion died down, Airron said to Raina, "I never thought I would say this, but it's great to be at school."

"I never thought I would hear you say it." Raina beamed at him. There was no opportunity for more. Airron's other friends closed around him to welcome him back.

Inside the school, even the teachers went out of their way to inquire about Airron's recovery. Mr. Flynn shook Airron's hand warmly in the hallway. "We've missed you in class. So good to see you back," he said sincerely.

"Thanks. Good to be back, and I really mean it," Airron said with a smile.

Mr. Leech was standing to the side, chest thrown out and shirt as tight as always, smiling whitely in case there was a larger audience somewhere that he hadn't spotted yet. He clapped Airron on the shoulder really hard, perhaps to show how strong his muscles were. Airron winced, he was not ready to be roughed up yet.

"Welcome back, Airron isn't it? Heard about your accident. Those scars will fade, I hope. You're the mayor's son, aren't you? I'm Mr. Leech, you can call me Wade." The teacher nodded his head wisely for no particular reason.

Mr. Flynn clenched his teeth together so forcibly that April heard a grinding noise. "Come along, Wade, we'll let Airron get to class. He has missed enough school."

The two teachers walked down the hall side-by-side. Mr. Leech was strutting along in pants as tight as his shirt. They were so tight that he actually had to wiggle a bit when he walked. Mr. Flynn was kind of hunched over, as if he wished himself invisible.

"That's your teacher?" Airron asked Raina incredulously. "You're in his class?"

"That's usually how it works," she said dryly.

"Poor you. Do you learn anything?"

"Not really, but I might someday, by accident. You never know." Raina smiled ruefully and they hurried to their room. The school day had begun.

When the final gong sounded, the mayor arrived to escort Airron home. The rest of the week followed a similar pattern, Airron was flown to school and home each day. No more strange or alarming events occurred, to everyone's relief.

They were all in a lively mood on Friday and Airron capped things off by announcing that he could go to Raina's house after school. He was even allowed to walk with them. For the first time in too long, it felt like a real weekend.

Salm turned up with Twiggy and Paddy. When they overtook Heather and Willowna, Raina invited them over, too. They were pleased to accept, but they wanted Finnegan and Gil to come along. From that point on the numbers swelled steadily.

"Are you hosting a gathering?" Raina's mother asked, when they arrived home accompanied by a rather large number of elves, and more seemed to be popping out of the trees every time she turned around.

"Not really, we're hanging out," Raina grinned. "And lots of elves are bringing food from home, so we don't have to feed them all."

"I should hope not, we don't have that much food, believe me. And your father and I are going out this evening. He has another guard duty and I am going to keep him company. DewDrop is at a sleepover, so you will be on your own. Salm, you are the eldest so you are in charge. Make sure you behave yourselves," Mrs. Poole warned, watching as Seamore and Perriwinkle came down the path, dragging a zucchini between them.

The gathering turned into an unplanned party and it was loudly declared to be in honor of Airron. Some classmates even brought musical instruments. April was surprised that a number of them could play songs, and quite well.

When night settled in, Salm poured out nectar for the fireflies, and lit a campfire on the shore. He ran into the house and came back toting a sack of dried corn kernels. Elves took turns tossing the kernels into the fire and catching them when they popped with an explosive bang and flew out.

It did look like April's whole class had turned up, possibly Salm's whole class as well. April thought she spied Figgy Forester, but if she did, he ducked out of sight. He had a habit of being elusive whenever April was in the vicinity. Even Cherry made an appearance at Starla's side, when the gathering was in full swing. Raina's party was probably the last place Cherry wanted to be since there was only enmity between them, but the elf seemed in no hurry to leave.

Raina was determined to get Airron swimming after they finished dancing together to one of the slow songs. She waded in and stood up to her neck. "Come on, Airron. You can still swim, can't you?"

"I'm not supposed to swim. Your father said so himself. No water on the leg wounds yet, no mucking about in water," Airron said, standing regretfully on the shore.

"Oh, well that's no fun. I'll come out, then."

"No, have a swim. I need to rest for a few minutes, anyway." He sank onto the sand beside Peter, trying not to look exhausted, but he clearly was.

"Okay, I won't be long." Raina dunked under, gone in the lap of a wave. There was something spooky about the black surface of the water at night and April joined the boys, not Raina. Airron lay back and closed his eyes. He might have even fallen asleep.

It was a great party and showed no sign of winding down. The moon inched overhead, casting its cold blue light onto the scene. Music was still being played, the fire was roaring high, lots of elves were dancing, but slowly now. Starla was partnered with Ray, and April couldn't see Cherry anywhere. Maybe she had slunk home.

April was as relaxed as could be, sitting in the sand and nibbling a popped corn when the gathering was spoiled in the worst possible way. She closed her eyes in pain, her head spinning, devastated by what she was feeling. Without a doubt, it was the same dangerous sensation as before. It simply wasn't fair!

At least they were all together—except they weren't. Raina was under the dark water alone. April swung toward Peter and spoke urgently in his ear. "It's back," was all she had to say.

Peter swore, he never swore. They both scanned the area. Nothing looked out of place, as always.

"We have to get Raina out of the water, she's alone down there," April whispered, not wanting to cause a panic. "I'll swim out and find her. She shouldn't be too far away."

"Okay. But be careful, April. And I'll try and get everyone together, safety in numbers," Peter said.

"Get Airron in the house, maybe everyone can fit in the house," April said, rising. "And tell Salm, he can help."

April ran across the sand and splashed into the water. It was impossible to see below the opaque surface, which was dancing with orange light reflected from the campfire. The bright glints hid whatever lay beneath. It was not going to be easy to find Raina, but April would find her.

She lowered completely under the cool water and tried to sense her friend. She couldn't. As always, that particular magical ability didn't work below the water. April dove deeper and swam straight away from the shore, feeling for Raina with her arms and listening for bubbles with her ears. Even her skin was alert for any disturbance in the natural water flow. Periodically, she surfaced for air, and tried to spot Raina above the water. Although the search was proving fruitless, April was reassured by how calm everything seemed.

The next time she surged up from the water to gasp in a lungful air, that had all changed. The world above wasn't black anymore. It was bright and fiery, as if the sun had decided to rise in the middle of the night, and much nearer to the earth than it ought. A chorus of shrill screams marked a sharp contrast to the silence under the water. April couldn't figure out what was happening until she spun around to face the shore.

The blinding light was coming from the campfire, but it wasn't a simple campfire any longer. It had grown all out of proportion, flaring up toward the night sky even as April watched. Elves were shrieking and running for the shelter of the house, away from the fire that appeared to be sprouting arms, of all things.

The flaming appendages reached out toward the small lake, where they caused the most impossible reaction with the water. The water didn't put the fire out, as it should do. Instead, the fire set the lake's lapping waves ablaze, and that was only the beginning. As if the water was dry tinder, the fire spread quickly across the rippling surface, travelling in

April's direction. This was not merely a reflected illusion of firelight, this was *real*—searing hot and crackling with sparks. April had been watching with such fascination that it took a moment to grasp the fact that she was in grave danger.

Peter waved frantically from the shore. There was no way to reach him, short of swimming through fire and April was not willing to try that. She preferred the opposite direction—away from the fire, toward the more distant shore. And she still had to find Raina, who probably had no idea that she was in peril.

Airron did. He tried to lunge around Peter. Luckily Peter caught hold of him and refused to let go. Salm pelted up from behind and threw another arm around Airron, who was fighting to remove his robe. Flying over the inferno would have been as dangerous as trying to swim through it. April stopped watching their scuffle when the flames leapt higher and tumbled over each other, as if they were alive and reaching out to lick her.

"Cat's claws," she swore and flipped around like a fish, stroking away from the surging heat. As hard as she swam, the fire was faster. Sparks allowed the flames to spread in leaps and bounds.

When the fire was almost upon her and stinging her back, the water warmed unnaturally. With no choice, April hauled in a huge breath and dove straight down. She'd had no near drowning experiences in four months, so she was probably overdue.

Yet, if she could find Raina in time, they could share the breath drawn in through Raina's gills. It was the only desperate possibility that April could come up with on the spur of the moment, and she only had a few moments left.

The fire cast an eerie light down from above, but April still could not spot her friend anywhere. With a cramping chest, April kicked deeper still, fighting to cover as much distance as possible before she ran out of her small ration of air. Her limbs grew heavy and weak. The fire surged past overhead, effectively trapping her below water without any chance of air, and without Raina. The brighter light had illuminated the deepest water, proving April was alone.

She closed her eyes against the expanding black spots. There was no way out of this, she knew it with a terrible finality that robbed her will. She would never see her friends again, not even one last time. Her lungs squeezed with force, as if a fat bunny had hopped on her chest. She needed to breathe the water, there was nothing else to breathe and her lungs were forcing her to inhale—so she did. She gasped in a full breath of water.

As if in a dream, the real world faded away and April was falling into a black abyss inhabited by a monster with a hundred razor sharp claws. They stabbed deep into April's back and dragged under the skin. She arched away from the monster and screamed in agony. It sounded loud, even underwater. April writhed in pain and waited for the end. But it never came.

The pain slowly eased and April did not drown—at least, she didn't think so. But she should have drowned. What was happening? Her lungs were full of glorious oxygen. But how had it gotten there? Unless …? Twisting an arm behind her back, April felt the skin under her top. Her fingers discovered a pattern of raised edges, radiating out from her spine. They certainly hadn't been there before, she would have noticed. They were pulsing opened and closed, breathing all by themselves. They were located exactly where Salm and Raina's gills marked their backs.

Incredibly, April now had gills. No wonder her back had felt like it was tearing open. In a way, it had. She immediately stopped thinking about that exact process. And in spite of having gills, she wasn't out of danger. The fire was flaring above, the lake was growing steadily hotter and Raina still had to be found.

Now that her wits were somewhat returned, April resumed her search, kicking deeper. The water was a little cooler at the bottom of the lake, but seemed as deserted of life as the surface. What if Raina had already succumbed to the hot water? What if she had tried to get back to shore through the flames? Frantic, April skimmed over the lakeweed in an expanding spiral pattern, combing through the rubbery vegetation.

When her fingers touched still flesh beneath the weedy tangle, April was almost too terrified to look. Sobbing, she dragged on a limp arm and hauled Raina clear of the dark fronds. Raina's eyelids fluttered and a few bubbles trailed from between her lips, proving she was alive. "Raina, wake up! Please wake up," April begged, forgetting that she couldn't actually talk underwater. It was weird when bubbles popped out of her mouth instead of words.

April shook Raina by the shoulders, but there was no reaction. Raina was not going to wake up anytime soon. And the lake showed no sign of running out of flames. April had to find a way to get them both ashore before the water started boiling. Gripping Raina's arm tightly, April towed her friend's limp body through the lakeweed in the only direction she could think of—toward the creek beside Raina's house. It flowed into the lake and should provide a supply of cooler water, if they could make it.

The closer they got to the shore, the shallower and hotter the water grew. April kept kicking and towing Raina along, although the longer she was trapped below water, the more peculiar she felt. When she laughed out loud at a dead fish, April realized she was getting quite giddy. And then she giggled at the stream of bubbles coming out of her mouth. There was nothing funny about a dead fish. And bubbles weren't that funny, were they? How could she laugh at a time like this? And at a poor, dead fish? Maybe it was the bubbles that were funny. Yes, that was it—bubbles tickled.

April tried to stop giggling, because she was using up all her air, gasping for breath through her gills now. Towing Raina must be more strenuous than she had realized. April stopped to rest, but it didn't help. The gasping only got worse. And the water was unbearably hot. She felt like she was drowning all over again, in a Giant's simmering pot of elf soup.

April studied the flames overhead hazily, trying hard to think when her head felt stuffed with dandelion fluff. Normally, a fire needed air to burn, but this was not a normal fire. Maybe this fire was fueled by the oxygen in the water, using it all up. It would explain why April was having trouble breathing and why the fish were dead. April had to get Raina out of the lake, fast!

"Don't stop, keep going. Don't stop, keep going," April chanted and tried to kick harder with legs that felt as mushy as overcooked string beans. She scanned desperately ahead but her vision clouded over.

April grew so sleepy that she must have drifted into a stupor, like Raina. Strong hands gripped her shoulders and warm lips sealed over her mouth. A ration of air was forced into her lungs. April opened her eyes and Salm's pale face wavered into view. Even through the cloudy water, he looked tremendously relieved that she wasn't dead. He nodded once and began to tug her through the water. And if Salm had reached them, they had to be near the creek!

She strengthened her grip on Raina. They were both towed along. Salm stopped and pressed his lips to hers again, and it felt very good and warm, but April didn't need his air. She shook her head. He looked at her questioningly. Since she couldn't talk, she gripped his hand and placed it on her back, under her shirt.

When he felt the gills, his eyes widened dramatically in surprise. April nodded and pointed ahead. He flashed her a grin and they started swimming together, towing Raina.

The water cooled by degrees and breathing through her gills grew easier. April panted in and out until her lungs stopped cramping and she could kick properly, keeping pace with Salm. In no time, they were swimming against the current into the actual creek, where the water was a normal temperature. The luminous orange light faded to black.

Salm swam still further upstream, then angled toward the land. He lifted April up and onto the shore before she was expecting it. She kept clinging to Raina's wrist, afraid to lose her grip.

"April, let go!" said Airron. He pried April's fingers apart and lifted Raina ashore. She was still unconscious, but as least she started coughing and breathing as soon as she was laid on the moss.

"What's wrong with her?" Airron cried.

Salm sat down heavily on the shore and pressed his chest, fighting to catch his breath. "Hard to breathe … in the lake."

"Fire's using up … oxygen in the water … I think. Not enough left … to breathe," April stammered, as winded as Salm.

Salm turned to stare at her. "April?"

"Huh?"

"How do you … I thought Raina must have been helping you breathe, but she couldn't, could she? How did you get gills?"

"Tell you … in a minute." April would, once she had her breath back.

Peter rushed up then. "You made it, Salm. You found them! Is Raina going to be okay?" he asked. Raina was very obviously in the worst condition.

"Should be," April answered, even though she didn't know for sure. She only hoped, as they all did. If hope had any power, Raina would be fine. A chorus of shouting had them all swinging around toward the house.

Airron groaned, "What now?"

"Hey, it sounds like my Dad." Salm stumbled up and gazed downstream. It sounded like a lot more elves than his father; it sounded like a crowd. But Mr. Poole's voice rang out over the rest, shouting wildly for Salm and Raina. The fiery lake must have lit up the whole of New Haven, drawing elves from as far as the town circle.

"Sit down, Salm. I'll tell your Dad that he's needed over here," Peter said, and hurried away. Salm sat right back down and April didn't even try to stand. Her legs still felt useless and her skin was starting to sting in the night air. Airron scooted closer to take Raina's hand. They were all in a state of shock.

Mr. and Mrs. Poole were quick to arrive. Mr. Poole stared down at Raina, his face stricken. He looked like her father, not a Healer at all. Mrs. Poole bit her lip and crouched down beside Raina. "Marsh? How is she? What's wrong with her?"

He gathered himself with effort. He checked Raina's breathing with shaking hands, he looked quite faint with relief that she was breathing. "Grab me a torch," he ordered Peter, who was the only elf in condition to run errands. Peter took off again and Mr. Poole continued his examination as the flames on the lake finally began to shrink away.

"Tell me what happened," Mr. Poole ordered Salm.

"I'll try, but it is hard to believe," Salm said. He did his best to describe how the lake had started burning, trapping Raina and April under the surface. He said that April had rescued Raina and that he had pulled them from the water. Salm had done a lot more than that, but he wasn't the type to sing his own praises.

Before he could mention April's new gills, Mr. Poole said, "So there was not enough oxygen to breathe?" He transferred his gaze to April in confusion. "But you were trapped underwater and you are not a merrow, yet you are ... still here? How can that be?" He was gently asking why she wasn't dead.

"I sort of ... grew gills, or got gills, when I couldn't breathe. My back really hurt and then I had gills. It was strange, kind of like magic," she guessed.

"Do you still have gills?"

"I don't know." April twisted her arm around and checked, but couldn't feel anything. "I don't think I do."

Salm peeked down the back of her shirt, and ran a hand over her skin. "No gills. They're gone now," he confirmed.

"Well, that is very peculiar. Usually gills are a permanent fixture, not here one moment and gone the next. Magic is the only explanation, isn't it?" Mr. Poole's attention was caught by Peter, returning with a torch. Mr. Poole did something strange then. He opened each of Raina's eyelids and flashed the light over them.

Again, he seemed greatly relieved by whatever he saw. "Her pupils are responsive. Her brain has not been deprived of oxygen for long enough to cause damage. I see no reason why Raina should not make a full recovery. But she might be more comfortable waking up in her own bed." He stood up smiling and pulled Mrs. Poole to her feet. She was smiling and crying all at the same time.

"Do the rest of you need treating?" Mr. Poole checked.

"I'm okay," said Salm. "I wasn't in the hottest water."

"April?"

"I'm fine."

He did not accept her word. "Your skin does look mildly scalded and may soon feel quite painful. I'll leave a special cream for burns in your room."

April wasn't about to refuse, her skin felt quite painful now. "My thanks."

"And Airron, you didn't overexert yourself?"

"Nope."

"Good, good." Mr. Poole handed Salm the torch, lifted Raina as if she weighed nothing, and strode off with Mrs. Poole.

Their small group stayed behind, as unmoving as a circle of stones, stunned by how the gathering had ended. A number of adults were examining the lake now and dousing the shrunken campfire. Darkness closed in on all sides.

"So it's back, again," Peter murmured, his voice in harmony with the unnatural quiet of the night. All the insects had fled.

"Yes," everyone agreed, depressed.

"And I'm starting to notice a pattern," Peter continued.

"What pattern?" Airron asked.

"In the choice of victims. Salm was the first, wasn't he? I think Sprite just happened to be in the wrong place at the wrong time, because she was with Salm. Airron—you were second. Sage Scarab was third. And now Raina and April. The creature seems to be targeting us." Peter motioned to all of them.

Salm picked up a pebble and heaved it at the creek in frustration. "But why?"

Peter had an answer. "I think it has to do with the forcefield."

"We did all help to save the forcefield," April realized, "Sage Scarab, too. And the creature wants the thunderwand. It's all about the forcefield."

"That's what I was thinking," Peter said.

"I'd guess you're on the right track with that thought." Sage Scarab made them all jump when he stepped silently into view from behind a dandelion. "Checking along the creek for clues," he explained.

"This thing doesn't leave clues, does it?" Peter asked.

"Not so far. Did find some popped corn, though." Sage Scarab sat down and chomped on his slightly sandy snack. "How are you all holding up?"

"We're holding up," Airron said. "As long as Raina is okay, and Mr. Poole says she should be."

"Good." Sage Scarab nodded and chewed. The corn sounded unpleasantly gritty, but he kept eating it.

"It's peculiar," April mused, thinking about all the attacks. "This creature has a tremendous amount of power. It could be causing a lot more damage than what we've seen, but it isn't."

Airron gaped at her as if she had suddenly sprouted another head. "It burned a lake, April. That's pretty extreme."

"I know, but think about it! The bees at the museum were only told to fly around. They could have been told to sting all the students, but they weren't. Airron, I'm not so sure about you. The mice did almost kill you, didn't they? But the fire on the lake tonight only happened when Raina was underwater. Imagine if it had happened earlier, when lots of elves were swimming, lots of elves without gills. Or imagine if the creature had burned the forest instead. And Salm, you were banged around, but never almost killed. And Sage Scarab, you were left hanging from a tree, not harmed either. And you were pretty helpless when we found you. The creature could have done anything to you, but it didn't. See what I mean?" April surveyed their faces in the dim light.

Sage Scarab hummed and hawed before he agreed. "You've got a point, I suppose. Scary creature! Could be doing a heck of a lot more damage. Question is—why isn't it? I'll have to think on it. Come on now, stop lounging around. Parents are waiting."

Peter held out a hand to help April up. When he gripped her arm and pulled, she had to bite her lip so she didn't yelp loudly. Unless that cream in her room worked miracles, she was going to have to sleep standing up. Her hot, tight skin felt like it belonged on a much smaller elf. April walked gingerly through the darkness, since even bending her arms and legs caused discomfort.

The kitchen was quite stuffed with waiting parents and even some elves that April had never met. The room had become the headquarters for the investigation. Welly was presiding at the kitchen table, with Ms. Larkin-LaBois by his side. Both elves looked almost too relieved when April appeared. Had they believed her harmed?

"Ah, there you are!" Mr. Poole tossed an arm around Salm, who flinched with pain. In the well-lit kitchen, Salm's skin was unnaturally red. He was more burned than he had let on. "You will be pleased to know that Raina is resting comfortably and I have every confidence that she will wake up as good as new." It was the very best news.

Head-Sage Falcon then requested a full account of everything that had happened, if April and Salm were up to it. They did their best to answer his questions while elves bustled in and out and kept interrupting. Peter and Airron were hustled away by their fathers with no chance to even say good-night.

As soon as elves stopped asking questions, Salm managed to slip away, and April soon followed. The solitude of her room was welcome, after all that had come before. Candles were already lit and the promised vial of cream was sitting prominently on the box dresser. April tested it on her arms and her stinging skin felt instantly cooled. She smoothed it on wherever she could reach and then felt too restless to sleep. April paced for a bit then gave in to the urge to check on Raina.

April tiptoed into Raina's room and sat on a cushion beside the bed for the longest time, happy to simply watch her friend sleep, tucked safely under her blanket. Raina had so nearly been lying forever at the bottom of the lake. It had been such a close call.

When her eyes grew heavy, April rose to leave. She wasn't alone anymore. Salm was standing in the doorway, not moving. He looked sort of lost, not like Salm at all. "Salm?" April whispered.

"Hey, April. Is Raina okay?" His dark eyes looked kind of startled. The night had been hard on all of them.

"Yes. Are you okay?"

"Umm, I guess. Couldn't sleep. Not used to my family almost dying." He turned aimlessly toward the stairs.

April followed him all the way down and couldn't think of one comforting thing to say. Salm was moving stiffly. "Salm, your skin looks really sore. Do you want some of the cream your father gave me? It works." She could help with his physical pain, at least.

"Okay." Salm followed her then, all the way back upstairs to her room. April handed over the vial and Salm stared at it blankly.

"You just smooth it on," April instructed.

Salm smiled unexpectedly, as if she had said something funny. "I know." But he made no move to open the vial. At least he looked happier, April didn't like it when Salm looked lost. "April …"

"Yes?"

"I don't know what I want to say. I mean, I know what I want to say, but I don't know how to say it … but thanks for what you did tonight, for saving Raina. When you went underwater without gills and the flames trapped you, I honestly didn't think I would ever see you, either of you, alive again," he admitted frankly.

"Salm, don't thank me, I hate that," April protested. "You're the one that got us both out. You saved my life and Raina's life. You did it Salm, not me." It always made April feel uncomfortable when she was thanked for stuff she had done, especially when she hadn't done it at all. And for some reason, she felt shy with Salm at that moment. It had something to do with the way he was looking at her.

April took the vial out of his hand and opened it, for a distraction. "It doesn't smell very good, kind of like rotting vegetation, but it really does help."

She handed it back and Salm crinkled his nose.

"Good. I have a few sore spots on my back," he said sheepishly. "But I can't rival your colour."

"My colour?" April stepped over to the mirror. "Good grief, I look like I've been soaked in raspberry juice. And there is something different about my hair." The ends had definitely been singed. She could smell the burnt odor when she held them up, and they were all frizzy. The fire had gotten much too close.

"Burnt hair?" Salm asked sympathetically.

"Burnt hair, red skin," April said in disgust. As usual, she was a mess.

Salm grinned again. "You look cute all pink."

"You must have singed your eyeballs if you think that."

"Nope, don't think so." Salm applied some of the cream to his shoulders, then tried to reach his back. He couldn't do it properly.

"Give it here. I'll do it," April offered. She spread the cream carefully on Salm's skin, which was redder than normal, but not quite as red as if it had been marinating in berry juice. Even though his gills were almost invisible in the candlelight, they were easy to feel when she rubbed her hand over them. "Are your gills okay?" April checked, tracing one of the lines carefully.

"Uh … ya." Salm jerked. "Tickles."

April removed her hands. "Sorry."

"It didn't hurt, just tickled. Gills are sensitive. Here, let me return the favor." Salm took the cream and turned April around.

"My thanks. My back is the sorest. Are there any marks left, where I had gills?"

Salm raised the back of her shirt and smoothed the cream on while he examined her skin. The cream did feel especially good on her back and Salm was careful not to hurt her. He examined every inch of her back as if he was a scientist.

"What are you looking at? I'm not really burnt on my back, am I?"

"No, well a bit. But I'm looking for your gills. It's really amazing that you had gills and now they're gone. There are some really faint greenish lines where gills would have been. The cream makes them show up, but they're really hard to see otherwise," he murmured. "There's a line here and here." He traced a finger gently out from her spine, as she had done to him. It didn't hurt, it tickled. A lot.

"Stop, Salm!" April turned around laughing. She held out her hand for the vial, staying safely out of reach. When she looked up at him, Salm had the most unusual expression on his face. It was very intent, April didn't know what it meant. No-one had ever looked at her that way before. It was probably because she was ridiculously pink for an elf. "Can I have the cream back?"

"Maybe you'll have to come and get it," Salm said softly. He seemed to be playing some sort of game.

When Mr. Poole cleared his throat loudly from the doorway, Salm jumped an inch. He looked as guilty as if he had been caught sneaking out of the house in the middle of the night.

"April, you found the medicine, I see. Is it working? If you are too sore, I can give you something else to ease the pain, something stronger to help you sleep," Mr. Poole said, although his eyes were narrowed on Salm.

"No, the cream is great. I'll be able to sleep fine. My thanks."

"Good. Sleep well, then. Salm, I'll see you to your room. Now." Mr. Poole was behaving peculiarly as well. Salm stared fixedly at the floor and followed his father.

April layered the cream on the rest of her for a second time, from the tips of her pink pointy ears to the soles of her tender feet. She settled cautiously into her bed. She was deeply asleep within seconds of resting her head on the puffy cotton ball pillow.

8. Basketberry

The next morning, Raina was brought up-to-date on all she had missed the previous evening, because she had been unconscious. Finding out that April had manifested magical gills was exciting news. She had to have a look at April's back. She had a hard time spotting the faint marks left by the gills that were no longer there, even when Salm pointed them out to her.

After breakfast, Mr. Poole had news. Unfortunately, it wasn't good news. "We were summoned to town early this morning," he began, his tone was so serious, they all paid full attention. "Another attempt was made to steal the remaining part of the thunderwand last night. I believe the fire on the lake was meant to lure us away from guarding the rod, which it did. But we were not so foolish as to leave the device unprotected. So the creature was unsuccessful for a second time. Alas, we learned nothing new from this latest attempt, except that the creature is tricky and determined, and still in our world." Mr. Poole frowned, deepening the lines that always marked his forehead of late.

Salm was sent outside to tidy up the party mess since he was the healthiest of its three hosts. "I'll help you, Salm," April offered, and went along. Raina wasn't allowed to help. Her father sent her back up to her room to rest and recuperate.

In the front garden, a row of ants was busy carting away any leftover food, including whole popped corn kernels. The insects were a big help and April tried not to get in their way as she gathered wet towels and piled up forgotten school packs. So many packs had been left behind that she could probably forget to do her own homework without getting into trouble.

Raina snuck outside and supervised their cleanup until Salm became so annoyed with his sister, he threatened to toss her back in the lake. Luckily, Airron and Peter turned up before that happened.

Together, they tackled the rest of the mess, then sat down to relax on the shore. The water was kind of flat looking, but a few fish were jumping in the middle, proving some life had survived. A deep sooty hole marked where the campfire had grown all out of control. It would take time for green vegetation to flourish and hide the scar on the land. Until then, it would be a very visible reminder of their near tragedy. April turned her back on the unsightly mark. She didn't see or hear the elves that flew down from the sky until Raina exclaimed, "Skylar! O'Wing! What are you doing here?"

Prince Skylar tucked his red and gold wings behind him before he sat down close beside Raina. He immediately reached over and took her hand. "Raina, you must know that I would be deeply concerned when I heard that you had been injured." He searched her face earnestly. "I had to see for myself that you were all right."

Raina may have blushed. It was impossible to tell since every inch of her skin already looked like it was blushing. "Oh, Skylar, that's so nice of you. But I'm fine. I don't even remember most of what happened. I had to be told. It sounds like I missed quite a night, but not a nice one."

"Definitely not a nice one. Well, I am pleased to see with my own eyes that you are recovering." He smiled to show his dimples, and his golden curls gleaming under the sun. His affection for Raina was plain on his face. Airron might have growled. Skylar might have heard him because he said, "And Airron, you are looking much healthier than the last time I saw you. It is good to see that you have made a full recovery."

"Thanks," Airron said, rather grudgingly.

"April? How are you after your near drowning?" Skylar asked.

"Fine. I'm glad you dropped by. We need to talk to you, both of you, about something important." If their theory from the previous night was correct, it was possible that Prince Skylar and O'Wing were also in danger, since they had participated in saving the forcefield. Neither elf had been as directly involved, but that was no guarantee that the creature would leave them unharmed.

"Something important?" Skylar dragged his gaze off Raina's pretty pink face and glanced warily at April.

"It might be," April admitted. "But not bad news, not really bad news anyway, more the possibility of bad news. Maybe."

"Would you like someone else to explain?" Airron said.

"Hey, I can explain fine," April protested.

"Doesn't sound like it to me."

"That's because you're interrupting me. Anyway, Skylar and O'Wing, Peter noticed that the creature's attacks seem to be targeted at *us*."

Airron took over, even though April had been explaining just fine. "And we're guessing it might be because we helped save the forcefield. It does want to get its creepy claws on all three parts of the thunderwand."

Salm jumped in. "So we've deduced that it is attacking us because we saved the forcefield. It is one of the things we have in common, which means you two could also be at risk."

O'Wing considered the information and frowned. "True, only those involved with the forcefield have been attacked. Well I hope you are wrong about us being in danger." O'Wing shot a glance at Skylar. "You're going to have to be well-guarded at all times, Prince, until this creature is caught."

"I will have you know that my father has finally agreed that the guards following me everywhere is an unnecessary precaution, although I suspect he employs you to keep me safe, since you have become my shadow," Skylar said.

"Friend and shadow," O'Wing said, with obvious affection.

"Regardless, the timing of this threat couldn't be worse."

"Tell it to the creature that's causing all the trouble," O'Wing said. "It's not my fault."

"You too, O'Wing," April said. "You have to be kept safe, too."

"I can take care of myself," O'Wing insisted, trying to look tough—and he did, because of his very crooked nose and extra years. He was twenty.

When Skylar asked about the burning lake, Salm described the previous evening and revealed the startling fact that April had had gills for a short time, before they disappeared again. Having magical gills was unheard of in New Haven. It was unheard of in the Outer-World, too.

"April, why didn't you grow gills the other time you almost drowned, when I pulled you out of Ceyenne Creek?" O'Wing asked. It was a good question. She hadn't produced gills any of the other times she had almost drowned in this world.

"I don't know. I don't know why I got gills this time. It happened all by itself."

"I bet it was the ceremony," Raina blurted out excitedly. "That's what changed about you. You did transform! I knew the ceremony did something. April 1st is your birthday, too."

"You're a merrow after all, April. But a magical one," Salm said.

"Really? I guess I am. And I'm in the right family!" It would be fun to swim underwater with Raina and Salm, as long as it wasn't so painful every time she needed to manifest gills. Hopefully she didn't have to drown, either. She really hoped it would be easier to get gills the second time, but she wasn't brave enough to test that theory quite yet. Last night was too vivid to even consider diving into the lake and trying to drown herself.

Like most recent weekends, they were forced to stick close to home because of the threat against all elves, and possibly them in particular. On Sunday, Raina insisted they catch up on homework. Most of the forgotten packs had been picked up, so April did her work, but reluctantly.

Their skin colour was almost back to normal on Monday, so they didn't have to go to school looking like two boiled crayfish. In the first class, Ms. Merry-Helen announced that there would be no field trips until further notice. Not one student was surprised. They would have been astonished if she had scheduled more field trips.

Since it was Monday, Mrs. Myrrh introduced a new sport called Basketberry. After she divided her class into four more or less even teams, they played the fun game. There was lots of running and throwing, and points were scored by tossing the berry into your opponent's basket, while they tried to guard it. April's team lost the first game badly. The final score was an embarrassing twenty to two.

Afterwards, April sat on the sidelines and watched while the two other teams played. They were evenly matched and the score remained tied for the longest time. Peter and Violet were playing the forward positions and worked together to move the berry across the field. They ducked and dodged, tossing the berry between them until they were in front of the opponent's basket.

Only Cherry was in position to stop the game-winning point. Violet took one step and underhanded the berry to Peter. He caught it on the run and gave every indication that he was sending the berry back to Violet. Instead, he feinted left and aimed to score. Cherry leaped at the same time and in the same direction. The berry made it into the basket, but Cherry and Peter collided with force. Peter was bigger and had more speed behind him, Cherry was knocked down. She landed hard on her behind.

Ms. Myrrh blew her whistle loudly and declared the game ended, before she rushed over to check for damaged students. Considerate as always, Peter reached out a hand to help Cherry up, saying, "Sorry about that, are you okay?"

She eyed his hand as if it was covered in dung and looked about to refuse his help, very rudely. But she didn't. Cherry latched onto Peter's hand and stared into his eyes with a fierce expression. A wave of dizziness washed over April. She leaned against a fern until her head cleared.

Peter walked over, looking a little dazed himself. He'd probably had the wind knocked out of him when he collided with Cherry. "Are you okay, Peter?" April asked.

"Ya. Cherry was acting weird." He glanced around uneasily, probably to make sure the elf wasn't sneaking up on him with a sharp thorn or something. "She was really mad, but she didn't shout or anything."

"She looked really mad," April agreed.

They rounded up Raina, Airron and Salm, and started home. The trek took much longer now, because they had to walk Peter home, Airron home, and themselves home. April wasn't overly concerned about the creature when they hiked through the forest that Monday. If it followed its usual pattern, nothing terrible would happen until the end of the week. She should have remembered that New Haven's unwanted visitor thrived on striking when they least expected it.

***

It was a dream—it had to be a dream. No, not a dream—the worst kind of nightmare. The evil creature was inside April's head, making her feel so sick that she wanted to crawl out of her own skin. She was ice cold and burning hot, all at the same time. She tried to push the thing out of her mind. Her head spun with the effort. Her body was paralyzed. She was trapped inside a deep hole with the terrifying creature as her only companion. Malevolent green eyes shone down from above, blocking out the moon and the stars. April tried to scream, but even her throat was paralyzed. She trembled with the effort to make any small sound. It began to rain. The rain turned into a deluge. Far away, voices were shouting and hands were shaking her, as if she was a rag doll. But no matter how strongly she fought, she couldn't escape from the nightmare.

Then suddenly April was really falling through space, the landing jolt snapped her back to the waking world most effectively. Her eyes flew opened, freeing her from the black prison. She didn't know where she was at first, but a number of concerned faces were staring down at her.

There was Raina, Salm, Mr. and Mrs. Poole, and even DewDrop. The little elf looked terrified.

April reached up to touch Raina's face, afraid it was an illusion. No, Raina was solid. April dragged a shuddering breath into her lungs. "Did you drop me out of the window?" she gasped, all mixed up.

"No, we dropped you onto your bed. If that hadn't worked, the window was next," Mr. Poole answered, with a concerned frown. "What happened?"

"I don't know." April struggled to sit up. Her head was still spinning dizzily. She swallowed hard, trying to keep her stomach where it belonged. She wiped a shaking hand across her brow. "I'm wet?"

"Water, a lot of water," Raina admitted sheepishly. "It usually works …but not this time. I couldn't wake you up at all, so I got help."

"None of us could awaken you. It was as if you were drugged. Except that you were obviously distressed, fighting something in your sleep." Mr. Poole crouched down and stared into her eyes. He lifted both her eyelids, like he had when Raina had been unconscious. "Everything looks normal."

"I guess I had a bad dream. I think it was the … the creature, it was inside my head—trapping me in sleep." Even saying it aloud pulled the nightmare too close.

Raina took her hand and squeezed it. "Is that what it was?"

"Yes, I was trapped with the evil creature. And it had green eyes." She hugged her knees tighter. "How did it do that? How did it get in my head? Or was a dream?"

"It sounds like you experienced a very vivid nightmare, a night terror," Mr. Poole concluded. "You could have been reliving the trauma of being trapped under the burning lake. It is not uncommon after such an ordeal. Are you all right now?"

"Yes. Are we late for school?" The sun was quite high; the night was long over.

"A bit. Don't worry, I'll send a note." Mrs. Poole patted April's arm. "Or you could spend the day in bed, if you need to recover."

"No, I don't want to spend any more time in bed." April was quite alarmed at the thought. She didn't think she ever wanted to sleep again. "I'll get up, have breakfast." Food might eliminate the sick feeling and hot tea might get rid of the shivers. How long had the creature been in her head before the morning arrived? No—it had only been a bad dream. The creature had never been inside her head.

"Right, we will meet you downstairs. Raina, stay with April. Don't leave her alone until she is feeling herself." Mr. Poole pushed Salm ahead of him out the door.

Raina dug out April's favorite overalls, sensing the need for comfort.

"My thanks, Raina." April tugged them on. She left her hair loose. It was wet anyway.

"So you're feeling okay now?" Raina asked from her perch on the bed.

"Sort of okay, more awake at least." April sat down beside her friend. "Raina, it was so real. Not like a nightmare at all. And the creature was so powerful and mean. It's a really awful thing."

"I'm sure it was a nightmare. My dad said so. But it really upset you, didn't it?"

"I thought I would go mad, trapped with it," April admitted. "It was worse than being trapped under the water. At least I wasn't alone under the water. I had you, even if you were sleeping. The worst part of being trapped in that well was being alone, alone except for the green eyes."

Raina put an arm around her. "At least it wasn't real, it was a bad dream. You probably won't even remember it by tonight." But April knew she would. It wasn't something you forgot in a day.

When they got downstairs, Salm was waiting to walk with them to school. All three were going to be late. Raina grabbed their packs and some berries to eat on the way. They automatically detoured toward Airron's house, only to find him already gone.

"He flew, you are late," Mrs. Fay-Finch said, before closing the door in their faces, rather abruptly and much harder than necessary.

"Wasn't that friendly?" Raina muttered sarcastically. "Should we still pick up Peter? Or do you think he's gone ahead?"

"Peter can't fly so we better go and check." After her most recent experience, April didn't think any elf should walk alone in the forest. They jogged to Peter's house and found it deserted.

"But how did he get to school?" Salm said, and hammered on the door again.

"Well, we don't know, do we? Maybe Airron flew over to meet him." Raina sounded annoyed because she was worried. They all were. "He's not here, Salm. You're knocking loud enough to wake the dead. Let's go."

April didn't appreciate Raina's choice of words. She double-checked magically. Peter was not in his house. The meadow was empty when they reached school. Even the corridors were deserted, they were that late. They waved goodbye to Salm, who headed for his own classroom.

"Do you think we'll get in trouble? I forgot to get a note from my mom," Raina whispered right before they entered their room. April didn't think Mrs. Merry-Helen would give them a hard time, she was too cheerful. They slipped quietly to their table and pulled out books; the lesson was already in progress.

April was sharpening a charcoal stick when Raina hissed, "Peter's not here."

Airron cleared his throat loudly from his usual spot, one eyebrow cocked questioningly at Peter's empty cushion. Apparently none of them knew where Peter was. They probably didn't have a minute to waste. April jumped up and the teacher stopped talking about some sort of insect with a sticky tongue.

"Is there a problem, April?" the teacher inquired, smiling brightly. Most teachers would have been irritated by the interruption.

"Has anyone seen Peter this morning?" April asked, without preamble.

"Peter? The quiet boy? He has not been in class," the teacher answered.

April looked around the room and all her classmates shook their heads. Cherry didn't bother to respond. She shared a private smirk with her tabletop.

April tried several other questions. "Has anyone seen him this morning? Does anyone know why he's not here? Or where he is?" She received the same negative response.

Raina rose and shoved April towards the door. "We have to go. We'll bring a note tomorrow," Raina told the teacher.

Airron joined them. "Me too."

"But you may not leave class without permission. If there is a problem, we must inform Headmistress Hawthorn. Wait! Stop!" Mrs. Merry-Helen called when they darted out the door. It looked like the teacher might give chase.

"Forget waiting. We have to find Peter, fast!" Raina declared.

They sprinted all the way to Peter's house. It was the logical place to start searching. Airron pounded at the door, but the house still appeared deserted. Again, April concentrated on the house and surrounding forest, but she still couldn't sense Peter. "He isn't here," she said.

"You checked—magically?" Raina verified.

"I checked."

Raina nibbled her lip worriedly. "Should we go see Peter's parents at work? They might know where he is?"

"No, we're already here." Airron reached for the door handle. "Let's have a look in Peter's room. Maybe there's a clue that will tell us where he went."

"I think that's the best idea," April agreed.

Airron opened the door and led the way. Not one of them was comfortable about entering the dwelling without permission, but it was necessary. The kitchen seemed too quiet, the whole house echoed with emptiness. Half a cup of berry juice sat on the table, looking lonely somehow.

"Peter's bedroom." Airron pointed down the short hall and scooted ahead.

The very last thing April expected was to hear Airron say, "He's here. He's sleeping in. All that panic for nothing. Hey, Peter, wake up! You're unbelievably late for school. And we're probably in a lot of trouble for coming to find you."

April moved forward, gripped by a strong sense of foreboding. She stopped in the doorway, terrified of what she would see. Peter was fully dressed and lying on his bed, but he wasn't sleeping. She would have sensed him if he were sleeping. If she couldn't sense Peter, it was because the living part of him was gone from this world. It was too late to help Peter.

"No." April closed her eyes against the awful truth.

Airron shook him around, but got no response. He stopped and backed away from the bed. "He's stiff and cold. Is he dead?" Airron asked in a most detached voice.

Raina stepped closer. April couldn't move. Peter certainly looked corpse-like. He was as white as snow and as still as a stone. Raina held her hand over his mouth for a long minute, next she pressed an ear against Peter's heart. April knew Peter was no longer with them since she couldn't sense him, and waited to hear the fateful verdict.

"Oh, thank goodness, Peter's alive!" Raina cried.

"What? Are you sure?" April gasped.

"Positive, his heart is beating and he's breathing." It certainly sounded like he was alive. "But he seems to be very deeply unconscious. He's not sleeping. Well, no one could sleep through all the noise we made banging at the door and shouting through the house ..." Raina's jaw dropped and she gaped at April, "Except April—this morning!"

Airron sank onto the only cushion. "Huh? What are you talking about?"

"The same sort of thing happened to April this morning. We couldn't wake her up at all," Raina stressed.

"Is that why you were late for school?" Airron glanced inquiringly at April.

"Yes. It was like the evil creature was in my head trapping me in a nightmare, trapping me in sleep. And I felt really sick ..." April trailed off, stunned by a revelation. "No! No, that wasn't it at all! It wasn't me!"

"Of course it was you. I was trying to wake you up." Raina sounded confused.

"It was me in bed, but the creature wasn't directly inside my head. It was inside another elf's head." April looked significantly at the bed.

Raina caught on. "Peter's?"

April nodded. "Yes, Peter's. I was sharing his nightmare. It wasn't mine at all. No wonder I can't sense Peter, it's like he's with the creature even now, the creature who I can never sense ...I couldn't figure out how it could have gotten into my head because it shouldn't have been able to. Not that it should be able to get into Peter's -" April's brain was starting to hurt.

"Maybe ... maybe you could share Peter's nightmare because of the creature? It must have some form of dark magic, like Drake Pitt, and you could communicate with him," Raina said, thinking aloud.

April had been able to read Drake Pitt's thoughts in an unprecedented way, because of his dark magic. And he could sense gold. So could Peter, but Peter didn't have dark magic. So it must be the creature that had allowed her to link with Peter in dreams. Maybe. April had too many questions and no answers. She finally convinced her feet to move forward and she touched Peter's arm. It was cold and clammy. He was not in good shape. She felt ill all over again, looking at the waxy mask that his face had become.

"But why is he like this? What's made him this way?" Airron demanded.

"It has to do with the evil creature that's causing all the trouble in New Haven. I know that much." Alas, April didn't know more. "Do you think if we picked Peter up and dropped him on the bed it would wake him up?" she asked Raina. "It worked for me."

"Yes, but you were a lot more lively. You were tossing around, like you were fighting something in your sleep. You weren't all still and cold, but I suppose it's worth a try. I don't think it could hurt Peter."

Airron rose restlessly. "Let's try it, we have to do something."

"Okay, but if we can't wake him up, I'll send for my father," Raina said.

It took all three of them to drag Peter to the end of his bed and sit him up.

"He's a lot heavier than he looks, isn't he?" Airron struggled to shove Peter into a standing position from behind, while April and Raina supported Peter on either side. "Okay, let me get out of the way before you drop him."

Airron scrambled aside and they pushed Peter onto his bed. He fell stiffly backwards, his whole body rigid. There was no sign that he knew what had happened—not a flicker of an eyelid, not a twitch, nothing.

"You woke right up when we did that. And you weren't all stiff," Raina said. "I think it's time to get my father."

Someone banged hard on the door. They all leaped an inch off the ground. "Oh no! Who could that be?" Raina gasped in fright.

April thought she recognized the heavy hand. "It sounds like Sage Scarab."

They stepped into the kitchen at the same moment that the door exploded inwards. Sage Scarab barreled through, almost knocking them over. Heady and Wade Leech were on his heels.

"Why the heck didn't you answer the door? Are you all deaf? We were thinking the worst." Sage Scarab scowled at them in turn, checking that they were unharmed

Heady stepped forward, glancing around what she could see of the house. "Did you locate Peter?" she asked.

Mrs. Merry-Helen must have alerted her that they had all left school without permission, because Peter was missing. She had been quick to investigate. Was Mr. Leech her bodyguard?

"We found Peter, but something's wrong. He's this way." The small crowd followed Raina down the hall and squeezed into Peter's cozy room. They could have used Airron's spacious bedroom at that moment. Peter was exactly as they had left him, kind of tumbled onto his bed.

Mr. Leech peered closer. "Is he dead, then?"

"No, he's not dead!" Raina snapped at her teacher.

"Well, he does look dead," Mr. Leech stroked his hair, ruffling it up.

Raina gaped at him. "Do you think we would be standing around if he was dead?"

Mr. Leech looked mildly offended. "Well, perhaps not, but no need to get snippy."

"Snippy? Snippy!" Raina was about to lose her temper.

"Enough, please." Heady studied Peter gravely. "Do you know what is wrong with Peter?"

Raina turned her back on Mr. Leech and said, "We don't know. We can't wake him up. I was going to get my father."

"I'll fetch him," Sage Scarab offered. "I'll get him here fast as a tick."

"Clayton, perhaps Wade should accompany you through the forest," Heady suggested a little too eagerly. Was she trying to get rid of the teacher?

"If you say so. Can you keep up?" Sage Scarab eyed Mr. Leech, lips pursed.

"Oh course. I jog one quarter mile each day, if you can believe that." Mr. Leech flexed his collection of muscles. "Feel this." He pointed at a bulging arm.

"Uh … no, thanks." Sage Scarab lowered his eyebrows and glanced darkly at Heady. "Thanks for the escort, I owe you one."

Mr. Leech waved merrily and followed Sage Scarab, jogging down the hall with springy steps. "I expect Sage Scarab will want me to cook dinner for him now." Heady claimed the only cushion in the room. The younger elves settled onto the edge of Peter's bed to wait. April felt Peter's forehead, it was no longer cold but burning hot. She knew exactly how he felt because she had experienced it herself—icy cold and burning hot, all at the same time.

"Tell me everything you know," Heady said. They did, including their wild guesses and half-formed theories.

"So, you believe Peter's condition can be blamed on the unwelcome visitor that is causing the other unfortunate events," she concluded sadly.

"Yes. I'm sure of it. Absolutely sure." April did know that much. There was no doubt that New Haven's trespasser had struck again and Peter was now the one paying a horrible price.

9. The Ant Test

Peter's condition remained unchanged in the time it took for Mr. Poole to arrive, accompanied by Peter's parents. Mr. Poole didn't ask questions. He simply shooed everyone back so he could examine Peter for himself.

Sage Scarab trailed in last. He edged away from Mr. Leech, as much as the small room would allow. "No change?" he muttered to April.

She sighed heavily. "No. None at all."

Mr. Poole lifted each of Peter's eyelids and flashed a torch over them, even though daylight was streaming in through the small, high knot-hole of a window. He proceeded to feel Peter's skin temperature and press a hand over his heart. Next, he reached into his sack for a fine thorn, which he poked into Peter's palms and the soles of his feet. Lastly, he pulled out a small vial and held it open under Peter's nose. There was no response at all.

While he performed the checkup, Raina told her father all that they had discovered. Mr. Poole nodded more than once, but did not comment. When finished his examination, he pulled a blanket over Peter and surveyed the room packed full of elves. "How about we find somewhere with a little more space," he suggested.

"Of course." Mrs. Stone showed them into the sitting room.

Mr. Poole did not speak until they were all settled. "I really don't have much to report," he began apologetically. "Peter appears to be in an unnaturally deep sleep. His pupils are dilated wide, as if he has been drugged or poisoned. I have never seen these exact symptoms, so I cannot even guess what has caused his physical condition. We will need to investigate everything he came into contact with this morning."

Mrs. Stone sniffed and wiped her eyes. "I don't know if we will be much help. We left for work early and didn't even ... didn't even see

Peter. We didn't say goodbye." She was a breath away from breaking down completely.

Mr. Poole took her hand, the only comfort he could offer other than his words, which were not overly inspiring. "Peter may wake up on his own—at any time. I do not believe he is in immediate danger. However, the longer he is unconscious, the harder it will be for him to awaken. I recommend that we try various stimulations and attempt to wake him up ourselves. I know he appears completely unresponsive, but it could still work. I would like to try, if I have your permission."

Mr. and Mrs. Stone didn't need to think about it, both nodded and hurried back into Peter's room.

"Dad, we already tried dropping him, like we did with April. It didn't work at all," Raina said.

"No, it will take more than dropping Peter to wake him up. He is in a different state than April, a different state altogether. The question is why?" He shook his head. "I wish I knew."

Heady rose with a jerk. "Well, if there is nothing I can do to help, I should return to the school."

"I'll see you safely back," Mr. Leech volunteered.

"Yes, you do have several classes to teach," she reminded him.

He thought hard and came to the same conclusion. "You're right. Yes, I do."

"Come along then, Wade. And you three?" Heady glanced at them. "You do have school, as well." April felt too worried to return to school. She wanted to stay and help Peter, if there was a way to help him.

"Ah, give the young ones a few minutes. I'll see them back," Sage Scarab offered. "You've got Wade there, to keep you company and guard you." The Sage's eyes twinkled wickedly.

"Fine. When you three are sufficiently recovered, return to school with Clayton." Heady strode out with Mr. Leech on her heels. She was walking briskly and Mr. Leech was jogging again. It looked rather like he was chasing her.

Sage Scarab chuckled as he watched them leave, then he made a beeline for the kitchen, his favorite room. They followed Sage Scarab, since Mr. Poole would certainly want some time alone with Peter's parents. April was not surprised to see the Sage peeking around in search of food. Nothing was in sight, not even one berry.

"Do you think Peter ate breakfast? It looks like his juice is on the table," Raina said, as if it was a clue.

"Shouldn't let perfectly good juice go to waste." Sage Scarab reached out a hand.

Raina slapped it away. "Don't even think about drinking that juice! My dad said we have to check everything Peter came in contact with. The juice could be poisoned."

He opened his mouth as though about to argue, then thought better of it. The juice stayed where it was "Might as well help out, I'll check the food." Sage Scarab began energetically opening all the cupboards and sticking his head right inside. "There's a few peas here. Don't think he'd eat peas for breakfast, do you?" Sage Scarab didn't wait for an answer and gobbled down a pea while they stared at him, open-mouthed. "Hey, I'm starting to feel a little woozy, better sit down." He swayed around the kitchen, clutching his head. Then he grinned and straightened up. "Ah, just kidding. Trying to cheer you up. Lighten the mood."

April would have gladly let him drink the juice at that moment. He returned to the cupboards and sampled other lunch and dinner foods. He remained perfectly healthy and declared them all safe for elf consumption. April sniffed the juice on the table. It smelled like raspberries, it smelled good.

"Don't you think of drinking it," Raina warned her.

"I won't. But let's try something." April carried the cup outside, where she scanned the ground until she spotted some ants. She poured out a few drops of juice where the insects were sure to smell it. She sat down to wait, straddling the raised root outside Peter's door.

"Good idea." Sage Scarab settled beside her, munching on a carrot round now. They all watched the ants listlessly and worried about Peter. April kept remembering her terrifying nightmare. If Peter was trapped in that place, he might never recover.

One ant ambled over to the juice and lapped at the liquid. It ingested a good quantity before it walked away. "Better keep an eye on it for a few more minutes, to be sure," Sage Scarab advised, with no sign of moving himself.

April, Raina and Airron scrambled up and tailed the ant along the edge of the undergrowth. So far, it appeared healthy. If the poison had been in the juice, it was probably fast acting. Peter had only drunk half the glass before he had returned to bed.

The ant marched a zigzagging path, then scuttled deeper into the weeds, showing no signs of distress. Without warning, it ducked around a rock and disappeared down an anthill, as if it knew it was being followed.

"Well, I think we can eliminate the juice," Raina decided. "That ant walked around for a long time and it's still perfectly fine."

"It's not the juice." Airron agreed, pulling Raina close for comfort. She kissed his scarred cheek and rested her head on his shoulder for a moment before she straightened up.

Disheartened, they retraced their steps. Airron scooped something off the ground and tossed it to April, saying, "You dropped your chain."

She caught the glinting gold and touched her neck, her tag was exactly where it should be. "No, I'm still wearing mine. This isn't mine." And chains like hers did not exist in New Haven, only in her former world.

April looped it gingerly over one finger and raised it up for a good look. This chain didn't have a tag. It had a small crystal vial sealed with a golden stopper. The proof that it came from her world was engraved on the stopper lid, in a script that only she could read.

At first glance, the vial appeared empty. April lifted it up to the sunlight and squinted. A small drop of clear liquid was illuminated in the bottom. Residue of what had been poured out?

"This came from my world," April murmured. "Another elf would have worn this, once upon a time. An elf from my world." She stroked the chain, absorbing the improbability of finding it *here*.

Raina leaned close. "April, what do the symbols on the lid say?"

"They say 'August'. I wonder why they say a month?"

Raina rolled her eyes enthusiastically. "April, you're named after a month—three months. Did you ever know an elf named August?"

"I don't think so. August," April repeated the name. "No, I can't remember an elf named August." she said, more emphatically. Holding the chain made her feel sad. It represented a link to her past and a whole world that no longer existed. All the elves she had ever known were gone now.

Raina lifted the chain out of April's hand for a closer look. "April, does this mean that another magical elf is causing all the trouble in New Haven? An elf from your world, an elf named August?"

"No," April replied with certainty. "It's not an elf doing these things. I would sense the presence of another elf. No, this is something entirely different."

"Like an imp?" Airron suggested, supporting his theory.

"Maybe an imp." April considered the vial. "They like shiny things. They steal. They wouldn't think twice about taking things off a dead body."

Raina immediately dropped the vial into April's hand. They returned to Peter's house with more questions than answers—yet again.

"Took you long enough. How's the ant?" Sage Scarab squinted up at them. He hadn't moved a muscle, but he was enjoying a good bask in the sunshine.

"The ant is fine, but we found something." April dangled the crystal in the air.

He straightened up. "Cripes! Where the heck did that come from?"

"It was on the ground." April removed the gold stopper from the vial. A pungent, sickly-sweet odor had her replacing the lid fast, trying not to breathe.

"Careful now, you don't know what's in there or how it works," Sage Scarab warned sharply. "Could work by smell, like sneezeweed."

April nodded and waited, but nothing happened. She didn't faint or sneeze or collapse into a coma. The mysterious liquid would have to be tasted and she wasn't about to do that. "I have to repeat the ant test," she murmured. Except that Sage Scarab had drank the rest of Peter's juice while they had been following the ant around. He was very lucky that the ant had remained healthy.

April shook her head at him and grabbed the glass back. She tapped the last few drops of juice onto the ground, then she added half the residual liquid from the vial, making sure to hold her breath. She closed the stopper and returned to the root to wait.

"Ants aren't having a good day, are they?" Sage Scarab observed.

"The first one didn't mind the meal, lucky for you," April chided, but she had a bad feeling about this second test. Sure enough, an ant marched over for a snack. It drank deeply for about half a minute before it keeled over, legs rigid.

Raina cried, "That's it! That must be what poisoned Peter."

"Yes. Sorry, ant." April felt awful for harming the innocent insect.

Raina picked up the ant gently, placing it in her palm. It stretched longer than her hand, stiff as a branch. She patted it regretfully and turned toward the door. "We better show my dad. Maybe this will help him figure out how to wake up Peter."

April hoped so with all her heart. Peter was the fourth of her four closest friends to be harmed by the destructive thing that had invaded

New Haven. Each attack had been different, but all from the same source. Peter's condition did seem to confirm their theory that the creature was only targeting the elves involved in saving the forcefield.

They found Mr. Poole in Peter's room, still trying to wake him up. Peter was so pale and lifeless that it hurt to look at him. "No progress yet, I am sorry to say. Are you returning to school now?" Mr. Poole asked, when they hesitated in the doorway.

"Not yet. We found something outside, something really important, Dad." Raina displayed the ant and had his full attention. April handed over the chain while Raina described the ant tests.

Mr. Stone took charge of the ant and examined it closely. Mr. Poole showed more interest in the vial, holding it up to the light. "Yes, yes, this could be most helpful. A very lucky find. Leave the poison with me for some further tests, and the ant, of course. Now, all of you go and wash your hands thoroughly."

Sage Scarab hustled the younger elves out of the room to wash their hands—thoroughly. April pointed out that he should really wash his hands, too. It was done with poor grace. Then he made good on his promise to escort them back to school.

"You do realize that this creature has now struck all of us directly," Raina said, trying to set a snail's pace. The longer it took to reach school, the better. "And it may still hurt Skylar and O'Wing."

"Maybe, maybe not. Surprised it hasn't confronted any of you lot directly," Sage Scarab said, trying to hurry them up. "Always sneaking around. Never showing its face."

April listened to the others talk with half an ear. She was deeply upset by Peter's condition, and she couldn't dispel the fear that all the attacks might be her fault somehow. By coming here and altering the forcefield, had she shifted some invisible balance between the magical and the non-magical world? It did seem more than a coincidence that after thousands of years of peaceful existence, a strongly magical creature had slunk into New Haven to wreak havoc so soon after April's arrival. The elven realm had needed April and her magic to save their forcefield, but maybe she wasn't supposed to stay here. Magical and non-magical elves had been unable to live together in the distant past. Was there an unknown reason for that segregation?

It was a relief to reach school and forget her tormented thoughts. The lunch gong had yet to ring, so the meadow was empty. Airron ran inside to retrieve all their packs from Mrs. Merry-Helen's classroom. Neither April nor Raina wanted to face the teacher after running out on her.

Airron was back in minutes with all three packs slung over his shoulders. "I was lucky that the room was empty. I ran in and grabbed the packs—free and clear. Didn't see Hairy-Melon and she didn't see me!"

"Please don't call her that, Airron," April begged.

The gong sounded to start lunch and the meadow filled up with elves. Their classmates hemmed them in, wanting to know what had happened to Peter. Raina did not go into details about the poison. She simply reported the basic facts of Peter's condition. Everyone was shocked and saddened to learn that he was in a deep sleep, unable to waken. Peter might be quiet-natured, but he was popular with all their classmates, except Cherry.

Elves spread out to eat lunch and Salm scooted in closer, to ask for more details than they had shared with the whole class. Raina told him everything, and concluded by saying, "We think it's what April was sensing this morning. It wasn't a nightmare. The creature wasn't in her head, but in Peter's head somehow and April sensed it, maybe because of the creature's dark magic or Peter's magic or … who knows?"

"But Peter is going to recover, isn't he?" Salm said. "I mean, Dad healed you, Airron. I'm sure healing Peter will be a piece of pie. Right?"

"It's different with Peter. Dad doesn't know what to do. But they're testing the contents of the vial that we found." Raina opened her lunch listlessly.

Salm scowled and picked at his lunch with little interest. None of them were hungry. "I don't think I should let any of you out of my sight. Next time, come and get me in my classroom before you go running off, so I can help at least." Being left behind on the night they had rescued Sage Scarab was still a sore spot with Salm.

Even though she wasn't hungry, either, April absently opened her mouth to nibble on her raisin. It didn't smell like a raisin—it smelled weird. April's hand stilled. She knew that smell! It was sickly-sweet and pungent. Her raisin didn't smell like a raisin at all. It smelled like a poisoned raisin.

"Don't eat any of your lunches! Don't touch them!" April knocked Raina's muffin out of her hand. Salm flinched and dropped his flatbread as if it was on fire. "Not you, Salm, I'm sure your lunch is fine. It wasn't left alone in a classroom like ours, was it?"

"No, been with it all morning." He picked up his bread and frowned at it.

"Let me check anyway." April leaned forward and sniffed his bread. It smelled like bread, earthy bread. "It's okay, you can eat it."

"Are you sure?"

"Positive. But clean if off first."

Raina held up her own raisin and sniffed it delicately. "It smells like a raisin. Why do you think there's something wrong with the food?"

"Because my raisin is poisoned! It smells exactly like the stuff in the vial."

Raina sniffed April's raisin. "It does! But mine smells fine. Let's check all the food." Airron and Salm leaned over to smell April's raisin, so they would be able to recognize the scent of the poison. They thoroughly sniffed all the food, even though the elves seated nearby turned to stare at them as if they were nuts.

"Only your raisin seems to have been tampered with, April," Raina concluded.

Salm looked puzzled. "One question. How did the creature get into the school to poison your lunch? It poisoned Peter before school and the vial was left behind at his house, so the timing doesn't work, does it? Your packs were only left in the classroom after Peter was poisoned," he stressed. "And if some weird creature tried to enter the school, it would have been seen, wouldn't it? There are too many students all over the place for it to move around unnoticed. I don't think the creature could have poisoned April's food."

"I hate to say it, Salm, but you might be right." Raina packed away her own perfectly normal smelling raisin. She had probably lost her appetite.

"Of course I'm right," he grumbled. "But if the creature didn't do it, who did? Only an elf could walk around the school in the middle of the day."

April leaned even closer. "And that elf must be in contact with the creature! How else would they get the same poison?"

"Right. So who hates New Haven enough to ally with the creature that is trying to shut down the barrier and destroy our world?" Salm said.

Drake Pitt would have been the most likely candidate, except he was no longer alive to destroy New Haven.

"As much as Cherry resents us, I can't see her going that far," Raina said. "If she helped the creature shut down the forcefield, she would suffer as much as anyone. I can't think of one elf who would want to end our world!"

"Unless ... could an imp trick an elf?" Airron asked April.

"Not in a thousand years. But an elf could trick an imp, any day of the week."

"That's no help in this situation." Airron said. And he was right.

The gong sounded. Lunch, such as it was, was already over. April stored her raisin back in her pack to give to Mr. Poole. They all rinsed their hands in the lake before they hurried inside. The afternoon classes seemed irrelevant when Peter was so gravely ill and April had trouble paying attention, except in Sports. They were playing Basketberry again, and she had to stay alert or the opposing team would clobber her.

It was April's turn to play as a forward, partnered with Perriwinkle. Unfortunately, Cherry was guarding the opposing basket. The elf took great pleasure in mowing April to the ground every chance she got, and she made sure she got a lot of chances. Near the end of the game, more by luck than skill, April and Perriwinkle managed to keep the berry and maneuver it close enough to score. April was about to aim the berry into the basket, when she hesitated. Perriwinkle should have this chance. Elves always teased him in Sports, because he wasn't very athletic.

As Cherry surged towards her, April returned the berry to Perriwinkle, who looked so surprised he almost dropped it, but he didn't. "Throw it!" April shouted and lunged between Cherry and Perriwinkle, granting him enough time.

Cherry slammed into April and they both went down hard, with April on the bottom. She didn't see what happened next, but a lot of cheering proved that Perriwinkle had indeed scored.

The small victory angered Cherry. Then again, she always seemed mad at April. While April was still flattened on the ground, Cherry hissed, "You can't help poor, poor, Peter, can you. You can't help any of your friends. What good are you?" Cherry shoved herself to stand with a rough hand planted on April's face. It was deliberately placed.

Tempted to bite the hand, hard, April froze. She wasn't about to bite a hand that smelled like ... poison. The familiar smell was too distinctive to mistake for any other scent. Cherry had been in close contact with the same poison that had incapacitated Peter and been applied to April's raisin! April's nose wasn't having a hallucination—noses didn't do that.

April flinched away from Cherry's hand and stumbled to stand. Too stunned by what she had discovered to keep playing, she feigned an injury and limped off the field. Peter was in grave condition and Cherry was involved. Maybe she was involved in all the attacks. She probably was.

Raina was on the sidelines. She looked April up and down. "Are you okay? Did Cherry hurt you?"

So angry that it almost overwhelmed her, April simply shook her head wordlessly. She needed all her self-control to calm down and keep her temper. She certainly didn't want to create a wild storm. New Haven had enough to deal with. And as much as she wanted to confront Cherry and force the truth out of her, April didn't think that would be the wisest course of action. She had to find out what Cherry was up to, without letting the elf know that she suspected her. That was the best way to help Peter.

"April?' Raina was looking concerned.

"I'm okay. We'll talk after school." It was not the time or place to discuss what she had smelled on Cherry. It was Raina's turn on the field anyway.

When the final gong sounded, April hurriedly rounded up all her friends. As soon as they were alone in the woodland, she stopped walking. "What's up? Do you sense the creature?" Raina asked, eyes darting around fearfully.

"No! I've been waiting to talk to you forever, well, since the Basketberry game but I had to wait until we had some privacy. Listen, when Cherry shoved me - "

"Which time?" Raina asked.

"Near the end of the game, but it really doesn't matter, no talking," April decided. "Now, when Cherry knocked me down ..." She paused to check the forest and make sure they couldn't be overheard.

"April, spit it out," Airron said.

"Fine then. Cherry smelled like the poison. She had some on her hand. She is the elf that put poison in my lunch," April blurted out. "She is the elf in contact with the creature that is trying to destroy New Haven. She's probably helping this thing to end her own world. She's responsible for what happened to Peter—probably to all of us!"

"Good grief, that makes no sense, April. Are you sure?" Raina asked.

"Positively sure, the smell is unmistakable. It was on *her*!"

"I believe you," Salm said, taking her word on faith.

Raina was less certain. "We need to think about this," she stressed. "Figure out what it means. It's not real evidence, is it? It's your word that you smelled poison on Cherry. I don't know if anyone will believe us."

"Believe me," April corrected her.

"But she was mad at Peter yesterday, wasn't she?" Raina recalled.

"And that day Big Lake swirled, she was there," Salm said.

"And she was at our party when the lake burned," April cried.

"My theory about an imp could be right, if Cherry is the brains behind the operation," Airron said smugly.

"They could be working together," Raina agreed.

April nodded her head. It would explain everything, except ... "Cherry might want revenge on us, but to destroy this whole world? Why would she do that?"

"We'll have to find out, won't we?" Salm said.

"Yes, we will." It was unanimous.

"But first, let's go see if Peter has miraculously woken up while we've been slogging away at school," Airron said. They detoured to Peter's house, only to find him in the same sad state as the morning.

Peter remained deeply asleep for the rest of the week. They checked on him each day after school and Mr. Poole kept them updated on his progress. Unfortunately, there wasn't any progress to speak of. And the ant was still asleep, in spite of endless attempts to revive it in Mr. Stone's laboratory.

April and Raina tried to keep an eye on Cherry with the boys' help. They didn't want her out of their sight for even a second, but short of following her everywhere and camping outside her house, it wasn't impossible.

Raina slept over in April's room each night, in case she managed to make contact with Peter in her sleep again. April hoped it would happen, even while she dreaded reliving the awful experience. But her sleeps remained entirely peaceful. She didn't even have one weird dream.

On Friday, Airron accompanied them home, but it didn't feel like a weekend. It felt like a blue Monday. With Airron, after the first few days they had known he would recover. It was not that way with Peter. It was starting to look like he might never wake up. Mr. Poole didn't say that he was out of ideas, but it was clear nonetheless.

Right after dinner, Raina was concerned enough to talk to her mother and father about Cherry smelling like the poison in the vial. She shooed

DewDrop out of the room first, then told them what April had smelled on the elf. April produced her raisin.

Mr. and Mrs. Poole listened skeptically to Raina's words, then Mr. Poole shook his head. "Raina, you are jumping to conclusions. Many things smell the same or almost the same. A smell is not proof. And if Cherry did smell like the poison, maybe she brushed against something the creature touched, especially if it was able to sneak unseen into the school to tamper with April's lunch. There is no proof in what you smelled on Cherry, April," he said regretfully.

"But Dad, Mom ..." Raina whined, she didn't get to finish.

"Cherry is a young girl. She would not aid in the destruction of New Haven," Mrs. Poole stated firmly. "You don't like Cherry and you are letting your prejudice affect your judgment. Now, the four of you can clean up the kitchen. Your father and I are going to have a nightcap with some of the Sages. We won't be late. Watch your sister."

"Nightcap?" April said, after the parents left the room. "They're going to try on hats?"

"No." Raina heaved a sigh and banged shells together. "They're going to have drinks. I knew they wouldn't believe us. I should have kept my mouth shut."

After they finished clearing up, Raina called a meeting of her own. April fully expected her to grow up to be the mayor someday, or maybe the Head-Sage. The minute DewDrop went to bed, Raina herded them outside and lit the area with fireflies. The four friends sat in a close circle, missing Peter and his ideas and advice—and *him*. Salm did not have a date. He was sticking close after all that had happened.

As soon as they were settled, Airron asked, "What is this meeting about?"

"It's about Peter. We have to think of a way to help him. I know the adults are doing their best, but it's pretty obvious that they're stumped. We know Cherry is involved. They don't believe it." Raina shook her head in frustration. "I'm convinced Cherry knows what the creature is, and maybe she knows where to find it. But she's not going to tell us, is she?" No-one disagreed. "It's been almost a whole week since Peter was poisoned. If the creature is getting ready to strike again, Cherry might be meeting with it. I think we need to watch her over the weekend—the *whole* weekend."

"But how can we follow her without being seen? And your parents would notice if we were missing," April pointed out.

"I'm not saying it's going to be easy or even possible," Raina said. "I'm only saying I wish we could follow her, and that we might learn something. I don't want to ask Skylar or O'Wing to help, even though they can fly, since they might be targets, too."

"We could enlist some other outside help," Salm said.

"Who would believe us?"

"Sage Scarab might," he said. "And he can follow anyone around in the forest, unseen. He's already patrolling the woodland. It wouldn't be very different from what he's doing now." It was a good idea, as long as it didn't put the Sage in further danger.

Airron surprised them by suggesting an unlikely ally. "And we could ask Starla to let us know if Cherry seems to be up to something. I think she would help."

"Is your mother still trying to make you date her?" Raina cried.

"No, my mom gave up on the idea when Starla started dating Ray, the night of your spectacular fire—I mean gathering," Airron corrected himself hastily. "But Starla and I still talk when my mom invites her over. Starla doesn't hang around with Cherry as much as she used to. Cherry seems to make her nervous lately, so I think she might help us."

"Okay, so we need to find Sage Scarab to ask him." Raina leaned forward eagerly. "We can probably find him tomorrow, and we can ask Starla tomorrow. But that leaves Cherry free to do whatever she wants tonight. We need to watch her tonight. I hate to say it, but I think we'll have to sneak away again."

April thought about the last time they had slipped out at night, to rescue Sage Scarab. At least this time the Pooles weren't home to notice if they were acting suspiciously. And they had Salm's help.

"Are you sleeping over in my room?" he asked Airron.

"Yes, I told my parents I was, since I'm not allowed to fly home alone at night."

"Good. Now, should all of us go to watch Cherry or should we take it in shifts?" Salm asked.

"We all have to go," April said firmly. "It has to be all of us, together, otherwise it's too dangerous. At least I can keep checking that the forest is safe, or sense if the creature in about to do something, not that I've ever been able to stop it from harming anyone. I know I'm useless against it but -"

"Shut up, April." Raina sounded exasperated. "But you're right, we will be safer all together." She sighed. "Sneaking out of the house again, with that dangerous thing roaming around. Not my idea of a fun Friday night."

"I only hope this will help Peter," Airron said, which was the whole point of the plan.

They arranged to meet as before, but they only went to bed after the parents came home. They headed for their respective rooms, trying to act sleepy without overdoing it. April didn't notice any suspicious glances directed their way by either parent, so it seemed like they had succeeded.

An hour after the parents retired for the night, they met in the front garden. "This is becoming a bad habit," Salm whispered in April's ear when he handed her one of two unlit torches. "Let's go guard Cherry."

"I don't think we're guarding Cherry, I think we're guarding ourselves," April muttered back. They walked to the first fork in the path before April magically lit both torches. "Okay, where does Cherry live?" she asked, when nobody moved.

"Umm … I don't know," Raina declared. "Salm, you must know?"

"Why would I know?"

"You've dated everyone. Haven't you ever dated Cherry?" Raina waggled her eyebrows.

"I have not dated everyone, and I wouldn't date Cherry if you held an arrow to my heart," Salm bit out angrily. "Anyway, Cherry moved somewhere else when her father died. She couldn't live alone, could she? She was only fourteen."

"Airron, do you know?" Raina asked hopefully, since he was the last one left.

"I don't know where she's living now. I know where her old house is located, but it's vacant now. My mom was talking about it just the other day, saying what a shame it is that such a grand house is standing empty, going to rot. And it has so much land around it."

Their predicament was almost funny. They had overlooked the most obvious part of their plan. They couldn't watch Cherry if they didn't have a clue where to find her.

"I don't believe this! Now we have to sneak back in the house to go to bed." Raina sounded fed up, and maybe relieved.

Airron tossed an arm over her shoulders. "At least we'll get a good night sleep. Tomorrow we can find Scarab and enlist Starla's help."

April only hoped that tomorrow wouldn't be too late. They turned around to retrace their steps. Salm didn't move. "You know, if I was Cherry and I needed to meet this creature in secret, what better place than a deserted house, my house, a house I know better than anyone, a house with a lot of empty land around it," Salm said leadingly.

April didn't need to be bonked on the head with an acorn. "And if I was a creature new to this world, what better place to hide out than in that very same house."

Airron turned back around. "Does this mean we aren't going to have a proper night's sleep, after all? Peter better appreciate our efforts when he wakes up!"

With the slight adjustment to their plan, they headed for Cherry's old house. It was in the same direction as Airron's house. The hour was late and they didn't see another elf the entire time they were travelling. When Airron slowed his steps, Raina asked, "Are we getting close?"

"Yup, just ahead."

Salm extinguished his torch into the damp soil. "Keep your torch lit, April, so we can see, but keep it low so it will be hidden," he whispered.

"Okay." April checked the surrounding forest. She couldn't sense anything threatening in the area. "It seems safe enough," she confirmed quietly.

"Good." Raina's voice cracked with tension. "Good. I guess this is it."

They approached the dwelling, staying hidden in the encroaching vegetation at the edge of the path. When the house came into view, it had a lonely, neglected air, emphasized by the stark moonlight, otherwise it was quite beautiful.

The light-coloured wood almost glowed. Several graceful wings of the house were taller than the rest, at three stories, but not nearly as tall as towers. It certainly didn't look like the sort of house that Drake Pitt would have resided in. He had been more suited to Airron's dark and brooding treehouse.

This dwelling didn't suit Cherry, either. Maybe it had been her mother's choice. Maybe she had been a kinder, gentler elf than her husband, or Cherry—who certainly appeared to be following in her father's footsteps by plotting the downfall of New Haven.

Sticking close together, they crept forward. April concentrated magically on the dwelling itself. "No elves in the house," she murmured.

"What about the creature?" Salm asked.

"I can never sense it, unless it's using magic. That's when I get that creepy feeling. It could be sitting right beside us in the dark bushes and I would have no clue," April remarked. Raina gulped and clutched Airron's arm so tightly, he whimpered.

Salm gave April's hand a comforting squeeze and borrowed her light. "Okay, let's check inside the house for evidence that the creature has been staying here, and let's hope it's not inside now."

In a crouch, Salm led the way directly to the front door. It didn't want to open. He strained to force it ajar with a creaking protest of unused wood. If the door was warning them not to enter, they did not heed the message.

10. Brag

When they were all inside Cherry's house, Airron shoved the door closed. April relit the second torch, making the shadowy room appear slightly less eerie. "Okay, should we split into pairs, search the house in half the time? Then get the heck out of here?" Airron almost succeeded in sounding fearless.

April knew a bad idea when she heard it. "No, we stay together the whole time. The creature could be in any room in this house. I can't sense it, you know that!"

No-one argued.

It was a big house with way too many rooms to check. Every time they entered a new one, April's heart pounded so hard that it was all she could hear. Finally, all the downstairs and second-storey rooms proved creature-free, with no evidence of a squatter.

"I guess that leaves the third-story rooms," Raina murmured. "I hope there aren't too many of those."

"If I were the creature, that's where I would stay—more secure," April said and started up the nearest staircase, as stealthily as possible. The steps did not cooperate, each individual plank creaked a loud protest.

"Cripes, we couldn't sneak up on a deaf worm in this place," Airron grumbled, when they were almost at the top.

April paused on the last step and listened intently. She couldn't hear a thing over their own noise. Since they had already lost any element of surprise that might have worked to their advantage, April sprang boldly into the room, just in case something was lying in wait.

There was nothing lying in wait, but there was an unusual lack of a floor. April's froggish hop carried her forward and straight down. She dropped the torch and reflexively grabbed for anything to stop her fall. Her fingers latched onto the last bit of intact planking, right in front of the door she had just foolishly leapt through. The torch kept falling and falling for the longest time. It fell past ground level and kept on going. It never hit bottom—it fell until she couldn't see it anymore.

"Stay back!" she shouted, trying to hang on with her fingertips. "There's no floor!" It didn't look like there was a roof either. Stars twinkled overhead.

A torch was extended and her friends peered into the room, directly above April. "There's no floor!" Raina gasped.

"I already said that," April wailed. "Grab my fingers, I'm losing my grip."

Salm was quick to crouch down and grip her wrists securely, straining to haul her back up over the edge to safety. There was not a lot of solid space between the gaping hole and the top of the stairs. When Salm jerked her up, she fell into him, nearly sending them both tumbling down the long flight of stairs at his back.

"If it's not drowning, its heights and … and great long stupid falls," April stammered, leaning against Salm's solid frame. "That pit has no bottom. Did you see the torch fall? It fell forever." She scooted back against the door jamb, trying to pull herself together.

"It's your luck." Salm sounded shaky himself.

"My bad luck," she sighed.

"Hey, look over there against the far wall." Airron pointed with their last light.

Most of the room was a big hole, but there was a narrow edge of flooring around the hole, beside the walls, as well as a larger intact section on the far side of the room. They could actually walk all the way around the room if they stuck close to the walls, if they didn't walk straight across and fall into the gaping pit.

"I'll go check it out." Salm cautiously stepped onto the ledge sideways. With his back pressed against the wall, he made his way around the pit to the intact section of floor.

April bit her lip hard, cursed under her breath and followed Salm. "That's not only a hole, you know. It's a trap," she said, glowering at the blackness.

"And a clever one, at least at night," Raina said.

Airron followed April, holding Raina's hand tightly all the way. When they stood together on the small patch of floor, it was obvious that something had been living there. A pile of leaves had been hauled inside and shaped into an untidy nest.

"Yuck." Raina pointed out a scattering of small bones and insect exoskeletons. April felt a little uncomfortable looking at the remains. She had been forced to survive on similar fare not so long ago.

Airron held the light close to the nest and they searched for clues. April plucked a coarse hair off one of the leaves. It was ash grey and definitely not an elf hair. And there was a distinct odor coming from the nest. It reeked of rancid filth, damp rot and worse.

"You know, Airron, it does look like an imp is camping here. And it certainly smells like it. They aren't very clean." April had smelled an imp before, and it had smelled an awful lot like this messy nest.

Salm kicked leaves around to make sure nothing was hidden beneath. "Too bad the two missing rods aren't here."

"I'm surprised they aren't," April mused. "I would expect the creature to keep them close. And what closer place than where it's living." She stepped toward the only window, right above the nest, and peered outside. She was getting the distinct feeling that they should leave soon. The creature could return at any moment. Unless it had actually been here when they arrived. Maybe they had scared it out the window, or up through the giant hole in the roof. It could be perched overhead right now, April realized with a shiver.

"Hand me the torch." She leaned backwards to grab it, then extended the light through the window, following it out with her head and shoulders. The roof of a lower wing of the house lay directly below. Strong vines grew up the outside wall—all the way to the window. It would be as easy as scaling a ladder to enter this room from outside. The creature could sneak up on them from the stairs, the window or the roof. And what about the weird pit? Maybe it lived down there. Maybe it had tunnelled into New Haven and not followed April at all.

April concentrated once more on the surrounding area and was alarmed to discover that an elf was approaching the house through the forest, fast. She yanked the torch back inside and lowered it from sight. "An elf is outside. It must be Cherry coming to meet the creature. We have to get out of this room!"

"But we need to stay close enough to overhear them," Raina insisted, terrified but determined.

"But not this close!" Airron said. They turned towards the door, then faltered. Something was rustling around below the stairs.

"Oh! Oh no!" Raina whimpered. "April, what's down there?"

April couldn't sense a thing. "I can't tell, so it must be the creature that's causing all the trouble. It is here." She motioned towards the window. "We can climb down outside, there are vines on the wall. Quick!"

"Quick it is." Airron hoisted Raina onto the window ledge first. Raina swung down, her pale face disappearing from sight.

"Airron, you next!" Salm said. Airron scrambled after Raina and slid from view. "Come on, April. Your turn." Salm jerked his head at the window. An all too familiar creak sounded—the creature was on the first step.

"No, Salm! You go first! Pull me up after." April shoved him toward the window as a second creak seemed as loud as a scream to her ears. Salm looked about to refuse when a third creak followed fast. There was no time to waste arguing.

"Follow me." He slipped quietly up over the window ledge. April held the torch high so he could find a vine to grab.

April was trying to remember how many steps ascended to the room, when the fourth and fifth creak sounded a whole lot closer. Salm reached urgently for her hand as he slid partway out the window, then everything went wrong. A loud shout from below the window caused them both to jump. Salm disappeared from sight as if he had fallen. April tried to catch his hand and missed. She dropped the torch instead. It landed flame down and extinguished itself. Heavy feet raced up the last few steps. April leapt for the window. She didn't make it.

Something slunk into the room.

April froze. She didn't move a muscle and barely dared draw breath. Whatever had arrived knew about the hole, it stopped in the doorway and snuffled wetly. April was quite petrified when the creature began skirting around the hole toward her. It must have some degree of night vision, while she had none.

Determined to even the odds and finally see this tormentor, face-to-face, April concentrated hard and fast on reigniting the torch with her magical ability. It flared brilliantly, more like a campfire than a mere torch. She grabbed it up and held it aloft like a shield, her back against the wall. Her wild gaze zeroed in on what was standing much, much too close.

Airron was proved absolutely correct—the creature was a green-eyed imp! And it was quite a sight. It wore nothing but a stained loincloth over its gray hunched body, and the baggy diaper didn't cover nearly enough of anything. It was the same height as April, in spite of the hunching. This imp was either smallish, or April's memories were warped by her child's height, the last time she had stared up at an imp. Protruding lips curled back to reveal an uneven row of pointy gray and yellow teeth. April was pretty sure it wasn't a smile and she didn't smile back. She couldn't have smiled to save her life.

The imp took one step forward and wrinkled its nose as if she smelled bad. April almost gagged on the strong reek emanating off its own body. This thing didn't smell like it had bathed since birth. Bony grey fingers tugged on a thick droopy ear, then one such filthy digit aimed straight at April, like an arrow.

When the imp spoke, it did so in a slow, lilting pitch. "April bad elf," it proclaimed, proving it knew exactly who she was. "Brag." The imp stroked his patchy chest as if he was grooming.

"Your name is Brag?" April guessed, trying to pinpoint the window in her peripheral vision.

"Brag." He stuck out a thick gray tongue and slowly licked his mouth, before he put the tongue back where it belonged—out of sight.

April tried to feel brave. This was her chance to find out what was going on. "Brag, did you follow me here?"

"To house?"

"No! Did you follow me into New Haven—this world?"

"Okey dokey. Brag follow April," he said agreeably.

"What? No, I don't want you to follow me! Did you follow me? Here? Before?"

"To house?" the imp asked dimly.

"No!" She gave up and changed her question. "Why are you here, harming elves?"

"Bad elfies trample Brag's garden. April bad, Peter bad, Raina bad, Airron bad, Salm bad. Bad elfies bad."

"I am not bad and I didn't trample any gardens," April denied.

The imp chattered his teeth sharply and April slid a small step closer to the window, in case he tried to take a chomp out of her or something. And how did he know all their names? April could only think of only one elf who would have been happy to supply that information. "Is Cherry bad?" April asked.

"Don't know Cherry bad elf."

"Are you sure you don't know Cherry?"

He looked sneaky. "Brag not know Cherry bad elf," he said, as if it was a hint. The pointless conversation was going nowhere, and April had a more important question.

"How do we wake Peter?"

"Peter not wakey-wakey. Forever sleep. Peter bad, trample Brag's garden."

"No!" His words made her heart ache. "Forever sleep? No, that can't be right. There must be a cure. What is the cure—tell me!" April cried desperately.

"No cure here." He scrunched up his face and stared vacantly at April. "April sky eye, not belong here."

If there was a way to cure Peter, the imp was not going to say. April tried another question. "Um ... Brag? Why do you want the thunderwand?"

"Brag want thunderwand?" he asked in surprise.

"The metal shiny sticks, from the museum. Why do you want them?" she asked, edging even closer to the window.

The imp's unblinking green gaze narrowed. "Brag has need," he snarled low in his throat. The question had made him angry and his words were still too vague to be useful. He wiggled one finger at a small pile of sticks on the floor. The collection flared and began to burn, filling the room with smoky light. The imp rubbed his huge hands together. "Playtime! What to do? What to do? What to do?" he chanted, hopping from one skinny leg to the other, in rhythm with his singsong words. His hopping was moving him steadily closer to April.

She was pretty sure that she was not going to enjoy Brag's playtime. Nor was she learning anything that would help Peter, or anything useful at all. Unless her magic would work against the imp in a direct confrontation, there wasn't any point in hanging around. Welly had told her to have faith in herself and her abilities, but it was difficult to feel confident when confronting the unpredictable imp alone in a dark creepy house.

The window was her best chance to escape. April was right beside the opening now and Brag didn't appear to notice; he was preoccupied with deciding what to do for playtime. As long as he was paying her no attention, she might as well try and get away now.

April flung herself onto the ledge. She crouched, prepared to jump into the vines. Unfortunately, Brag had made up his mind that it was time to act. "Playtime," he sang, thrust both hands forward and wiggled all ten of his fingers.

The vines below came to life, lengthening dramatically and squirming around like a nest of enraged snakes. If April leaped into them now, they would surely wrap her up as tightly as they had trapped Sage Scarab. If she went back into the room, she would face Brag. April was stuck on the thin ledge, unable to go forward or back.

"What to do? What to do? What to do?" Brag pranced gleefully. His dark shadow kept him company, dancing large on the walls. The scene was right out of a nightmare.

April searched the ground below. She didn't see her friends anywhere in the dim moonlight. Had the elf that she'd sensed earlier harmed them? April concentrated magically, trying to locate them. Three elves were travelling rapidly away from Cherry's house. A fourth elf was circling above. Airron—it had to be Airron! April looked up in time to see him swoop into view.

"Get ready to jump!" he hollered.

Brag heard him too, and reacted with speed. He swung his arm over his head, and flung it in April's direction as if he was pelting her with a berry. A sizzling bubble formed and rolled through the air toward her, swelling as it got closer. Instinctively, April focused on it, trying to pop it before it reached her. The bubble didn't even notice her magic and almost seemed to feed on it, expanding and rolling faster.

There was no time to wait for Airron. April launched off the ledge with her arms in the air. She started to plummet before he caught her hand with one of his own, completely off balance since it left him with only one flying arm and a lot more weight.

"Grab my neck," he cried, swinging her upward as they tumbled out of control. April flung both arms around his neck, freeing his second wing. The sizzling bubble rolled by overhead and burst. April could feel the wave of magic tingle past her skin, but it was too diffuse to cause any damage.

Airron regained control and glided up, into the safety of the darkness. "Don't let go!" he ordered. He must be joking if he thought she needed to be told. She nodded weakly against his neck.

"Heights again!" she remarked, her voice shaking.

"At least it's dark, you can't see how high up we are."

"I don't have to see to know. You saved my life, Airron."

"Well, someone had to do it. Stop strangling, would you? I do need to breath. Where are the others? Can you tell?" he asked.

April loosened her grip and concentrated one more time, even though her brain felt like leftover turnip mush. "Below, a little to the right, not too far ahead."

Airron was starting to puff heavily from the effort of flying their combined weight. "Talk me down to them, okay."

April did. "Start going down, a little more to the right. Straight down, I see a torch. Who has another torch?" April finally remembered the other elf and guessed it wasn't Cherry after all. "Sage Scarab?"

"He does seem to turn up when we need him most, doesn't he?" Airron said.

"I guess that's part of his magic." Although his timing could have been better.

Airron banked and straightened up, landing with his feet under him. It was a pretty smooth landing, all things considered. Accurate, as well. Raina grabbed both of them before they had even stopped moving.

"Airron, you did it! You rescued April. Are you okay?" The question applied to both of them.

Airron was exhausted by his efforts, but he nodded valiantly as Sage Scarab and Salm hurried up. Sage Scarab didn't hug anyone, he was much too mad. "Both of you in one piece, are you? Luckier than you deserve to be. Let's get the heck out of here. April, keep checking the forest, every minute. We'll talk when I've got you safely home. Move. Move faster!"

Sage Scarab drove them through the forest at a punishing pace, ranting under his breath all the way to the Pooles' house. Once there, he banged the door open and slammed it shut with no regard for the fact that it was the middle of the night. "Cripes, I swear you're determined to drive me into an early grave. What the heck were you thinking, tracking down the monster in the middle of the night? With no help at all? Into the kitchen, all of you. Least you can do is feed me while you tell me what you learned about this critter!"

He stormed into the kitchen, while Raina and Salm tried their best to shush him. The morning would be soon enough to confront their parents.

But that was not to be. Mr. Poole rushed downstairs in his night shirt, hair standing on end and carrying a big stick. Mrs. Poole followed close on his heels, lighting candles as she went. When she saw the four of them—fully dressed and obviously returning to the house in various states of dishevelment, she shook her head in defeat. "Don't tell me. Don't you dare say a word until I'm sitting down," she warned. "Oh, Salm. Are you hurt? Again? Go and sit down in the kitchen."

Now that April could see him, Salm did look to be in the worst condition with fresh bruises and scrapes, a distinct limp, and a bump sprouting on his forehead.

"All of you, kitchen, now, sit," Mr. Poole ground out.

They went and sat down in the kitchen, and April really needed to sit down. The night was catching up with her.

Mr. Poole held his temper, barely, and opened his medical sack, saying, "What happened tonight?" Apparently not one of them wanted to say, so no-one said a word.

He eyed each of them in turn and Sage Scarab said, "Don't look at me, I only came in at the tail end. Clean up duty." He carried a basket of cookies to the table, munching on one. "To tell you the truth, I wouldn't mind hearing this tale myself." He sat down, chewing loudly in the silence.

Mr. Poole sighed. "Salm, you can start. I want to know exactly what went on this evening, and it better be the truth."

Salm didn't know quite where to begin, but he gave it a try. "Okay, um … well, we … um, we snuck out of the house because we believe that Cherry Pitt is in contact with the creature that is creating the problems in New Haven. We were going to watch her, but we didn't know where she lived exactly." Salm flushed, clearly embarrassed to admit this fact.

Sage Scarab snorted in disgust, or laughter, or both.

"Uh, ya, well … anyway, we came up with the idea that Cherry might be meeting the creature at her old house, which is vacant, and kind of isolated," Salm mentioned lamely.

"Where better to confront something that can kill you for fun," Sage Scarab agreed. The sarcasm was overdone.

Salm ignored it. "We …uh, searched the house. As it turned out, the creature was living in one of the upstairs rooms and it almost caught us. Well, it did catch April. You'll have to ask her about that part. I fell out of the window before I saw what happened, or even what the thing is." Salm had wisely left out an awful lot, like the bottomless pit trap.

All eyes turned to April. She said, "Airron, you were right. The creature is an imp."

"Told you so." Airron kept his gloating to a minimum.

"His name is Brag and he thinks all elves are bad, especially us, for trampling his garden—whatever that means. He sort of denied knowing Cherry, but he was in her house, wasn't he. That must mean something." At least April thought it did.

"So, what did he look like?" Airron asked.

"Almost exactly like the picture in your book. And he smelled really foul. Well, you smelled the nest. You can imagine." April was getting sidetracked.

"You stood and conversed with this vile and dangerous creature?" Mrs. Poole cried, choking on the drink she had poured for herself.

"Yes, but only because I couldn't get away, and I thought Brag might tell me something helpful, about Peter," April stressed.

"And did this imp tell you anything that will help us to deal with it? Or help Peter?" Mr. Poole asked.

"He went on about elves trampling his garden, and how bad we all are. He wants the thunderwand, said he needs it, but he didn't say why. He didn't make a lot of sense. He likes to say the same thing over and over, kind of like he's singing, and he dances while he talks." April shook her head in frustration. "Brag does have powerful magic, but I think he has limited ideas about how to use it. He tried to trap me by turning the vines into snaky plants, like he did with Sage Scarab. He made fire, and he threw some sort of power bubble at me, but it didn't hit me because Airron flew me away. He saved my life."

"Just glad I had wings. Did the imp say anything to help Peter?"

Mr. Poole leaned forward. "Yes, did he tell you how to awaken Peter?"

"He wasn't very clear. I didn't understand a lot of what he said," April answered evasively.

"What exactly did he tell you," Mr. Poole pressed.

"He called it a 'forever sleep' and said there was no cure in this world, then he said I didn't belong here," April revealed reluctantly.

Mr. Poole ran a harried hand through his thinning brown hair. "April, not so long ago, you said that once upon a time an elf from your world had the ability to heal elves magically. Do you think that could be an ability you possess, or all elves from your world? I believe Peter is suffering from a magical affliction, so maybe you could help him." He Poole sounded desperate.

"I really don't think so. Curing elves was a very special magic. The way that the elves from my world talked about it, it was an extremely

140

rare gift." April wished she could heal Peter, but didn't see how it could be possible.

"But have you ever tried?" Mr. Poole pressed.

"Well, no, I've never tried. I wouldn't know how. Do you think I should try and wake up Peter magically?"

"There isn't anything to lose," Mr. Poole said grimly. Peter must be in terrible shape.

"Could I at least try waking up the ant first? In case something goes wrong?"

"Good idea. First thing in the morning," Mr. Poole said. "Now, we need to wake the Sages and the entire High Court and decide how to deal with the imp that is living in the Pitt's vacant house. Maybe if we flush him out, he will leave our world. We also need to question Cherry about her involvement with this creature." He glanced at Sage Scarab.

Sage Scarab stood and brushed cookie crumbs off his stomach. "I'm on it. I'll start with Falcon, see what he thinks. He won't mind being woken up in the middle of the night. All part of the job."

"The imp won't be there now, he'll be hiding," April stated with certainty.

"We'll take a look anyway, search the place, bring along a bunch of the King's archers for protection. Might stop the critter with an arrow." Sage Scarab looked rather bloodthirsty for a moment. "Anyway, you said it's not bright, might continue to hang around. You never know." He turned to leave. "You four get some sleep, and don't you dare get out of bed until daylight."

"Don't worry, I have plans to chain them to their beds," Mr. Poole said, sounding serious.

"Sage Scarab?" April had to tell him something before he left. He grunted. "When you search the upstairs room where Brag is nesting, be really careful when you go inside. There's a ... a trap when you step through the door. A deep pit. It might be bottomless."

"A bottomless pit you say? Cripes, lucky none of you fell down it. Never would have seen you again. Thanks for mentioning that. Anything else I should know?" His voice was as dry as dust.

April glanced at her friends and they all shook their heads quickly. There was no point in mentioning that April had fallen into the pit. It certainly wouldn't help their credibility.

Mrs. Poole rose with aplomb and adjusted her nightshirt. "Bottomless pits? Evil imps? I am too exhausted to yell at you now. I will yell in the morning. Get to bed and stay there! You have half the night left, use it properly."

Since April could barely keep her eyes opened, she was happy to obey. And she would need her strength for the morning. She left Salm getting some grudging medical treatment from his father and headed straight to bed.

***

It was another nightmare. April was trapped at the bottom of a deep, black lonely cold hole. She was dying of thirst. She knew she would never leave the hole. It would become her forever grave. She was growing so weak, she wanted to feel sunlight and breathe sweet forest air. An ant crawled endlessly in circles around her. A horrible face looked down at her from the world above the hole. Brag's face. He opened his pointy teeth and clicked them. "Peter bad, Peter bad, Peter bad," he said, over and over.

The memory of the dream was still with her when Mrs. Poole shook her awake. She was drenched in cold sweat. The sun was barely rising over the lake. "It's time, April. Marsh is going to take you to the laboratory. You should have a bite of breakfast. I'm sure you'll need your energy."

April sat up, pulling her blanket around her knees. She was shivering from the dream. Mrs. Poole took a good look at April and sat down beside her. "Are you all right?"

"Bad dream," April mumbled.

"No wonder, after last night. April, no matter what happens, I know you will do everything you can to help Peter. No matter what happens, remember that you've done your best." It didn't sound like she was optimistic about April healing Peter. April didn't have a lot of faith in her ability to heal him either. But she would try. There was nothing to lose by trying. Mrs. Poole patter her shoulder and left her to get dressed.

After dunking her head in the basin of water, April dried off and pulled on her overalls, feeling the need for comfort. Peter had been suffering terribly in his dream world, she had to get him out of that hole. She had to heal him magically. No—she had to get him out of the hole! April froze with one overall strap pulled over her shoulder. Imps and holes? An imp looking down into a hole?

April pressed her temples and strained to remember the illustration in Airron's book. It was no good, she had to look at the page again. Now! April dashed madly down the spiralling stairs, getting quite dizzy. She almost flew up the steps to Salm's room and ran in without knocking. Both Airron and Salm were asleep, cozy under their blankets.

April dropped to the ground beside Airron. She shook him awake much too abruptly. "Airron, Airron, wake up! It's an emergency."

He sprang to his feet. "What? What's wrong?"

Salm bolted up, too and echoed, "What's wrong?"

"Airron, you need to fly to your house. Get the book that you showed us with the pictures of the imp tormenting the villagers and looking down into the hole. I need to read it right away," she said urgently. "It could help Peter! Can you get it? Now?"

"Okay, not a problem." Airron stepped over to Salm's window and stood on the ledge. He spread his wings and soared away, yawning. He was still half asleep. He would be lucky to not fly into a tree.

"He makes it look so easy," April said, collapsing down on the edge of Salm's bed to wait. Salm looked worse than the night before. The bump on his forehead had grown and his bruises were colourful in the clear morning light. "Oh, Salm! Did you fall all the way out of that window to the ground?" she asked.

Salm grimaced. "Only to the lower roof."

"Well, I think you got the worst of it last night. Don't get up, I'll be right back!" She ran back downstairs and fetched cups of juice and berries.

Mr. Poole looked up from his breakfast. "Are you ready to go?"

"No. I have to read something first. I won't be long." April carried the snack up to Salm and ate with him while waiting for Airron to return. They hadn't even finished the berries before he soared back in through the window with a pack slung over his neck. Airron must have flown as fast as he possibly could, because he was quite winded when he slumped back onto his blanket.

April handed him a cup of juice and the last berry, in exchange for the book. "My thanks, Airron." She started flipping frantically through the pages.

"The pages are marked," he said.

Several thin strands of dried grass stuck out of the middle of the book. April opened to those pages, filled with hope. She located the picture of an elf staring down into a hole, remembering her own statement from the

143

night before, about Brag having a limited bag of tricks. Maybe they were shared from imp to imp, from one generation to the next, since the creatures were not very clever when left to their own devices. April had never read the myth that the picture illustrated, but did so now.

A drowsy Raina wandered in while April was immersed in the tale of how an imp fed an elf a poisoned apple and trapped him in the bottom of a well, while he was in a drugged sleep. It wasn't a real well, but a dream well. The imp came each night to torment him after moonrise. The imp told the villager that he would never leave the forever hole, unless the moon set before the imp visited him in the night. If the imp did not visit for one whole night, the villager could climb out of the hole.

April closed the book with a thud. Everyone jumped, they were half-asleep. She hadn't meant to scare her friends, but now that she had their full attention, she had news to share. "We have to find Brag if we want to save Peter. And it will have to be tonight. I don't think we have much time left," she said.

"Tonight? Again? Are you sure?" Raina asked.

"Yes, tonight. Brag put Peter into a drugged sleep, I think. And the imp is keeping Peter trapped in sleep, in a deep well, by visiting each night while they are both dreaming. The only way to free Peter is to stop Brag from visiting him in dreams for one whole night, then Peter can climb out of the hole and wake up. The myth says so." April felt like she was babbling, but must have made some sense because heads nodded, if uncertainly.

"I think we better read this for ourselves." Raina lifted the book off April, effectively dismissing her. "You go with my dad and see if you can do anything to help Peter magically. Sage Scarab promised he would keep an eye on Cherry, so we've got that covered. Meet us back here as soon as you're done."

"Okay." April ran down the stairs, full of hope about what she had read in the book.

11. Midnight Picnic

M r. Stone's laboratory was an unremarkable gray stone structure located on the fringe of the town circle. April had visited the circle many times, and she had never even noticed the nondescript building.

Peter's father was pacing anxiously, awaiting them. The ant was ready on a table, installed in a cozy little box on a soft square of cloth, with another one pulled up to its mandibles. Mr. Stone looked embarrassed when April mentioned that the ant looked comfortable. It looked a lot more at ease here than it did pacing endless circles in the dream world. Unfortunately, nothing magical that April tried could wake up the ant, but she didn't harm it either. Mr. Poole and Mr. Stone agreed she should go ahead and try to wake up Peter. They set off for his house.

Under the gentle morning sun, the forest was filled with the vibrant sounds of insects and life. It should have been comforting to walk through the woodland, yet April resented the perfect day, as if it mocked Peter's suffering, as if it mocked all their troubles. Clouds and cold drizzle would have been more appropriate.

Mrs. Stone was sitting on a cushion, reading to Peter as he lay like death. He looked almost shrunken somehow, and so much worse than the last time she had seen him. April couldn't manage any sort of greeting when Peter's mother rose. "Do you think this will work?" Mrs. Stone asked, almost pleading.

"I don't know, but I really should be alone to concentrate," April told his mother apologetically.

Mr. and Mrs. Stone left with such hope in their eyes that April felt like a fraud. She had no expectations that this would work. She closed the door quietly and slid Mrs. Stone's cushion up against the bed. April settled upon it, then didn't know what to do. There was a cup of water beside the bed and April poured drops between Peter's dry lips when she remembered how thirsty he had been in the dream. When the cup was empty, she placed her palms on Peter's forehead, pressing down to make strong contact. She closed her eyes and concentrated on Peter's thoughts, deeper and deeper, until she left her own thoughts far behind. She must have tried for half an hour, but could make no connection at all. She might have been pressing her palms against an empty pillow.

Trying a different approach, April laid her hands over his heart. If she couldn't learn anything from his mind, maybe she could learn something from his body. Focusing with renewed energy, April concentrated on what was happening to him physically. That too proved hopeless. Healing him was well beyond April's scope of magic.

She rested her head briefly on his cold chest, listening to his heart thud slowly and laboriously. His skin was so cold and smooth, it felt like wax—it felt lifeless. Except Peter was very much alive and trapped inside his own body, suffering.

"We're going to help you, tonight," April whispered, even though he couldn't hear her. Several tears escaped to travel aimlessly down her cheeks and it felt like her own heart was being cruelly squeezed.

Unable to face the disappointment on the Stones' faces, April simply shook her head in passing and walked straight outside. Mrs. Stone was the one who followed her into the front garden. April fought to gain control over herself before she turned to face Peter's mother.

Mrs. Stone stood there, like a wounded sparrow. "How is Peter? Could you help at all?"

April had to tell her something. She stepped close and whispered, "Tonight. We're doing something tonight. If it works, Peter will awaken at first light tomorrow. But please don't tell anyone, we're not supposed to …" She trailed off. She really shouldn't say what they weren't supposed to do.

Mrs. Stone nodded once and didn't ask even one question. "I won't say anything. Perhaps that is not the right thing to do, but if you can help Peter …" She left the rest unsaid. "Farewell, and be careful April." She reached out to grip April's hand, then returned to the house.

When April arrived home, Raina, Salm and Airron were lounging on the shore of the lake with the book still opened between them. She was bombarded with questions as soon as she sat down. "I couldn't do a thing for Peter. He's not doing very well. We have to take on Brag," she said, and motioned at the book. "Did you find out anything useful about imps?"

"I don't know if we would recognize important information," Raina said. "We can't even figure out how you know about the hole, and Brag needing to visit each night. Peter's not in a hole, he's asleep in his bed."

"I know, but I shared his dream again last night. Peter is still trapped in a deep well with Brag staring down at him. Even the ant is stuck down there. The myth is truth, I know it is. So we have to find Brag and keep him awake all night. If Brag doesn't visit Peter in dreams, Peter will wake up—climb out of the hole," she said. "Did the book say anything at all that might help?"

Raina pulled it onto her lap and flipped pages. "Let's see, there was something about a prince or princess kissing an elf trapped in forever sleep, the kiss is supposed to wake them up. But that's no help, we only have a prince and I don't think Skylar's kiss would wake up Peter. We would need a princess and New Haven doesn't have one of those at the moment. Um, imps are powerful, but not clever. The book compares them to naughty, thoughtless children." Raina snorted in disgust. She did not agree. "They aren't frightened of very much, well, they don't have to be, do they? Imps are frightened of Giants, and their magic doesn't work at all against Giants. I wonder why that is? Hmm, well it doesn't help us anyway. Let's see … they like to collect gold and precious jewels and any shiny things. Imps are shy about being seen and prefer to stay hidden. They think they are clever, but they're not." Raina paused thoughtfully.

"Easy to trick?" Airron said with a smirk.

Salm grinned back. "Elves can be pretty tricky."

"We need a great plan, a foolproof plan," Raina stressed.

Salm nodded. "Absolutely foolproof."

The four friends put their heads together for the whole afternoon, plotting. In the end, they had a plan. It wasn't foolproof, far from it, and it wasn't all that clever, but it was the best they could come up with. Plan in place, they had some preparations to make.

They rose stiffly off the moss when Mrs. Poole called them for dinner. Mr. Poole rushed in late and loaded his shell with assorted vegetables and flatbread, as if he hadn't eaten all day.

"How was everything in town?" Mrs. Poole asked, after he had devoured enough to slow him down. He had been eating like Sage Scarab.

He swiped his mouth and swallowed. "The Sages and the High Court are in a high uproar about the imp. Falcon had quite a job calming them down, but he managed in the end."

"Did they look for the imp?" Raina asked casually.

"Sage Scarab took an armed troop of the King's guards to search the Pitts' old house from top to bottom. It proved deserted. The imp has moved on. Falcon himself went and had a long talk with Cherry. She denies any knowledge of the imp, and there is not one shred of proof that she is involved."

"Oh, she's involved all right, up to the tips of her pointed ears," Raina snapped resentfully. But her words alone were not proof.

After dinner, they began the first stage of their plan. "We'll clean up. Go and rest, you've had a long day," Raina told her parents. "I'll bring you a nightcap. Salm can put DewDrop to bed."

"But I don't want to go to bed," DewDrop whined.

"Not yet," Salm said. "Later. We can play a game first."

"Okay!" DewDrop scampered up to her room with Salm, leaving the kitchen free for them to pilfer the supplies necessary to carry out their plan.

Raina searched through the cupboards and pulled out bottles, examining them closely. April supplied two cups and Raina poured a generous amount into each.

"You take it in to my parents," she whispered to April. "They won't question you about how full the cups are, because you don't know any better."

"I know better!" But April carried the two cups into the sitting room anyway. And Raina was right, her parents didn't say a word, but they did look into their almost overflowing drinks with arched eyebrows.

Back in the kitchen, April helped stuff a sack with the best snacks they could find. Then they squeezed in two bottles of the strongest fermented drink in the house. One of them was fermented baneberry.

"That better be enough," Raina remarked tensely. "What if it's not enough?"

"It will have to be, won't it," Airron said.

April ran up to her room and retrieved her sack of gold. She carried it downstairs in her pocket, discreetly hidden. They forced the gold into the pack, too, making it very heavy. They hid their supplies in an empty cupboard. Ready and waiting.

"Now we should play a game until my parents go to bed," Raina suggested softly. "It would look more natural. More normal."

"I'll go see if Salm is ready. Do you want to play sticks and stones?" April asked.

"Sure, anything."

April retrieved the game and peeked into DewDrop's room. DewDrop was snuggled against Salm's side while he read her a story. Her eyes were drooping. The scene looked so safe and cozy that April wanted to crawl onto the bed and snuggle against Salm's other side, listen to the story, and forget all about Brag. But that wouldn't help Peter. Salm winked when he saw her. April tiptoed away before she disturbed the little elf.

Mr. and Mrs. Poole looked as sleepy as DewDrop when April passed by and held up the game, trying to smile innocently. "Would you like another nightcap drink?" she asked.

"No, no, that was more than enough," Mrs. Poole said hastily. "I'm nodding off as it is. None of us managed a decent night's sleep last night. Tonight will be different."

"Yes." April left the room quickly because she didn't think she was a very good actor. She was having trouble keeping a straight face, due to nerves no doubt. Airron set the game out on the table. Salm joined them, but they were too distracted to actually play, knowing what they would face in a few short hours. It wasn't long before the parents wandered in to say good night. At least it looked like a real game was in progress.

"Are you sleeping here again?" Mrs. Poole asked Airron.

"Yes, I told my parents. Someone has to make sure these three stay in bed." Airron grinned.

Mr. Poole narrowed his eyes. "Make sure that you all do."

"Don't worry, we will," Raina lied.

"Don't worry? Hard not to. Well, good-night then." Mr. Poole escorted his wife away. She really was almost asleep on her feet.

Raina whispered, "Almost time."

April's breath caught in her throat. She was dreading a second encounter with Brag. He was an unpredictable creature, with enough power to terrify her down to her tiniest toes. Power without brains was a very dangerous combination. Alas, Brag had to be faced if Peter was to escape from forever sleep. And April had more brains than the imp—she just hoped it was advantage enough.

They waited an extra hour to be sure that the parents were deeply asleep. When Salm checked and heard snoring, it was time to go. Salm lifted the heavy pack out of the cupboard. Raina handed out four torches before she blew out the candles. As silent as their shadows, they slipped from the house. Again, they travelled down the path for a safe distance before daring to light their torches.

"You know, it's awfully easy to escape from your parents. That's two nights in a row," Airron said lightly.

Raina couldn't disagree. "It was easy."

"I would like you to remember that particular fact when our world is safe again. We could take a hike up to Blueberry Hill some late night," Airron proposed. "How does that sound?"

"Interesting," she said.

April asked, "What's Blueberry Hill? I've never heard of it."

"No, you wouldn't have. There are still some things about our world that you don't know and I have no intention of telling you." Raina said, sounding flustered.

"Why not?" April looked at the faces of her friends in the torchlight. All three were as close-mouthed as adult mayflies, and those insects didn't even have a mouth in their final stage of life.

"Look, I'll tell you about Blueberry Hill another day, when you don't have a date with Brag," Raina said. "But now is not the time, believe me."

"So, where should we look for Brag?" Salm said, getting them back on track. "Is it back to Cherry's old house?"

April nodded. "I think we should try there first. The house has already been searched and the elves have left. Brag might believe it's safe to return to his nest."

"I hope you're right. And I hope Sage Scarab keeps a close eye on Cherry. We certainly don't want her turning up and wrecking our plan," Raina said worriedly.

April didn't want to think about the plan going awry. So many things could go wrong and with one wave of his filthy fingers, Brag could destroy them all.

She concentrated on the forest continually, yet sensed nothing unusual. When they reached the edge of the trees surrounding Cherry's former dwelling, three torches were snuffed. April kept her light and Salm shifted the pack from his shoulder to hers. It was so heavy, it almost tipped her over. This was it—there would be no turning back now.

"Remember, stay out of sight. If anything goes wrong, run," April warned. "You won't be able to help against Brag's magic, so get out of here if the plan doesn't work."

"April, we're not going to leave you alone with Brag, if he's even here." Raina adjusted the pack higher on April's shoulder. "We're smarter than the imp even if we don't have magic. We'll figure something out. We're not going to abandon you. Now, stop talking nonsense and go see if Brag is skulking about." Raina hugged her tightly. So did Airron. And so did Salm. April didn't want to let any of them go.

"This is going to work," Salm whispered in her ear.

"Yes. Okay, okay. We can do this." April gulped hard and hurried across the moss, directly toward Brag's window.

She placed the pack below his lair and flashed the torch around in circles. He would see the light if he was inside or anywhere nearby. April collected sticks and build a small campfire. She settled cross-legged on the ground to wait. Her heart was pounding so hard that she didn't think she would hear a rampaging boar if it galloped by. Brag would probably have to tap her on her shoulder to announce his presence.

April unloaded the contents of the sack and set out a lovely picnic, even filling the two cups with fermented drink, although hers was only for show. If Brag wasn't here, she would have to pack it all up again. If he wasn't here, April didn't have a clue where to search next. And they had to find Brag this night. Peter was almost out of time.

When her mouth grew too dry to swallow, she took a sip of the fermented drink. It tasted as horrible as the last time she had tried potent baneberries, compliments of Cherry. In a way, they had Cherry to thank for this plan. April was trying to trick Brag in a similar way to how Cherry had tricked her several months ago, by getting the imp so intoxicated that he could be tied up and kept awake all night long.

When a scrabbling noise proved that something was climbing down the wall, April released a pent up breath. Brag was here! She casually picked up a berry tart and it slipped through her fingers. She tried again and managed to control her shaky hand.

The imp's smell arrived before he did. Brag scuttled into the firelight smiling so widely that his face looked split in two. "Brag come play."

"Greetings, Brag. I want to play," April said. "I brought a picnic. Are you hungry and thirsty?"

"Picnic hungry." Brag scampered closer, crouched down and grabbed the tart right out of her hand. "April friend?"

"Yes," she said agreeably, and handed him a second tart.

She hadn't expected the imp to have manners, and he didn't. Brag stuffed both the tarts into his mouth at the same time, squishing some of the jam up his nose in the process. It made him sneeze violently, all over April. She stared in dismay at the red slimy globs stuck to her overalls, unwilling to brush them off with her hand.

April swallowed hard and picked up her cup. She slurped loudly, smacking her lips to make it seem delicious, adding an enthusiastic, "Yummy."

Brag eyed her drink covetously, reached over and stole it out of her hand, sloshing it onto her overalls. He took a big mouthful and spewed it right back out, on April. It was quickly followed by the whole cup, dumped over her head.

"Hey! What did you do that for?" she cried, leaping to her feet. After two minutes with Brag, she was a sticky mess. On the bright side, she was still alive.

"Drink rotten," Brag snarled, wiggling his dangerous fingers.

"No! No, it's not. It's supposed to taste like that," April said desperately. The plan was already going awry. If Brag would not drink the fermented baneberries, April was in a world of trouble. "Only the first cup tastes bad, then it gets better and better. It's a kind of … of magic drink. The more you drink the better it tastes, I promise. Here, drink more, you'll see!" April extended the second cup gingerly, half-expecting to get blasted by the imp's magic.

Brag huffed a bit, accepted the cup and gulped the whole thing down. He gargled with the last mouthful, smacked his lips together and licked them thoughtfully. "Not good." He looked disappointed.

"That's because you have to try more. You didn't drink enough yet." April poured more. Brag downed the second cup just as fast.

"Better, maybe. Maybe not." But he accepted a third cup and slurped that down, then helped himself to more food. April refilled both cups to the brim while Brag proceeded to eat like a starved wolf, ripping and tearing with his sharp teeth. "Why picnic?" he mumbled between rips. It had taken him long enough to ask.

"I came to make a deal with you." April handed him one of the cups. He spilled as much as he drank, then cleaned himself up by licking his chest, with a tongue that could come much too far out of his mouth.

April's stomach clenched at the sight. She shifted her gaze to study the starry sky until Brag was finished his grooming. "A deal with Brag," she reminded him when it seemed like he had forgotten what they were talking about.

"No deal, bad elf."

"But you don't know what the deal is yet. It's a very good deal for Brag." She switched his empty cup for the full cup. He held it in front of his face and stuck his tongue into it. "Brag, pay attention! I tried to cure Peter, I can't wake him." She reached behind her back and produced the sack of gold, opened at the top. "This gold is for Brag if he will wake up Peter." The gold was another prop to keep Brag drinking and amenable.

It did not have the desired reaction. Brag squealed with high-pitched laughter and fell over. He rolled around, kicking his big dirty feet and laughing, which sounded more like tortured screams than humor. April was thoroughly sprayed with wet crumbs, fermented drink, and worst of all, Brag's drool.

"April pitiful puddle of gold. Brag have lake of gold," the imp hinted in his sneaky voice, with a sly peek at the sack. As much as he had belittled April's gold, he still wanted it. Greed was plastered across his face.

"Where did you get a lake of gold?" April asked curiously.

"Secret."

"Brag can have my small puddle of gold, if you share the secret." April pushed the gold closer, and handed him yet another refilled cup. He slurped and considered her proposal, then grabbed the sack.

"Lake of gold to hurt Airron, Raina, Peter, April, Salm. Bad elves trample Brag's garden." Brag stuck his fingers into the sack and stirred the coins around happily.

"Which elf paid you a lake of gold? Cherry?" Who else would want to hurt the five of them?

He giggled. "Brag not remember."

April was running out of patience, and feeling a little more confident since Brag hadn't tried to kill her yet. "You do so remember. And what about Sage Scarab?"

Brag looked blanker than he normally did. He picked up a gold coin and tried to push it onto his baby finger like a ring. The hole was too small and it got stuck on the tip. He tried to pull it off with his teeth and bit his finger instead. He was losing some of his coordination; it was a promising sign.

"What about Sage Scarab?" April repeated.

"Who Scarab?" Brag's words were slurred.

"The old elf, wrapped in vines and hung from a tree. Remember?"

"Brag remember." The imp burped. "Scarab follow Brag, Brag wrap him up. Make trees cry sap. Playtime."

"Ya, the cat was hilarious." April uncorked the second bottle and Brag extended his cup eagerly, bottom up. April righted it and filled it. Brag grabbed the bottle instead.

"Bad elfie have good drink. Magic drink." Brag tilted his head sideways and tried to pour the fluid into his ear. April grabbed the bottle back.

"I told you it was good. Now, I have a different deal for Brag. A better deal," April emphasized, hoping he would spill his secrets now that he was intoxicated.

"More playtime?" The imp snatched the bottle back.

April borrowed his words. "Playtime deal. If Brag wakes Peter up, April will get Brag what he wants *most*." She waited for him to catch on.

He couldn't figure it out on his own. "What Brag want most?"

"Third shiny metal stick."

"Third metal stick. Brag fix mistake," he squealed, set the bottle down carefully, and tried to clap his hands together. They missed each other entirely.

"Yes, third stick. April get." She was starting to talk like the imp.

"Other elfie not get stick," he confided sadly, leaning towards April as if she was his best pal. "Brag burn lake, elfie not get stick."

"Is Cherry the elf that was helping you?"

Brag clapped a hand over his snout. "Oops. No Cherry bad elf. No no no. Don't know Cherry bad elf."

April didn't argue, there was no point. "Brag, listen, I have magic. I can get stick. Good deal? I'll even bring the third metal stick to where you hid the other two. Where are the other two shiny metal sticks?" April had no intention of handing over the third wand, but if the offer helped her to learn the location of the stolen two, all the better.

Brag didn't answer, he poured more fermented drink into his ear and then clanked the bottle against his head. "Maybe deal." Brag clinked again and stuck his tongue sideways, trying to lap the liquid out of his ear. He began to sway back and forth on his bony rump.

"Okay, deal. Good deal." April nodded as if a bargain had been struck. She hoped their picnic was almost over. It had been the worst picnic ever. "Brag, did you follow me here?" she asked, while she had the chance.

Brag didn't answer. He sealed his mouth around the bottle and drained the whole thing, after which, he burped long and loud and threw an arm over April's shoulder. She flinched when the fermented drink flowed out of his ear and splashed warmly onto her shoulder.

"Good deal, playtime deal," Brag slurred, right before he fell over backwards taking his arm with him.

The imp had passed right out from the strong drink, and that had been the plan. But April really wished he had answered her most pressing questions before he lost his wits.

With fumbling hands, April reached into the bottom of the pack and yanked out the strongest cord they had been able to find. Gritting her teeth, she flipped the imp onto his stomach. He needed his hands to perform magic, so April pulled them behind his back and tied them as tightly as she could, even wrapping the cord around his fingers, trapping the digits together in multiple knots. As soon as the last knot was secure, April stood up and waved, so her friends would know it was safe to approach.

They sprinted up and she said, "I can't believe plying him with fermented drink worked. We have to restrain him quickly!"

"Quickly it is," Airron said. He and Salm hoisted the imp off the ground. They carted him toward the nearest tree. Using thicker cord, they tied his ankles together and hung him upside-down over the lowest branch.

Raina giggled nervously. "It was pretty funny when he poured the drink over your head."

April scowled at her friend. "It wasn't funny! And he ruined my overalls, he sneezed jam out of his nose." April pointed at the gooey splatters and Raina backed off.

"You've got something gross in your hair, too," Airron pointed out helpfully. He was tall enough to look down.

"Take it out?"

"Not a chance."

"Okay, what now?" Salm prompted, less inclined to joke around.

"Now, the fun part." April sighed. "We have to keep Brag awake for the rest of the night, so he can't visit Peter in his dreams." She grabbed a stick and poked Brag sharply in the ribs. That woke the imp up. He howled and wriggled wildly, before closing his eyes again.

"Hey, Brag!" April prodded him again. He jerked and forced his eyelids open. His eyes had transformed from brilliant green to blood red. His eyes could change colour! "We didn't finish our deal Brag, wake up."

The imp's answer was to snarl and snap. He struggled to free his hands and grew enraged when he realized that his arms were bound tightly. "Bad bad bad elfies," he screeched and swung himself violently back and forth. The motion upset him, and he closed his eyes and vomited.

"Good grief," Raina cried, leaping away. Everyone went with her.

Brag wasn't ready to give in yet. A sharp cracking noise was accompanied by a fiery spark from behind his back. The imp screeched in pain. He had foolishly attempted to use magic with his hands all tied up, and had zapped himself in the rump. Brag's screeching faded to whimpers and he didn't try that again. Instead, he fell asleep.

April had to step close again, but she placed her feet carefully. She had enough gross stuff on her without stepping in worse. She prodded him again, then shouted loudly near his ear. Brag woke up and tried to zap her. He had forgotten he shouldn't do that. This time he hit one of the branches in the tree overhead, it exploded and the hot embers came raining down. April jumped aside, but Brag couldn't. He whimpered, rather piteously, until the embers on his skin cooled to gray.

When the woody dust settled, April tried to reason with the imp. "Look Brag, all you have to do is stay awake. If you do that, I won't bug you at all, okay?"

Brag closed his eyes and started snoring, again. April poked him with the stick, again. It was the start of the longest night imaginable. The four elves took turns poking and shaking and tossing water on the imp every time he shut his bleary eyes. He threatened them with all manner of torment, showing more imagination than April would have believed possible.

The sun must have slept in the next morning because it took forever to rise. When the beautiful orange light finally glowed on the horizon, April was filled with hope that Peter might be able to awaken now, if the myth was in fact truth, as she believed. But Brag had to be kept awake until they knew for sure.

Since Airron had the only pair of wings and was by far the fastest, he flew directly to Peter's house to verify that Peter had escaped from his forever sleep. If Peter wasn't awake, he was going to fly straight back to them. If Peter was awake, Airron was going to continue on to Welly's home and alert him that they had Brag in captivity. They didn't know

156

what to do with Brag now. Lastly, Airron was going to drop by Raina's house and inform the Pooles that their wayward offspring were unharmed. He was not looking forward to that visit at all.

"They'll never let me sleep over again, you know!" he had shouted, before gliding away.

They continued to prod Brag halfheartedly, in case the sun had to be fully up or something. The imp kept trying to bite them with his sharp teeth. He had chomped the poking stick enough times to shred it.

Airron did not return immediately, which was a very promising sign. When he finally glided down and landed, before any of the elves he had alerted, he was grinning from ear-to-ear. They didn't have to ask about Peter, the answer was on his face. "He wanted some berry fizz, first thing he said!" Airron declared, hugging Raina jubilantly.

April's eyes squeezed closed. The relief was so great that it felt like pain.

"Really? We did it? Peter's awake?" Raina said. "That's great! Can we stop poking Brag now?"

Brag certainly thought it was a good idea. "Stop poking Brag," he whimpered.

"We'll stop. Now go to sleep," April ordered the imp.

He obeyed instantly and looked almost peaceful, swaying gently in rhythm with his snoring.

"Peter's awake! We did it!" Raina skipped toward the far side of the garden, away from the imp, displaying more energy than seemed possible. It didn't last. She collapsed to the moss in a mixture of euphoric exhaustion.

"Yup, we really did it. Woke up Peter and captured the imp." Salm sank down beside her.

Raina hugged her brother. "It was a good night's work, wasn't it? A great night's work. Mom and Dad can't be mad at us, can they? Airron, did my parents say anything?"

"Um ... they weren't pleased." That had to be a huge understatement. "They'll be here soon, you can talk to them yourself," Airron added evasively. "And Head-Sage Falcon said to wait for him here. I don't know what they'll do with Brag. We captured him—they can figure out what to do with him."

Soon, they were all lying down and relaxing. It was very hard to stay awake. It turned out to be impossible. They were napping when Sage Scarab and Welly arrived with a troop of the King's archers. The whole group rushed out of the trees as if they were entering a battleground, making so much noise that it woke April up.

The new arrivals stopped dead, looking bewildered by the more or less tranquil scene before them. Brag was still sleeping peacefully, if loudly, hanging upside-down in the tree, while his captors slumbered on the moss.

Welly stroked his long white beard into place and approached their foursome. April struggled up and dusted off, and realized exactly how disgusting and sticky she was. She tried to look alert. They were very lucky that Brag hadn't escaped while they slept. That would not have looked very good. Then again, if Brag had escaped, they probably wouldn't be alive to tell the tale.

Sage Scarab stomped up faster than anyone else. "Swear I left you in bed, with orders to stay put," he fumed.

"That was yesterday," Raina pointed out, "Not last night."

"Still weren't supposed to get out of bed."

"Greetings." Welly was more polite when he reached them. "I don't know quite what to say, but I will leave the scolding to your parents, and Clayton. You've had another interesting evening." He tilted his head at Brag. "I see the creature is captured. Well, it is past time to meet this visitor to our world. Introduce me." His eyes were on April.

"Okay, if he'll wake up." April had her doubts.

She was attempting to rouse Brag, when the Pooles arrived on the scene. April pretended she didn't notice when they began shouting at Raina and Salm. She stayed focused on the imp.

"Hey, Brag! Wake up again. If you wake up one more time, you can sleep as long as you want."

Sage Scarab angled his head sideways, trying to see what Brag looked like upside-right. Welly coughed and backed away. It must have been due to the smell. After being exposed to the imp all night, April figured she was immune to it, or her nose was permanently damaged.

Brag cracked his eyelids opened, revealing a marbled combination of leaf green and blood red. He wriggled around helplessly, then settled for glaring and snapping his teeth at his new audience. "Bad bad bad elfies," he whined.

"A good elf wants to meet you Brag, so be nice," April warned him. "Head-Sage Falcon, I present Brag, the imp." She made a proper introduction, in spite of the circumstances.

"Brag, you have been causing great harm in my world, trespassing where you have no right." Welly's voice was colder than April had ever heard it. His words might have been chipped from ice.

"Bad elfies no right, no trample Brag's garden. Elfies for gold, good deal." Brag stuck his long tongue out at the Head-Sage, and squeezed his eyes closed tight.

Welly ignored the gesture. "Why are you here? Why are you hurting elves?"

The imp started snoring so loudly, he drowned out any further questions. It was obviously fake snoring.

"Do not take your eyes off the imp," Welly directed the archers, who moved to circle Brag at a safe distance back, arrows at the ready.

"April, this way." He guided her toward where her friends were still being taken to task, beside the ruined picnic.

April lagged behind. She was too tired to get yelled at. She wanted to go home and get into bed more than anything, except for having a shower. She couldn't wait to scrub off Brag's spittle and the sticky fermented baneberries, and worse. But it didn't look like any of that was going to happen quite yet.

Mrs. Poole leaned over and sniffed April. "You've been drinking fermented drinks," she said

"Um … not really. Brag poured some on me," she said. "We were trying to get him intoxicated, to tie him up, so he couldn't use his hands for magic."

"Those bottles look familiar." Mr. Poole nudged one of the empty bottles with his toe.

"We had to borrow them, for Brag," Raina said defensively. "We shouldn't be in trouble, we're heroes." It was not the right thing to say, nor the right moment to say it.

"You planned this!" Mr. Poole exploded, losing his temper. "It was premeditated! You snuck out of the house again, in the middle of the night, to confront a creature that could slaughter all of you with a flick of his finger. You take our drinks to have a picnic with it! And you believed this to be a wise idea? You … you …" He clearly didn't know what to say next or who to say it too.

"It was the only way to save Peter. There was no other way," April interjected. "It might not have been wise … but it worked." Perhaps it was the wrong moment to mention that, as well.

"But you could easily have paid four lives for one. Four lives for none if your mad scheme hadn't worked."

"But it did work, Dad," Raina said.

Mr. Poole seemed to deflate. He sighed heavily and shook his head, as if beaten.

Welly scooped up April's gold in the awkward moment that followed. "This is your gold, I presume?" She nodded. He handed it over. "Let us discuss this in another location. Over there." He led them away from Brag and away from the picnic mess. "Come, sit down. I need to know everything that you learned from the imp before your parents take you home." Welly inclined his head respectfully to the Pooles. "Sit, please."

They all sank onto the moss and April reported what she had learned from Brag, but it wasn't much. Brag had revealed little that was helpful. She had no idea where the two missing thunderwands were hidden, or why Brag was even in New Haven to torment them. She could offer no proof that Cherry was involved. But they had saved Peter and captured the imp. It was what they had set out to do, and what really mattered.

"Elves have been trampling in Brag's garden? What do you think that means? Where is his garden?" Welly asked. He seemed to feel it was a key bit of information.

"I have no idea. Maybe he'll tell us more when he wakes up," April said.

"Perhaps he will. But what do we do with this imp now?" He looked to Sage Scarab.

Sage Scarab, in turn, eyed the creature. "Can't release him. Too bad he's so disagreeable, could do a lot of good with all that power." He shook his head regretfully. "Think you can reform the critter, Welkin?"

"I regret that I do not believe that to be possible."

Sage Scarab shrugged. "Let's haul him back to town for now, keep him tied up and guarded in the underground chamber. Nothing else for it."

"And don't forget that imps lie all the time," April said. "Imps can't make or keep promises. And keep his hands and fingers tightly tied, he needs them to do his magic. And don't stand too close to him, not that you could. Maybe you could give him a bath, I don't think he's ever had one. And he likes fermented drink, it would keep him subdued anyway." She stopped giving advice when Sage Scarab marched away.

"I won't thank you for capturing the creature. I do not think your parents would approve." Welly actually winked before he strolled after Sage Scarab. A long and uncomfortable silence followed his departure.

"Well, let's get you home. I must stop and check on Peter. You can have a short visit, if he is up to it." Mr. Poole's anger had faded and he simply seemed deeply weary, as if he had been the elf to sit up all night, prodding Brag with a stick and listening to the high-pitched howling.

12. River Surfing

Peter was sitting up in bed and feasting as if he hadn't eaten in a year. He looked embarrassed when his friends crowded in, and shoved his platter aside. His face was thinner and winter-pale, but his eyes glowed with happiness.

"About time you woke up, Peter. You overdid the sleeping in just a tad," Airron complained, trying hard to sound unmoved. Boys were like that.

"I hear I almost slept to death. I had the most boring attack of anyone," Peter griped. But April knew he hadn't. He had suffered terribly in the bottom of the well.

"How are you feeling Peter?" Raina asked.

"Really glad to be awake. I can't wait to get out of this bed." He swung his legs over the edge, bending them around. Peter was shy. Clearly, he didn't want to talk about what he had been through. "So tell me how you woke me up. The last real thing I remember was eating a crab apple for breakfast. I found it on the stoop, all ripe and polished. I thought my mom left it there. It was poisoned?"

"Drugged, almost the same thing," April said

"But how did you wake me up? I thought I was stuck in the well forever."

They took turns entertaining Peter with the details of their adventure. Peter was astonished by the amazing tale. It was a lot more fun telling the story to him than telling it to parents. Airron finished up by describing how they had spent the night tormenting Brag to keep him awake, so that the imp couldn't visit Peter in his dreams. Airron made it sound like a hilarious time had been had by all, except Brag, of course.

"I can't believe that the four of you took on the creature, for me? You shouldn't have, you know. It could have so easily gone wrong." Peter looked worried, after the fact.

"Peter, it's over and done. We beat the imp," Airron said. "Now shut up about it!"

"Right. I won't complain about being rescued." Peter allowed Salm and Airron to pull him stiffly into a standing position. He swayed back and forth before finding his balance. "What day is it, anyway?" he asked.

They actually had to think about it since they hadn't slept a full night in two days. Raina figured it out first. "It's Sunday. Oh, school tomorrow." She frowned in disappointment. The weekend had disappeared.

"So I really did sleep almost a week? Six days," Peter said in amazement.

"Yup, missed one week of school," Airron said. "But I beat you there. I missed the most school."

"Ya, but I don't like to miss school," Peter pointed out. He was walking slowly around his bedroom when Mr. Poole shouted abruptly that it was time to leave.

Raina grimaced. "He's still a little mad."

"He is," Airron said. "I'm going to stay here with Peter. You go ahead."

"We'll visit you after school tomorrow, Peter, if you're not there." April hugged him goodbye, absorbing how alive he felt compared to the last time she had touched him.

"I won't be there, I can barely stand. This is just for show," he whispered in her ear, adding, "You could do with a shower, you're very sticky."

"And probably smelly," April laughed and left the room smiling. Now that Peter was out of danger, it felt like a one pound weight had been removed from each shoulder.

Before she could leave the house, Mrs. Stone wrapped her in a tight embrace, uncaring about April's stickiness and smelliness. "Thank you, thank you, thank you," she said, crying tears of joy.

"I'm just so glad it worked." April hugged her back, sharing her joy.

As it turned out, Peter didn't return to school until Wednesday. And the entire week was peaceful now that Brag was captured. The only problem was that no-one in New Haven knew what to do with the imp. Releasing him was out of the question and they certainly didn't want to keep him imprisoned forever.

Brag's week in captivity soon stretched to a month and the younger elves embraced their freedom with enthusiasm. April didn't worry about the imp, leaving that to the adults.

When Heady came to take her out of Ms. Larkin-LaBois's class on a Thursday afternoon, Brag was the last thing on April's mind. Heady greeted April's teacher in the manner of a dear and trusted old friend, before coming to the point of her classroom visit. "Would it be a problem if I borrowed April for the remainder of the lesson?" she asked.

"Please do. We are completing our family trees. April is doing an alternate assignment and does tend to have extra time on her hands." At that moment, April was helping Peter with his project since he had missed so much school. She was trying to draw some of his ancestors, he was trying not to laugh at the awkward stick figures with really big heads and sticking out shell-shaped ears.

"April, bring your books," Heady said briskly. When April was herded straight out the front door of the school, she got worried. Heady was looking stern, but then she usually did.

"I'm not in trouble am I? I haven't done anything I shouldn't lately," April said.

"Glad to hear it. No, Falcon would like to see you this afternoon. I will escort you to his office." Heady didn't elaborate. When they arrived, Sage Scarab was already installed on one of the luxurious cushions. Heady sat down too, clearly intending to stay.

"Welcome, April, thank you for coming. We have a problem," Welly stated, without the usual niceties. He was looking frazzled, right down to the tip of his beard, which was not in its usual neat curl. "Brag is restrained in the underground chamber of Seelie Court, as you know, but he will not survive our tight security forever and we cannot release him. After a month of imprisonment, he would surely destroy our whole world and every last elf in New Haven, as he delights in informing us. Do you know how far away we would need to transport Brag for our world to be safe?"

April didn't even have to think about it. There was only one answer. "Farther than you could ever take him."

Welly frowned. "Are you certain?"

"Yes, I'm positive. You could never take him so far away that he couldn't come back," she said.

"If we transported him outside the forcefield, would you be able to arrange for a raven to fly him so far away that he could not return?"

164

April shook her head. "A raven would never let an imp get that close. Most forest creatures stay very far away from imps, as far as they can. Brag could probably force a raven to give him a ride, but then he could just as easily make it bring him back here. So that's no help. And I doubt Brag would cooperate. I don't know what would work to get rid of him. Brag's magic is simply too powerful."

"Can you think of any other way to solve this dilemma? Is there anything in the Outer-World that might be of help to us?" Welly asked.

Short of importing a Giant, which would be a hundred times worse than the imp, April had no ideas. "Anything we could do, he could undo. I can't think of anything."

"Well, I would appreciate your giving it some additional thought."

"Okay, I will, I promise. Umm … has Brag spoken about Cherry?" April asked, not sure if she should. Cherry had been keeping a low profile at school. She hadn't started any fights with April or anyone else.

"Brag has not mentioned Cherry. Perhaps the imp was acting alone."

April knew otherwise. Brag had known the names of the five elves that Cherry held responsible for her father's death. And Brag had known all about the wands and where to find them. He had known things only an elf would know. His plotting had been too clever for his brain, and Brag had been staying in Cherry's house. April mentioned all these facts.

"We are well aware, April," Welly said.

"We're not fools," Sage Scarab cut in.

Welly shot him a quelling glance. "We are keeping an eye on Cherry, even though we can only suspect her involvement. However, without Brag, she has no terrible power to commit such dark deeds any longer," he said.

"I guess." April tried not to feel frustrated. But it irked that Cherry had most likely harmed other elves and still sat so smugly in school. "Has Brag revealed the location of the two missing wands yet?"

"The imp has said any number of things, not one of which has proven true. He sends us on a futile hunt every other day. The rods are never where he tells us they are, and it is always a different location," Welly said wearily.

"That sounds like Brag," she said.

April knew she hadn't been any help at all, now or over the last month. She had tried to forget Brag even existed, leaving the adults to deal with the imp. But she knew more about magic and the Outer-World than anyone else in New Haven, and she should be helping.

"I'll try to think of something. Could I speak to you alone for a minute?" April had another question that could not be asked in front of any other elf.

Welly inclined his head. "Of course."

Sage Scarab 'harrumphed' and stomped out, as if personally insulted.

Heady was more understanding. "I must return to school anyway," she said, and closed the door on her way out.

"April?" Welly prompted then.

"Remember the elf that you mentioned before? The elf that … knows things before they happen?"

He smiled. "I do remember. I am not senile yet."

"Has she said anything about this? About Brag? About how it will all turn out?" April really wanted to know.

"Not a word that I can repeat." It was an ambiguous answer.

"Oh. But she has said *something*?"

"Something or nothing. It is often impossible to tell the difference."

"But can't you ask her to be specific?" April pressed.

"It does not work that way." His dark eyes eluded her gaze. "April, she only tells me what I need to know. I do not always understand her visions. She does not always know how to interpret what she sees. It is the vaguest sort of magic, if it is magic at all. I am sure that we will work things out for ourselves. Look what you and your friends have already accomplished," he reminded her. "Brag is no longer endangering New Haven. Our only issue now is what to do with the imp. If you think of anything, please come and speak with me." Welly did raise his eyes then, exposing the same underlying misery as last time they had spoken. April was the one to look away, afraid of what she saw. Maybe the elf who could see glimpses of the future had seen something terrible, and Welly didn't want to tell her.

As much as she did not want to know, April had to ask one more question. "Welly, did Brag say if … if he followed me here? Did I bring him into this world?"

The question appeared to catch him off guard. "April, you have conversed with this creature." She nodded. "Then you know that he will say two very different things in the same breath. His words are nothing but noise to fill the silence, and not to be trusted." He hadn't answered her question. "I do not want you to dwell on this. Think of it no more. If the imp did indeed follow you into our world, you are not the one responsible for his deeds. Now, we will talk again soon, I am sure." He rose.

She was being dismissed. April returned to school and met up with her friends in the meadow. They discussed their weekend plans on the way home. It was fun to have danger-free weekends again, and they were making the most of them.

"River surfing on Saturday!" Raina insisted. April hadn't tried this activity yet.

"Thrills on Blueberry Hill—Saturday night." Airron grinned wickedly and raised one eyebrow.

Raina furrowed her brow. "I don't know Airron. I don't know if we should."

"Sure we should," Airron said.

Salm backed him up. "Sounds good to me." They were ganging up on Raina.

"It would," Raina snapped. "Who would you bring, Salm? Blossom? Sprite or Iris or is it Ivy?" Her voice had a definite bite as she scooted under a droopy branch.

"None of your business."

"Blueberry Hill?" April said. "Wouldn't you want to pick blueberries during the day? I mean, how do you find them at night? Do you feel around in the dark?"

Airron burst into laughter, as if April had said something hilarious. Raina glared at him. "I'll tell you about Blueberry Hill later, April. I promise. So stop asking questions."

"Well, you're going to have to tell her sometime, aren't you? She is fifteen," Airron said teasingly.

"Why do you have to be fifteen to pick blueberries on Blueberry Hill?" April said, even though Raina had told her not to ask questions.

Her friend shot her a quelling glance. "Later, April."

"What should we do Friday night? That's closer." Peter was changing the subject, it was obvious.

"Oh, I've volunteered us all to work at school," Raina mentioned.

"What?" Airron cried. "Work? On Friday night? At school? Are you nuts? And exactly who did you volunteer?"

"Well, the four of us. Not Salm because he's not in our grade. And our grade is doing the Fairy Lights decorations. Almost the whole class will be there to help. It's fun work," Raina insisted.

"There's no such thing," Airron argued.

"Of course there is."

"Is this another festival that I don't know about?" April asked, hoping it had nothing to do with blueberries.

"Didn't I tell you about the Fairy Lights Frolic?" Raina asked in surprise.

"You didn't. I don't know about the Fairy Lights Frolic and I don't know about picking blueberries."

Raina ignored the blueberries. "The Fairy Lights Frolic is a traditional gathering held once a year to celebrate new life and rebirth. It comes after the Harvest Moon Festival," she explained.

"I think you mean it's to celebrate spring, which you don't get in your world," April said. "Although you're missing a season between the autumn harvest and spring. That's when it's winter in the Outer-World, when everything freezes over. Your world has mixed it all up again. How did they forget a whole season?"

"Don't know. We don't have seasons so it doesn't matter." Raina couldn't have been more unconcerned. "Do you want to hear about the Fairy Lights Festival or not?"

"I do."

"First of all, beautiful lights are installed around Blossom Tree Circle. Fairies fly up and string the lights in the trees, which is why they're called fairy lights."

April asked, "Will you do that, Airron?"

"If they need me. Flying is always fun. Always willing to fly."

"See, that's fun work," Raina said.

"The flying is fun, not the work," Airron countered, stubbornly.

"What's Blossom Tree Circle?" April interrupted.

"A special ring of trees, you'll see it soon enough." Raina was more interested in talking about the festival than the location. "Anyway, once upon a time it was the night that fairy brides magically appeared to their husbands for the very first time, within the circle of flowering trees, and all the petals would rain down on them. But that was when marriages used to be arranged by the parents. Only the royal family still make such traditional arrangements. I'm glad it's not a common practice anymore," Raina declared.

"Me, too," Airron said. "Or I'd be stuck with Starla, for sure."

Raina did not deign to comment on that. She continued, "There are all kinds of myths about it being a special night. The most well-known tale is about a fairy called Cupid, who shoots elves with magical arrows to make them fall in love. That's the myth anyway. Nowadays, couples that are planning to wed announce their betrothal on that night and all the elves join in the celebration. But the petals still rain down from the trees, and it's not only fairy brides anymore, but pixie brides and merrow brides—all elven brides." Raina blushed slightly. "But traditionally, fairy brides are still considered the most special. And …" She trailed off.

"And what?" April asked.

"Well, it's hard to explain. For a week or two before the gathering, elves get all goofy—the boys, mostly."

"Goofy?" April didn't understand. Raina was not being as informative as usual.

"You know … I guess you don't know. Before the gathering, elves get really preoccupied with dating. It happens every year. Some elves even get into fights for stupid reasons. The boy elves. And lots of elves decide that they want to get married, all at the same time. No-one can explain why. Maybe it's because of the full moon, or maybe it is Cupid, although no-one has ever seen him or his magical arrows."

"It doesn't sound like the moon or Cupid. It sounds more like a magical spell," April said. "And a really powerful one if it has lasted for thousands of years."

"Really? Could magic do that?" Raina gasped.

"Yes. So we're doing the decorations for this night? When elves get all goofy and fight and fall in love because they are under an ancient magical spell? And they might get shot with arrows?" April summarized. "And it's coming up soon?"

"It is," Raina said. "But I've never thought of it quite that way before."

April had one more important question. "So elves should have started acting goofy already. Um … Raina, do we get all goofy too?"

"No, no, of course not. We're not old enough, and we're girls." In spite of her words, she didn't sound positive.

Walking through the woodland, April thought about this latest festival. She had never before heard of a fairy named Cupid, who made elves fall in love by shooting them. It sounded kind of crazy. She really hoped that this was one myth that held no truth.

"April, why did Heady want to see you?" Peter asked, distracting her from her thoughts.

"Oh, Welly wanted to ask me some questions. They don't know what to do with Brag. They can't keep him tied tight and guarded forever. They wanted to know if they could take Brag far enough away for our world to be safe from him."

"Is it possible?" Peter asked.

"No, nowhere is far enough away." April stopped to tug her braid off a branch where it had gotten stuck. "I don't know what they'll do with him. I'm supposed to think about it. You can think about it too, Peter, if you want. You always have good ideas. Maybe you'll come up with something."

Peter looked pleased to be asked, or maybe pleased to think about getting rid of Brag. They arrived at his path and he said, "I'll think about it. See you tomorrow!" He left with a wave of his hand.

Airron twirled Raina around, stole a kiss and went with Peter. Raina ambled away, a bemused expression on her face. "I guess some of the boys are getting goofy," she said, looking distinctly goofy herself.

Friday night was fun work, Raina was right. Almost the entire class stayed to help and there was as much fooling around going on, as there was actual work being done. Ms. Larkin-LaBois was one of the supervising teachers and Heady had remained behind as well. Mr. Leech apparently felt they could not do without his expertise and muscles. He circulated amongst them, hauling the baskets of fluorescent, glowing flowers that students were attaching one by one onto the long rows of vines stretched to zigzag back and forth across the meadow.

There were thousands of flowers to be tied on, so it was lucky there were so many hands to help. And the tying on process was such a simple task that they could spend the whole time talking. The girl elves were very excited about the Fairy Lights Festival and inclined to giggle. The boys didn't giggle at all and weren't nearly as good at tying on the flowers.

When they were about halfway through the task, Ms. Larkin-LaBois and Heady handed out cups of berry fizz. April stood up to look at the finished section of the vines. They were glowing brilliantly and it looked like half of the meadow was thickly carpeted with rosy stars.

"They really do look great, don't they?" April said in amazement. She had never seen anything like it.

"They do," Raina agreed.

They got back to work and while they tied flowers, Raina organized their plans for river surfing. A number of classmates invited themselves along. Raina didn't mind. "That's great! The more the merrier. Anyone can come," she broadcast.

By the time they finished the fairy lights, it was very late. The forest was as dark as it always was at night. Airron and Peter insisted on walking them all the way home. As soon as the school was left behind, Airron grabbed Raina, tickled her and chased her into the trees. He was acting very silly.

April and Peter walked along more sedately. Peter seemed unsure of himself and didn't talk much, not that he was ever talkative. But since his week trapped in forever sleep, he was even quieter. His body had recovered, but his spirit still needed more time.

"Are you sleeping okay yet?" April asked. The previous week, Peter had confided to having nightmares and trouble falling asleep. He had joked about being afraid to go to sleep, but it probably wasn't a joke.

"It's getting better, slowly. I didn't expect to get over it right away, I don't think it works that way, does it?"

"No," April agreed. She couldn't honestly say that she was completely over her five years alone in the forest, or what had come before. "It takes time."

"Yes, time. Each week is better than the previous one," Peter said, "But I don't think that I'll ever forget."

"No, you probably won't. Some things stick with you. They become part of who you are." April wasn't sure if that was good or bad, it probably depended on the thing itself and how an elf dealt with it. Cherry had taken the death of her father and turned it into revenge and hate against other elves. That wasn't good at all.

"Have you come up with any ideas about how to get rid of Brag?" Peter asked.

April shook her head, idly watching the flickering shadows created by the torch light moving through the leafy dark forest. "No, and I have been thinking about it, a lot. If there is a way to get rid of him, it eludes me. You haven't thought of anything?"

"No, not a thing. And I wish I could. Knowing the imp is still inside New Haven ... well, I wish he wasn't."

"Me, too."

They were almost home before Airron and Raina caught up, giggling and covered in bits of foliage. Airron took the lead then, escorting them gallantly to the front door and seeing them safely inside.

April slept in the next morning. When Raina woke her up to go river surfing, a picnic lunch was already packed. Even Salm was awake and finishing breakfast. They walked over to Airron's house, where Airron and Peter were waiting on Airron's high balcony, basking in the sunshine.

"Ready?" Raina shouted up.

"We've been ready for at least an hour. What took you so long?" Airron stepped off the balcony and glided down to them, since he was robeless. Peter had to march all the way down the spiral staircase, around and around the thick tree trunk, toting the pack. He looked grumpy when he got to the bottom.

Lots of elves were at the river ahead of them. Some were already in the water, balanced on smooth strips of bark while the current rushed them along.

"Is it safe?" April asked, studying the scene.

"Perfectly. That's why we come here instead of Ceyenne Creek." Salm nudged April. "Go get your shorts on. I'll find a strip of wood and show you how it's done!" He headed into the nearest trees.

April tugged her overalls off, already wearing her shorts underneath. Raina pulled off her own top layer of clothes while Airron followed Salm, to search for wood. Peter simply stood like a statue, staring out over the water.

"Peter? Aren't you going to get some wood? To surf?" April asked.

"Will you take a ride with me?" He sounded almost angry.

"Sure, of course."

Peter dropped his pack and marched off. Raina watched Peter keenly for a moment. "April, remember what I was saying about boys getting goofy?"

"Yes."

Salm hurried back before she had a chance to say more. Raina shook her head and whispered, "Later." Clearly, she did not want to talk in front of Salm. He had a worn, flat piece of bark balanced on his head. It was taller than he was.

"I found the perfect piece of surfing wood. Someone must have hidden it here, but it's mine now." Salm yanked off his shirt. "Come on, April. You'll love this. No heights, but there is lots of water!" He took her hand. She must have been moving too slowly.

They raced for the river and Salm showed her the best spot to wade in and catch the current. April perched on the front of the board with her legs dangling in the cool water, filled with anticipation. The sun was beaming down and all around, elves were laughing and chattering. It promised to be a lovely day.

172

Salm gave the wood a shove and leaped on top, all in one motion. He rose and balanced on his feet as the board picked up speed, skimming over the waves. "Try standing up, we'll go faster," he said.

Standing on the unsteady board while it bounced along proved impossible, April was tossed backwards and knocked Salm right off the wood. The current pulled her under and April felt an overwhelming moment of panic, and then she had gills, just like that. Her back hurt a little bit, but nothing like the first time, and she hadn't almost drowned. Getting gills the second time couldn't have been easier!

As soon as April surfaced, she told Salm, "I got gills again. It was really easy this time!"

He grinned back and said, "Then we can go in the faster, deeper water!"

April nodded eagerly. Knowing that she was perfectly safe in the water, she could relax and fully enjoy the activity.

Surfing really was a lot of fun, but not as easy as it looked. April had a hard time staying on her feet and staying on the board because everything moved. The water moved, the board moved and Salm moved. The current was nothing compared to the deadly force of Ceyenne Creek, but it was strong enough to make swimming, and even wading a challenge. April loved every minute. She tried to remember other times when she had felt so content. They were few and far between.

When Peter surfed by and spotted them walking back up the creek, he leaped off his board and waded ashore. "April, ready for a ride with me?" he said, sending a challenging glance at Salm.

April nodded eagerly, she really enjoyed surfing and she was excited about her gills. April had been carrying Salm's board. Peter took it and tossed it carelessly toward Salm. The board almost hit Salm in the head.

Peter ignored Salm's cry of outrage and clasped April's hand. "We'll use my board. Come on." He tugged her toward the creek and right into the water. April scrambled onto the wood and crouched on her toes while Peter got them started. The wood surged forward and Peter reached for April's hands to guide her up. It was unexpected when he wrapped both his arms around her, holding her steady against him. They raced into the rushing wind and spraying water until a ripple knocked them right off the board.

April popped out of the water laughing. "We didn't get very far, did we? We'll have to try that again."

"Fine with me."

They made a number of runs down the river, managing to stay on top the whole way down. Peter was in high spirits, not grumpy as he had been in the morning. When they were quite starved, they waded ashore. Raina was already unpacking the picnic and organizing it on leaves.

April couldn't wait to tell Raina her good news. "I got gills again and they work a lot better now. As soon as I'm underwater, they appear. I don't even have to drown."

"That's great, April. Now we can swim together!" Raina tossed flatbread to the boys. For once, they had brought plenty of food.

After lunch, everyone grouped together. Salm build a campfire. Brag was in captivity so it was perfectly safe. Elves lounged around the flames and dried out, deeply appreciative that New Haven was safe once more and that they could do this at all. Later, there were surfing races. Salm and Ivy proved the fastest as a couple and Finnegan was the fastest alone.

Dusk was falling when they packed up everything and started the hike home. At least this creek was much closer to town than Big Lake. Walking home was not much further than walking to school.

"Well, I'm really looking forward to tonight," Airron said, as soon as they were away from the creek. "Blueberry Hill!"

"Should we have mentioned it to everyone else?" April asked.

"No, Blueberry Hill is not for crowds. It's for small groups, very small groups," Airron emphasized. "Didn't Raina explain anything to you?"

"No, I didn't!" Raina answered for her, "I didn't have a chance, did I? And I don't think we should go there tonight. It's asking for trouble."

"How can picking blueberries cause trouble?" April asked. No-one answered.

"But I've been looking forward to it all day. You're not going to disappoint me, are you?" Airron pleaded. "Come on, it'll be fun."

Raina looked tempted, but still hesitated. "I don't know. I think all you boys are getting goofy. Salm sure is."

"I am not," said Salm.

"And even Peter," she added.

"Don't be ridiculous," Peter said.

"Are you getting goofy?" Raina asked Airron.

"Not any more than usual. Come on, let's go and have fun, Raina," he cajoled her. "We've all been a little short of fun lately, haven't we?"

"True." She really looked torn. "Oh, okay. But I have to go home for dinner first! And you better eat at your own house, I need time to clean up and get ready."

They arranged to meet at the fork in the path after moonrise, then make their way to Blueberry Hill. That was the plan. The fact that they never made it to the hill was not their fault. The blame belonged to someone else entirely.

13. Sticks and Sticks

Dinner had started without them. Mr. and Mrs. Poole were eating alone, with one candle on the table. It was the only small light in the room. The kitchen was almost too dark to see the food. DewDrop was conspicuously absent.

"So, you made it. We thought we would be alone for dinner. DewDrop is at a sleepover," Mr. Poole mentioned, rather curtly.

"We're just going to eat and run. Wow, truffles!" Raina winked at her parents. Salm smirked and grabbed three shells out of the cupboard.

"So, you are all going out after dinner? How nice." Mrs. Poole perked up and pushed the food across the table. They served themselves and gobbled down dinner as if they hadn't eaten all week. "So, where are you going this night?" Mrs. Poole was slowly savoring every bite of the delicacy.

"Maybe Airron's, or maybe Peter's. We'll see where we end up," Raina said evasively. April glanced at her friend in surprise. Why didn't Raina simply say they were going to pick blueberries?

"That's fine, dear. Don't be too late." Her mother didn't question her. Now that New Haven was safe, there wasn't anything to worry about.

As soon as Raina finished her last bite of truffle, she motioned for April to follow her to her room. Raina proceeded to brush her teeth meticulously and change into a pretty red dress. Then she brushed her hair and looked in the mirror for a long time. Lastly, she applied some flower perfume. She made as if to dab some on April, then pulled her hand back hastily. "Best not," she murmured almost to herself.

From her perch on the bed, April asked, "Why are you getting all fixed up to pick blueberries?"

"I want to talk to you about that, before we go to Blueberry Hill. That's why I thought Airron and Peter should go home for dinner. It's lucky they did, actually. I think my parents want to be alone. That was a romantic dinner we interrupted. They're probably being affected by what we talked about earlier. Even though they're old, they still get goofy every year. Now Airron is showing signs. So are Salm and Peter," Raina said in disgust.

"Raina, why didn't you tell your parents where we're going?" April asked. "What's the big deal?"

"It's not a big deal really, but they might not approve. Listen, about Blueberry Hill … " Raina came over and sat beside April on the bed.

"We're not going to pick blueberries, are we?"

Raina sighed before she answered, "No, that's not what elves do on Blueberry Hill. It's a different sort of place."

"Why is it so hard to tell me? Is it something bad?"

"It's not bad, but it is something you don't know about." Raina took a resolute breath and actually opened her mouth to finally explain. Salm had impeccable timing when he stuck his head through the door, impatient to be off.

"What's holding you up? Mom and Dad can't wait to get rid of us. They're about to throw me right out the window. Come on."

Raina glared at him and stood up. "We'll talk later, although it might be too late," she muttered under her breath. She was talking to herself a lot lately.

As soon as they reached the ground floor, they were ushered out of the house like unwelcome ants at a picnic. Mr. Poole shut the door firmly behind them. If the door had contained a lock, it would have been clicked in place.

"Do you think we spoiled their romantic evening? Did they let you grab a torch?" Raina asked Salm. They were stumbling about in the dark.

"Yes, but I don't think I have a flint stone." Salm tripped over something.

"Oh, just give it to April." He did so, and April sparked the torch. She handed it back.

"Thank you so much." He graciously offered his arm for her to hold. April obligingly tucked her own through his. Did he think she needed help to walk? A second torch flashed back and forth, from up ahead.

Airron and Peter were waiting. They always seemed to be ready first. "About time," Airron said, picking Raina right up off the ground and swinging her around until they were both so dizzy, they couldn't stand up. He was getting progressively goofier.

Peter, on the other hand, looked downright grouchy again and glared at Salm. "Five's a crowd," Salm said, an edge to his voice.

"Too true," Peter agreed coolly, moving to April's other side. He tucked her available hand into the crook of his arm.

"I can walk," April said. She was ignored.

They marched along towards Blueberry Hill. Judging by the direction, it must be located on the other side of the town circle. Airron was carrying a bulky sack. He passed it to Peter after he figured he had carried it for long enough. Peter carried it for about five minutes before he shoved it at Salm. Salm did not appreciate the gesture. "I used to like you, Peter."

"Likewise," Peter said curtly. They left it at that and marched forward on stomping feet.

When they reached the glowing lights of town, Salm said, "Cut through the town circle. It's quicker than going all the way around to get to Blueberry Hill."

"Been there a lot, Salm?" Airron snickered.

"Not that much. It's not like I hang out there."

"That's not what I've heard," Raina needled him.

On the opposite side of the circle, they began climbing. The angle of the slope grew steadily steeper, providing a more picturesque view of the town from above. It would have been a lovely hike except that Peter and Salm had started shoving the pack back and forth between them, and shoving each other. They were getting more and more aggressive. April scooted ahead since it was safer to walk alone.

When Salm knocked Peter over with the pack, things came to a head. Peter lunged to his feet with a roar and tackled Salm to the ground. Salm grabbed Peter around the neck and the boys rolled down the hill, swinging fists at each other as they disappeared into the darkness.

Raina simply shook her head at them, placed her hands on her hips and declared, "Super goofy."

Airron nodded smugly beside her. "Aren't they?"

"Why are they fighting over the pack? Are they going to hurt each other?" April cried, distressed. The boys were fighting like enemies over carrying a pack. It made no sense.

April was considering magical ways to stop their fight when something so terrible happened, the tussle was instantly forgotten. She sank to her knees, eyes closed in pain, unable to believe what she was feeling. It couldn't be true, but it was. There was no denying the awful sensation.

"April, what's wrong?" Raina crouched down beside her "Are you upset about the boys fighting? It always happens at this time of year …" She trailed off when April lurched to her feet, shaking her head to clear it.

"Brag," April gasped out.

Raina didn't understand. "Brag?"

"He must have escaped."

"What? Oh no! No, he can't have!" Raina wailed.

"He has. Or else there is another imp in New Haven."

"Oh no! Airron, can you do something about those two?" Raina pointed downhill, where furious cursing and impacting blows could still be heard.

"I'll give it a shot." Airron ran into the darkness.

He was successful, returning with Salm on one side and Peter on the other. Peter had a bloody nose and Salm was developing a black eye, but they weren't fighting any more.

"Brag?" Salm asked, his face looking anguished.

April nodded. It was either Brag or another imp. Her gold coins were on Brag. "I have to go and check the place where they were guarding him. If Brag has escaped, he's going to want to do a whole lot of damage." He would destroy the whole elven realm, and he had the ability to do so.

Salm kicked the stuffed pack that was laying on the ground now. "Let's go, then," he said flatly.

April didn't move. "Listen," she said as firmly as she could. "I'll go alone. There is no point in risking all of us, is there? Brag is going to be really, really mad. Let me go and check out what's happened. Wait here and I'll be right back." Her friends were all healthy and uninjured, more or less. April wanted them to stay that way. And Brag was going to be a nightmare after his time in captivity.

"Forget it. Let's go." Salm took off running.

As usual, April's logic was ignored. They all jogged down the hill to the town circle, faces tight and fearful. April ran faster, trying to be first, at least. The feeling had subsided now, as if Brag had used one great burst of magic and that was all. At least he wasn't tearing a path of destruction through New Haven.

When they reached the town circle, their small group edged between two buildings and crouched in the dark, trying to spot trouble. Everything looked calm. "Where exactly are they keeping Brag?" Peter whispered.

"In Seelie Court. Below ground."

They leaned further forward, bringing that structure into sight. It looked as placid as the rest of the circle. A few couples were sitting by the fountain, arms wrapped around each other. Some were even kissing.

"It doesn't look like anything is wrong, although it does look like Cupid has flown by," Raina breathed softly.

April rose to her feet. "Let's stroll over to Seelie Court as if we don't suspect a thing, and take a closer look. Maybe I am wrong about this. I could be wrong." But she knew she wasn't.

They wandered into the circle as if they had all the time in the world. Even standing right in front of Seelie Court, it presented a perfectly tranquil façade. Venturing inside was the only way to discover what had happened. Gulping hard, April approached the door and leaned against it. The thick wood swung smoothly inward, revealing an empty corridor. They all filed through the archway.

"Shouldn't there be guards around here somewhere?" Raina said.

"Should be," Airron agreed. "Maybe they're below ground." Or maybe something had happened to them. The stairs were located near the end of the corridor. They were dark and unlit. April didn't think that was a good sign. She reached her hand toward Salm, and murmured, "Torch."

He placed it in her hand. She lit it and started forward.

Single file, they descended the long, narrow stairs until they reached bottom and were funneled into the dank, claustrophobic chamber that April knew all too well. Thanks to Drake Pitt, she had spent three awful days sealed inside that prison.

The scene that greeted them took a moment to figure out because it was so absurd. It was definitely the place where Brag had been kept, the lingering stench proved that. It was also obvious that Brag was no longer there. An elf was tied up and gagged in his place. Mr. Leech blinked at them furiously and tried to smile whitely, except he had dirty cloth blocking his mouth.

Raina's jaw dropped in disbelief. "Mr. Leech?"

Two other elves were incapacitated. One was wrapped up in a root that had grown in through a crack in the wall—or it had cracked the wall. Another elf had his head resting serenely in his dinner, as if it was a pillow. He was snoring peacefully. April recognized O'Wing under all the sauce.

April tried to shake him awake while Peter pulled out his pocket blade and cut loose the elf that was trapped by the root.

180

As soon as the elf was released, he pointed an accusing finger at Mr. Leech. No one had been in a hurry to untie the teacher or even remove the filthy gag. "It was him. It was him! Leech did it. Untied the imp so he could stretch his hands. I only left the room for a second." The elf marched up to Mr. Leech, flexing his own fingers as if he intended to strangle the teacher with his bare hands.

Salm did his best to restrain him. "Rocky? Your name is Rocky, right?"

"Ya, it's Rocky," the elf growled.

"Rocky, when did Brag escape? How long ago?" Salm asked urgently.

"Not long. More than a quarter hour, less than a half hour," the elf estimated.

It looked like Mr. Leech was trying to tell them something. Since O'Wing was still too groggy to answer questions, Raina reluctantly removed Mr. Leech's gag, and his restraints.

The teacher immediately slicked his hair into place and smoothed the wrinkles from his clothing, saying with a sniff, "The imp promised he would do no harm, he assured me magic doesn't work below ground."

"Elf magic doesn't. Imp magic is another story. Imps lie," April said.

"Yes, I was warned about that. But the imp assured me that he was not lying this time. In fact, he promised he was not lying," Mr. Leech said.

"Good grief," Raina cried, then took charge, very efficiently. "What's done is done. Rocky, go find the Head-Sage and explain the situation. That would be the most help." She moved him away from the hapless teacher, right out the door.

With Rocky alerting elves that Brag had escaped, Raina addressed the most critical issue. "Okay, where would Brag go? What would he do first?"

Mr. Leech stopped polishing his teeth with his finger, and said, "The imp did go on and on about some metal stick."

"What? Where is the last rod?" Raina cried.

"My Dad said they returned it to the museum, when everything was safe again ..." Airron trailed off in dismay.

April was already running for the door, along with everyone else. It took less than two minutes to reach the museum. They raced into the display room fully prepared for what they would find—or not find. The last rod was gone!

"Haven't we done this already?" Raina wailed, tossing her hands in the air.

"Peter!" April grabbed him. "Can you track it again?"

"I don't see why not." He lifted a torch off the wall and led the way, straight out the back door. They pelted into the undergrowth. Peter immediately veered left around a mossy rock.

"I've got it," he shouted and sprinted harder, pulling away. Salm held the second light and they stayed as close to Peter as they could, weaving through the dark vegetation, still shocked by the sudden and disastrous turn of events.

After an hour of hard running, Peter had very bad news. "Brag is heading for the barrier. He must have hidden the other two devices somewhere near the forcefield."

A distant rumble of thunder confirmed it. It was also a very clear indication of Brag's intent to shut down the forcefield. The sky began to spit rain. The ground turned slick, making it hard to run.

"This evening is not going as planned," Airron bellowed. "How can the imp make the devices work? I thought only you could do that, April."

"I thought so, too. Brag's magic is very powerful, but it's not good magic. If he can make the devices work, I don't know how he's doing it. Although the scroll did say the forcefield was created with more than one magic. Maybe imp magic provides the strongest power. I don't know! Can we make it to the barrier in time, do you think?"

Peter slackened his pace slightly, allowing them to stay together. "We have to try," was all he said.

They ran for another hour and April didn't think she could keep going, but everyone else was managing the feat, so she did, too. The rain worsened and soon, they were slogging through mud. Fighting for energy, April forced her legs to keep pumping while the thunder steadily increased in volume and frequency, and the rain kept pelting down. At least the storm was taking a much longer time to build than when April had used the devices, so maybe they had a chance.

But as fast as they sprinted, it was not fast enough. The storm reached a crescendo before they arrived at the barrier. The wind blew them back, waves of rain almost washed them away, and one blinding bolt of lightning crackled down and lit up the night, illuminating the profile of a jutting hill, the tallest hill to the east—the hill that had caused all of New Haven's problems in the first place. There was a deafening clap of thunder, the ground shook hard and the lightning turned off. The deed was done.

April wanted to sink to her knees in defeat, but she kept following Peter. If they could get the wands back, she could fix the barrier. Or maybe Brag wouldn't be able to pull them out of the hilltop. Drake Pitt hadn't been able too. If Brag couldn't either, they had a chance to put things right.

April was surprised when Peter did not lead them up the hill housing the Echoes. He bypassed it and headed straight toward the barrier, pulling ahead again. He could really run.

"Why this way, Peter?" April shouted, before he got too far away.

"I'm following the devices. Brag must have carried them down already, because they've gone this way. Hurry!"

So Brag had been able to remove the devices and now he was stealing them away from New Haven. Heartsick, April kept running. "Peter, wait. Don't get too far ahead," she called.

He didn't hear her and his torch disappeared from sight. She spun around, surprised to find that everyone else had dropped quite far behind, for no apparent reason. They were even going the wrong way. April turned around and still couldn't spot Peter's torch at all. What was happening? She opted to run back and find out what was going on, since Peter had disappeared.

When she reached her friends, she didn't understand why they were simply standing still. All three looked kind of nauseous. Raina grabbed April when she emerged from the darkness. "Where's Peter?" she said urgently, scanning behind April.

"He got too far ahead and I lost sight of him. Why did you stop running?"

"April, the imp did something we didn't expect," Raina wheezed.

April looked around, she couldn't see anything unusual. "What did he do?"

"The forcefield—it's still on! It's still working, but it's functioning the way it used too. We can't travel through the barrier any longer. We had to stop. Peter will be back in a minute, too. He won't be able to continue."

"What's Brag about? Do you think he made a mistake?" Airron asked, pressing his hand to his chest as if it hurt.

"No." April understood it all in a flash—and it made perfect sense. "No, I don't think he did make a mistake. I think he fixed a mistake. Brag does know how to work the thunderwand. He did exactly what he wanted to do. No wonder Cherry was willing to help him in exchange for harming us. Brag never wanted to shut down the barrier. He wanted to put it back the way it was—the way it used to be. Fix the mistake!" April could have kicked herself for overlooking the obvious.

Salm nodded. "Stop elves from trampling in his garden—the territory outside the barrier. He thinks it belongs to him and elves are walking around out there for the very first time in eons."

"He doesn't want elves in his garden. He wants to trap us inside the barrier again," April said, "Well, you, not me. That's all he wanted." If she had known, she might have helped the imp herself.

Salm propped himself against a tree with a groan, requiring the support. Raina sank down onto a handy stone. They still had to recover from their close contact with the forcefield. "I hope there are no elves outside the barrier now, they won't make it back, will they?" Raina said sadly.

"I heard Ms. Summers was back, and I saw Figgy yesterday at the river, or was that today? Anyway, he disappeared, but he was there," April remembered. Hopefully, no other elves were outside. The novelty had sort of worn off after the initial rush to explore the Outer-World.

"Peter's taking too long. He should have been back by now," Airron said, sounding really worried.

Raina bit her lip and stared ahead, but no torch lit the darkness. "Yes, he should have come back. April, you're the only one who can get to Peter. He won't have long in the barrier, and I don't think he's going to make it back on his own."

"I'll find him. I'll get him out, don't worry." April started running. Her legs nearly buckled under her and she couldn't see. She ran back to Salm, who was holding the last torch. "Sorry, I'll need it to run, its dark." Salm already knew that. She grabbed a stick and stuck one end into the torch until it caught fire. Salm got the stick, April kept the torch. "Make a campfire so I can find you again," she shouted, dashing off.

April retraced her steps to where she had last spotted Peter's torch, and tried to sense him. All she could sense in this pocket of low ground was the Echoes' combined heartbeats, forming the barrier. It masked everything else.

"Slug slime," April swore and kept running, searching as much of the forest floor as she could. It should have been easy to find him, he couldn't have gotten far with the barrier back on. About to search in another direction, April finally spied a pinprick of light and stumbled towards it, terrified of what she would find.

It was Peter's torch and he was lying flat on the ground, struggling for breath. "April," he coughed, "What happened? …the others?"

She grabbed his hand and squeezed. His hand was as limp and cold as a dead fish, and he didn't have the strength to return the pressure. "They're fine, Peter. The barrier has been altered back to the way it used to be. I guess you figured that out?"

Peter nodded and closed his eyes. "Alone again, like … dream," he slurred weakly. "And here you are." He was babbling.

"Peter, we have to get you back inside New Haven. Can you walk at all? If I help you? Can you stand up even?"

He tried to shake his head. It fell to one side. "No, sorry."

"Do you mind if I drag you? I don't think I can carry you. You're pretty heavy."

"Go ahead. Sorry … can't help."

"It's okay. Stop apologizing." April grabbed his ankles and started dragging. Mercifully, Peter passed out and didn't have to witness how slow their progress was. At this rate, it would take hours to get him out of the barrier, and he didn't have hours. Judging by his shallow breathing and blue-tinged pallor, he might not even have minutes.

One second, April was tugging Peter along at a snail's pace, the next second they were both hanging upside-down in midair, arms dangling. Brag was either smarter than the average imp or luckier than he deserved to be. April had not been able to catch Brag, but he had been able to catch her.

The imp looked different from her upside-down perspective, and a bit like a bat. He smiled and opened his mouth wide all at the same time. "April bad elf, bad elf April," he chanted in glee, clapping his hands together. He did not call her a friend anymore.

Panic gripped her, until she looked at Peter hanging helpless, unaware of what was happening. She needed her wits to find a way out of this dilemma. Peter wouldn't survive otherwise. Her own prospects didn't look so good.

Fighting for composure, April met the imp's green gaze. "Greetings Brag. Fancy meeting you here in the middle of the barrier," she said as calmly as she could.

"Playtime," Brag sang, grinding his teeth together as if he was sharpening them.

Imps didn't actually eat elves, did they? The imp pointed his finger at the ground and created a fire right underneath April. Maybe she was about to be cooked, but he hadn't said eating time. He had said playtime.

"What … what kind of playtime?" April stammered

"Playtime playtime." As usual, Brag's answer was no answer at all.

April decided she was better off not knowing and said, "Brag, no more elves will trample in your garden. Why don't you let me and Peter go and we'll never trample in your garden again. Good deal?" It was worth a try.

"No deal," Brag snapped.

The smoke wafted upwards and April choked, it was also getting kind of hot. When she spotted something in the smoky air, April blinked her stinging eyes, trying to see. Bubbles? Yes, three bubbles holding three rods floated into view. No wonder Brag had been able to move so fast, he had floated the devices instead of trying to carry them. Maybe he had floated himself, as well. That thought gave April an idea—a wild idea that just might help Peter.

Brag pointed his fingers at the smoke and wiggled them, creating ten small bubbles in the air at one time, one for each finger. He levitated them up to April and burst them in her face releasing thick puffs of smoke. The imp crowed in malicious delight. He really had a twisted sense of humor. April held her breath and swung back and forth flapping her arms furiously, trying to clear the smoky air.

When she could breathe again, she said, "Small, weak bubbles." She shook her head piteously at the imp, belittling his magic.

Brag pouted. "Only playtime bubbles." He yanked hard on her dangling braid.

"Ouch! Cut it out! Brag could never make big strong bubbles. Bubbles big and strong enough to hold an elf. Brag is too weak," April scoffed, really hoping he wouldn't notice that the three bubbles holding the three wands were easily big and strong enough to hold three elves instead.

"Brag not weak. Brag good at bubbles."

"Brag could never make a bubble big and strong enough to float an elf," April taunted, "Never ever."

"Could so! Brag float April to moon," he threatened, his teeth chattering in anger.

"Yes, float April. Don't float Peter." She was talking like Brag again. "Peter is afraid of … of bubbles. Don't you dare scare Peter," April ordered the imp, trying to sound as bossy as Raina could.

"Will so float Peter. Big bubble easy as teeny-tiny bubble." Brag wrinkled up his snout of a nose and aimed all ten fingers at Peter. Peter stopped hanging suspended in the air and fell into a glimmering sphere that formed in the air below him. Peter didn't even notice, but he looked a lot more comfortable curled in the bubble than hanging in the air. It was also entirely possible that the magic bubble would block the deadly effects of the barrier. Peter did look like he was already breathing easier.

April smiled admiringly at Brag. "It's a beautiful bubble, Brag," she said and meant it.

"Brag good at bubbles."

It truly was a lovely show of magic, especially if it protected Peter. But now April had to keep Brag's attention away from Peter while she got just mad enough to create a slight breeze, blowing towards New Haven. It shouldn't be hard to get mad. Brag did have her suspended in mid-air over a smoky fire.

But first she had to distract him. "Brag was very tricky to escape from smart elf," April complimented the imp. Flattery rarely went amiss.

"Bad elf say call him Wade. Bad elf Wade not so smart. Brag smarter," the imp boasted.

April wasn't going to argue the point. The imp might even be right. "Well, Brag was very clever to escape and steal all the metal sticks and fix the mistake to stop elves from trampling in his garden." The blood must be pooling in her brain because she was starting to feel dopey and dizzy. She needed to feel mad.

"Walking time," Brag said.

"Walking time?" April repeated stupidly.

He flicked a baby finger. April plummeted to the ground. Brag was not thoughtful enough to provide a soft landing, but she did miss the campfire.

"Ouch! Thanks a lot, Brag." The landing had hurt and it did make her mad. April struggled to her feet and dusted off, concentrating furiously on the emotion.

"Walking time. Carry torch." Brag shoved the light at her, then picked up a sharp stick. He poked her in the stomach to start walking. He hadn't forgotten about how they had kept him awake all night.

"Hey. That really hurts! My stick wasn't that sharp," April fumed, her anger growing. The light gust of wind was barely noticeable, but it was enough to move the bubbles—all four of them. April had only been thinking of Peter, yet the thunderwand bubbles floated along with him.

April couldn't have stopped them if she wanted to. Now it was time to keep the imp fully distracted.

April grabbed the stick out of Brag's hand, broke it over her knee and tossed it into the fire. "That stick is too sharp. Find a duller one," she ordered and stomped away from New Haven, away from the escaping bubbles, half-expecting Brag to blast her to bits then and there.

"Brag find better stick. Bigger stick. Sharper stick. Pointier stick. Pointy as teeth stick!" He scoured the ground with curled lips, bent at the waist. April peeked over her shoulder. She couldn't see the bubbles at all in the night sky. They were on their way through the barrier's innermost layer. They were on their way to New Haven. Breathing a little easier, she picked up a nearby stick.

"Hey, Brag? Is this a good stick?" April motioned him over.

He scuttled closer and examined the bit of branch. The imp snorted in disgust, grabbed it out of her hand, threw it on the ground, jumped up and down on top of it, picked it up again, and broke it into eight pieces. He tossed them in the fire.

"Too small. Not pointy like teeth."

"I'll just keep looking then." April bite her lip and almost giggled. It was nerves. Both of them continued to search for a stick for the longest time, until Brag deemed one suitably big enough and pointy enough. He tested it on April's back. She made sure to flinch and cry out in pain, very dramatically.

Brag was delighted. He made good use of his stick to march her away from New Haven. The imp had forgotten all about the bubbles.

While they hiked through the long night, April had a lot of time to think about how to stop Brag from ever returning to New Haven. She wished for Peter's ideas, or Salm's straightforward approach to problems, or Raina's organized thinking, or Airron's confidence. But she only had herself, and a magic too weak to match Brag's power.

The longer April thought about how to stop Brag from revisiting New Haven, the more hopeless the situation seemed. He simply had too much magic. He could do whatever he wanted. The only way he *might* not return was if he believed that the New Haven elves would never trample in his garden again—ever. And he would need the missing thunderwand to ensure that. No, that was wrong. There was more than one way to guarantee that elves never left New Haven again. More than the thunderwand was necessary to alter the barrier. April was necessary. The thunderwand didn't work without April. Without April, they were useless. Without April …

"Without me," April whispered. Finally, she had a solution, but it was the worst one she could have dreamed up. April closed her eyes and wished she had never thought of it. She wished it out of her head, but it wouldn't go.

Brag was content enough for the moment, poking her in the back regularly. But he was not going to be entertained forever. And her back could only bear so much poking with a sharp stick, although April barely noticed the pain now. She was so numb with what she had to do to save New Haven, she couldn't feel anything but heartbroken.

They trudged along hour after hour, until the horizon lightened and glowed orange. They didn't encounter any dangerous creatures since they were still inside the outermost layer of the forcefield, the transitional layer that warned large or dangerous creatures away—the fruit of the peach, as April thought of it.

The sun edged fully over the horizon before Brag stopped walking and got a vacant look on his face, the kind of look you get when you're trying to remember something you may or may not have forgotten. He tugged on his droopiest ear and scratched his head, then scratched it harder.

April didn't want the imp to realize that she'd had anything to do with Peter and the devices floating away, so she tried to look as vacuous as Brag. The imp turned in a circle, then turned an accusing green eye on April. "Bubbles gone."

"Bubbles gone?" April furrowed her brow and spun in a circle herself. "They were here a minute ago, weren't they? I'm sure they were. Maybe they floated ahead? Maybe we were walking too slowly. We should hurry and catch them." She pointed away from New Haven and took several optimistic steps.

"Bad elf April lie. Bubbles not come," Brag snarled and sounded downright feral. It was time to bargain for New Haven's safety.

"Brag, listen. This is important. Very important. Are you listening? This is a very good deal for Brag. Best deal ever," April emphasized.

He jabbed a finger in her direction. Suddenly, she was hanging upside-down, suspended in mid-air again. Brag's eyes turned as red as fresh blood. "Bad elf April lie."

"But I'm telling the truth *now*. Playtime, Brag. Listen, then you'll know I'm telling the truth. It won't hurt Brag to listen for one minute.

You have nothing to lose and everything to gain. Best deal ever. I'll prove it."

He crouched down on the ground, looking bone-weary. "Bad elf talk."

April had to keep her explanation as short and simple as possible, so he would understand. "Brag doesn't need the metal sticks anymore. The thunderwand won't work without me—without April. The forcefield can't be altered without my magic." She gestured at herself. "The forcefield will never let elves leave New Haven again, ever." The last part was almost impossible to say. "Elves will never trample in Brag's garden again, never again ... if Brag has April."

"April sky-eye elf." Brag squinted at her eyes and smiled slowly. He got it. "No April, no magic, no elfies trample Brag's garden. Never ever. April not lie."

"April not lie," she confirmed sadly. New Haven would be safe now. She closed her eyes and waited for whatever Brag would do. Nothing happened for the longest time. April peeked through her eyelids. Brag had fallen asleep, leaving her hanging.

While she had the chance, April tried to use her own magic to escape from her invisible bonds. She was fed up with being upside-down. She concentrated on releasing her ankles in every possible way she could think of. Alas, her magic didn't have any effect. She couldn't even figure out what was holding her up in the air.

April closed her eyes again and hung limply, helpless. A warm trickle flowed down her forehead into her hair. She had never cried upside-down before, and the drops running over her forehead felt weird.

Sleep floated April away like a cloud. It had been a long night and there wasn't anything worth staying awake for now. Her friends would guess her fate when Peter made it back to New Haven in Brag's magic bubble and April did not return. They would know she had faced the imp and lost. But New Haven had won, so it was okay. Maybe she would sleep through Brag blasting her out of existence with his powerful magic. That would be best.

14. Upside-down

"Wakey-wakey time." The sun was directly overhead when the imp prodded her with his favorite stick.

April had a pounding headache from the hours of being upside-down, proving that she was still very much alive. Her head felt all weird and tight, like a lot of invisible fingers were tugging on her hair. She told Brag exactly what he could do with his stupid, pointy stick, too grouchy to care if she angered him.

Brag hugged the stick protectively, as if it was a cherished pet. He even gave it a little kiss and said, "Walking time."

"What are you talking about? Walking where time?" In answer, April got spun in dizzy circles until she was lowered to her feet. At least he didn't drop her on her head, but her head still felt weird. "I really don't like you, Brag. You're mean."

He took that as a compliment and bobbled his head in agreement. He pointed back towards New Haven. "Walking time," he repeated.

"Have you completely forgotten what we talked about last night?" April said crossly. One of them was confused and she didn't think it was her.

"Brag get gold. Lake of gold."

April screamed in frustration, stomped her feet until she jarred some feeling back into them and took off after the imp. Brag had started walking without her. She groped her head, because it still felt strange.

Her fingers couldn't figure out what was going on with her hair. Something was very wrong. It was standing up, stiffly. There were even leaves sprouting off of her hair. "What did you do?" April cried, as soon as she caught up.

"Brag make pretty," he said.

"Did you turn my hair into tree branches?" April shrieked. A mirror would have come in very handy right then.

Brag patted the top of his grizzled, patchy head. "Brag hair not good for playtime. Bad elf April hair long as snakes. Fun for playtime."

At least he hadn't turned her hair into snakes. She felt it more carefully and thoroughly. It did still feel like hair. Maybe it hadn't been turned into tree branches, merely wound tightly around tree branches.

She could figure it out later. She had more pressing matters to discuss with Brag, before they reached New Haven. "Brag, you can't go back to New Haven. Elves will never trample in your garden again, that's the important thing. Forget about the gold, you have me. That's more important." April didn't understand why Brag was taking her back with him anyway, he should be getting rid of her—permanently. Walking her back to New Haven was stupid.

"Brag's gold." He shot a sneaky-eyed sideways glance at her. There was more to this than Cherry's promised payment. "Bad bad elfies. Tie Brag up. Long long time." Brag's lip curled up to his nose when he let that slip.

"Ah. Revenge?" April guessed.

"Playtime," Brag snarled.

It meant the same thing. He wasn't ready to forget about his month in captivity, it seemed. It would take more than offering herself in exchange for the lost thunderwand to get him to leave New Haven in peace. April needed to find another way to stop him. The only bright side was that Brag hadn't yet tried to blast her away. For the moment, he was focused on gold and revenge.

"Brag, why did we walk so far away from New Haven, if you meant to go back?" April had to ask.

"Brag take shiny metal sticks far away."

"Oh." April didn't point out that he had forgotten to bring the shiny metal sticks along. It had been a lot of walking for nothing. And she had another question that she might as well ask. "Brag, did you follow me to New Haven?"

"Brag follow April," he confirmed.

Her heart sank. So all of this had been her fault. "But why?"

"April lead, Brag follow. April go faster." He jabbed her in the back with his stick.

"What? No! Not now. Did you follow me to New Haven before?"

"Before when?"

April groaned in sheer frustration. "Before today. Before now. The first time! The very first time you found New Haven. Did I lead you there? Did you follow me?" How much clearer could she make it?

"Nopey-dokey."

April wanted more than a 'nopey-dokey'. She wanted details. "So how did you find New Haven?"

"Brag follow elf."

"But not me?"

"Not April bad elf."

They were finally getting somewhere. "So who did you follow?"

"Brag not know name. Stupid elf ride snappy turtle."

Figgy? Figgy had led the imp to New Haven. April wasn't responsible after all. She felt great relief, and she didn't blame Figgy, as she would have blamed herself. Figgy knew nothing about the outside world or magic. Leading the imp to New Haven had been an accident. April was just glad it wasn't her fault that Brag had found the elven realm.

They forded a small stream and quenched their thirst. April found a few berries growing on the bank. Brag grabbed them and shoved them into his mouth before she could eat even one. And then they were marching again. It was like the previous night in reverse, and April couldn't think of even a bad idea to stop the imp from reentering New Haven and causing all manner of mayhem in his quest of revenge.

The afternoon was half-over when they crossed through the second and innermost layer of the barrier. April knew they were back inside New Haven, because she almost stepped in the charcoal circle of a recent campfire, exactly where she had left her friends. She stuck a toe into the coals. They were cold. Her friends were long gone.

Brag pointed straight ahead. "You want to get the gold first?" April guessed, hoping that was the case.

"Gold first."

It granted April more time to come up with an idea to stop Brag. If she couldn't best the imp by matching wits with him, she didn't deserve to win.

Brag aimed unerringly for Cherry's old dwelling. He knew the way, even in the darkness that pressed in around them. The moon was fully overhead when they arrived at the lonely, eerie house. April concentrated on the area and it proved as empty as it looked—nobody was watching the place. Elves probably believed Brag was long gone. They were going to be sadly disappointed.

"Up." Bragged pointed with his stick.

April climbed the vines and he didn't make them come alive. She tumbled through the window. Brag scrambled into his nest of leaves, looking happy to be home. April felt a sharp pang inside, as if she had swallowed a thorn. She wanted to go home so badly that it hurt. If Brag fell asleep, maybe she could slip away? No, she couldn't leave him unattended. She had to stay by his side. If the right opportunity presented itself, she could stop his destruction. She couldn't go home yet, no matter how badly she wanted to.

"Brag, where is the gold? What are we waiting for?" April crouched against the wall, halfway between the imp and the bottomless pit, unsure which was the lesser of two evils.

"Elfie bring gold."

He must mean Cherry. "But how will she know you're here? She might think you've left this world, for good," April pointed out, in case Brag hadn't thought of that.

"Elfie know," he said, without bothering to explain how. "Upside-down time. April not escape."

With a flick of the imp's index finger, April hung suspended in the air yet again, feet where her head should be. He really did have a limited bag of tricks, but this time he added an interesting twist. Cackling wildly, he floated her across the room—toward the gaping hole that looked like a Giant's open mouth, hungry to devour her.

"Brag? Oh no! Please! Not over the pit, anything but that. I can't escape from your magic anyway. You know I can't! Don't put me over the pit!" But it was too late, April was dangling over the pit that was so deep, it didn't have a bottom. She couldn't breathe. She screamed instead, for the longest time. When a violent crack of thunder shook Cherry's house, April managed to stop screaming. She fought to regain some measure of control. She didn't want to damage New Haven, especially when she might not be around to repair any magical fallout.

Brag yanked his fingers out of his ears. She must have been really loud. "Brag go away. Brag come back. Then April go away. April not come back. Never ever." The imp pointed down into the hole and snapped his fingers. "No bad elfies trample Brag's garden."

So he hadn't forgotten about getting rid of her after all. He was just biding his time. "No, not down there." April shuddered and couldn't stop shaking.

"Brag go away. Brag come back. Bad elf April go down hole. Bad elf April not come back." He waggled his fingers at her and climbed out the window.

April gazed down into the hole and it felt like she was already falling. The hole expanded before her eyes and reached up to swallow her. The torch slipped from her slack fingers and fell into the black pit, and April fell with it, at least in her mind. It was a relief when the blackness swallowed her up completely.

***

April awoke up in the same nightmare she had left behind. She was alone with the bottomless pit. What if Brag's magic wore off before he came back? What if he never came back and the magic lost power? What if he came back and dropped her in the hole, like he had promised? What if … "Shut up, April," she said, her voice a sob.

"April? What are you doing hanging there? And talking to yourself?" The second voice was definitely not hers, but it was familiar. It was coming from the top of the stairs behind her back. Flickering torchlight moved to light the room.

"Figgy?" she said. Figgy Forester edged around the wall, followed by his two friends. Maybe April was dreaming. "Figgy, Cedric, Robin? Are you really here?"

"Yes, of course. We heard you screaming. We hid as the evil imp left by the window. We came to rescue you. Is that okay?" Figgy sounded unsure.

"It's fine. I do want to be rescued. The sooner the better. Now would be good."

There was a long moment of silence. The torch light was extended closer. "What's wrong with your head?" Figgy asked.

April had forgotten about that. "I'm not sure. I think Brag turned my hair into tree branches. Or wrapped it around tree branches."

"It looks very strange," Figgy said, then turned to his winged friend. "Robin, you want to see if you can rescue April?"

"I'll give it a try," Robin said and rose off the floor. He had a hard time flying in the enclosed space. He flapped hard to stay in the air as he glided towards her. April reached out and he clasped her hand. It felt wonderful to touch another elf's hand. Robin tried to tug her over to solid ground. Alas, her body didn't move. She stayed anchored in place. He

195

had to release her and land before he plummeted into the bottomless pit himself.

"Well, that didn't work, did it?" said Figgy.

"Maybe the imp is the only one who can release me. It is his magic," April said sadly.

"Wait! I have an idea." Cedric hung out the window and rooted around. He came back with a long section of vine. He stepped as close as he could. "Catch!" Cedric tossed one end of the vine to her.

April caught it. "What now, Cedric?"

"Loop the vine around your waist and the three of us will pull. Maybe it will just take more strength to move you."

"Okay. Great idea, Cedric." April wrapped the vine tightly around her middle and knotted it securely. The three elves lined up and dug their heels into the floor, pulling with their combined strength. April should have moved, but she didn't, not one inch. Brag's magic was stronger than muscles.

"Rescuing you is going to be harder than we thought," Figgy said and turned to consult with Robin and Cedric. April could hear the murmur of their voices, but not the actual words. Figgy turned back and said, "April, do you have any ideas? Have you tried your own magic to break free?"

"Yes. It doesn't work against the imp's and Brag said he was going to drop me into the bottomless pit as soon as he gets back." April felt as helpless as her three would-be saviors looked.

Figgy got a funny look on his face, an *idea* look. "Will the imp come in through the window?" he asked.

"Probably. He uses it more than the stairs. Why?"

"Will he return soon?"

"He didn't say. Why?"

Figgy didn't answer. He held a whispered conversation with his two friends. April strained her ears, but couldn't make out a word. "Figgy! Tell me. I'm the one hanging here, over the bottomless pit!" she hissed, stabbing her finger down.

"Quiet! We're working out the details," Figgy snapped, then ignored her. April counted to ten slowly. It was lucky she was stuck in place.

"Figgy!"

"Hang on."

"Did you say that on purpose?" April's voice rose indignantly.

"What? No! We're working on a plan." Figgy turned back to his friends and kept talking. He was the only one. It sounded more like he was trying to convince them that his idea would work.

"Can you tell me the plan?" April asked, after another ten count.

"Fine. Listen carefully," Figgy ordered. "Make sure the vine is tied really tightly around your waist. When the imp comes back, and hopefully he will use the window, and hopefully it will still be dark and hopefully he won't notice the vine - "

It was a lot of hopefullys. "Imps aren't very observant," April interjected, hopefully.

"Okay. Good. We'll hide down the stairs and hang onto our end of the vine. Or maybe we should tie it to something? That might be safer ... anyway, the imp will return and drop you into the bottomless pit and the vine will stop you from plunging all the way to the bottom, not that there is a bottom, well, there must be a bottom somewhere, but that's not important to the plan. As long as the imp doesn't notice the vine in the dark, and as long as he doesn't watch you fall down the hole, and as long as you don't make any noise, we can haul you back up, real quiet!" Figgy gloated smugly over his plan.

"Good grief! You want me to fall down into the pit?" April didn't like his idea at all. As far as plans went, it was highly dangerous. "I really don't want to do that, Figgy."

"You'll only fall a little way into the pit. Do you have a better idea?" Figgy sounded highly insulted that she didn't like his plan.

Cedric asked eagerly, "Yes, do you have another idea, April?" He wasn't very impressed with Figgy's plan either, it seemed.

"I don't. It's really hard to think upside-down. All the blood has rushed into my head. And my hair branches are really tight. They're pulling on my head," April muttered weakly. "What if the vine breaks? What if—um ... did anyone else hear a noise outside the window?"

"Well, I would say it's lucky somebody around here has a plan," Figgy said before the three elves scurried around the pit and dove down the stairs with their end of the vine. April twisted her end around, trying to hide the knot and dangling vine behind her back. It still showed in the torchlight coming from the stairs. Torchlight?

"Figgy! Snuff the torch," April gasped.

Thank goodness he heard her. The room darkened. A rustling noise confirmed that something was climbing up the vines. Her fast-beating heart was pumping so much blood into her brain that it felt about to

197

explode. Her head spinning, April tried to sense who or what was climbing in. She should have checked earlier. It was not the imp, it was elves. They were trying to be quiet, but they weren't doing a very good job. Lucky for them, Brag wasn't lounging in his nest.

Four shadows slipped into the room. "Look, the fire has warm coals, and we heard that thunder noise!" said Raina's voice. April could guess who was with her.

"Maybe Brag came back. Maybe he brought April." Salm sounded really upset.

"I'm here," April called, more than a little embarrassed to be discovered in her present position, bested by Brag.

"April? Oh my goodness, you're okay! Where are you?" Raina sounded so happy. April was even happier, after believing she would never see Raina again. A torch was lit off the coals, illuminating the room. Everyone blinked at April and tilted their heads to the side. They looked funny upside-down, not that they were. And Peter had made it back to New Haven in his bubble. He looked perfectly healthy.

Given the circumstances, it was impossible to share a proper reunion.

"April? What are you doing hanging over the bottomless pit, upside-down? How are you doing that? And what the heck is up with your hair?" Airron asked. Raina simply clapped both hands over her eyes and peeked between her fingers. Salm turned pale.

"That's Brag's doing. He said he made it pretty. And hanging here, it's Brag's magic, and I can't free myself. I have tried, I don't like hanging here, you know." The vine around her waist tugged, reminding her. "Figgy!" she shouted, louder than she should have. Three heads popped cautiously up from the stairs.

"What's going on?" The question came from both sides of the bottomless pit.

Figgy was the one to explain. April didn't try. She was getting another splitting headache from both hanging by her heels and the branches digging into her head.

"April?" said Figgy, when he was finally finished his long-winded explanation.

"Still here, not going anywhere," she said.

"So, we're going to stick with my plan," Figgy said.

"Unless someone else has a better idea. Does anyone?" April asked, and then, "Um ... did anyone else hear a noise outside the window?" She could have cried. She really could have.

Everyone made for the stairs. All the torches were snuffed. Seven elves crowded the stairs now, but they didn't make a peep of sound. April tried to sense who was coming. This time she could sense nothing, and knew it was Brag.

April's nose confirmed the imp's presence before he pointed his finger and restarted the fire. "Bad elf April," he greeted her, as soon as they could glare at each other properly in the light.

"Awful imp Brag," she retorted.

"Drop dead time. Playtime." He rubbed his hands together as if to power his magic, as if he was getting ready.

"Hey, where's your lake of gold? Weren't you meeting Cherry? I mean the unknown elf?" April might as well find out what she could, while she had the chance.

"Secret," Brag whispered, and stuck his finger into his mouth. He sucked on it trying to make a 'shh' noise.

"You're supposed to put your finger in front of your lips, not inside your mouth to say 'shh'," April corrected him.

He pulled his finger out with a wet pop and shuffled closer. "Brag miss April bad elf." He sniffed loudly. "Brag sad."

April thought she heard a snort from the stairs. Brag glanced that way.

"It's okay, Brag," April said quickly, drawing his attention back to her. "You have to drop me in the pit so no more elves will trample in your garden. I understand. Now get it over with. I don't like hanging here. Drop me in the pit," she ordered.

Brag hesitated and tugged on his ear. "April understand?"

"I do. I do understand. I want you to drop me in the pit."

"April sure?"

"Yes. April sure. Drop me in the pit," she ordered.

"April weird. April bossy. Okey-dokey. Brag not watch, Brag miss April. Brag sad." Was that a tear glinting in his eye?

"Good. Don't watch. April won't miss Brag. Brag is mean, Brag hurt April's friends." She closed her eyes, bit her lip and willed herself not to scream. She was falling before she realized that she had been released from her magical bonds, and she did scream. She couldn't help it. She dropped for what felt like an eternity. Worse yet, there was something alive in the pit. It tore across her back and landed on her shoulders, clinging tight with sharp talons. The thing was only dislodged when she jerked to an abrupt stop, on the end of the vine. It had held!

April bounced against the side of the pit several times, dislodging chunks of packed earth. The lumps made it sound like she was continuing to fall and fall and fall. "No bottom, I knew it." Upside-right again, April pressed her forehead against the cool earth. She touched her back with a shaking hand to make sure the pit creature was really gone. Her fingers felt only her own clammy skin, damp with fear. Whatever had landed on her wasn't there now.

Nothing happened for the longest time and April clung to the wall unmoving. It was great to be upside-right again. "Bright side," she whispered and waited to be hoisted back up, petrified of what lay below. Still nothing happened. Maybe she was supposed to climb out of the pit herself. There had not been enough time to go over the smaller details of Figgy's plan. And surely Brag had left the house by now.

Tired of waiting, April grabbed the vine, dug her toes into the side of the pit, and strained to haul herself upward. She climbed silently. It was a peculiar pit, aside from being bottomless, because the packed earth went all the way up to the top floor of the house. It shouldn't have done that. There should have been more house under the top floor, not earth. Oh well, April had enough to worry about without trying to figure out the mysterious pit.

When she was almost at the top, the vine started to move. April was dragged up the last couple of inches and over the edge onto solid floor.

"April! Brag left." Raina put an arm around her shoulder. April clutched her friend as if she would never let go.

"Raina! It's so good to see you and … and … are you sure Brag's left the house?"

"Yes, he packed some things in a sack and went out the window. He looked really sad after he dropped you down the hole. I don't think he wanted to stay here anymore." Raina's voice was barely audible and no torches were lit, to be safe. Brag's fire was burning low again, April must have been down in the pit longer than she had realized.

"There was something alive in the pit," April gasped. "I think we should get away from here, talk at home. I can't wait to get home."

"Yes, everyone better come. Figgy, Cedric, Robin, you too. Maybe my parents won't kill us if we have company. We snuck away again," Raina confessed. April couldn't believe it and started to laugh.

They numbered eight when they rushed through the forest on light feet. Salm led the way with only one torch, held low. No-one knew which direction Brag had taken and they certainly didn't want to run into him by accident.

The moon was directly overhead when they tiptoed into the house. They needn't have bothered with stealth. Mr. and Mrs. Poole were waiting at the kitchen table, looking like two boiling storm clouds. The parents weren't expecting such a large group—and they weren't expecting April.

"Oh my goodness!" Mrs. Poole leaped up from her cushion. "April, you're back, unharmed! You're here!" She embraced April tightly, then pulled back and gazed at April's head. "What's wrong with your hair?"

"Brag played with it. I'm hoping he didn't turn it into tree branches," she said.

Mrs. Poole touched the weird hairdo. "No, your hair is only woven around branches, a lot of branches." She gave her head a little shake. "We were thinking the very worst, when you didn't come back, when the imp ... and then the rest of you disappeared, yet again, sneaking out of the house." She was starting to sound mad, working up a head of steam.

"Welcome home, April. Are you uninjured? Aside from the hair?" Mr. Poole asked, in case she needed healing of some sort.

"I'm fine. But really hungry."

Snacks were set out. Figgy, Cedric and Robin were greeted and urged to sit and eat, too. April feasted and told her story. She revealed the bad news, that Brag had returned. "I was hoping to convince him not to come back, but I couldn't," April said with regret.

"And now the imp is here?" Mr. Poole sounded fed up.

"Yes. For revenge, because we held him captive. And for his payment of gold. That's why he came back."

"Ah. Did you see Cherry meet with the imp or present him with gold?" Mr. Poole asked. April shook her head. "Did you see the gold?" April kept shaking her head. It was the imp's word again, without any proof.

Figgy was eager to talk about his role. "We saw the evil imp for ourselves, but he was alone in the forest. We rescued April from him. It was my plan that stopped April from falling down into the bottomless pit," he emphasized.

April hadn't gotten around to expressing her gratitude. She had been too busy eating. "Yes, my thanks Figgy. It was a great idea. I may have had some misgivings, but it worked perfectly. You saved my life, all of you. You were really brave against Brag."

Figgy shrugged nonchalantly, as if he saved lives every day. "Well, best be off. It's getting late." It wasn't getting late, it was late. Mr. Poole walked the elves out. Her friends looked nervous again. They expected to get in real trouble now.

"April, you said there was something alive in the pit? What was it?" Raina might have been truly curious or she might have been trying to delay her mother's wrath.

April had almost forgotten about the mysterious creature in the pit. She reached over her shoulder and felt her back.

"I don't know. It felt like it cut me with talons or claws. But I can't feel anything now. Do you see anything?" April swiveled on her cushion so Raina could check.

"No, there aren't any marks. I wonder what's down there. It's an unnatural pit, isn't it?"

Mr. Poole returned and surprised them by not shouting or even saying a word about grounding them forever. "Get some sleep, all of you. I am going to wake the Sages and the High Court. I will let them know that you are safely home, April. Falcon was most upset by your disappearance, well, we all were. Now we must find a way to deal with this imp once and for all, before he takes his revenge on New Haven. We will also have to hide the three rods at once, perhaps in three different locations," he mused.

"I don't think you have to worry about the rods so much," April said.

"Why not?"

"Brag knows that I'm the only elf in New Haven who can make them work, and he thinks I'm down the pit. He believes the wands are useless now."

"I think we will hide the wands, regardless. In case you encounter Brag again, if you sneak out of the house to confront him. Need I say more?" Mr. Poole arched an eyebrow.

"Uh, no," April mumbled. Hiding the rods was a very good idea after all.

Still in his nightshirt, Mr. Poole headed for the door. He didn't get far. Sage Scarab walked in without knocking, probably because it was the middle of the night. He stomped into the kitchen and glared around the table. His eyes widened on April's head, but he didn't comment. He had more important matters on his mind. "April, glad you made it back. Bring the imp with you?"

"No, the imp brought me with him."

"Shame. Critter's like a rotten smell—determined to linger. Matter of fact, that's not far off, is it? Marsh, we better rouse everyone. The mayor will want to hold a gathering, middle of the night won't matter." Sage Scarab stomped out. Mr. Poole hesitated to follow.

"Go, I'll make sure these five stay put. Airron and Peter, you'll have to sleep over. Marsh can let your parents know you're here." She walked him to the kitchen door." Be careful, dear. And do get dressed." Mrs. Poole kissed him on the cheek and then followed him out, probably to make sure he didn't forget his clothes. The room was silent for a long minute.

"Whew, I think we got off *really* lightly," Raina said.

April sagged into her pillow, exhausted. She couldn't wait to sleep late the next morning, then she remembered, "Oh, we have school tomorrow, don't we?"

"Unless school is cancelled. It might be cancelled," Raina said.

"Not a chance." Airron yawned.

"Come on, April. Bedtime. You look done in. And you won't be able to sleep with tree branches on your head. We'll have to cut your hair off, or untangle it."

"I don't want to cut it off. It can be untangled, can't it?"

"Let's give it a try." Raina followed April upstairs.

April finally had a chance to look in the mirror and see what her hair was doing. It was standing up a lot higher than she had realized, and laced with cross branches. Leaves and flowers sprouted off the branches. In spite of how ridiculous it was, it did look rather pretty. Brag was something of a hairstylist, it seemed. But to rest her head on her pillow, it had to come out.

Raina got to work, untangling April's hair from the network of tree branches. It took a long time. When she was finished, Raina looked done in herself. She tossed the branches out the window into the lake.

"Thanks, Raina. You should get to bed. You look exhausted."

"So do you. At least now you can sleep."

"Yes, and I'm so glad to be home." They shared a long hug, said their goodnights and went to bed. They slept for the whole night. The parents must have been delighted. The weekend was over and they never had reached Blueberry Hill.

15. Fairy Lights and Flower Petals

School wasn't cancelled, not even for one day. Nothing terrible happened on Monday or Tuesday or Wednesday. As the weekend edged closer, it was as if Brag had vanished into thin air. There was neither hide nor coarse hair of the imp. New Haven was almost as tranquil as before Brag. Only one thing disrupted that peace—the boys at school kept acting goofy and getting into fistfights.

There was some debate over whether Saturday night's Fairy Lights Frolic would still take place. A gathering was held in town to decide the matter, and most elves were thrilled when it was announced that the celebration would go ahead as scheduled.

In recognition of the special night that they would be participating in as young adult elves (Mrs. Myrrh's words), Sports class had become dance class. The whole week was devoted to the ancient art of fairy dancing. On Monday, the teacher reviewed the basic steps used for most dances. Everyone knew them except April. On Tuesday, the whole class performed the easiest circle dances. No-one messed up, except April. On Wednesday, the steps became more involved, elves had to weave in and around long lines of other elves, hand linked together in a long chain. There were a number of collisions and lots of falling down, mostly because of April. But it had all been good fun. No elves were injured in dance practice.

On Thursday, Mrs. Myrrh paired students up for couples dancing, which required elves to follow steps with their partner, as well as dance around in a set pattern with the other couples. Mrs. Myrrh partnered April with Seamore, which did not turn out to be a very good idea. April was the most inexperienced dancer and Seamore was the most uncoordinated, unless that was April as well. The pair was constantly mixing up all their classmates, dancing every which way.

After one too many collisions with other couples, Mrs. Myrrh split up April and Seamore. April got to dance with Gil and Seamore was sent to dance with Aurora, who didn't look at all pleased with the new arrangement. April had a great time after the switch. Gil guided her lightly around the meadow, always knowing where to spin or kick or leap. All April had to do was follow him and remember her basic steps.

"You're a really good dancer," April complimented Gil.

He smiled and tossed her into the air, in unison with all the other couples. "I've been dancing all my life. I don't even have to think about it."

April wondered if she would ever get that good at dancing, and doubted it.

On Friday, the dancing became truly challenging. It was still couples dancing, but it was further complicated by switching partners many times right in the middle of all the steps. April was fine when Gil was guiding her around, but when she had to remember the moves herself, she was hopelessly turned around. She even ended up trying to dance with Cherry, who shoved her into a cluster of dancers, messing up the entire class.

Then Ray and Cosmo began fighting with each other over who got to dance with Starla. Cosmo even punched Ray in the nose, knocking him flat. Mrs. Myrrh simply sent the boys to opposite sides of the meadow and resumed dance practice without missing a beat.

By the end of the class on Friday, April didn't feel at all prepared for dancing under the Fairy Lights. She needed a lot more than one short week of practice. She needed about a year.

April and Raina walked home alone, since Airron had stayed at school to do more fun work. Fairies were needed to fly around and string the fairy lights into the trees. Peter and Salm had also remained behind, to haul the vines around on the ground while the fairies strung them into the branches high above.

"It gives us time to get ready tonight," Raina told April, hurrying her along.

"Get ready for what?" April asked.

"For the dance, tomorrow."

"But that's tomorrow. Why do we have to get ready now? It's not like getting ready for the gathering where you got your gills, is it?" That had taken hours and hours.

Raina smiled. "No, it's not as bad as that. Tomorrow, we'll wear traditional fairy clothes, so we need to get them ready. And we should wash and style our hair, and stuff like that. It's fun to get ready," she stressed. "And I'm fifteen this year, so it's different. Airron and I are going on a real date. I want to look pretty."

"You always look pretty." April was usually a mess, but Raina tended to be well-groomed at all times.

"Thanks." Raina looked pleased by the compliment.

"Do boy elves do the same thing?" April asked curiously.

"Well, I'm sure Airron will change his robe. But it's not the same for boys," Raina explained. "They get goofy and fight. Girls get dressed up. It's just the way it is."

"If you're going on a real date with Airron, who should I go with?" April asked.

"Yes, that is a bit more complicated. We never had our Blueberry Hill talk. I guess now is as good a time as any." Raina wrinkled her nose and looked very resigned to what she was about to say.

"What does picking blueberries have to do with dating?"

"Well, it's like this ..." Raina began, but didn't get any further. A nearby fern trembled. April had forgotten to check the forest. She tugged Raina backward, in case it was Brag.

But it wasn't Brag. Figgy popped onto the path, with Robin and Cedric on his heels. The three elves seemed to spend all their time wandering about the woodland.

"April, there you are, we were looking for you. Greetings, Raina." Figgy strutted up, not nervous of April at all now that he had saved her life. He should have been leery of Raina, who looked like she wanted to stuff him down a mole hole for interrupting her.

"Hi Figgy, Cedric, Robin." April hadn't seen them since the evening she had escaped the bottomless pit.

"A quick word, April, over there. In private." Figgy took her arm proprietarily and moved her away.

"Oh, sure." April went down the path with Figgy, curious about why he wanted to speak to her alone.

"April, as you know, the Fairy Lights Frolic is fast approaching," he began.

"Yes, tomorrow."

"Don't interrupt. Since I saved your life, I think you should go with me." It was not a request, he had already decided.

"You mean ... like on a date?"

"Yes. Well, you are pretty famous around here, and it would look good to have you on my arm. Impress everyone. A real hummingbird feather in my acorn cap, if you know what I mean. And I did save your life. I'll pick you up at seven."

April didn't know what to say. "Um …"

"Yup, seven on the dot. Don't be late. Dress pretty." Figgy turned on his heel and sauntered away. Without another word, he retrieved his companions and disappeared into the wall of greenery.

April stood rooted. It looked like she had just agreed to a date—a real date. She didn't know if she wanted to go on a real date with Figgy, but she was fifteen. She should probably be going on a date, like Raina. But with Figgy? He was awfully bossy. Oh well, he hadn't really given her a chance to refuse.

April noticed Raina watching her, bug-eyed. "Did Figgy ask you on a date?" Raina demanded. April didn't know how she had guessed.

"Yes, to the Fairy Lights Frolic. Although he didn't really ask, he kind of told me I was going with him."

"And what did you tell him?"

"Nothing much. He didn't give me a chance. He's picking me up at seven."

Raina gaped. "You're going to go with him?"

"Well, he wants me to go with him and no-one else has asked me."

Raina shook her head and started laughing really hard. "Well, that solves one big problem," she muttered, almost to herself.

"What problem?"

"You know what? Never mind. Let's go home and get ready, now we have two of us to fix up. It will take twice as long."

"Maybe longer," April said. She needed a lot more fixing up than Raina. There was no denying it.

They passed the time until dinner in Raina's bedroom, examining her traditional fairy clothes. She dug out some smaller ones for April and insisted April try them all on. Every last article of clothing was green. It seemed to bring out the green streaks in April's hair. "Do you have any other colours?" April asked, not sure that she should be wearing the particular hue. She didn't like it when her hair looked green. New Haven elves never had green hair.

Raina plucked at the skirt of April's costume to flounce it up. "Traditional fairy clothes are green. That's the only colour they come in."

"And are they all so pieced together, so layered?" April examined herself in the mirror. It looked like she was wearing leaves, as if she was camouflaged.

"Yes, that's the style." Raina held up two similar outfits. "Which one should I wear? This one or this one?" They both looked the exact same—leafy and green.

"The one on the left?" April guessed.

"That's what I thought, too." Raina tossed the rejected outfit aside and laid the chosen one flat on her bed.

"You know, Raina, I think the tradition of these clothes comes from my world. We only wore clothes that helped us blend in with the forest, so we could remain unseen and safe. Leafy and green … in the summer anyway," she stressed.

"You weren't leafy and green when we found you. You were wearing fur, smelly fur." Raina grimaced in remembrance.

"Yes, but that wasn't by choice, I had nothing else to wear and it wasn't summer in the outside world. And you didn't find me, I found you," April said.

"We found each other. Good thing, too. Now, we need to make two crowns of flowers, to wear over our hair. If we find some flowering vines, we can coil them around then add more flowers. It's the easiest way. But we should do that tomorrow, so the flowers don't wilt." It sounded like more camouflage.

"Which costume should I wear?" April asked, not able to tell if one was better than the other.

"Wear the one you have on now. It's definitely the prettiest." Maybe she was guessing, like April.

They stored away the rejected clothes and April returned to her bedroom to change back into her normal shorts. She draped the fairy outfit over her window ledge for her first date—with Figgy Forester.

There was a real dinner waiting downstairs, even though it was Friday. The main course was the egg-shaped fruit of the water lily flower. Mrs. Poole said it was a delicacy. It tasted like popped corn and was very filling. DewDrop was really excited about seeing the fairy lights and the flower petals rain down. It was all she talked about until she put so much food in her mouth that she couldn't speak at all.

"Will Salm be home for dinner?" Mrs. Poole asked Raina. They had started eating without him.

"He should be. Stringing the lights doesn't take all night. Airron and Peter might come back with him."

"Of course," Mr. Poole murmured dryly. He got up and added more shells to the table. The three boys rushed in halfway through the meal.

"I'm starving, that was hard work," Salm said, settling on his cushion and serving himself a huge portion. "You wouldn't believe how heavy those flower vines are when they're all coiled up."

Mrs. Poole cleared her throat, it was a hint. Salm handed the shells over to Peter and Airron. They matched Salm's heap of food.

"How did it go? Decorating the trees with lights?" Raina asked Airron.

"I did a great job. The fairy lights have never looked so well-placed," he boasted. "But we're not finished yet, this is a dinner break. We have to go back for another hour or two. It will be the best display, ever. You'll see for yourself, tomorrow night."

"I'm looking forward to it," Raina assured him.

Salm stopped eating and looked straight at April. "Are we all going to go together, then?"

Raina glanced at her brother, her eyes dancing with mischief. "No, we're not. Airron and I have a date, we'll be going alone. And April has a date."

Salm turned to glare at Peter, Peter glared back at Salm. "I thought we were all going together," Salm said.

"Not to the Fairy Lights Frolic. Not now that we're fifteen," Raina declared.

"When did you ask April?" Salm demanded of Peter.

Peter looked confused. "I didn't ask April. When did you ask her?"

"I never asked her."

Airron looked from one to the other, and grinned. "Interesting. April, who asked for the honor of escorting you to the Fairy Lights Frolic?"

"Figgy," she said.

"Figgy?" Salm gasped

Peter stared at her blankly. "Figgy? Figgy Forester?"

"Yes, Figgy. He asked, sort of ..." She trailed off.

Salm looked affronted. "But he's a year older than me."

"And he's ..." Peter apparently didn't know what Figgy was.

"A stranger?" Salm supplied.

"A stranger," Peter agreed. April looked between them in confusion.

"And he's kind of annoying." Salm was not being very nice.

Peter scowled darkly. "He is annoying—very annoying."

"Figgy is not a stranger. He's kind of nice, sometimes. And he helped save my life last week," April reminded them. "And he asked me to go. No-one else asked me to go. I've never been on a date before." They knew that, of course. She certainly hadn't expected Salm to ask her, he

209

was like her brother. And she hadn't expected Peter to ask her, they were close friends. Then again, she wouldn't have expected Figgy to ask her, not in a thousand years. Maybe it was the goofy affect.

Mr. Poole shared a concerned glance with his wife. "Figgy is a year older than Salm."

"Yes, he is. Perhaps you should all go together, even though you are on dates," Mrs. Poole stated firmly. The 'perhaps' really didn't apply.

"But Mom, that's not fair!" Raina cried indignantly.

"You are lucky to be going to the gathering at all, given the number of times you have snuck out of this house with the sole purpose of placing yourself in jeopardy. It would not be wise to argue about this," her mother warned.

Raina was smart enough to drop the subject, but she made it obvious that she was disgruntled by staring sullenly at her plate.

"Raina, you have talked to April about dating, haven't you?" Mrs. Poole said.

Raina sighed and looked up. "Not really. Almost. I keep trying and someone *always* interrupts."

"Well, I suggest you do it before tomorrow. And you will all go together." Her decision was final.

"Me too?" DewDrop asked. She had been watching them talk with an avid expression.

"No," her father snapped. "You are much too young, thank goodness. Your mother and I will take you. We will all be at the gathering," he stressed.

Raina slumped in defeat, but she had dug the hole of worms for herself.

The three boys ate quickly and rushed off to finish decorating the trees with lights. Raina dragged April upstairs to finish preparations for the dance. And talk, it seemed. "I think I better tell you about dating. Or else my mother will do it." Raina made that sound like a horrendous alternative.

"Okay." April sat down on her bed ready to listen. Raina joined her. First she nibbled on her lip, then her fingernail, as if lost for words. April had rarely seen her lacking words.

"Is there a secret ritual involved in dating?" April guessed, to help Raina out.

"No, not really. I think I'm supposed to talk to you about kissing and stuff."

"Kissing? Do elves kiss on dates?"

"You've never been kissed, have you?" Raina asked frankly.

April shook her head. "Not really. You and Airron kiss?" April had seen them, lately.

"We kiss," Raina confided, as if it was a secret.

"Because you're dating," April concluded. It seemed simple enough. Apparently it wasn't.

"Well, there's kissing, and there's kissing." Raina wrinkled her nose. "Maybe my mother would be better at this."

"You're doing okay. Elves kiss on dates." It couldn't have sounded easier.

"But you don't have to kiss, only if you want to," Raina stressed.

"Okay, elves kiss on dates if they want to. I can do that. But I don't think I want to kiss Figgy." April thought she understood perfectly, until Raina started pacing.

"The kissing is usually on the lips," Raina warned her.

"Your Mom and Dad don't kiss on the lips."

"They probably do in private, but I really, really don't want to think about that!" Raina paused for a moment. "That should be all you need to know for now. That went well, didn't it?"

"I guess." It didn't sound like a big deal. Raina hadn't said much. She had barely said anything.

"Except …" Raina had forgotten something.

"Except what?"

"If an elf gets fresh, you can slap him," Raina explained. "But not too hard. And don't lose your temper, you wouldn't want to strike him with a firebolt."

"Fresh?" April didn't know what that meant. She understood fresh fruit and vegetables, but not fresh elves.

"Um … if an elf tries to do more than kiss or kisses too much. You'll know if it happens. Let's talk about something else."

"Okay. What does it feel like when Airron kisses you on the lips?" she asked, curious.

"April!"

"What? I'm only asking. I don't know any of this stuff, do I?"

Raina stopped pacing and sat down. "I know you don't know this stuff." She sighed. "That's a hard question to answer. It feels right, like we belong together. And Airron's a good kisser, not too wet. Kind of … oh, it's hard to explain. But that reminds me, if you are going to kiss, you do want fresh breath. You can keep a piece of mint leaf in your pocket and chew it before you kiss. But remember to spit it out first, secretly. You don't want your date to see you spitting stuff out. You don't have any more questions, do you?"

"Chew a mint leaf, spit it out. Kiss—on the lips, if I want too. No, that's it," April decided, except … "Is that what elves do on Blueberry Hill? Kiss?"

"Yes."

"But elves can kiss anywhere, can't they. All you need is lips. Why go to a special place?"

"Because it's romantic," Raina stressed. "Blueberry Hill is supposed to be very romantic—for kissing. You don't have more questions, do you?" It sounded like an order.

"No," April said.

"Good, great. Okay, let's finish getting ready then." They completed preparations for their dates and went downstairs for a snack before going to bed early, since Raina said they would be up very late the next night. Mr. and Mrs. Poole called them into the sitting room before they reached the kitchen.

"What?" Raina asked shortly. Was she expecting more warnings about the frolic?

"Did you have that talk with April, honey?" her mother checked.

"Yes."

"Good, good." Mrs. Poole didn't ask for details. Kissing was obviously a topic elves avoided talking about.

Mr. Poole reached into his pocket and pulled out the gold chain with the crystal vial. "April, I thought you might like this back, for tomorrow night. It comes from your world, so you should have it. It belongs to you, more than any other elf." He placed the chain into her hand and April stared at it. The chain still made her feel sad, it was a tangible reminder of a whole world that had been lost.

She slipped it over her head to join her own gold chain. The cold crystal against her warm skin made her shiver. "My thanks."

At seven the next evening, Raina, April and Salm were ready and waiting in the sitting room. The first knock sounded precisely on time. Mr. Poole answered it for them. Peter and Airron strode in wearing almost identical leafy green clothes. The main difference was that Airron wore a shorter than normal robe and Peter wore a vest and shorter than normal pants. And Airron wore a smile, while Peter wore a moody scowl.

"Are we here first?" Peter demanded, peering around.

"You are," Salm needled him. "Sweet of you to be so punctual. Are you my date?"

A second knock sounded before Peter could respond. It was probably a good thing. Based on Peter's expression, the words he was about to produce might not have been very polite. Peter certainly seemed to be more affected by this infamous night than the other two boys.

Mr. Poole ushered Figgy into the room. "Greetings. April, you look ... very traditional. Let's go." He backed towards the door, anxious to leave.

"Okay, I'm ready." April made to follow him.

"Figgy, may I have a word with you?" Mr. Poole asked politely, motioning towards the kitchen. Figgy had no choice but to go along, not really. Mr. Poole steered him into the kitchen like a cornered cricket. Raina was having a hard time not laughing.

"How come he never did that to me?" Airron asked.

"My father knows you a lot better than he knows Figgy. And I know a little bit more about dating than April," Raina said.

"Hey, I thought you told me everything I need to know?" April interjected.

"Well, there's knowing and there's ... *knowing*. And I only told you about introductory dating," Raina said.

Salm raised his eyebrows at his sister. "Introductory dating? Are you teaching classes? What did you tell our April?"

"Mind your own business."

Salm grinned wickedly. "Hey, I should be the one teaching classes, I have a lot more experience at dating than you. I could even demonstrate."

"Ya, I've heard all about your experience. Girls talk," Raina hinted.

"Nothing but good things, I'm sure."

"Not hardly. Why don't you make yourself useful and go rescue Figgy. Once Dad gets started, he doesn't know when to stop. We'll wait in the front garden."

Salm didn't emerge with Figgy for another five minutes. Mr. and Mrs. Poole followed and waved from the door, calling, "We will see you at Blossom Tree Circle."

"As if we could forget," Raina grumbled under her breath.

Figgy immediately tossed an arm over April's shoulders and yanked her close. It felt like she was in a headlock. Figgy wasn't tall for an elf, he only came up to Peter's eyebrows, and Airron's chin. But he was still taller than April, and wiry strong. April stayed where she was, guessing they were supposed to walk like this on a date.

Airron observed them and tucked Raina's arm through his. Salm eyed both couples and stepped towards Peter.

Peter sidled away. "Don't even think about it. I am not your date."

Salm gave chase—around the garden and down the path. When the rest of them caught up, the two boys were winded and dirty, it looked like they had been wrestling. At least there was no blood.

Raina shook her head in disgust and they continued on their way, blending into the forest that surrounded them on all sides. The leafy green camouflage worked especially well in New Haven, which had an abundance of flourishing growth.

Figgy talked nonstop when Salm asked him what he was doing now that he had finished school. After a twenty minute monologue about doing almost nothing, he asked Salm the same question.

"I'm not finished school yet." Salm looked momentarily troubled. "This is my last year and I don't know what I want to do. I don't want to be a Healer like my father. I'd faint if I had to look at a lot of blood, or even a little blood." He shuddered. "I can't decide what I want to do, that's the problem. And I'm running out of time if I want to arrange an apprenticeship with any elf other than my father."

Discussing their respective futures lasted all the way to the magically lit circle of trees. April stopped listening to Figgy's latest monologue about himself and stared around the perfect ring of straight, white trunks. These trees didn't even look like trees. Aside from being too white and too straight, they had no leaves at all, only pure white blossoms. The flowers grew so thickly, the branches appeared coated in snow. It was a fantastic sight, enhanced by the countless vines of fluorescent pink blossoms. They had been woven around and around the ring of trees. The enclosed circle of ground was so flat and smooth, it could have been mistaken for the surface of a still pond.

Blossom Tree Circle was a magical place, straight out of traditional elf lore. As soon as April stood within the ring, she could feel the magic seeping out of the ground beneath her feet and shimmering in the sky above. New Haven elves probably couldn't feel the magic in the same way, but they sensed the place was very special. It was reflected on their faces.

"Wow," April breathed in awe. It was so much more than she had expected, and the trees hadn't even started raining petals yet. She couldn't wait to see that.

"It is beautiful, isn't it?" Raina whispered reverently. She glowed in this place. All the elves had a similar aura.

"It is." April was unable to tear her eyes away from the trees.

"She's never seen it before," Raina remarked to Figgy, excusing April.

Figgy smiled warmly at April. "Oh, that's true, isn't it?" He looked a lot more handsome all of the sudden. He seemed taller and his carrot orange hair gleamed golden. April blinked, trying to clear her eyes of the shimmering haze of magic. She looked at each of her friends in turn, Raina was stunningly beautiful and all the boys were perfectly handsome. Every last elf looked almost too good to be true. No wonder fairy brides were reputed to appear to their husband for the first time in this place. A love match would be guaranteed.

Raina turned to Airron. "You were right, you did a super job with the flowers. The circle has never looked better."

"I did it for your eyes alone," Airron vowed romantically. Was his behavior also being influenced by the magical circle?

"Hey, he did have some help you know," Salm grumbled.

The pair ignored him, having eyes and ears only for each other. April wouldn't have been surprised to see Cupid hovering overhead, firing off his arrows of love.

"April, let's dance first. I want everyone to see us together. We can eat later." Figgy didn't offer her a choice and wasn't acting mushy like Airron. Maybe elves had to feel true affection to be influenced in that way.

A dozen flutists provided the music for dancing, evenly spaced around the perimeter of the circle. They were wearing pink robes and crowns of pink flowers. Pink and white seemed to be the dominant colours for the evening.

"I'm not a very good dancer," April warned Figgy.

"Well, do your best. I'm good enough for both of us." Figgy pulled her into the position for couples dancing and started them moving with a flourish of fancy kicks and leaps. Figgy proved as light on his feet as Gil. April followed him easily, feeling graceful herself, especially when she looked up into the magically lit trees spinning overhead when she whirled. No, it was this place—even she could dance better than usual here.

"You're a really good dancer," April told Figgy.

"Told you. You're not doing so bad yourself." They kept dancing and April felt hypnotized by the trees. Figgy was the one that called a halt once everyone had seen them together. He guided April over to tables of finger food and drinks, where they loaded a leaf with fancy bites, then shared them.

When April spotted her friends, she urged Figgy over to join them. Together, they watched the other dancers flow by as the circle filled up with elves.

"Hey, there's Sage Scarab." April was surprised to see him dancing gracefully and not eating. She recognized the elegant white-haired Sage Rose in his arms. Welly passed by in his wake, sedately spinning Heady.

"Oh!" Raina exclaimed, clamping a hand over her mouth to suppress laughter. They all followed her wide-eyed gaze. Mr. Leech was whirling by, partnered with a statuesque elf in a costume as tight as his own. She had almost as much hair as April, but it was very curly and very blonde and piled very high on her head. Both impressive elves danced around with their chests thrown out, April was surprised that there was enough room for two such large chests in the small space between their arms. All the boy elves got a little bug-eyed when Mr. Leech steered his dance partner in their direction.

"Greetings." He looked truly magnificent tonight and dimpled at his date. "Hope you don't mind meeting a few more of my admiring students. Sorry, I don't remember your names." He waved a breezy hand over all of them. Airron ducked quickly, he had come within a fraction of an inch of being felled by the bulging arm. "Rocks-Anne DeVine, more of my admiring students."

April glowered at him, since he was the elf responsible for setting Brag free to harm New Haven and hang April upside-down over the bottomless pit. She was definitely not an admiring student. She couldn't be less admiring if she tried.

The boys gawked at Rocks-Anne. Her tight costume seemed to be missing some leafy green layers from the upper front and center. They gulped out, "Pleased to meet you."

"Likewise, I'm sure," Rocks-Anne drawled, her smile rivaling Mr. Leech's for sheer perfection. "Wadey, are we going to get that drinky. I swear I am absolutely overcome." She flapped her hand around over her heaving chest and fluttered her lush eyelashes like bird's wings. Surely the dancing hadn't been that strenuous?

Wadey Leech and Rocks-Anne DeVine strutted away. They certainly were an eye-catching pair and many elves turned to stare when they passed by.

"April, do you want to dance?" Peter asked. "Figgy, you don't mind?"

Figgy said curtly, "Well, just one, make it quick."

Peter escorted April through the crowd of elves to the center of the circle. The dancing was now so crowded that there was no pattern to the movements. Elves moved wherever there was room. Bodies pressed around on all sides. It was cozy and claustrophobic at the same time. At least April didn't mind being squished into Peter, better than Figgy who she did not know very well, and wasn't sure she liked overly.

"Are you enjoying the frolic?" Peter asked.

"Yes, I can't wait to see the petals rain down." April looked up, but nothing was happening yet.

"The petals fall at midnight, on the dot. Still a couple of hours to go." Peter whirled her around into an opened space. April kept twirling until she got dizzy. After their dance, Peter returned her to Figgy, but Salm intercepted her.

"April, my turn." Salm was an enthusiastic dancer, spinning April all over and almost colliding with countless couples, and he kept making her laugh. It was fun to dance with Salm. April returned to Figgy, so winded that her much smaller chest was heaving in a fair imitation of Rocks-Anne DeVine's.

The hours until midnight flew by. April danced mostly with Figgy, since they were on a date. A number of couples announced their betrothal beneath a mistletoe canopy set up for that very purpose. Then those couples performed a moondance around a pole, holding onto colourful ribbons while a choir of elves serenaded them, their pure voices joined in perfect harmony. April wondered if that unearthly sound was because of the Blossom Tree Circle magic, too.

And when the full moon rose directly overhead and beamed down into the very center of the circle, every single flower petal drifted slowly to earth, carpeting the ground in a thick layer of perfumed white. It looked like giant snowflakes in the soft glow of the fairy lights. April stood transfixed until the very last petal tumbled through the air and a cheer replaced the profound silence that had fallen over the crowd.

"Wasn't it breathtaking?" Raina asked, leaning against Airron with his arms wrapped around her from behind.

April nodded, that was certainly one word for it. "Raina, you do know that this is a very magical place and a powerful spell makes all the flower petals fall together, don't you? No wonder elves want to get married when they come here. The circle makes elves glow with outer beauty and dance with grace. This place has so much magic, I'm surprised Franken didn't torch it ages ago."

"April, what are you talking about?" Raina asked blankly. Her starry eyes were blinded by the circle's spell.

"Never mind."

Apparently the dancing was finished because it would have been hazardous to spin around on the slippery carpet of petals. The youngest elves began pushing the petals into huge piles, helped by their parents. They ran at the piles, leaping high and landing softly, only to disappear completely when they were buried inside them. DewDrop was in the thick of the activity, giggling and rolling around in the petals. April was tempted to join her, it looked like the most fun. But she was fifteen and on a date. It probably wouldn't be considered appropriate behavior to play in the petals with DewDrop.

The oldest elves left first, calling goodnight as they faded into the trees. Mr. and Mrs. Poole wandered over to see if they were ready to depart, and to check on them. It was obvious. "We will go ahead and meet you at home. Don't be long and stay together," Mr. Poole cautioned, handing Salm an extra torch. DewDrop started whining about wanting to stay with them. She whined all the way out of sight. She was overtired.

"Let them get farther ahead," Raina murmured, standing motionless until they couldn't hear DewDrop any longer. Then they meandered through the forest, in no hurry to end the evening. They could sleep in all they wanted the next morning.

Raina sighed happily. "It was such a lovely night. I'm glad Brag didn't do anything to spoil the gathering."

"I don't think he could have done anything inside the circle, even if he wanted too. There's way too much good magic, I've never felt anything like it. The ground is soaked with it." April didn't know how else to describe the circle's powerful aura, and not one of her friends had been consciously aware of the magical ambiance.

"April was babbling about that before," Raina said in an aside to Airron.

Figgy tossed his arm over April's shoulders again. He walked slower and slower, April had no choice but to match his snail's pace. Raina and

Airron strode ahead, and Peter and Salm went with them because Raina kept shoving them along. Soon, April couldn't see them at all. And she was all alone with Figgy.

Figgy looked down at April with a smirk. "So, did I show you a good time?"

"I had a nice time. The falling petals were amazing. Why did we slow down?"

"We're on a date." He leered. "It is expected that we would want to be alone."

"Oh. Is this when we kiss, if we want too?" April asked Figgy nervously. She had forgotten to chew a mint leaf.

Figgy frowned and peered at her face in the torchlight. "Kiss? You want me to kiss you? For real? I suppose I could do that, I guess."

"You *guess*?" April might have been feeling insulted. Figgy certainly didn't seem eager to kiss, he made it sound like a chore. April didn't want to kiss him, but wasn't he supposed to want to kiss her? April tried to pull free. She was getting a crick in her neck.

"No, I can kiss you. I can do that. Can't wait to tell my friends that I kissed you. Looks good on me. Come here." He yanked her closer with his eyes closed and his lips puckered. He looked funny. Is that how elves were supposed to kiss? Raina hadn't said anything about closing your eyes and puckering your lips all up. Suddenly, Figgy's eyes flew open and he backed off. His strangling arm released her.

"You stopped. Did I do something wrong?" April asked.

"You did lots wrong," he said. "But that's not it. It's ... I'm not used to looking at light blue eyes—caught me off guard. I've spent my whole life looking at dark eyes, so light blue eyes are ... kind of weird. And when we get so close, they seem bluer, brighter, like lights. It's off-putting. And that green hair is strange too. Looks greener tonight, for some reason." Figgy was not making a whole lot of sense, but April understood him perfectly.

She was definitely insulted and hurt now, even though she hadn't really wanted to kiss Figgy. "Was I supposed to shut my eyes, like you? So you wouldn't have to look at my weird eyes?"

"Good idea. Close your eyes and I'll try again." Figgy tugged her closer, almost setting her on fire with the torch.

Enough was enough. April shoved him away, hard. "Forget it, Figgy. Keep your lips away from me or I'll strike you with a firebolt!" she said, struggling to control her temper.

Figgy back off then, and kept his lips to himself. "Cripes, no need to get mad. You should have closed your eyes in the first place, is all. I probably could have kissed you if you'd closed your eyes like you're supposed too. You've never kissed before, have you?" He made it sound like an accusation.

April shook her head. It was probably pretty obvious.

"Well, do a better job next time and someone will probably kiss you." Figgy paused awkwardly and cleared his throat. "You can find your way home from here, can't you? I've got further to go, so I'll take the torch. Night." Figgy strode away without a backward glance, leaving April standing alone in the dark.

If this was a typical date, she was not impressed. But she didn't mind the minutes of solitude. She felt a little bit like crying for some reason. Figgy couldn't stand to kiss her because she was different from all the other elves in New Haven—because she had weird eyes and hair. Cherry had said repeatedly that April's eyes were ugly. But April couldn't help having blue eyes, it wasn't something she could change. And the only way for her to not have green hair was to cut it all off. She certainly didn't want to do that. She couldn't help being different.

April started walking and tripped over a pebble in the middle of the path, hurting her toes. She limped slowly through the darkness, deeply regretting that her first date had ended on such a sour note. When she reached home, her friends were sitting outside in a relaxed circle. Nectar had been poured out and fireflies gently lit the area. April stomped up and sat down with a flounce.

"Where's Figgy?" Raina asked.

April mumbled, "Gone home."

Raina looked like she was dying to ask what had happened, but she didn't. Airron did. "What happened? Did you send him packing? Give him the old heave-ho? Did he get fresh?"

"I don't know what fresh is, and no, I don't think he got fresh. I think he got the opposite of fresh," April bit out. She might have pouted.

"Now, now, what went wrong?" Airron scooted over and pressed her head onto his shoulder, overly commiserating.

"Stop it. I want to be mad." But April allowed her head to stay where he had placed it.

"Did Figgy get fresh? Did you have to slap him?" Raina gasped.

"No. There was no kissing. And how come you didn't tell me that you have to close your eyes when you kiss? And pucker your lips all up?" April demanded.

"Did you forget to tell her to close and pucker? That is basic Introductory Dating information," Salm told his sister. "You can't kiss without puckering."

"How come no kissing?" Airron nudged her with his elbow.

"Because Figgy prefers brown eyes, I guess. As if there's something wrong with blue eyes, as if blue eyes are too weird to kiss," April huffed with renewed indignation.

"Well, Figgy's a fool, isn't he," Salm proclaimed. "Don't pay any attention to him. He doesn't know what he's about. There's not a thing wrong with your eyes, quite the opposite."

"Did he just leave you in the forest?" Raina asked incredulously.

"Yes, and he took the torch, although I did threaten to strike him with a firebolt," April admitted.

For some reason, everyone thought that was hilarious and started laughing. As always, the laughter was contagious and April started laughing with them.

She didn't feel sad or hurt or angry around her friends. They never seemed to care or even notice that she was different. When the laughter finally stopped, she said, "You know, I don't think I want to kiss or date yet, anyway. I like things the way they are. I like having friends better than dates." She wanted to simply enjoy having friends for the first time. And she'd never had a childhood, not by any stretch of the imagination. So she didn't have to act fifteen if she didn't want too. She could jump in piles of flower petals if she felt like it. There was lots of time to be fifteen. She could wait until she was sixteen or seventeen or eighteen.

16. Heap of Gold

A second week passed by with not even the faintest whiff of Brag. It was a lovely respite from all that had come before, but unexpected. Brag had disappeared as if he had never been. April was pleased that he was missing, yet at the same time, his mysterious absence unsettled her. She couldn't walk through the woods without jumping at every shifting shadow, and the forest floor was a patchwork of shadows.

Now that the Fairy Lights Frolic had come and gone, elves were level-headed again. The boys had settled down. There hadn't been one fistfight at school. All the previous safeguards were back in place. No elves were allowed to walk home from school alone, and once they got home, they had to stay put. There were no trips of any kind. 'House arrest' Raina called it. She was chafing against the lack of freedom, and had grown quite testy and inclined to throw small objects.

Cherry, in contrast, remained suspiciously subdued at school. She came to class every day and did her work, as if it was the most pressing concern in her life. She was so placid, it looked like maple sugar wouldn't melt in her mouth. As far as April was concerned, that wasn't logical either, unless Cherry knew something they didn't, something about Brag. Maybe Cherry knew that he had left New Haven for good, but Cherry couldn't report such news since she had denied knowing the imp. If she had given Brag his gold, he might have left. And he did believe that he had gotten rid of April permanently. Maybe the imp had decided that was revenge enough.

On Friday, Airron and Peter had arranged to go to Raina's house instead of directly home. As they walked along with Salm, Raina huffed about her parents being too over-protective. "Brag's been gone two weeks. Two weeks! He must be gone for good! How much longer do you think we'll be stuck at home? Until we're fifty?"

"Poor Raina, life's tough!" Airron laughed.

"I almost wish the stupid imp would show his grizzled, gray snout and get it over with," Raina said testily.

Airron did not agree. "Bite your tongue," he said succinctly.

"Do you really wish that Brag would make an appearance?" Peter's question sounded serious. His expression was hard to read.

"Oh, I don't know. I do and I don't. I hate all this waiting and being cooped up. But I guess Brag is worse, isn't he? Why?"

"No reason." Peter had gotten very tight-lipped and a deep crease had appeared between his eyes.

Raina stopped walking and turned to face him. "Peter, why did you ask then? It's not like we could find Brag, even if we wanted too. He's not at Cherry's house and April can't sense him, can she?"

"No, she can't."

"Peter!" Raina stomped her foot, ready to start throwing him around. As much as he tried to hide it, Peter knew something he was not telling them.

Salm was the one to rescue him. "Raina, he'll tell us if he wants—if he thinks we should know. Give him a break. Come on." Salm started walking faster, they weren't supposed to linger anywhere but safe home.

Peter took a few steps and stopped again. "Maybe I should tell you. I don't know what to do about it." He sighed as if the fate of New Haven was his alone to decide.

"Peter?" April was truly curious now, especially when he wouldn't meet her gaze and looked downright guilty and a little bit shifty.

"What?" he asked, still undecided.

"Are you going to tell us this big secret or not?" Raina shouted in frustration.

"Sorry," Peter apologized. "But if I am going to tell you, it should be here. Not at your house. We've been safe the last two weeks, this could change things." He spotted a comfortable ledge of white fungus on a nearby tree trunk and went to sit on it, his legs dangling. It was large enough for all of them. They surrounded him.

Raina spoke first. "Peter, how could things change?"

He said, "April."

"What?" she asked.

"No—April." He repeated her name in a different way. He wasn't talking to her, he was talking about her. "April's safe now, isn't she. Brag thinks she's gone. And April is the one who would have to confront Brag, if we knew where he was, and I don't think April has a chance against the imp's magic." Peter looked shamefaced when he said this, but it didn't hurt April's feelings. She held the same opinion herself, in spite of Welly's words of support. "We were lucky to catch Brag the first time, I don't think we would be so lucky a second time, if we knew where he was. Think about it," Peter said.

"Oh." Raina got it. All of them did. Peter must have some idea where Brag was hiding, but he didn't want April to face the imp again.

"You know where Brag is?" April was afraid to hear the answer.

"I might. I'm not positive. I know *something*," Peter revealed. "I've known something for a couple of weeks." He had seemed distracted at school. April had assumed he was still recovering from his own encounters with the imp. But it was more than that.

Raina wasn't mad anymore, she was scared. "Peter, what do you know?"

"It's the gold. There's a lot of gold where there didn't used to be any gold. A whole heap of it has been sitting in one spot for almost two weeks, not moving. I've sensed it." With his thumbnail, he absently carved a design into the soft white fungus that was their couch. "It is a lot of gold."

Airron was flabbergasted. "And you haven't claimed it?"

"Of course not, Airron. It's probably Brag's gold, or Cherry's gold. It's not my gold. And it's an important clue. I'm not about to go and tamper with it, am I? I don't know what to do about it. And now you know, too."

Every eye fixed on him for a long moment. He had been carrying this secret for a long time and he hadn't told even one of his closest friends.

"Should you inform the Sages?" Raina asked.

"No," Peter answered decisively. "I think the gold is better left alone for now. Everything is safe and quiet. They'll only want to hold a gathering anyway. That never seems to help."

"Where is the gold, Peter?" April asked. It would have to be checked out, by her.

Peter didn't answer, he looked at Raina. Raina shook her head firmly. "No. We don't need to know. New Haven is safe, let's leave it alone. Don't tell anyone where it is, Peter. Especially April. As long as our world is safe, leave the gold alone."

A relieved smile lit Peter's face. "That's what I thought." He had shared his burden, it was lighter now.

"But - " April was cut off after the first word.

"No buts!" Raina shoved April off the fungus. "Not another word. Let's go." April went, but she planned to discuss this heap of gold with Peter as soon as Raina's pointed ears were out of range.

It took a surprising amount of effort to get Peter alone. Both Raina and Salm kept a close eye on April over the weekend and even Peter avoided being alone with her for even a minute. By Sunday, April was convinced that her friends knew what she was plotting and they were refusing to cooperate. It was frustrating. She only wanted to go and look at the gold, nothing more. What harm could there be in looking at a pile of gold? She wasn't about to take any. And it was unlikely that Brag would be hanging around the gold after so long. Maybe the gold had been abandoned, which would mean something had happened to Brag. It could confirm that the imp was gone for good, couldn't it?

When April finally did get to talk to Peter alone, she had Prince Skylar to thank. It happened on Tuesday when Salm stayed at school for a detention and Airron had to fly directly home because his mother was hosting a special family dinner for a couple of stuffy old aunts and uncles (Airron's words). Peter walked April and Raina all the way home, not sure how he would get to his house later, but after two and a half Brag-free weeks, they were all feeling more secure.

The three friends were stepping into Raina's front garden when Skylar swooped down out of the sky. "Head's up!" he shouted in warning.

"Skylar!" They were all delighted to see him, it had been too long since the last occasion.

"What are you doing here?" Raina asked, but welcomingly.

"Nothing but a visit. I've missed you, all of you." He meant Raina in particular. It was obvious he still had a special regard for Raina, even though any future between them was impossible. Raina didn't have wings and never would. Skylar's important position as future King made it impossible for him to date any elf, unless they had wings. Prince Skylar had not even made an appearance at the Fairy Lights Frolic, and April suspected that was because Raina was dating Airron.

Raina led Skylar along the shore. "Has your father been keeping you busy?"

"Yes, more than is warranted. He says it is because I am getting older." Skylar pulled a face.

"Well, we've been busy with Brag, I suppose you've heard all about it?"

Raina and Skylar continued to chat, they had a lot to catch up on. And April seized her opportunity, she locked arms with Peter and steered him in the other direction. Peter dug his heels in but April was very determined. She had been trying to get him alone for days. "Peter, I want to talk to you," she said, trying to sound as bossy as Raina could.

"I know. I don't want to talk to you. Not about the gold. Not about the location of the gold. I'll talk to you about anything else, but not that." Poor Peter sounded desperate.

"At least tell me if there has been any change—any action with the gold?"

"No." He tried to tug free.

She held his arm tighter. "No you won't tell me? Or no there hasn't been any change?"

"No change," Peter said.

"Oh. None at all?"

"Not even one small nugget. Can I go now?" He gave his arm another tug.

April did not let go. "No, not yet. So, is the gold close to here?"

Peter glanced around for help, but Raina and the Prince had forgotten all about them. Peter was on his own. He shrugged. "Depends what you mean by close."

"Peter, I don't want to do anything about the gold. I only want to look at it, for clues. It might tell us if Brag has disappeared. I mean, no-one has even gone to look at it, have they?" she assumed.

Peter flushed all the way up his forehead and down his neck. The tips of his pointed ears reddened. It was a flood of red. "Have you visited the gold?" April accused, outraged.

"No. Maybe. Oh, all right, yes," he confessed with obvious reluctance.

Peter had visited the gold, and he must have gone alone. He had placed himself in peril to protect her. "Peter, you shouldn't have. That was a really risky thing to do! I can't believe you did that! When did you go?"

The red deepened. "Uh … at night."

"Good grief! You went alone? At night? That's just stupid." April felt deeply angry with Peter. After all he had been through with Brag! He had almost died twice—and he had gone to visit the gold alone, at night! It felt like she was about to lose control of her temper in a big way, a big stormy kind of way. She might have to jump in the lake to cool off. April shut her eyes and counted to ten, breathing slowly. Counting really did help.

"April? Are you mad at me? Please don't be mad at me."

April sat down on the shore abruptly and Peter joined her. He ran sand through his fingers and waited for her to speak. It was her turn. "I'm more scared when I think about what you did. Scared and mad, sometimes they go together."

"Well, I feel scared when I think about you taking on Brag again, but I think he is gone. The gold is sitting there, undisturbed. I didn't try and touch it or anything. I watched it from a distance. It does look abandoned, but I don't know what that means."

"I think it means Brag is gone. Peter, I would like to go with you to see the gold, maybe I could sense something," April said. "You've proven its safe by going yourself. So now I can go. We won't tell anyone else, we can go together." April thought it was a perfect plan.

Peter didn't. He shook his head adamantly and said, "No!"

"No what?" Raina had snuck up on them, with Skylar.

"Nothing. Have a seat." Peter was transparently relieved to have the company and scooted over to make room, even though the entire expanse of the shore was free for the sitting. The four friends crowded close together and enjoyed a visit until dinner.

April was frustrated by the interruption, but fully intended to continue her conversation with Peter before he left for home. She figured it would be easy to get him alone again, since Prince Skylar was inclined to usurp Raina's company when Airron was not around.

It didn't turn out to be easy, it turned out to be impossible.

Both Skylar and Peter ended up staying for the meal. Mrs. Poole was unnaturally flustered and kept apologizing for the food, even though it was delicious. Prince Skylar had that effect on elves. As soon as the meal was over, both boys left together. April didn't have a chance for a private moment with Peter.

April briefly considered telling Raina what she had learned from Peter, but decided against it. She wasn't ready to give up, and still hoped to persuade Peter to take her to see the gold. In spite of her determination, however, it took two more days to get Peter alone again.

This time, Ms. Larkin-LaBois was the elf who orchestrated the opportunity. The family-tree project was finally finished and the teacher asked April and Peter to carry all the large bark squares to their home classroom, where they would be tacked on the walls together with the merrow and fairy family-trees.

"Sure, we'll take them," April said, speaking for Peter, too.

They gathered the projects from tabletops around the room. April expected some scathing comment from Cherry when she collected the elf's work. Cherry didn't even notice, the elf was napping at her table with dark circles under her eyes. She looked exhausted. Maybe she wasn't sleeping well because she was feeling guilty about her actions. April hoped so.

When they passed by Raina's classroom, they could hear Mr. Leech droning on about the tenth generation of Leech's. April had to hurry away when she started giggling. Even Peter stopped looking anxious and laughed.

They stored the projects in the corner of the empty classroom and April nabbed Peter's sleeve when he looked ready to run. "Peter -"

"No."

"But I didn't ask anything yet," April pointed out.

"No," he repeated.

"But you don't know what I'm going to say."

"I do so." He probably did.

"But Peter ..."

"No."

April was starting to get mad at him again. "At least tell me if there has been any change with the gold. You can tell me that, can't you?"

"I guess. There's been no change," he admitted.

"And you haven't gone back to see the gold again, have you?" April pressed, worried that he might have.

He smiled ruefully. "No, and I don't think I could. Once was scary enough."

"You were very brave to go alone, Peter. But it wouldn't be scary if we went together. The gold still hasn't moved, so it must be safe to go and look at it. Right?"

"It has been a long time." Peter looked undecided. "Maybe it would be safe to go and look. Let me think about it, okay?"

"Well, don't think too long. And stop avoiding me when I want to talk to you. It's not very nice," April told him.

Peter sighed and looked at April as if she was a few trees short of a forest. "I always want to talk to you. But I want you to be safe even more. Come on, April. Ms. Larkin-LaBois will think we've gotten lost in the school."

"Oh." She didn't know what to say. Mr. Leech was still talking about the tenth generation on their return trip. "How can he still be talking about

Leeches? Hasn't he run out of ancestors yet? How many Leeches can there be?" April whispered.

Peter thought for a moment. "Tenth generation? Two parents, four grandparents, eight great-grandparents, sixteen … thirty-two … sixty-four…"

"How many in the tenth generation?"

"One thousand and twenty-four, I think. Yup, one thousand and twenty-four." He chuckled. "Just think, if you'd gotten your gills a little sooner and found out you were a magical merrow, you would be in that class."

"Yikes! It was a lucky escape, wasn't it? Poor Raina."

On Friday, April tried not to pester Peter. She waited until lunch, planning to ask him if he had made a decision then. When Ms. Larkin-LaBois sent for April right before lunch, she couldn't believe it. It was as if even the teacher was conspiring to stop her from talking to Peter. April arrived at her bare office only to find Welly there. Ms. Larkin-LaBois motioned for April to enter.

"Greetings. You wanted to see me? Now? I can come back later, if you're busy," April said.

Ms. Larkin-LaBois tilted her head toward a cushion. "Have a seat, April. We would both like to speak with you."

"April, it is a pleasure to see you again. How are you faring these days?" Welly asked. There was no twinkle in his eye. Was that because of Brag?

"I'm faring well. It's been quiet, hasn't it?" she said.

"It has been quiet and we are all most thankful. I was visiting the school and thought it would be the perfect opportunity to check if you had sensed anything of the imp or noticed anything amiss? Anything at all?" He watched her keenly, almost as if he suspected something.

"No, nothing is amiss," April replied more-or-less honestly. Peter's gold was not amiss. It was sitting quietly in the forest and causing no trouble whatsoever. And the gold was not her secret to tell. She didn't even know where it was. And she certainly didn't want other elves visiting it, in case Brag was lying in wait. "Everything is normal. Brag seems to have disappeared," she tacked on, trying not to look guilty.

"It does appear that way, but looks can be deceiving. April, you must continue to be vigilant and act with caution at all times. Brag may still be in our world, we have no proof that he is not." Welly's grave words sounded a lot like a warning.

"I know. I will." April had no intention of acting incautiously. If she visited the gold to search for clues, it would be done with the utmost caution.

By the time April left the office, she was convinced that something was troubling Welly. He was usually the happiest of elves, now he seemed depressed. Neither was Ms. Larkin-LaBois the slightest bit cheerful. They had made a morose pair and April was glad to escape the heavy atmosphere of the little room, and step outside into the sunshine.

The usual lunch spot was filled up with too many elves to allow for a confidential word with Peter. April glared at Peter even though it wasn't his fault. He leaned closer. "We'll talk after school," he promised.

"We could talk now," April said, but he wouldn't.

The afternoon proved overlong. It often did on Friday, but April found it dragged worse than ever because she couldn't wait to hear Peter's news. The curiosity to know what had become of Brag was building up inside her. She was sure that a visit to the gold would provide some clues, maybe prove that Brag had left for good. More than anything, April wanted to know that New Haven was safe again.

Citing Friday, Mrs. Myrrh announced that she had planned a special one-day activity. April studied the new sports equipment and her heart skipped a beat of two. A series of vines had been draped over the water, from the uppermost boughs of the tallest trees that ringed the lake. This sport looked like it involved both heights and water. April was ready to sneak away from school if students were supposed to climb as high as those vines.

"Peter, let's get out of here," April whispered, trying to steer him into the undergrowth.

Peter refused to cooperate. "Mrs. Myrrh will notice if we go missing. I don't want to be in a lot of trouble on Monday. I really don't want a week of detentions," he said.

April didn't either, but it was a price she was willing to pay, to slip away with Peter. Before she could convince him, the teacher strode closer. "Line up, class. One nice straight line, hurry up." An ear-splitting whistle had students leaping into position.

April ended up at the very end of the row with Raina.

"Why do you think those long vines are hanging out of the trees, over the lake?" Raina asked. "You don't suppose we have to swing on them, do you?"

April gulped, staring way, way up. "I think we do."

"Oh, that looks exciting. A nice change from Basketberry and dancing, don't you think?" Raina had obviously forgotten who she was talking to.

"Class, quiet! Now, pay attention. If you look up, you will see a series of vines, securely tied onto the branches above." All the students looked up. April tried to spot if the vines really were tied securely. It was impossible to tell from the ground.

"You will climb the trunk of the tree to the branch holding the vine. Once there, you will firmly grip the free end of the vine. It is looped over the branch for the first group of elves. The rest of you will need to haul it back up before you can take your turn. Now, where was I? Ah, yes, grip the free end of the vine—firmly. Vine firmly gripped, you will leap and swing out over the lake on your vine, toward the next vine. You are going to try switching vines in mid-air, again and again. Bonus marks for any students that make it all the way to the tenth and last vine. You can land in the lake after that. Fairies! No flying allowed, that would be considered cheating. So, who's first? Who wants to show the class how it's done.

A lot of rearranging took place. April had no intention of participating at all, so stayed at the end of the line, but she thought it would be fun to watch the rest of the class swing on the vines.

In Sports, it was easy to spot the fairies because the five girls wore shorts and halter tops, leaving their wings free in case they needed them, and the three winged boys (Airron, Ray and Cosmo) were bare-chested as always. The rest of the class wore regular shorts and tops. For this activity, the eight fairies had all ended up at the front of the line, probably because if they messed up, they could fly. The ten merrows claimed the next spots, since they couldn't drown. Seamore kept rippling his gills, as if to limber them up for the water. The pixies came last, and then April, who still tended to think of herself as a pixie, even though she was a magical merrow.

Ray went first, climbing the bark with ease and swinging from vine to vine until he ran out of vines. He mustn't have wanted to get wet because when he released the last vine, he did not dive into the lake. He flew back to the class with a flourish.

The other fairies had no trouble with the activity, they were used to being in the air. Some did splash into the lake for a swim. Airron didn't, he flew back as dry as when he had left.

231

The merrows had a lot more trouble swinging on the vines. Seamore had a close call, he let go of one rope too soon, missed the next rope completely, and almost crashed into a tree trunk.

Raina showed no fear when she took her turn, but she only made it as far as the fifth vine before she plummeted into the water like a stone.

The pixies weren't any better at swinging through the air than the merrows. Peter made it all the way to the end, but he was one of the few pixies that managed the feat. Cherry participated, but from the way she dragged herself up the tree, it appeared that she still wasn't getting any proper rest. When she reached the third vine, she simply let go and dropped into the water.

In a surprisingly short time, the whole class had jumped except April. She had hoped that no-one would notice, but it became rather obvious when Ms. Myrrh tapped her birchbark clipboard with a charcoal stick and pointed to April. She was marking their participation.

Raina stepped up behind April and nudged her. "Come on, April, you can do it. You've climbed the Giant tree, and you climbed the tree when the cat was chasing us, and you fell into the bottomless pit, didn't you? This is nothing. And you do need the marks." April really did need the marks, but did she need them that badly?

"I promise I'll fly up and catch you if you miss the water," Airron offered, joining them. "You can't be the only one in the class too scared to jump! Looks bad on you. Everyone will be calling you one of those Outer-World chicken birds."

And she was making the whole class wait. "Okay, I'll try, I guess. But make sure you get ready to catch me. You have to promise."

"I promise," Airron vowed with a hand over his heart and a gleam in his eye.

April wished he would take this a lot more seriously. She clenched her teeth and started climbing. It was time she got over her fear of heights. It really was embarrassing to be the only elf in the class too frightened to participate. And this tree was nothing compared to the bottomless pit. There was even water to land in.

Still, the higher April climbed, the more she regretted her decision. No amount of marks was worth this. She was tempted to climb back down and might have, except for the humiliation factor. Everyone was watching, and waiting.

"Weasel whiskers," she cussed under her breath and kept going.

April reached the branch and with clammy hands verified that the vine really was securely tied. She straddled the limb and started hauling up the long vine. Staring way down made her stomach churn, so she closed her eyes. Closed eyes were much worse—her head felt like it was spinning in circles. Her aversion to heights had not been cured by falling into the bottomless pit. If anything, it seemed worse. April opened her eyes again and found the end of the vine had arrived. She almost dropped it.

Some of the class started shouting for her to hurry up. She was taking too long and most of them wanted to jump again. April rose unsteadily. "Get it over with. Tight, grip the vine tight," she whispered. Mrs. Myrrh had said so. April clasped the vine as tight as she could in trembling hands. She was still taking too long and the shouting got louder. Some of it sounded encouraging, but much of it sounded impatient.

April strangled the vine, closed her eyes and leaped without any grace at all. It was more of a flinging herself off the branch headfirst. She forgot to open her eyes and was over the lake before it seemed possible. The motion of the vine yanking her back toward the shore alerted her that it was past time to switch vines. Her eyes popped opened. The second vine was already too far away to grab. And the vine she held was pulling her back to the tree. She really didn't want to smash into the trunk. That would hurt and it might break bones. She tried to release her grip, except her hands didn't cooperate. By the time April convinced them to let go, she was almost over the land again. Then she was falling. It felt like the bottomless pit all over again, right down to the pit creature scratching her back and digging talons into her shoulders. The hallucination felt so real, the pit could have been happening all over again.

April hit the shallow water by the shore with a hard smack, belly first. It really hurt. Not ready to face a critical audience, she swam down and into deeper water, using the time to recover and cool her stinging stomach. Her gills materialized and took over breathing without any conscious effort on her part. When her legs felt steady again, April swam ashore almost unnoticed by the class. They were swinging from the vines again, and not one at a time now. At least three elves were swinging overhead.

Mrs. Myrrh waved April over as soon as she stepped on land. "No more jumping for you. Do you know how close you came to hitting the land? And the tree? No? Well, go sit down and keep out of the way." She sounded a bit mad.

April was happy to obey. She claimed a sunny spot in the sand and watched her classmates having a great time while she dried off and grew sleepy. She was dozing when a loud scream woke her up. April leapt to her feet, automatically scanning for Brag and expecting the worst. It wasn't Brag.

Raina strode over and provided an explanation. "Seamore landed on Cherry. You missed it? Too bad. He dropped out of the sky like a stone and landed on her head." Raina didn't even pretend to be sympathetic.

Mrs. Myrrh had run right into the water. The nearest students were hauling the injured pair out, while the whole class crowded close. Seamore was dazed, but proved to be fine when he sat up and rubbed water out of his eyes.

Cherry didn't so much as twitch. She lay as limp as a strand of wet hair, with a big bump erupting on her temple.

"Oh dear," Mrs. Myrrh said. "Raina, we need your father. Ray, could you fly to the Healer's office in town and tell Mr. Poole that we require his assistance? Tell him it is an emergency. Heather, locate the Headmistress, would you. Check her office."

Ray was gone in a flash of bright wings.

"The rest of you, no more jumping. Seamore, can you walk? Perriwinkle, lend him a hand. Class is dismissed early. Gather your packs, you can leave now. Go!"

The school day was almost over anyway. The gong would sound in less than half an hour. April and her friends collected their packs and watched from a distance when Mr. Poole rushed through the meadow. He bent to examine Cherry, while Mrs. Myrrh hung over his shoulder like a vulture. Several of Cherry's friends waited around to hear about her condition. Marigold sobbed dramatically, and Lily rubbed her on the back. Starla didn't stay at all. She really didn't spend much time with Cherry these days.

"I wonder if she's okay." Raina said. Her father looked concerned, even from afar.

"She'll be fine. It's only a bump on her hard head," Airron said. "And she deserves it, after what she did to us."

They were all convinced of Cherry's guilt. Thanks to Cherry, he had visible scars, one that would mark his handsome face forever. And Peter had scars on the inside, even though he rarely talked about it. And Raina had almost died in her own lake. Not to mention all the poor fish. Cherry had left her mark on all of them, by allying with Brag.

"Let's go," Airron said curtly.

"Wait, I want to talk to my dad for a minute. I think he's almost done." Raina was right. Mr. Poole stood up, dusted off, and had a few more words with Mrs. Myrrh before he walked toward the school.

"Dad!" Raina called. He altered course. "How's Cherry?"

"I think she will be fine. But she did take quite a severe blow to the head. I doubt that she will regain her wits before the sunrise."

Airron snorted, but didn't comment other than the snort.

"Are you going to leave her there overnight?" Raina asked.

"No, no. A couple of fairies will fly her to her aunt's house on a stretcher. They have been sent for. I will check on Cherry in the morning. Come on, I'll walk home with you. Wouldn't mind finishing early today, it is Friday. Oh, and there's Salm. Ready to go?"

April didn't mind walking home with Mr. Poole, but she did mind being robbed of her opportunity to talk privately with Peter, yet again. She needn't have worried, as soon as they reached home, Peter wanted to talk, but not to her alone. He wanted to talk to all of them, except Mr. Poole, on the shore of the lake.

"What is it, Peter? You didn't even let us get snacks," Raina complained, as soon as they were seated in a circle.

"Go and get snacks then, there's no rush. I didn't realize you were hungry." Peter might not be in a hurry, but April was.

"Raina can get snacks later. We need to talk first." April motioned Raina to stay. "I've been waiting for days. Will you take me to see the gold or not?"

"Peter!" Raina gasped. "You wouldn't do that, would you?"

He looked sheepish. "Well, no. Not if I thought there was any risk, but it has been almost three weeks, hasn't it? And if we all went together, the five of us, I think it is time to find out what's happened to Brag."

The others hadn't been expecting the news, but April was pleased with Peter's decision. She felt it was the right one. "If we prove Brag is gone, everything can go back to normal. We won't have to stay home all the time, or be scared," she said, backing up Peter. "And it has been nearly three weeks. That's almost a month, isn't it?" It wasn't, but close enough. April waited tensely for Raina's reaction. She couldn't tell which way her friend was leaning.

Raina didn't keep them in suspense. "I think you're right, Peter. Enough time has passed that it should be safe to go and look, if we go together. But no way are we going at night, if my parents found us sneaking out again …" she trailed off, eyes wide. None of them wanted to face that possibility.

"Sounds like a plan." Airron nodded decisively. "When should we go?"

"Soon, and get it over with," Salm said, which was how April felt.

"I guess it depends on how far away the gold is and how long it will take to walk there and back. Peter?" Raina asked. "Do you know exactly where it is?"

"Umm … yes, I know exactly where it is." He flushed, giving himself away.

Raina eyed him sharply. "Peter! Did you already go and examine the gold?"

He didn't answer—an answer in itself.

"Alone. At night. To protect me," April revealed. And they worried about her! They should be worrying about Peter.

"I don't believe it! Peter, that was a really crazy thing to do. I can't believe you did that. You're usually smart, but that was dumb." Raina looked deeply disappointed in him.

"It wasn't that far away, only about an hour's walk," Peter muttered defensively, pointing southeast. "It's not like I walked to the forcefield and back, or anything. The gold is close, we could go tomorrow! Do you want to go tomorrow?" He was trying to change the subject. It was obvious.

Raina eyed them each in turn and every head nodded. "Okay, tomorrow it is, in the afternoon," she decided arbitrarily.

"Tomorrow afternoon," April repeated, feeling a pang of nerves. She would have preferred to go alone, in case Brag was hanging around, but after three weeks it did seem unlikely.

17. The Best Laid Plans

Airron and Peter showed up right after lunch the next day. Their small group sat idly around the lake for a bit, to make it look like they weren't planning anything, especially anything sneaky. They rose aimlessly and Raina called through the window that they were going for a short walk. That was when their plan stopped going as planned.

"Wait a minute," Mrs. Poole shouted and hurried outside. "Your father and I are going out for the afternoon. One of you will have to stay with DewDrop. Raina? Salm? April?"

They looked at each other in dismay. "But ... when will you be back?" Raina asked.

"I don't know. Does it matter? You have to stay close anyway. We will be back when we are back. Why don't all of you watch DewDrop? Take her for a walk with you." Mrs. Poole smiled brightly and returned to the house, unaware of what she had done.

They returned to the shore to reconsider their plans. "One of us could stay with DewDrop, and the rest of us could still go," Raina proposed uncertainly.

"Are you offering to stay behind?" Salm asked.

Raina snorted. "Not a chance. I was thinking of you."

"But I'm bigger and stronger," Salm said. "More protection if anything goes wrong."

"But I'm smarter," Raina shot back. "Brains are better than muscles."

"Hey, I've got as many brains as you. More. And I'm stronger. I should go," Salm insisted.

Neither elf wanted to stay behind with DewDrop. And April had to go, she was the only one with the ability to sense more than eyes could see. "We could go at night -" April began, and got no further.

"No!" It was unanimous, except for April.

"There's always tomorrow," Raina said lamely. "Peter, is tomorrow okay for you?" Peter didn't answer, he was staring off into space. "Peter?" she said loudly.

He jumped. "What? Hey, what's that over there?" Peter pointed toward the Poole's front garden. They all turned around to look—at nothing.

Raina frowned. "I don't see anything. What did you see?"

"Uh … something, right over there. Keep looking," Peter ordered. He sounded odd.

April turned back around to ask what he had spotted and lost her voice. She saw something too, but it wasn't in the Pooles' garden, it was in the opposite direction entirely. Her eyes widened in alarm and she stared at the small unnatural bubble. It had Brag written all over it. Her friends could not see this.

"Hey!" She pointed toward the garden. "I thought I saw something too. Over there!"

"What are you talking about?" Raina sounded annoyed now. "I don't see anything. You and Peter must be imagining things."

"No, I did see something, right there." April insisted, looking anywhere but at the bubble. Thank goodness her friends were still facing in the opposite direction. She peeked over her shoulder. The bubble drifted closer and burst, and not a moment too soon.

Raina spun around and faced the lake again. "Well, I don't see anything, except you acting really weird."

"Oh, well I thought I saw something. I guess my eyes were playing tricks. So, we'll go tomorrow? That's fine. No rush. Tomorrow is probably better anyway. We can relax today." April stopped babbling before she gave herself away.

It looked like Brag was still hanging around after all. It was lucky that their expedition had been delayed by Mrs. Poole. It gave April a chance to investigate alone, and keep her friends safe.

"Same time tomorrow, I guess?" Raina assumed.

Airron nodded. "Sounds good to me."

"Ya, tomorrow," Peter said tersely. He didn't look so good. April darted a glance at his face, he darted a glance back. April gaped at him— he knew! Then she got it. Peter had seen the bubble first! He hadn't seen anything in the Poole's garden either. He knew about the bubble, and he knew she knew, and neither was at all happy about it. If April hadn't been so freaked out by the bubble, she would have clued in sooner.

"Well, I'm going to head home, since we're not going gold hunting," Peter said. "I have some chores, not to mention a pile of homework. Lots of homework." He rose and stretched, a little too nonchalantly.

April knew exactly what he was up too. She sprang to her feet. "I feel like a walk. I'll walk you home."

"That's okay, you don't have to."

April smiled stiffly. "I know I don't have to, but I would really like to."

"It's okay, I feel like being alone." Peter smiled back, ever so politely.

"But I feel like a walk," she said, through clenched teeth.

"Don't trouble yourself," Peter said.

"It's no trouble." April shot him a warning glance.

Their conversation was being closely monitored by their friends. Three heads were swiveling back and forth between them.

"Sure it is. Stay here. Relax," Peter took one step away.

"But I don't want to relax. I feel like a walk. Maybe I'll take a walk … all by myself," April stressed, glancing southeast. Peter glared. She glared right back.

"Fine, you can walk me home then," Peter said grudgingly and stomped away.

"I will. Bye," April said and took off after him, leaving three very perplexed elves behind. "Peter, slow down. I'm going with you whether you want me to or not."

"I'm only going home, April. I'm not going anywhere else, believe me."

"But you saw it, didn't you?" She was sure he had seen the bubble.

"Yes, I saw the stupid thing." He slowed his pace now that they were out of sight and sound of the others. "April, you can't go. Brag thinks you're dead. You're safe now. You can't go."

"Peter, I'm the only elf with any measurable magical defense. I'm the only elf who has a chance of stopping Brag before he harms New Haven. I have to get lucky against him sometime! I am going, one hour southeast," she added, in case he tried to sneak away without her.

Peter groaned, "Me and my big mouth."

"You're the one that shouldn't be going, Peter. I should go alone." April was certain that she could find the gold now that she knew its approximate location.

Peter stopped walking and turned to her. Speaking calmly took a visible effort but Peter managed an even tone. "April, neither of us want

Raina, Airron, Salm or any other elf to be anywhere near Brag," he stated clearly. April nodded in agreement. "But you and I saw the bubble. We know that the imp is still around. You want to go and investigate alone, but I'm not going to let that happen."

April suspected where he was heading with this. "So we have to go together?"

"I'm afraid so. Unless we bring other elves."

"I don't think that's a good idea, Peter. The fewer elves at risk, the better. I should go alone."

Peter wasn't even going to consider it. "No."

"Please, Peter?" she said, laying a hand on his arm.

"Nope, and I think it would be better to wait until tonight. Night or day, it won't matter against Brag now, will it? And then no-one will know what we're up to. We can be gone as long as we need to. We'll have all night." All night with Brag sounded like a sleepover in a colony of fire ants.

"Okay, tonight it is." Maybe April could tie Peter up in the meantime.

They walked back toward the Pooles' house together and discussed their plans. Neither was willing to trust the other out of sight. Peter would stay and sleep over in Salm's room. He and April would steal away as soon as everyone else was asleep. They had never snuck out on their friends before. It was going to be a lot harder than sneaking out on parents.

When they walked back into the front garden, Raina, Salm and Airron were still sitting by the lake. "Peter, I thought you were going home? To do chores and homework?" Raina said. His departure had been peculiar.

"Changed my mind." He didn't say more and did a great job of acting like himself for the rest of the day and evening.

April, on the other hand, had to go to bed early when she couldn't keep up the strained pretense of normality any longer. The hardest part of the night came when Raina followed her upstairs to talk. "April, are you sure you're all right? You're not sick are you? You look a bit sick."

April hated lying to her best friend and felt awful doing it, but she didn't want Raina anywhere near Brag. "I do feel a little sick," April said. It wasn't a lie. "I'm going to go to sleep. I'll see you in the morning." Hopefully. She hugged Raina goodnight and tried to smile.

"Are you sure you're okay?"

"Positive." April lay down and shut her eyes, trying to hide her deceit.

"Well … okay. Sleep well." Raina snuffed the candle and left quietly. April pressed her face into the pillow and felt like a pile of old dung. Too anxious to sleep, she got up and paced in the dark. The moon rose overhead before the house was finally quiet. April flipped over the hourglass on her dresser and waited until a quarter of the fine silt had run through. Only then did she tiptoe downstairs.

On the last step, April faltered. A candle was burning and someone was stretched out in front of the door, snoring gently. It was … Salm! Why would he be asleep in front of the door? April detoured toward the backdoor. A body was blocking it, as well—Airron!

April slunk back to her room and sat down on the window ledge to think. Her friends must have been so suspicious of her behavior that they were barring the doors. They were much harder to sneak away from than parents. Mr. and Mrs. Poole had never slept in front of the doors. April was trying to decide what to do when she heard a faint splash. Below Salm's window, the moonlight reflected off a pattern of circular ripples. Peter was leaving without her! He was sneaking away.

"Not a chance," April muttered. She stood up on her window ledge. She had jumped into the lake once before, when escaping from Drake Pitt, but that time she'd had Salm to help. He had given her a good shove. This time she had to jump all by herself, before Peter left. It was strong motivation.

April launched off the ledge, determined to keep Peter from doing something risky to protect her. As she tumbled through space, her back hurt again. Positive that something had latched onto her, April flung an arm over her shoulder to dislodge the thing, and did indeed feel something foreign beneath her hand. She hit the lake and the force of the water must have knocked it off, because when she checked again, it was gone.

Completely unnerved, April bobbed to the surface and concentrated magically to locate Peter. She really didn't want to be alone in the dark right now. She was afraid of the mysterious thing that kept landing on her back. April sensed an elf by the water's edge. Peter hadn't left her behind after all.

"April," Peter called softly, as soon as she neared the shore.

"Here." She waded towards his voice and grabbed onto Peter in the faint moonlight. "Check my back! Make sure there's nothing on my back." Her voice quivered with fear. Something that you couldn't see, but could only imagine, was much scarier than something you could actually see.

"Turn around." Peter ran his hands over her soaked shirt. "I can't feel anything. Why do you think there's something on your back? Wait—tell me when we're further away from the house." He linked their fingers and started walking fast. No-one shouted for them to stop or gave chase. They had successfully eluded their vigilant friends.

When they were a safe distance into the woods and April tripped over a root, Peter said apologetically, "I had a torch, but it got wet. I can't believe Airron and Salm guarded the doors." He squeezed her hand in reassurance. "Now, why did you think there was something on your back?"

"Because there was something on my back," April said. "It felt like the pit creature again, but it didn't hurt so much. And I felt it at school— when we had to swing on the vines. I felt it then, too, but I thought it was my imagination. What could it be? Do you have some weird flying creature in New Haven that I don't know about?" April stumbled over a stone. It was hard to see anything but the largest shapes.

Peter didn't answer right away. A passing firefly lit his features, he was thinking. The firefly gave April an idea. She concentrated on the small insect. It wasn't very bright, except for the light it emitted, but it was willing to fly beside them when she asked it to.

Peter grinned in the greenish light. "Is that your firefly?"

"It is."

"Why didn't you think of fireflies on those other occasions when we were sneaking through the forest at night, without a torch?"

April shrugged, "I rarely travelled after dark in the Outer-World, so I've never used fireflies to light the way. You didn't think of it either."

"True. Magic sure does come in handy, doesn't it? Now, about this thing on your back, I have an idea. It's a crazy idea, but maybe not so crazy." Peter let that sink in.

A second firefly crossed their path and April asked it to come along, too. It obliged. They could see even better and the insects didn't alert anyone or anything to their presence—not like a torch.

"Okay Peter, what is your crazy idea?" April said.

"I think you have wings," he said.

"Are you joking?"

"No, I'm serious."

"But I don't have wings," April said. Peter knew that.

242

"You don't have gills when you're on the land, only in the water. Magical gills," he stressed. "Maybe you don't have wings on the land, only in the air. Magical wings."

Was it possible? April added a third firefly to their escort and Peter laughed quietly. They both knew what they were about to face, but the insects did look funny flying in a wavering formation. "But an elf can't be a pixie and a merrow and a fairy all at once, can they?" April had never heard of such a thing.

"Maybe they can if they have magic. You are born on April 1st, like a New Haven elf. With your magic, maybe you can have both wings and gills, and neither when you're on land." Peter made a good point. And he usually had good ideas. "You aren't like New Haven elves in other ways, April. Maybe you're not like New Haven elves in this way."

"I know I'm different. I try not to be." It was a bit of a sore spot. Peter didn't usually mention it.

"April, I didn't mean it in a bad way. You must know that." He turned left at a fork in the path. "I meant it in a good way. All my life I've wanted wings, but I'll never have them. I'll never know what it feels like to fly. If you have wings you should be really happy, that's all I meant. And you have gills too. You're lucky."

"Well, I don't think I have wings anyway. I think something landed on my back." The other idea was crazy.

"Three times? The three times you happened to be falling? The only three times you've fallen since the transformation ceremony? Three times is more than coincidence. I think you have wings."

"I would know if I had wings," April said stubbornly, and added a fourth firefly.

"Just consider it." Peter left it at that and led the way unerringly toward the gold as the raven flies, since he was drawn directly towards it. They walked for more than an hour because even with the fireflies, it was harder travelling at night. When Peter slowed down and touched her arm, April knew they were close.

"Maybe we should lose a couple of the bugs," he whispered.

April sent three of them away and asked one to hang around a little longer. It opted to go with its new friends. The bugs were probably going to have a party. "Sorry, they all wanted to leave together," April murmured.

The darkness seemed even blacker after the light. They waited for their eyes to adjust before taking cautious steps forward. "There," Peter breathed.

Faint yellow glinted up ahead. Gold under moonlight. April stood still and her nose told her all she needed to know. "Brag. He's here."

Peter gulped audibly. "Ya, I can smell him. I didn't smell him last time I was here." April stood with Peter for long minutes, neither sure what to do now. She thought she heard a piteous whimper. Then it came again, louder.

"It sounds like someone is in trouble," Peter said softly.

Brag might have wrapped up Sage Scarab for a second time, or trapped another innocent victim. They had to help, if they could. April nudged Peter behind her and eased forward, moving as if in slow motion.

"April ghost?" Brag's voice came from directly ahead.

"Brag?"

"April ghost!" He sounded happy to see her, even though he believed her a spirit.

"I'm not dead, Brag. I didn't go all the way down the pit," she said tersely.

"April ghost not dead?"

"Not even close. What's going on, Brag?" She couldn't see him, she could only hear him and smell him.

"April make fire?" Why didn't he do it himself?

She kicked a few sticks together and concentrated to create intense heat. She wanted to see. When the fire flared, it became obvious why he hadn't created his own light. The imp was skin and bones. His hands were tied behind his back and his ankles were bound to a branch that he must have been dragging around.

"Brag? Who's got you all tied up?" April asked, bewildered.

"Brag forever sleep," he whimpered, a lone tear leaking from the corner of one bloodshot eye. It trailed down his grizzled gray face and he caught it with his tongue.

"What are you talking about? You're awake. And you're the one who makes forever sleep. You made Peter sleep." April motioned towards Peter. He was staring fixedly at the imp. He had never met Brag face-to-face in the real world before.

"Brag wake up. Brag sorry, bad elf Peter. Brag sorry, April ghost." The imp looked about to sob his heart out, if he had one.

"I'm alive, Brag." April was trying to make sense of his few words. "So, if you've been asleep and you just woke up, who made you forever sleep?"

"Elfie stole Brag's potion. Stole Brag's secret."

"Elfie? And you woke up a day ago?"

The imp sniffed wetly. "Don't know. Long time, short time." He moaned and tried to pull his hands free.

"Makes sense," Peter said. "Cherry got bonked on the head yesterday."

"And she couldn't have visited Brag in dreams if she was knocked out," April said. It was yet more evidence of Cherry being the elf involved, not that they needed more. "He's been trapped in sleep for almost three weeks, I guess. That's a really long time."

"Forever." Peter knew better than anyone how long forever sleep felt.

"Brag thirsty mouth." The imp's lower lip trembled. He looked harmless, which proved that looks could be very deceiving.

"I can't believe I'm saying this, but I kind of feel sorry for the imp. He does look pitiful. Three weeks! I'm surprised he survived. I guess we'll have to take him back to town." Peter walked towards the pile of nuggets. April followed. It was a lot of gold.

"Welly is not going to thank us, is he?" April hoped returning the imp didn't make the Head-Sage even sadder than he had been of late.

Finding the imp in this state was the last thing they had expected. Brag could not harm anyone right now, but they were still stuck with him. And Cherry had bested the imp, it seemed. April hadn't been able to, except the picnic time, but Cherry had succeeded. No wonder she had looked so tired at school, if she had been visiting Brag every night in dreams.

"Wait here. I'm going to find him some water. We passed a trickle of a creek not far back." Peter must have a heart as big as the Outer-World to be kind to Brag after what the imp had done to him. Peter lifted a burning stick and took it along. April watched the small light flicker between the trees until it disappeared.

"April ghost?"

"I'm alive, Brag. I'm not a ghost. Peter is getting you some water, which is more than you deserve after how you tortured him. Then we'll take you back to New Haven and Welly will be stuck with you. You better be able to walk." No way could she or would she carry his filthy carcass.

"Brag sorry. Brag sorry for pit. Untie Brag?"

"I don't think so. I'm not Mr. Leech."

Brag understood the Mr. Leech reference, and he giggled weakly. April moved to the opposite side of the fire where the smoke blocked the imp's curdled stench. Peter was back in minutes with a pool of water cupped inside a leaf.

"Open up," Peter said, standing over Brag.

The imp tried his ploy on Peter now. "Peter untie Brag? Brag drink?"

"No way. Open up if you want the water."

Brag was too thirsty to resist. He opened his mouth as wide as a baby bird at feeding time. Peter emptied the contents of the leaf between the rows of pointy teeth. Brag finished every last drop as if it was nectar, then he drifted into true sleep—his mouth gaping wide. Peter tossed the leaf aside and moved to sit beside April. She leaned against his shoulder, exhausted. The forest was peaceful now that Brag was asleep, and the tension of what they would face was eliminated. Brag was all tied up and powerless.

"Not what we expected to find," Peter remarked.

"No."

"We might as well rest for a bit. Brag might be able to walk soon. We have lots of time to get back before morning. And he's still secured." Peter yawned. They settled down and stared at the campfire until it was nothing but a pile of glowing coals, not unlike the heap of warm gold behind them.

April's heavy eyes closed, lulled by the low chorus of insects and the whisper of rustling leaves—lulled into a false sense of security. She should have remembered that Brag was not the only dangerous being in New Haven. She should have remembered that every time she thought the situation was under control, it blew up in her face like a touch-me-not flower, whose capsule of seeds exploded at the slightest contact. But she didn't remember, she fell deeply asleep instead.

"Wakey-wakey! Playtime." Something tickled April's nose in the middle of a nice dream about river surfing.

"Ah!" Peter shouted loudly and jerked up. April was dislodged from his comfy shoulder before she was fully awake.

"What? What?" She stumbled to her feet, dismayed to see the first rays of the sun lighting the sky. And even more dismayed to see ... Brag! An untied Brag.

"Ah! Brag! How did you get loose?" April cried.

The imp smiled dangerously and held up his hands, he wiggled his fingers and even kissed them. "Brag make deal. Good deal."

Who had Brag made a deal with? April didn't see anyone but Peter, and Peter wouldn't have released Brag, not in a thousand years. April needed to check a little further. She closed her eyes and concentrated. An elf was moving through the forest in the direction of New Haven. And even further off, slightly to the east, three elves were moving toward them. April didn't have to be a genius to guess who the three elves were.

"One elf is leaving, and three elves are approaching," April whispered significantly to Peter, her eyes on Brag. Peter squeezed her fingers tightly. His hand felt unnaturally cold and clammy.

"Who did you make a deal with, Brag?" Peter managed a friendly tone.

"Elf."

"That would be Cherry bad elf?" April supplied.

"Not Cherry bad elf," Brag said in his crafty voice.

"Then who?"

"Playtime. Guessing time."

They did not have time to waste on this game. "Who, Brag? It must be Cherry," April insisted.

"Not Cherry *bad elf.*" Brag's hint was not subtle.

"Is it Cherry?" Peter asked.

"Maybe. Maybe not."

"Cherry good elf?" Peter tried.

Brag bobbled his head happily and finally named his partner in crime. "Cherry friend." It was no surprise.

"So, Cherry is your friend and she released you. Then who tied you up?"

Brag pouted. "Cherry elf."

Peter shared a confused look with April. She let him keep talking, he was doing a better job of it. "Why did Cherry tie you up? If she's your friend?"

"Brag not know." He tugged on his droopiest ear.

"And is she the elf that stole your potion, the one who trapped you in sleep?"

"Cherry friend," Brag said plaintively.

"Doesn't sound very friendly," Peter said.

"Cherry friend. Only friend." Brag was getting mad. April was surprised by his loyalty to Cherry after what she had done to the imp.

Then again, April knew how lonesome it was to live by yourself in the forest. Even an enemy might be a friend, compared to no-one at all.

Peter wisely moved the conversation along. "So Cherry tied you up, then she released you. Why did she do that?"

"Cherry friend untie Brag. Brag do … something," the imp said slyly.

"What are you supposed to do, Brag?" Peter sounded calm, but he wasn't. His body was rocking back and forth ever so slightly, almost vibrating.

"Secret." The imp walked up to a rock and turned it over with his big knobby toe. He grabbed up a many-legged white millipede. It was in his mouth in a flash. The crunching sounded sinister in the silent forest. The whole situation reeked of disaster. Their friends were walking into terrible danger. Brag was loose and Cherry had bribed him to do something awful.

Peter tried reasoning with the imp. "Brag, Cherry was really mean to you, trapping you in forever sleep for three weeks. A friend wouldn't do that. Why would you want to do anything to help her? You've got your gold, you're free. You don't have to do anything Cherry told you to do. Why don't you take your gold and go home to your garden, right now."

"Brag have gold." The imp spat out a couple of legs

April checked the forest again. The three elves were much closer. The single elf was departing at the same rapid pace, almost out of April's sensing range now. Brag snapped a beetle off a leaf and held it squirming between his fingers. "April help Brag. April carry gold. Brag leave. Good deal?"

April was pretty sure there was more to it than her carting gold around like a pack-mouse. They both knew he could float the gold away with a flick of his finger. Maybe the imp wanted her to leave New Haven with him since he no longer possessed the thunderwand. April was willing to leave with him, if it got him out of New Haven.

"Okay, Brag. Good deal. I'll help you carry your gold away, if we leave right now," April said. "Then Cherry won't know where the gold is, and you won't have to do whatever it is she wants you to do. But we have to leave *now*."

Brag swallowed the second beetle whole and bobbed his head. "Okey dokey. Now good."

April grabbed Brag's arm and picked up one of the nuggets, hoping to hurry the imp along. Unfortunately, the simple action started the most bizarre chain of events. Before April knew what was happening, the two of them were encased in a bubble and floating up.

"Oh. Oh no. Brag, let me down! What did you do?" April hadn't seen his fingers move and she hadn't taken her eyes off of him.

The imp scrunched his face up in alarm. "Bubble trap."

"Well it's your trap! Brag, make the bubble go down!" April wanted down, down to the ground. But they kept going up, up to the sky.

Peter waved from below and tried to follow the bubble, fighting his way through a deep and tangled field of clover. He was making slow progress. The bubble rose with ease and started to drift toward New Haven, without any breeze to move it.

"Brag, make the bubble go down, now," April said. "Please."

"Can't."

"Of course you can. It's your magic."

"Can't. Forever trap." He pouted. "Cherry friend deal, float April away."

"And you're trapped with me because I grabbed your arm?" April guessed.

"April fault Brag trapped." He glowered at her.

She gasped in indignation. "It is not my fault. I didn't make the trap. I didn't even know there was a trap. This is all your fault Brag!"

"Is not." He pouted.

"Of course it is. Now how do we get out of here?" April wanted to shake the answer out of him.

"Can't. Forever trap."

They were back to that, and April was beginning to believe the imp. The news made April queasy, as did the height. Nothing blocked her view of the earth far below. Peter looked small now. He had escaped the clover and was slogging through a boggy patch of earth. And then April spotted the three elves she had sensed—Raina, Salm and Airron. They weren't looking up and they were going to miss Peter. April waved wildly at Peter and pointed to his right. He adjusted his direction, even though he didn't know why she was telling him to go that way. With his eyes on the sky, he almost collided with Salm. Peter must have delivered the news immediately because all their faces turned up. April waved sheepishly. Brag waved, too.

"Brag, are you saying we're stuck in this bubble forever, if this is a forever trap?"

"No." Brag crinkled up his nose. "Guess where bubble go?"

"I don't want to guess. Where is the bubble going?"

"Guess," he ordered.

"No," April said sullenly.

"Guess."

"No!"

"Guess." Brag would do this all day.

"Fine. Up, the bubble is going up to the moon." It was a random guess.

Brag looked disappointed in her. "No. Bubble go down."

"Down? But down is good."

Brag shook his head violently. "No, no, no!"

"No? Why isn't down good?"

"Down pit." The idea terrified the imp. He turned to claw at the wall of the bubble like a mad thing.

"Stop that, Brag. It's not helping. Is this bubble really going to go down the bottomless pit?" April cried in dismay.

"Only one pit."

"Brag, listen. There has to be a way out of this trap, and I don't mean the going down the pit way. You must have overlooked something. Help me figure a way out of this," April said desperately.

But Brag had not told her everything. "Cherry friend help make trap."

"But how? How did she help?" April needed details.

"Help help. Brag tired." Before she could ask more questions, the imp curled up in a tight ball and began snoring in denial of his fate.

April was distracted when something surged close. Airron had shed his robe and flown up. "Airron!" It was great to see him. She didn't need to feel hopeless! Airron could stop the bubble.

He 'tsked' and shook his head as her predicament. "April, April, April. Imp got the better of you again?"

"He did." There was no denying it.

"Well, you can pop the bubble now and I'll carry you down. But I'll tell you right now, I'm not going to carry the imp. I can't carry two of you, and he'd probably kill me."

"Airron, I don't think the bubble will break. Brag says it's a forever trap. He says that Cherry helped make it, and he says the bubble has a … a destination." She avoided saying exactly where.

"Maybe he's lying. Try popping it." Airron glided lower, ready to catch her.

"Okay, I'll try." Maybe Brag was wrong about the bubble. And Airron would catch her if it burst. Brag could make himself another bubble, a regular bubble. Or not.

April took a steadying breath and gave it her best try, she used her sharpest fingernail, then she kicked as hard as she could. But the bubble barely wobbled—it was a really tough bubble. She shook her head. "It's not going to break, Airron."

"Maybe I can pop it from the outside. I'll borrow Peter's blade." A blade was a lot sharper than a bitten fingernail.

Airron spiraled down to Peter. It was incredible to watch Airron fly from above, really beautiful. April relaxed, not really worried anymore. If Airron couldn't pop the bubble, he could at least push it down to the ground and anchor it until they figured this trap out. Her friends wouldn't let her come to harm.

Airron was back in no time, clutching Peter's blade. "Get ready April. After I break the bubble, I'll have to swoop down and catch you, but I won't miss. I promise."

"I know you won't let me fall, Airron."

He nodded once, raised his arm and slashed at the shimmering magic. April was flung backwards, but not because the bubble burst. Some sort of shock wave surged outwards. Airron was catapulted back from the bubble at a horrendous speed, directly toward the ground.

"No!" April screamed.

Airron fell like a broken butterfly, spinning in circles, his wings limp and useless. He kept falling and falling, as if time had all but stopped. "No." April closed her eyes before he hit the ground. She could not watch her friend die. It would break her heart as surely as it broke his body.

18. Final Destination

"April ghost?" Brag tapped her on the shoulder. April couldn't talk to the imp. She couldn't stand to look at him after the tragedy he had caused. She stayed huddled against the side, eyes closed.

"April ghost? Airron okey dokey. Brag save bad elf Airron." What was the imp talking about?

April forced her eyes opened and willed herself to look, terrified of what she would see. It was not what she expected. Airron was sinking gently to the ground encased in a weak, shaky bubble. It burst as soon as it touched down. Raina, Salm and Peter were there when Airron landed. He was helped to his feet, shaking his head to clear it. Airron was all right!

"Brag save Airron," the imp repeated timidly, watching April with big eyes.

"Ya, after your trap almost killed him. But that was a good thing to do Brag, you saved Airron's life. Thank-you," April said since the imp had chosen to help. April wouldn't have expected it of him. She hadn't been quick enough to think of asking Brag to make a bubble, he had thought of it all by himself.

"April friend?" the imp asked hopefully.

"Sure." April was feeling almost kindly toward the imp, since he had saved Airron's life.

"Bubble trap Cherry idea." Brag tried to pass the blame. And Cherry had thought of everything. Maybe there was no way out of the bubble until they reached the bottom of the bottomless pit.

"Brag, tell me about the bubble. What will it do when it reaches the pit?" she asked.

"Bubble go down, down, down. Bye-bye Brag. Bye-bye April. Brag sad." He really was, tears flowed down his face.

"But why can't we just come back up again?" It was the wrong question to ask.

"No bottom. Not come back. Never come back." His lip quivered.

"But Brag, there must be a bottom somewhere, even if it is a bottomless pit."

"No bottom." Brag shook his head sadly.

"Oh, well, this is your magic. Why can't you break the bubble?" she asked.

"Brag magic and Cherry mumbo jumbo."

So Cherry really did have the power of dark magic, like her father. April had certainly suspected as much. And the imp couldn't break the bubble because it contained Cherry's magic and Brag's magic—together. Imp and elf magic, a very strange union. Her friends were keeping pace below the bubble, talking and gesturing. At least they didn't know April's final destination. Luckily, she hadn't told Airron.

Even though the bubble travelled sluggishly, time began to race faster and faster. Brag curled up again and had another nap. When the bubble drifted over the town circle, elves pointed up in disbelief. Raina dashed up to Welly's building, but no-one was there. It was Sunday morning.

Floating in the bubble took on a dreamlike quality. When Prince Skylar flew into view, it was a nice surprise. He must have spotted the bubble from his window. The King's Keep was located on the high hill overlooking the town and had a panoramic view of New Haven. Skylar flapped closer.

"Don't touch the bubble," April warned him. "It's dangerous."

"Really? April, what is going on?" Skylar eyed the imp.

"This bubble is a trap. Brag set the trap, now we're trapped," she explained lamely.

"But … can't you pop it. It would be my great pleasure to carry you to the ground." Skylar smiled, showing his dimples.

"I already tried. Airron already tried. Talk to him." April pointed down.

Skylar spotted the small group moving across the square. "I will return." He flew down and joined her friends. They talked and gestured some more, then Skylar flew back.

"How is Airron?" April asked.

"Recovering. But he said not to touch the bubble under any circumstances. They asked me to ask you where the bubble is going. Airron said you said that the bubble was going somewhere." Skylar flapped his crimson wings slowly, circling the bubble to keep pace.

It would be better if no-one else knew where the bubble was going. April shrugged evasively.

"April, where is the bubble going?" Skylar repeated.

She pointed vaguely in the direction that the bubble was drifting. "That way."

"Where will it stop?"

"I don't know," April lied badly.

Skylar didn't like her answer. He returned to the ground, there was some urgent conversation, then everyone stared up. April waved and tried to smile. Her mouth didn't work. They were far enough away that they couldn't tell.

Skylar returned. "Airron is pretty sure that you said the bubble had a destination, April." She was saved from replying when a fairy with leaf green wings soared into view.

The Prince was transparently relieved to see O'Wing. April was happy to see him, too. One last time. "What's happening?" O'Wing asked, flying too close.

Both April and Skylar shouted, "Don't touch the bubble!"

O'Wing raised his wings and braked. Skylar explained the situation and O'Wing studied the bubble. Brag was still napping, unaware that they had visitors. "So we can't pop the bubble and catch April?" O'Wing verified.

"No, and April won't tell us where the bubble is going."

"I did tell you, that way." She pointed, again.

"If April won't tell, let's ask the imp," O'Wing said.

"Leave him alone. He's sleeping. He's tired," April said.

O'Wing didn't listen. He yelled until the imp cracked one eyelid.

"Brag, don't say anything," April ordered.

"Hey, imp! Where is the bubble going?" O'Wing asked.

"Down bottomless pit. Bye-bye, Brag. Bye-bye April bad elf," Brag whimpered, curled up tighter and went back to sleep.

"Thanks a lot, Brag." April scowled at him.

O'Wing groaned. "Down the bottomless pit?"

"April?" Skylar soared close. "Is it true?" He stared sadly into her eyes with the shimmering wall of magic between them. It was hard to lie when you were looking into someone's eyes. She didn't say no. It was answer enough.

O'Wing flew as close as he could, until his wing brushed Skylar's. "Is there nothing we can do? Nothing you can do? Nothing the imp can do?

There must be something … magical? It's a … a flimsy bubble, nothing to it."

"I don't think there is anything we can do. This is a really good trap. Brag said Cherry helped him to create it, he said she has magic. That's why he can't break it by himself." April peered down at her friends again, Sage Scarab had joined them. "Skylar, O'Wing, please don't say where the bubble is going. Okay? And after, say goodbye for me …say …" April lost her voice when her throat closed.

"April, we're going to get you out of the bubble. Don't think we're not. But we won't say anything about where it's headed. I promise," O'Wing said.

The bubble crested a low hill and the town disappeared from sight. It was getting closer to Cherry's former home. Closer to the pit. Time was running out much too fast.

"Be right back." Both fairies coasted down to the ground and an intense debate followed. Sage Scarab waved his fist up at the imp. Brag didn't notice. He was still sleeping and accepting his fate too easily. Maybe April was guilty of the same thing. She had to keep trying to escape.

"Hey, Brag," April shouted. "Brag, wake up. Come on! Do you want to go down the pit? Talk to me." The imp rolled over and showed her his bristled back. "Brag, I can get us out if you help me. Tell me more about the bubbles. What did Cherry do? What magic did she use?" But Brag would have nothing to do with April.

By the time Skylar and O'Wing returned, the bubble had crested another hill. Maybe it was Blueberry Hill. April never did get there, and it didn't look like she ever would. "How is everything on the ground?" she asked, leaning her forehead against the magical wall. It was lonely in the bubble. Brag was not very good company.

O'Wing tried to sound at ease. "All is well. Airron is still dizzy, can't fly yet. Sage Scarab sends greetings."

"We didn't say anything about the bubble's destination," Skylar added, "But I believe Peter has realized all is not well. Sage Scarab also suspects something is amiss."

"I tried to find out more about the magic used to create this trap, but Brag's not talking." April motioned to the imp's back. "All I know is he can't break the bubble because of Cherry's hand in this. That's sort of what he said, anyway."

"Peter proposed something. He said you should get really mad," O'Wing said.

April shook her head immediately. "No, I can't tell firebolts where to strike. That would be much too dangerous for New Haven." If that was Peter's best idea, there was no way out of this.

"Have you tried your own magic?" O'Wing said desperately.

"It doesn't work against Brag's."

"But have you tried?"

"Yes, I've tried. Of course I've tried. My magic is useless." She sagged against the side of the bubble.

"Well, try again. What have you got to lose?" O'Wing said.

April motioned them back and closed her eyes to focus on popping her prison. She focused all her magic on one small part of the shimmering wall, but nothing happened. She opened her eyes and shook her head. She had known it wouldn't work, but had dared to hope anyway.

Skylar and O'Wing glided close again. April felt too sad to talk. She rested her head on her crossed arms and stared at the ground. Directly below, her friends climbed the hill and April wished with all her heart to be walking with them.

Red wings streaked under the bubble. Skylar swooped away, flying very fast for an elf. He looked like he was late for an important gathering. O'Wing coasted below the bubble and tried to hover. "April, listen. Skylar has gone to talk to Cherry, to see if she'll cooperate. You're supposed to tell Brag to keep trying to pop the bubble. If both Brag and Cherry work together, the bubble will pop, won't it?"

April sighed forlornly. "There's not enough time, O'Wing. And Cherry won't cooperate anyway. She'll never admit that she was allied with Brag. Never. And she won't want to help me." If April went down the pit, Cherry would probably host a big party.

"April, you're giving up. Cherry's aunt lives nearby, and Skylar has a lot to bargain with. He will be the King of this world. He could make Cherry's life very difficult or very easy. Tell Brag to try and burst the bubble," he insisted. "There's a chance that it could work, you have nothing to lose." O'Wing had said that before, he was still right.

April sat up and pushed her hair off her face. She shouted at Brag, loudly. He kept snoring. She shoved him with her feet, and shouted louder. She was so persistent, or so annoying, that he finally rolled into a crouch. The imp pursed his lips and blew air wetly through them, making a very rude noise.

"Pit time?" Brag snarled, as if their fate was her fault.

"No. O'Wing has an idea. You're supposed to try and burst the bubble and keep trying—don't give up. Skylar is going to find your friend Cherry. She'll try too. She's your friend, she won't want you to go down the pit, will she?" April didn't believe her own words, but as long as Brag did, that was all that mattered.

Brag looked doubtful. "Maybe, maybe not."

"If you both try, the bubble will pop, right?" April checked.

"Bubble pop. Big pop! Okey dokey, Brag try. Now?" he asked.

"Yes, now!" It would have to be now. The Pitt's deserted house had appeared in the distance.

"Okey dokey." Brag raised his hands and wiggled his magical fingers, all ten of them. He kept at it long after April would have given up. When Peter motioned O'Wing down towards him, it looked urgent. Maybe Peter had thought of a better way to break the bubble.

"Right back," O'Wing said, yet again. He soared down to the ground. Raina spoke rapidly, she was doing all the talking, not Peter. And Figgy, Cedric and Robin had joined them. It looked like Figgy had some suggestions of his own. He kept interrupting Raina. Even from a distance, April could tell that Raina was getting annoyed.

April turned back to Brag, the imp was still wiggling his fingers and chanting to himself. He should probably take a break until O'Wing returned, in case the bubble did pop, but April really didn't think Brag had a hope so she didn't bother telling him to stop. The imp was concentrating and looked almost happy. He had probably forgotten all about their destination now that he had something to occupy him. April made the mistake of glancing down. They were almost over the gaping hole in the roof.

"This is it," April whispered. At least she'd had some time to enjoy New Haven and have friends. It had been the best time of her life, but sadly, it had been too short. "Better than nothing," she whispered, trying hard to look on the bright side.

And then the bubble burst with an explosive 'pop' that must have been heard as far away as the Outer-World. The shockwave generated by the bursting magical bubble sent April and Brag spinning through the air. It knocked her senseless, until the sensation of falling was alarming enough to revive her.

"Brag, make a bubble! Two bubbles! Normal bubbles," April hollered. And then she saw him falling limply through space—so limply that there was no doubt he was unconscious. He wasn't going to be any help, and that weird thing had landed on her back again.

The bubble had burst, but the situation was not improved. If anything, it was worse. Unless Peter was right, unless she did have wings. There was only one way to find out. April reached behind and ripped the back seam of her top.

As soon as her back was bare, April felt something billow free and slow her down. Instinctively, she spread her arms wide. She slowed down dramatically. A turn of her neck was all it took to see what had stopped her fall. Wings! Her very own wings—and they were beautiful! Every brilliant colour of the rainbow had been crowded together in one place, and the colours sparkled with magical light. In all her time in New Haven, she had never seen wings like these. Peter was proved absolutely right.

April's heart soared as powerfully as her new wings. All of her was as light as air, lighter. She laughed out loud because she was not going to fall to her death after all. She was not going to travel down the bottomless pit, never to return.

And Brag kept falling, his limbs tangled together as if he was already broken. The imp had done terrible things, but he had saved Airron by choice, and he had been manipulated by Cherry. Maybe all he had really wanted was a friend.

April couldn't watch him fall and not try to save him. She didn't know how to fly, but she gave it her best effort. She tucked her arms and wings tighter, the way she had seen Airron do, and aimed at Brag. She picked up speed and the wind whistled past her ears. It was a diving fall. The big birds of prey did this in the Outer-World. But Brag was still too far below, tumbling toward the hole in the roof, as if the pit were sucking him in.

Trying to dive even faster, April squeezed her arms against her sides and clenched her teeth. It felt too much like she was plunging to her death, on purpose. "Brag, make a bubble," she screamed.

The imp did nothing, except fall. And it didn't look like April could reach him before he fell into the pit, unless she intended to join him. But she kept trying, she was gaining. The distance between them shrank by degrees. "Brag, wake up! Make a bubble!" she hollered.

He still didn't hear her words. When she could almost touch his toe, it was now or never. The roof was almost upon them.

April reached out an arm to grab the imp's ankle, but that proved to be a mistake. One suddenly opened wing threw her into an out-of-control spiral, and sent her crashing into another body.

Leaf green wings blocked her view as she and O'Wing almost went into the pit together. April collided with the edge of the roof and instinctively grabbed the solid wood. O'Wing's hand clamped around her ankle. They dangled precariously for several seconds before April latched onto the roof with her second hand.

O'Wing scrambled up awkwardly. He only had one free hand because he was gripping Brag's scrawny ankle. O'Wing had saved the imp! He dragged the unconscious Brag up onto the roof and fell backwards with a groan. Feeling dazed and dizzy from the fall and the impact, April collapsed bonelessly down beside him. She stared at the brilliant blue sky above and smiled. The morning had been a nightmare, but the nightmare was over.

"Uh, April? Something smells bad," O'Wing mumbled, after a minute or an hour had passed.

"That would be Brag," April said. "It's not me."

"I didn't think it was."

"Good."

"You didn't think it was me, did you?" He turned his head toward her.

"No." It was not the most brilliant conversation after almost dying.

When Skylar landed on the roof beside them, neither moved. "April? O'Wing? Are you unharmed?" he asked.

"I think I'm okay. I might be in shock," April said.

"Fine, sort of," O'Wing said.

Skylar grinned down at her. "April, you have wings!"

"Beautiful wings." She beamed up at him, a bit loopy. "Well, I did. They're gone now."

"Incredible. I saw them from afar and they were truly magnificent. And you saved the imp?" Skylar didn't sound sure that was a good thing.

"O'Wing saved Brag. I tried, but I wasn't fast enough. What happened with Cherry?" April asked, her brain starting to function again.

"She denied everything and refused to help," Skylar said.

"What?" It was certainly not what April expected to hear.

"Her aunt verified that Cherry hadn't left her room since Seamore knocked her out. So how did you escape the bubble?"

"Brag kept trying to pop the bubble with his magic, and then it popped." April struggled to sit.

Skylar offered a hand. "Perhaps he weakened it with his repeated attempts?"

"No." April knew better. It was Cherry. She had worked her magic after Skylar's visit.

To release Brag, she must have snuck out through her window during the night and slipped back in before anyone noticed her absence. April knew how easy it was to do that. But why had Cherry cooperated and released April from the bubble? It was beyond April to figure it out when her wits were as scattered as fall leaves on a windy day.

The sound of approaching elves carried faintly through the air, coming from below. It was time to get off the roof. April struggled to her feet. O'Wing made getting off the roof look easy. He gripped the edge and swung down to the intact floor below, inside the room with the pit. Skylar lowered the unconscious imp down to O'Wing, then he and April climbed down the join them.

With disgusted expressions and more than one comment about the smell, the two boys carted Brag between them down the stairs and out of the neglected house. When they gained the ground, April might have kissed the moss beneath her feet except she didn't have a chance. A whole crowd of elves flowed into the front garden, and April was thrilled to see all of them.

It was the happiest reunion imaginable. Raina didn't even yell at April for sneaking away without her. All she said was, "I'm so glad you're still here," and, "you have wings! Wings!" Airron was alive and healthy, and Peter had survived the night unscathed. Salm hugged her tight, but didn't try to talk over all the other elves who were talking at once.

More elves arrived on their heels. Welly, Ms. Larkin-LaBois and the Pooles rushed into the garden, demanding to know what had happened. It was a spontaneous gathering of the loudest sort. When enough questions had been answered to settle everyone down, Welly turned toward Brag, who was laid out on the ground. He addressed the issue of what to do with the imp.

Sage Scarab knew exactly what to do with him. "Tie the critter up while we've got the chance," he barked and tore a length of vine off a handy stem, intent on doing just that.

April understood his motivation, but deep inside she didn't think it was the best course of action. She had never gotten to know an imp before, but she had gotten to know Brag pretty well, and tying him up again didn't seem right. He was more animal than elf in many ways, and he was more child than adult in spite of his age, and he was definitely misguided. But he had saved Airron. He had some good in him. Not enough, but some.

"Sage Scarab," she said hesitantly. He grunted. "Maybe you shouldn't tie Brag up. Maybe you should leave him free."

A lot of shocked faces turned to gape at her. Everyone. Sage Scarab's wrinkled face was the most incredulous. "What the heck are you yammering about? You and the imp best buddies now? Or did you hit your head in the fall, knock all the sense out? Or was that bubble thing airtight?" He might have come up with more possibilities, except Welly raised a hand for silence.

The Head-Sage looked rejuvenated. He placed a warm hand on April's shoulder and said, "April, would you like to explain? You did save the creature's life, at great risk to your own."

"Actually, O'Wing saved Brag's life. I tried but I didn't make it." April wasn't sure if O'Wing was going to appreciate being known as the elf who saved the imp, but she couldn't take credit for something she hadn't done, even if that credit was blame. "And I think Brag might leave now, if we don't tie him up."

"Why do you believe this?" At least Welly was willing to listen, but it was hard to explain.

"Well, an elf did save his life. And he does have his gold now. He's probably missing his garden, and elves won't trample in it anymore if the forcefield stays the way it is. He's probably ready to go home. He's had a tough three weeks." It was the best April could offer. She had no proof that the imp would leave, only an instinctual feeling.

"He's had a tough three weeks?" Sage Scarab's voice cracked on the words. "We've had a tough three months! Or however long he's been roaming around, feels like forever. Wrapped me up in vines and near starved me, didn't he?" The Sage was quite incensed. "Almost killed all of you lot, some of you twice over!"

"I know. I know he did a lot of very bad things, but if we tie him up again—what are we going to do with him?" April said. "We'll be stuck with him forever. And he'll find some way to escape again, and he'll be really mad and want to destroy New Haven. But I think right now, he might just leave."

"You do have a point," Welly said. "But I fear what the imp will do to our world if he is left free now." He turned to study Brag, who looked harmless and rather hideous laying limp on the ground.

"It is a great risk, it is a gamble," Welly murmured almost to himself. He looked at Ms. Larkin-LaBois who was standing still and quiet compared to the rest of the elves. She met his gaze without expression and he sighed softly. Guidance? Had he been looking to Ms. Larkin-LaBois for guidance? If so, she had not offered any. Ms. Larkin-LaBois? Of course, it suddenly made sense that she was the elf who knew things before they happened. April almost said 'ah-ha', but she didn't. She thought she had it figured out, but she wasn't positive. And there were more pressing issues to be addressed at the moment.

"I know it's a risk to let Brag go. I know that." Maybe April was wrong. New Haven would be safe it they tied up the imp's magic hands, and New Haven's safety was the most important thing. The decision had to be made now, before Brag stirred. There was no time to hold a gathering.

Welly made the decision. "April, I cannot do as you ask. I cannot endanger this whole world again when we have the opportunity to prevent it. And you have no proof that Brag will leave. You do understand, don't you?"

"Yes." And she did. The Head-Sage had to think of everyone, that was his job and his responsibility. When the surrounding hum of voices went silent, dead silent, Welly swung around in alarm.

Brag was sitting up, yawning and stretching as if he was waking from the very best night's sleep. He scratched behind his ear, picked his nose, and chattered his teeth before he realized he had an audience, and quite a large one at that. They had missed their opportunity to restrain the imp.

He stared at the small crowd and hunched his shoulders, looking shy and frightened, until he spotted April. He scrambled to his feet and smiled to properly display his dangerous teeth. Elves stepped back, fast. April stepped closer, in case he tried anything.

"Brag not dead?" The imp pinched his own cheek as if to make sure.

April confirmed it. "Brag is alive."

"April ghost not dead?" Brag reached out and pinched her cheek, hard, with the same hand he had just used to pick his nose.

"Ouch! Yuck! No, I'm still not dead. I'm talking to you, aren't I?" April rubbed her cheek with her shirt hem, trying to clean it.

"Maybe. Maybe not. Hey, mine!" Brag's hand darted out and he ripped something off April's neck. She backed up and stared down. Her gold chains had been exposed by the rearrangement of her top and the imp had taken the newest chain.

"Your chain? Where did you get that chain, Brag?" April asked, not daring to demand its return.

He tilted his head and pulled his ear. "Find on ground."

"When Brag? A long time ago? It must have been a long time ago. Right?"

"Not so long time. Brag get gold and go home now." He dropped the chain around his scrawny neck and started walking away, just like that. It was what April had hoped the imp would do, but she hadn't expected it to happen so quickly. And now she didn't want him to leave, at least not before he answered some very important questions.

"Brag wait!" April went after him, although several hands reached out to restrain her. She shook them off. "Brag, where did you find the chain?"

"On ground, already said."

"But where exactly. Close? Far?" she prompted

"April save Brag. Brag tell truth." He held up both hands and April hoped he wasn't going to use magic again. He didn't, he used his fingers to count. His lips moved and he had to start over several times before he calculated his answer. "Not too close. Not too far," he said triumphantly. It was as accurate as he could be.

"And which direction? North, south, east or west?"

He pointed east, toward April's former home.

"Inside or outside New Haven?" she asked.

"Out."

"And when? When did you find it?"

Brag pulled a wrinkled-nose face. "Not so long time." He had already told her that.

"Brag! Was it months or years or what? Tell me more." She might have shaken him, if it had been anyone else.

"Don't know more. Brag go home now." He waved and started scuttling toward the nearest weeds.

"By home do you mean far away?" April asked, hoping home meant somewhere other than his leafy nest in Cherry's old house.

"Brag's garden. April friend save Brag. Brag go home."

"Brag, if you do find the elf who once wore this chain, can you tell them we're here," she said.

"Okey dokey." The imp hitched up his drooping loincloth and ducked out of sight.

"Oh, and it was O'Wing that saved you," April shouted lamely after him.

"Brag come back and visit," he sang in return. It was terrible news.

"Good grief." Raina was the only one who spoke. She stepped close and put an arm around April's shoulder.

April appreciated the contact, her knees were starting to feel more like water than knees. Everyone started talking at once, and April didn't try to compete. At least Brag was gone. Except he might come back for a visit. She really, really hoped not.

19 – Hibernation

The very next day, Peter confirmed that Brag's heap of gold was gone. On Tuesday, an important gathering was held. The Sages and the High Court reached a unanimous decision to leave the barrier the way it was for the time being. Elves travelling into the Outer-World had resulted in three months of trouble that could so easily have destroyed New Haven. The realm needed some time to recover. It was also decided that the thunderwand would no longer be kept on display at the museum. The three rods would be replaced with well-crafted replicas. The genuine magical articles would be secreted away, and only a few select individuals would know the secret location. April would be one of the select individuals.

On Wednesday, when they walked home after school, Airron and Raina veered off to have some alone time, or that's what Peter called it. It left Peter and April to have their own alone time, which gave them a chance to talk about all that had happened. Peter was looking happier and more at ease than he had since Brag's first appearance. April wasn't feeling quite so at ease. Astute as always, Peter asked her what was bothering her.

April sighed. "Oh, that chain Brag found. I can't help but think that there's another elf out there, searching for us." And April knew firsthand how difficult it was to survive in the harsh Outer-World, to be *alone*. It hurt inside her chest to know that another elf might be suffering as she had, and searching for a home. "An elf from my world," she murmured. "I just wish Brag had been able to tell us more."

"Me, too. You aren't thinking of trying to find the lost elf, are you?" Peter asked.

His question made her realize that the vague idea had been floating around in her head, she simply hadn't realized it yet. "You mean leave New Haven to try and find them? I don't know, Peter. It's a really big world outside. It would be impossible to find one elf, if they're even still alive."

"That's what I figured. Maybe the elf will find us. You did."

"I did. Maybe they will, too," April said. Or maybe Brag would point them in the right direction, if he found the elf, and if he remembered where New Haven was located.

April and Peter must have walked really slowly, because Airron and Raina were home before them. They were already in the kitchen sipping juice. Even Salm was home, scribbling on a pile of homework, and complaining energetically about school and teachers and way too much work. "At least we have holidays coming up," he mentioned, reaching for another page.

"School holidays?" April asked.

"Yes!" Rain declared energetically, "And we'll be able to leave home and have fun now that Brag is gone."

"But what school holidays? No-one told me. You don't have two summer holidays, do you?" In this world, it was entirely possible.

"No," Raina laughed. "That would be silly. We only have one month off for this holiday, about halfway through the school year. That's not summer. It's -"

"Don't say winter, you didn't even know winter actually existed until I told you," April pointed out.

"I wasn't going too," Raina said. "It's not winter or summer. It's actually supposed to be a period of rest and respite. There is even a myth about sleeping for the entire month, not that anyone does that, and the holiday has a really weird name. No elf knows why. It's called Hibernation."

"Hibernation," April repeated, unable to suppress a smile.

"Yes. Does that mean something? Outside?"

"Yes. It means winter." April shouldn't have been surprised. In a world that was always summer, New Haven had the autumn Harvest Moon Festival followed by the summer holidays, then the spring Fairy Lights Frolic and now winter Hibernation. The sequence of the seasons was completely mixed-up.

"Why is Hibernation winter?" Raina asked.

After April finished explaining about gigantic creatures like furry bears and even small insects sleeping for months at a time, until the weather warmed up, Raina simple looked confused. She refused to believe that frogs buried themselves deep in the mud until the thick ice

266

melted off the ponds, and that the fish actually survived in the frigid water beneath that ice.

Airron accused April of making up stories again. She denied it.

"Anyway, the point is that we have more holidays coming up next week and we're supposed to sleep in," Raina said.

It was great news. After the three months of Brag, April could really use some holidays and some respite. But there were still two more school days to get through, before the so-called Hibernation.

The tail end of the week was anticlimactic, April was sleepy and inattentive, but knew it would pass. It was because of the near fatal bubble ride, and the almost falling to her death, and the disturbing news of the lost elf.

Ms. Larkin-LaBois had an unexpected announcement for her class on Friday. April would have missed the words entirely if Peter hadn't nudged her to pay attention.

"I would like to inform you all that I will not be returning as your teacher after the Hibernation holidays," Ms. Larkin-LaBois said with regret. "I have enjoyed my time with you, however I was only here on a temporary basis. I suspect Ms. Summers will be back, since she can no longer explore and study the world outside. I will miss you all, but I have other obligations that demand my time and attention."

The class was slow to leave, taking the time to say farewell to her.

"A word, April," Ms. Larkin-LaBois murmured when April passed by the front table. April and Peter stopped. "Alone," the teacher specified, but nicely. Peter said his goodbyes and closed the door on his way out.

"Smart elf." Ms. Larkin-LaBois motioned for April to sit. "April, I wanted to tell you that if you ever need an ear, or feel the need for guidance, I am still available even though I am no longer your teacher. On occasion, my advice can be helpful. Welkin can tell you where to find me, if you have need."

"Oh. Okay." April had a lot of questions, but didn't know if she should ask any of them. Ms. Larkin-LaBois tapped her charcoal stick thoughtfully before she looked up and met April's gaze again.

"April, I would like to share something with you. However, what I am about to reveal is very private. Extremely confidential. It must not be repeated, not even to your closest friends. I would like your word. Do I have it?"

"Yes. I won't tell anyone," April promised, and kept on babbling. "You … you're the elf that knows things before they happen, aren't you?"

The teacher's thin gray eyebrows almost flew off her head. "As a matter of fact, I am. Amongst other things. But only one elf in this world shares my secret. How did you know?"

"I guessed, I wasn't sure. You have magic?" April already knew the answer.

"Yes, quite strong for New Haven. Quite strong, indeed. I've hidden that fact all of my life, as you can imagine. Only Welkin knows the truth, and only since the forcefield was injured. When the barrier was in danger of failing, it became necessary to reassure him that there was some hope for our world." She inclined her head towards April.

"Me? You saw me?" Welly had hinted as much, not so long ago.

"Five years before you came. I knew that you would be able to help us, but I did not know how it would end. Rather like this latest episode."

"Brag?" April said.

"Yes, I foresaw the arrival of something dangerous in New Haven, but I could not identify the creature. I believe his powerful magic interfered with my vision." She tapped her forehead, between her eyes.

"Did you know how it would turn out, with Brag? In the end?" April asked, very interested in this elf's unusual magic. Even in April's world, she had never heard of an elf with this particular gift.

"I saw some fragmented images, bits and pieces. Never enough. That is why I decided it was a good time to become a teacher. The task has proved more tiring than I would have expected." She smiled in a self-depreciating fashion. "But perhaps that is my age creeping upon me. I have many more years than I will admit too."

"You were at school because of me?" April asked in amazement.

"Yes, I thought I might be able to sense more of the events to come, if we were in closer proximity. Help and guide you, as much as I was able, if it became necessary." The elderly elf leaned forward intently. "I kept seeing you falling into the bottomless pit. I feared … I suspected, the tragic worst. I thought I saw wings, but I did not understand how that was possible, since you do not have wings, or didn't. And the wings were not part of all of my visions."

April thought about that. "Maybe you also saw the other times I fell in the pit. The first time I fell in the pit, I caught the edge. The second time I fell in, I had a vine tied onto me. The last time, I didn't really go into the pit, the wings and the roof stopped me."

"Ah, you've been in danger from the pit three times? I didn't know that. Yes, that would explain the discrepancy. Three times, imagine that. Well, you can see how the visions can be misinterpreted. I admit that I did not believe you would survive Brag," Ms. Larkin-LaBois said frankly.

"You thought I was going to die? Go right down the pit?" April gasped.

"I did believe it was a distinct possibility."

"Oh." No wonder the teacher had seemed burdened when she spoke with April. And Welly had been told! His eyes had held the same sad message. Now she understood. He hadn't been burdened about Brag, he had been sad about April.

"I did suspect that the transformation ceremony might have affected you in unexpected ways, especially when I learned that you had manifested gills when you needed them," the teacher murmured. "But to have wings, too? That doesn't happen in our world. An elf has one of the other, never both. So I did not expect you to have wings, and I believe that was the key to the imp leaving our world in peace," she said. But that didn't make sense either.

"But wouldn't Brag have fallen into the bottomless pit if I didn't get wings? And leave … that way. And I didn't save him anyway, O'Wing did."

"The imp would have survived by his magic, even if you, April, had not survived the fall. And O'Wing saved him because you were trying. Because you had wings. It was a key link in the chain of events."

April frowned. "But how could you see Brag surviving on his own— that never happened."

"When magic is involved, the future path is undecided until the events unfold. Your act of kindness in trying to save Brag is what ultimately saved our world. It was a selfless act, very selfless. Not many would have placed themselves at risk to save one who had caused such harm to them and those they care about."

"I didn't have a lot of time to think about it." April flushed in embarrassment. Many would call her actions foolish, herself included. But if her actions had saved New Haven, April hadn't been useless against Brag after all. And it hadn't depended on her magic, it had depended on her compassion. April's embarrassment turned to pleasure as the knowledge sank in. She hadn't been useless against Brag after all. It was a happy ending, of sorts.

"To continue, interpreting the future is more complex than one would imagine. I have a long lifetime of experience and I still have more questions than answers. The idea of interfering in future events fills me with dread, so it is rare that I will risk it." She paused for a moment, before she said softly, "The stakes must be very high."

"Oh." Being able to see the future didn't sound like it was much help, especially if an elf saw more than one future and didn't know which was the true future.

"Now, April, listen well. If you ever need my counsel, please seek me out. I want you to know that I will guide you if I am able. Promise me that you will remember my words," the teacher said, almost sternly.

April nodded, filled with foreboding. This elf knew something, it was as clear as the midday sun. She knew something about the future, something that she was not saying, and she didn't look happy about her vision. The stakes must be very high, if she was telling April to come and talk to her after she had just finished saying how she would not interfere.

"Okay, I promise." April wouldn't forget. She couldn't forget is she wanted too. "Does it have to do with the elf outside, the elf from my world?" she said, hazarding a guess.

Ms. Larkin-LaBois didn't flicker so much as one eyelash. "April, I trust you know and understand that I will not speak about this now. The events with Brag have already come to pass, so there is no danger. This future is another matter, another matter entirely. If you feel the need, you may come to speak with me, that is all I wanted to tell you. Now, Mr. Flynn will be wondering what has become of you."

The elf walked April to the door. She had said all she was willing to say.

Thanks to Ms. Larkin-LaBois, April was so distracted for the remainder of the afternoon that she alone was responsible for her team losing their Basketberry game in Sports, and it was the first game they'd ever had a chance of winning. And she was so distracted that she forgot her pack in Mr. Flynn's room.

"Owl pellets. I have to go and get my pack," April grumbled, after the final gong echoed to silence.

Airron laughed at her. "Where did you leave your brain today?"

"I have no idea," April huffed. "If I knew, I would go and get it, put it back where it belongs."

"Do you want me to come with you? Help you find your pack?" Peter grinned. Even Peter was teasing her.

"No, I can find it all by myself. I'll be quick. I'll catch up."

April dashed through the deserted meadow. Inside, the corridors were equally empty. No-one hung around school on the Friday before a holiday, it seemed, not even the teachers. Mr. Flynn was long gone, but April's pack was exactly where she had left it, beside her table. She'd had to step over it to forget it. About to pick it up, April felt an unpleasant tingle travel down her spine. She wasn't alone; a shadowy body blocked the doorway.

"April-May June July August," Cherry said, hate emanating off her.

April took an involuntary step back. "Cherry. What are you doing here?"

"I go to school here," the elf mocked sarcastically.

"You know what I mean." April frowned. Cherry had a way of making an elf feel stupid, especially April.

Cherry stepped further into the room. "Pretty deserted around here."

April wasn't too happy about that, herself. "What do you want, Cherry?"

She took the question literally. "I want you to leave New Haven. I want my father back, but that's not going to happen, since you killed him."

"I didn't kill him," April protested hotly. "I told him to let go of the rod before the lightning struck. He wouldn't and I couldn't stop the storm."

Cherry narrowed her eyes like a cat. "Whatever. Can't bring back the dead. Living with my aunt is a drag, she isn't like my father at all. He taught me all kinds of interesting stuff. You have no idea."

"I can guess," April bit out.

"Learned a lot from Brag, too. I'm going to miss the stinky little imp. He livened things up, didn't he?"

"You admit that you helped Brag threaten New Haven and hurt elves? Raina, Airron and Peter were almost killed." April couldn't believe that Cherry was speaking so frankly, then again, they were alone. All alone.

"As I recall, you almost went down the bottomless pit yourself. Almost—so close. The wings were unexpected, weren't they? Who would have expected you to survive the popped bubble? Not me." She shook her head regretfully.

"You popped the bubble to kill me?" April gasped.

Cherry just smiled coldly and said, "The pit has been boarded over, you know. I snuck over and had a look last night. It's all sealed up, so no-one will fall in. When I'm old enough to move back into my house, I think I might open Brag's pit back up. It's a fascinating feature in a house, don't you think?" she taunted.

"No." April said, unwilling to play along. But at least she now knew why Cherry had popped the bubble. She hadn't expected April to manifest wings and survive the fall. She had probably been watching from her window, hoping to see April plummet to her death.

April did have one pressing question, before she put a lot of distance between herself and Cherry. "Brag said you helped make the bubble trap. You have dark magic like your father, don't you?"

"I'd like to see you prove it," Cherry snarled, her pretty face looking ugly.

April couldn't and Cherry knew it. April edged around the elf, heading for the door. She had better things to do on this Friday than hang out with Cherry.

But Cherry wasn't finished. "Stay out of my way from now on. You are lucky to be alive, you don't have a clue how lucky. Stay far away from me or you won't be so lucky next time. Clear enough? Even for you?" The whole episode with Brag should have shaken Cherry to the core, but it didn't appear to have scraped even the surface of her cold arrogance.

April's temper snuck up on her, and she fought to control it. "No, you've got it backwards, Cherry. You better stay away from me—far away, after what you did. Or you won't be so lucky. You're the one that will be sorry. If you have any brains at all, you'll stay miles away from me and my friends," April shouted and strode toward the door.

"Like I'm scared of you," Cherry yelled after her. She didn't sound scared.

"Well, you should be. I won't let you hurt elves again." It felt great to yell at Cherry, but April had nothing else to say. She fled the room, then the school, hoping to leave the black cloud of Cherry behind. As soon as she caught up with her friends, the cloud evaporated.

"Took you long enough. Couldn't find your pack?" Raina asked.

"I found it fine."

"Then where is it?"

"Oh." April had forgotten it—again. "Uh, I don't need it. It's the holidays. I wasn't going to do any homework anyway." April didn't mention Cherry, or say a word about Ms. Larkin-LaBois's unspoken concerns about the future. They all deserved to enjoy their weekend and their upcoming Hibernation. Every time April thought about the holiday, she was inclined to giggle. Elves hibernating in the middle of summer was ridiculous. Winter was preparing to wrap its cold arms around the Outer-World even now, but New Haven wouldn't feel even a touch of frost. The magical realm would know nothing but eternal summer while the world around them froze to ice.

"So, where are we going?" April said.

"We were talking about what we should do tonight," Airron mentioned so casually, if April had had antennae, they would have been wiggling.

"And what did you decide?" she asked.

"We're going to my house. I'm going to give you some flying lessons. We can jump out of the top storey windows, they're really high up. Really high," Airron said. "So, are you game?"

"Nope. I'd rather picnic with Brag," April said cheerfully. "You would have to throw me out the window."

"I could do that. You don't weigh more than a bug." Airron took a quick sidestep, as if he was going to capture her then and there.

April took off running. No way was she testing her magical wings today. Never would be soon enough for that. Peter tried to tackle Airron, all he caught was Airron's ankle. Raina grabbed April's hand and they ran, laughing like children as they raced through the undergrowth into a field of daisies. They wove between the bright flowers under the warm sunlight, their feet barely touching the earth.

Brag was gone. New Haven was safe. And April was not jumping out of any windows! It was the perfect start to Hibernation.

The End

Join the author's mailing list for free monthly give-aways
and author/artist updates –
SrigleyArts.com

Continue the adventure with Book 3 – Message in a Bubble